Books of Merit

LAURIER IN LOVE

ALSO BY ROY MACSKIMMING

FICTION

Macdonald

Out of Love
 (translated into French as *Coups de cœur*)

Formentera
 (translated into French as *Formentera*)

NON-FICTION

The Perilous Trade: Publishing Canada's Writers

Cold War: The Amazing Canada-Soviet Hockey Series of 1972

Gordie: A Hockey Legend

To Joyce,

LAURIER IN LOVE

Best regards,

A NOVEL

Roy

ROY MACSKIMMING

Thomas Allen Publishers
Toronto

Library and Archives Canada Cataloguing in Publication

MacSkimming, Roy, 1944–
    Laurier in love / Roy MacSkimming.

ISBN 978-0-88762-614-2

1. Laurier, Wilfrid, Sir, 1841–1919—Fiction.
2. Canada—Politics and government—1896–1911—Fiction.
I. Title.

PS8575.S53L38 2010   C813'.54   C2010-903798-7

Editor: Patrick Crean
Text design: Gordon Robertson
Cover design: Sputnik Design Partners Inc.
Cover image: iStock

Published by Thomas Allen Publishers,
a division of Thomas Allen & Son Limited,
145 Front Street East, Suite 209,
Toronto, Ontario M5A 1E3 Canada

www.thomas-allen.com

The publisher gratefully acknowledges the support of
the Ontario Arts Council for its publishing program.

We acknowledge the support of the Canada Council for the Arts, which
last year invested $20.1 million in writing and publishing throughout Canada.

We acknowledge the Government of Ontario through the
Ontario Media Development Corporation's Ontario Book Initiative.

We acknowledge the financial support of the Government of Canada
through the Canada Book Fund for our publishing activities.

1 2 3 4 5   14 13 12 11 10

Printed and bound in Canada

And in all the difficulties, all the pains, and all the vicissitudes of our situation, let us always remember that love is better than hatred, and faith better than doubt, and let hope in our future destinies be the pillar of fire to guide us.

Wilfrid Laurier,
January 4, 1894

October 1933

This story owes its existence to an act of destruction. And so, this act of creation.

Although the story is my own, I appear only occasionally. What are we to make of that? A sad commentary on my significance! Yet I've always felt in danger of disappearing. Surrounded by the great and the near-great, I've sought my shadow within theirs. Perhaps this explains why I was so noisy, so obnoxious.

My father would have preferred I disappear altogether. My conduct, my very existence, embarrassed him. If only I'd been considerate enough to marry some nice respectable girl and move away to some obscure respectable town, where I could practise whatever law one practises in such places, too busy fathering children and supporting a growing family to make trouble, he'd have been far happier.

But I did nothing of the sort. I insisted on a public life. Ran for office numerous times, occasionally won. Wrote political manifestoes, essays, newspaper columns, editorials, letters to the editor—idealistic and scathing, hectoring and lecturing. Joined in founding the most principled newspaper of our age, in this or any other country. Married but had no children, never to become a plump and prosperous paterfamilias: but then there's no money in either journalism or politics, at least if one is honest. I married a woman who was barren—or was the flaw in myself?—and whose own father turned out to be a small-time swindler and jailbird. But where's the shame in that today, when the ancient civilizations of Europe are putting hoodlums, thugs and buffoons in charge of their destinies?

And so I've remained uncompromised, owing nothing to anyone but God. With no one to protect. Free to set down this story of the great and the near-great, who have so much to protect, so much to hide.

In the process I've set myself a single standard. I can't say whether it's a literary or a moral one, but in either case it's necessary. It is this: while describing people and events—people and events that may be familiar to you—I will write about them with rigorous objectivity. I will tell the truth, as revealed to me over time by those most closely involved, without letting it become distorted by my personal biases. And it's known I have some.

You may find the story doesn't always flatter one Sir Wilfrid Laurier, seventh Prime Minister of Canada. My absence of illusion about Laurier doesn't result from being his political enemy— although I was—but from knowing the great man too well. Although very few ever became intimate with him, I came close enough to realize Sir Wilfrid was scarcely the high-minded idealist, selfless statesman and perfect gentleman many Canadians imagined. He was, after all, the Quebec politician who best knew how to keep Quebec in its place. In my language we have a word for that.

But enough: I said I wouldn't let my biases seep through. For now I will disappear. I'll be as impartial as I can toward the two most important (although not the only) women in Laurier's life, his faithful wife, Zoë, and their dear "friend," Émilie Lavergne. I will tell my story through their eyes, based on their own accounts, confided to me later in life. Madame Lavergne and Lady Laurier knew their secrets were safe with me.

I am the only one who could have written this story, the only one with the requisite knowledge. Whether I have any insight into that knowledge I leave for you to judge. By the time I return, you'll have made up your mind.

2

July 1896

Pulling out of the wedding cake of Bonaventure Station, the Canada Atlantic Express lurches violently. Shudders, stops, lunges. Zoë wonders if something is wrong. But having promised him she'll accept everything as it comes, she remains silent.

They sit side by side at the head of the parlour car. Their chairs are upholstered in plush green velvet. Zoë feels enthroned, engulfed. She glances sideways. His eyes are serenely closed, head leaning back against the antimacassar. His long tapered fingers cover the back of her gloved hand. The grey top hat sits upturned on his lap, the matching gloves nestled inside. The demanding day is far from over. She doesn't need to study his beautiful profile to read his thoughts.

Passing the grey unpainted homes of Montreal's working class, the train settles into a steady, rolling motion. Zoë watches lines of laundry snapping in the hot breeze, dangerously close to ashes spewing from the engine. Party workers have attached festive red, white and blue bunting to the outside of their car. She watches it fluttering madly beyond the curtained windows.

The party has booked them a private car, added to the regular five o'clock train to Ottawa. They have it all to themselves—along with the entourage, of course. For now the swarm of hangers-on keeps a discreet distance. They number at least two dozen, several of whom have inserted themselves at the last moment, desperate to be seen and, even better, photographed with their leader on this historic day.

It will be like this from now on: perpetually surrounded by stout, bustling, self-important men. These black-suited eminences will form the carapace of her life, the soft shell she moves within. Some of them can be pleasant enough, even strenuously gallant toward her, but they too are always in a hurry, always bursting with the urgency of the moment, so anxious for Wilfrid's consideration that they barely spare her a glance. In that respect they're all the same, English and French alike.

The only one who behaves any differently is Joseph-Israël Tarte. He, at least, is aware of her as a human being. Blessed with a feline intelligence, Tarte treats her as a compatriot, an equal, deserving of more than gentlemanly respect. Also, he isn't stout. As Wilfrid says, Tarte has always been the exception, ever since their school days together at Collège de L'Assomption. She's begun to find Tarte's stutter rather charming.

The heat inside the car is withering, and Zoë longs for the cool of evening. She feels another rivulet detach itself from her armpit, slither down her side, soak into the tight binding of her corset. She whispers into Wilfrid's ear that she's dying to remove her long kid gloves.

Without opening his eyes, he murmurs, "Of course, my dear, you must do exactly as you please."

But she won't. There isn't a single other woman in the car, someone who would understand. In any case she feels a fierce pride in her stoic denial of her body. With this unremarked sacrifice, this powerful act, she begins her defense of their union, their citadel, their ultimate salvation, against the onslaught of the world.

It's a defense Zoë has been conducting all her married life. Innumerable skirmishes have taken place, some frightening, some painful. The all-too-predictable onset of Wilfrid's illnesses. The constant, hurtful gossip and innuendo about Émilie Lavergne. The merciless attacks of his enemies, who aren't above libel, bribery, even violence. Not long ago one of Wilfrid's supporters was kicked to death at a rally.

In Ontario they still accuse him of being soft on Riel, a sympathizer with treason. In Quebec they accuse him of speaking English better than French. Even her beloved Church denounces him, painting him as an apostate, an atheist (a "Barabbas," one curé called him), and declaring it a sin to vote for him. But those challenges are nothing compared to this one. After all the years as Leader of the Opposition, they're plunging into the fight of their lives, a war to the finish: the holding and using of power. Zoë has only a shadowy conception of what it will mean.

Wilfrid has tried to prepare her. A few days ago they were at home in Arthabaska, recovering from the campaign, celebrating her birthday. After lunch on the rear verandah, they walked across the broad lawn to Zoë's garden, and out of habit she picked up the small shears and began pruning her luxuriant pink climbing rose. He asked her to stop for a moment, to sit on the double swing and hear something he had to say.

As they swung back and forth, sheltered from the sun by tall maples, he spoke in a resolutely prepared voice. There will be enormous sacrifices to make in this new life of theirs. The demands on her time and patience and generous heart, already great, will only multiply. Absolutely everyone in Ottawa will seek her ear, her help, her intervention with her husband. Society will be relentless in expecting her presence, most importantly the vice-regal court presided over by Lord and Lady Aberdeen—and thank God the Aberdeens are staunch supporters, kind and loyal friends to them both, ever ready to make lively conversation in French. But always and everywhere will be the English. Every English hostess and charity queen will be consumed with curiosity and envy, anxious for the opportunity to size up the Prime Minister's wife, to invite her to be their guest of honour at luncheons and receptions and teas, where they will simultaneously show her off to their friends and try to reduce her to their level.

Zoë must never, Wilfrid told her, *ever* allow her doubts about her fluency in English, or her fear of her hostesses' motives and pretensions, to stop her from accepting their invitations. She must always remember: she's a far finer, more gracious lady than any of them. They will be fortunate to have her under their roofs. It is she, with her unassuming dignity and thoughtful kindness, who will set the tone for conducting oneself in the Ottawa of his new regime.

Zoë heard no mention of the sacrifices Wilfrid would be making, but she let that go. Face to face on the swing, he addressed her with reckless abandon, his sincerity spreading such a passionate flush over his pale features that fine beads of perspiration appeared on the irresistible curve of his upper lip. Zoë wasn't sure she believed his claims on her behalf, but she loved him for making them. Remembering those reassurances now, she feels distinctly better, physically relieved, as he squeezes her hand, excuses himself and leaves her to join the men.

The entourage has been kept waiting nearly an hour. Impatient as they are, they've learned to respect Wilfrid's insistence on the solitude he needs to rest, to reflect, to marshal his thoughts.

In addition to Tarte, with his lithe frame and pointed goatee and quick, glittering eyes, Sir Richard Cartwright is here, large and immovable, the primordial politician of old Ontario. Cartwright's walrus moustache always strikes Zoë as silly, yet she feels intimidated by his aggressive, hungry laugh. Frederick Borden's mutton-chop sidewhiskers are equally flamboyant and ridiculous: around the married Borden, however, rumours of women fly constantly, only the Lord knows why. And there are others, all ambitious, all eager for a cabinet post, and several new MPs from Quebec and the Maritimes whose names she doesn't know, and Mr. Murphy from McGill, the boyish president of the Federation of Young Liberal Clubs, self-consciously sporting a bowler hat.

The men cluster in groups around the big chairs, some sitting, some standing in the aisle, leaning down to hear and be heard above the clatter of the train. A few sip iced Tom Collinses brought by the Negro porter. They argue and swap gossip, coughing and spluttering through their cigar smoke, laughing uninhibitedly at their own jokes.

Zoë watches them spring comically to their feet as Wilfrid approaches up the patterned carpet. His gait is languid, adapted from long practice to the swaying of trains. With his height, he has to stoop to avoid hitting his head on the brass light fixtures suspended from the panelled ceiling. The last to rise in obeisance are Tarte and Cartwright: the one who attended school with him, the other who coveted his position. Of this group, only they, Zoë knows, can be certain of seats in the new cabinet.

The cabinet isn't big enough to contain all Wilfrid's key supporters from every province. This dilemma is costing him sleep now that the recounts are complete, his victory official, and Prime Minister Tupper finally, reluctantly, agreeing to resign. Meanwhile Wilfrid makes political small talk with those lucky or shrewd enough to have joined his victorious band preparing to take the capital.

Zoë picks up the newspaper Wilfrid was reading. It's the Toronto *Globe*, devoutly Liberal. The front-page cartoon portrays the ghost of Sir John A. Macdonald in his Windsor uniform and ceremonial sword—the same uniform, she recalls, that the late Prime Minister wore in his coffin—patting a poorly drawn Wilfrid on the back. Macdonald is grinning eerily and saying, "No man could more worthily fill the great office I vacated."

She finds it chilling.

She turns the page to an article reporting on the rebellion in Crete, where the people are throwing off centuries of Turkish rule, then sets the paper aside. She stares out the window. The landscape rushes by. Somewhere in that dense featureless bush, occasionally interrupted by small farms, is the Quebec–Ontario border. They might have crossed it already. She closes her eyes and lets her thoughts dwell on the morning just past.

They awakened in Montreal, in the familiar, pleasantly scented guest room of Wilfrid's oldest and dearest friend, Laurent-Olivier David. They breakfasted well, surrounded by friends and supporters who dropped by to extend their congratulations. Everyone was in a celebratory mood after the official announcement of victory the day before.

Two messages arrived at the breakfast table in rapid succession. A telegram came from Lord Aberdeen, calling Wilfrid to Rideau Hall to be sworn in. And the Mayor of Montreal, having learned the Lauriers were passing through the city, sent a note saying two Royal Navy warships, HMS *Intrepid* and HMS *Tartar*, were docked in the harbour. A reception for the British officers was planned for noon, and the Mayor, apologizing for the short notice, would be deeply honoured by the Lauriers' presence.

Wilfrid had been so looking forward to talking with Laurent-Olivier David in his friend's library, one of his greatest pleasures, but knew where his duty lay. As he told the breakfast assembly, it was important to get off on the right foot. David telephoned for a carriage to take them to City Hall.

Driving to the reception, Zoë watched their former neighbourhood pass by, outwardly unchanged. In those stone houses of old Montreal she'd once supported herself, although barely, as a piano teacher. They drove quite near the Gauthiers' home on rue St-Louis. She and Wilfrid, then a law student at McGill, had met and boarded and fallen in love there.

The courtship was long and initially inconclusive: the strangest wooing she'd ever known. At first Wilfrid watched her from afar, shyly joining the Gauthier family singsongs around the piano, casting hungry glances at her as she played. Eventually, since Dr. Gauthier's sitting room was constantly full of visitors talking politics, they ventured outside to find time alone. On warm bright evenings he'd take her arm to promenade past the shops on Notre-Dame, or linger under the Lombardy poplars on the Champ de Mars when a regimental band was playing. He invited her to attend his McGill convocation, and she sat in Molson Hall beside his proud father and stepmother visiting from St-Lin and listened to him deliver the valedictory address. Speaking in French, he told the largely uncomprehending audience that Canada's racial struggles were over: "There is now no other family than the human family, whatever the language they speak, or the altar at which they kneel." She felt herself easily the luckiest girl in Montreal. She'd never heard the name Émilie Lavergne.

And they talked, always talked. She'd never forget the feverish, exciting rhythms of his conversation back then, his ecstatic engagement with everything he saw and heard and read, the insistent pressure of his hand on her upper arm. They grew frighteningly close. She believed they'd go on like that forever. Yet he never once asked for her hand in marriage. When he abruptly moved away to practise law in distant Arthabaska, she was devastated. His departure drained the light out of her life.

Wilfrid's reason for leaving Montreal was the same reason he hadn't proposed: he'd been coughing blood. One wintry afternoon he'd collapsed across his desk at his law office, bright red liquid erupting from his throat, ruining sheaves of legal documents. He was convinced he'd inherited the family curse. His mother, Marcelle, had died of consumption when he was seven, followed by his sister Malvina. "I fear I am carrying in my lungs," he wrote Zoë from Arthabaska, "a germ of death that no power in the world can dislodge." He refused to subject her to a marriage cut short by mortal illness, leaving her in poverty, perhaps with children to raise alone. His doctor had advised him to get out of smoke-filled Montreal as fast as he could. He was following doctor's orders.

Yet Zoë didn't care if he had consumption, at least not for her own sake: she'd marry him all the same, embrace wholeheartedly whatever time they had, however long or short. But it didn't matter how she felt. He was gone.

From Arthabaska he continued writing impassioned letters proclaiming his love, but he was no longer present in her day-to-day life, and he didn't invite her to come join him. Unlike Wilfrid, Zoë couldn't live on emotions existing solely on paper, however beautifully expressed. Eventually she accepted a marriage proposal from Pierre Valois, a medical student, a good man, devoted to her. Still she cried herself to sleep every night over Wilfrid. She felt hopeless. Until Dr. Gauthier intervened.

Dr. Gauthier wasn't only their landlord, he was a stern and affectionate father to them both, given to a brusque, old-fashioned imperiousness. He sent Wilfrid a telegram summoning him to Montreal "on a matter of urgent importance." Arriving on the overnight train from Arthabaska, Wilfrid went straight to Dr. Gauthier's consulting room, where he was ordered to strip off all his clothes. At the end of a lengthy examination, Dr. Gauthier matter-of-factly informed him he wasn't suffering from consumption at all: his ailment was chronic bronchitis. It was a troublesome condition, requiring careful management, but it certainly wouldn't kill him. In fact, Dr. Gauthier observed tartly, he'd probably outlive Zoë, the way she was carrying on lately. Her misery and tears were making the whole household miserable. And now, wasn't it time he acted like a man?

Dr. Gauthier sent for Zoë, leaving her alone with Wilfrid in the consulting room. With bewildered relief they fell into each other's arms. They were married that night, since Wilfrid had an important case to argue in court the next morning in Arthabaska. . . .

She was about to indulge in the maelstrom of emotion surrounding their instant wedding, but they'd arrived at City Hall. Madame Laurier descended the carriage on her husband's arm, to be ushered inside and cheered by the overdressed crowd at the Mayor's reception.

The guest of honour was a British vice-admiral named Erskine. Heavily bearded, with an astounding quantity of gold braid on his chest, he was accompanied by several officers in ceremonial uniform, all visibly deferring to him. The Royal Navy men stood together with the Mayor, punch glasses in hand, preparing to repel boarders. As Wilfrid and Zoë proceeded through the throng, accepting congratulations from all sides, shaking hands with old colleagues, it became obvious to Erskine that his distinguished presence was being upstaged. All eyes were on Wilfrid: his magnificent forehead, his thick, wavy chestnut hair silvering at the temples.

Introduced by the Mayor, Wilfrid shook the Vice-Admiral's hand and asked a succession of questions displaying his knowledge of naval matters. He hadn't prepared a speech for the occasion. When he did speak, he'd told Zoë in the carriage, he'd be very brief. Constitutionally, he still wasn't Prime Minister.

The Mayor proposed a series of toasts to the Queen, her navy, her officers. Erskine made his reply. He stressed how much the British people and Her Majesty's government counted on Canada's loyalty. The Royal Navy patrolled the seven seas not only to defend Great Britain, he reminded everyone, but the entire Empire. He concluded heartily, if somewhat condescendingly, by congratulating Mr. Laurier on his accession to power in the Dominion.

In response Wilfrid kept his voice light and musical. The acoustics in the room were good, he didn't need to declaim. He'd taken just three sips of champagne punch, one for each toast. Zoë had counted.

He now appreciated more than ever, Wilfrid said, the significance of Nelson's words at the Battle of Trafalgar, "England expects every man to do his duty." He himself would try his utmost to do his duty, by both Canada and the Empire. And if ever the occasion should arise when Britain must stand against the world in arms, she could always count on the support of the Canadian people.

Vice-Admiral Erskine beamed as he absorbed these fine imperial sentiments. Then Wilfrid delivered the coup de grace: the Canadian people were free, he said, and they were loyal—loyal *because* they were free.

It made a good start, he told her afterwards.

The train slows on its entry into Ottawa, and Zoë realizes she's drifted off. They've enjoyed a good supper in the dining car: trout, boiled potatoes and asparagus, accompanied by a little Muscadet and a dessert of fresh strawberries with *crème anglaise*. Now the sun is setting. In the parlour car the atmosphere is still hot and close, acrid with cigar smoke. She hoists herself up in her chair and straightens her hat and notices Wilfrid is grinning.

"You shouldn't stare at me like that," she says. "I must look a fright."

"My dear, you look rested and refreshed," he replies. It's a description that fits him better.

Up ahead, around a bend in the tracks, she sees the bridge over the Rideau Canal and the Canada Atlantic station on the far side, enveloped in long shadows. The porters open the doors to the evening. A sound of distant cheering enters from up the tracks, coming from the station.

Young Murphy approaches clutching his bowler. He's excited. "There's a huge crowd at the station, sir. The railway wired ahead to warn us."

Wilfrid betrays his pleasure. "I'm surprised. Our arrival was supposed to be unannounced. I haven't prepared a speech."

"Somebody in Ottawa must have told your supporters, sir."

"There will be no police escort," Wilfrid observes.

Murphy beams. "No, sir. We're your bodyguard tonight."

The train comes to a halt, the entourage steps aside, the Lauriers emerge onto the rear platform, Wilfrid already waving. A great deep-throated roar goes up, followed by three cheers. Standing behind him, feeling the humid, sooty air caress her cheeks, Zoë watches faces in the crowd contort with happiness. The men in front press up against the train, pushed by the force of those behind. She feels marooned. Nobody appears to be in charge. She's alarmed that neither the police nor the Liberal Party have made arrangements for the leader's arrival.

Wilfrid raises his long arms high into the air, and gradually the mob settles down, except for a drunken cry of "Long live Laurier! To hell with Tupper!"

"My friends," Wilfrid begins in his best platform voice, "my friends, *mes chers amis*, Madame Laurier and I thank you for coming out this evening to welcome us. I must tell you, I had no idea there was going to be such a grand reception. When I saw you massed at the station, I asked my colleagues on the train, 'What city is this? Have we stopped at the wrong place?' Because I well remember the day, not so many years ago, when there were precious few Liberals to be found in Ottawa. Clearly that sad situation is no more! I feel enormous pride in the fact that two Liberal candidates have been elected to represent you in my new government."

As the cheering dies down, Wilfrid retains his triumphant smile and slips naturally into French. Ottawa, after all, is one-third French-speaking. He's on his second sentence when a voice bawls out, "For God's sake, speak English!"

Wilfrid stops in mid-sentence. Returning to English, he tells the voice, "I don't know who you are. But I did not fight and win this election, nor have I laboured in politics all these years, to elevate one language, one race, over the other. Our Liberal victory is a shared victory. Our two peoples made it together. Our country is a shared country, which we also made together, and nothing and no one will stop me from speaking my mother tongue—especially in our nation's capital." Which he proceeds to do.

"Now," he continues, "we have much ahead of us. His Excellency the Governor General has asked me to visit him at Rideau Hall without delay. Thank you! But by the same token, until I have seen His Excellency I am not yet your Prime Minister, and I may not speak as if I were. For now I will simply assure you that your loyalty is deeply gratifying. I will have more to tell all my good friends in the days to come. Madame Laurier and I will now try to reach our carriage, which I'm told is waiting to take us off for a good night's rest. I wish you all a happy evening!"

Zoë hopes the mob will respond by applauding and melting away, but it has no such intention. It stays right where it is, swaying like a happy drunk on unsteady legs, hoping for more. The only sign of movement comes from the very back, where men who couldn't hear properly are pressing forward for a better view.

Wilfrid turns to the troops behind him. With the physical courage of the young, Murphy leads several MPs in a charge over the railing and onto the platform. They clear a space for steps to be lowered, and Wilfrid descends first, then helps Zoë down. Forming a flying wedge like footballers, the escorts force a passage through the mob. Wilfrid takes her arm, patting it firmly, and together they plunge into the crowd.

Halfway to the station building, a fat man in a straw boater suddenly lunges to grab Wilfrid by the wrist. Zoë, who has schooled herself to think an outstretched arm never intends anything worse than a handshake, is frightened, then relieved as the man pumps Wilfrid's hand. They push on through the station building and out onto Catherine Street. They enter the first of several open carriages. Other members of the entourage pile into the carriages behind, and they all pull away amid wild cheering. Even though Zoë is used to election mobs, something about this crowd has shaken her: something different, manic, uncontrolled. She seeks Wilfrid's eyes for reassurance, but he's turned away from her, still waving, still smiling his fixed, dreamy smile.

Dusk softens the capital's raw streets as the carriage proceeds up Elgin. Mosquito hawks swoop high above the rooftops, releasing distant shrieks into the dimming air. The Russell House lies ahead at the corner of Sparks, another crowd lying in wait: hundreds massed outside the row of smart shops on the hotel's ground floor.

This time the cheering is casual and good-natured. The carriage halts before the main entrance, and Wilfrid rises from his seat. Zoë watches his face bathed in electric light from the hotel façade. Wrought-iron balconies and striped awnings rise above him in tiers as he smiles and nods in all directions and finally, unable to resist appeals for a speech, delivers a shorter version of his remarks at the station. The people seem satisfied to have heard, however briefly, the famous silvery voice.

Arm in arm they enter the hotel, the only home they've known in Ottawa. The lobby is bedlam. She's never seen it so packed. People swarm over the mosaic tile floor, jamming the grand staircase all the way up to the stained-glass window on the landing. Cigar smoke rolls out of the long bar off the lobby, propelled by raucous male laughter. Pastel nymphs frolic on the domed ceiling, oblivious to it all.

Men rush up to Wilfrid to grasp his hand. Zoë recognizes no one except Joseph-Israël Tarte, who has somehow got to the hotel ahead of them. He's already holding forth at the base of one of the Corinthian columns, his stutter subdued, gesticulating with both arms, enjoying his celebrity as architect of victory in Quebec. Tarte's strategy of open-air rallies, planted newspaper stories and bribery has been enormously successful, proving once again his favourite adage, "Elections are not won by prayers alone." Of course Tarte remembers to pray, too.

It's beginning to seem unlikely they'll ever get to their room when a familiar face appears out of the crowd: bearded, attractive John Willison, editor of *The Globe*. Ever since Wilfrid's difficult early days as party leader, when Willison headed the Young Men's Liberal Club in Toronto, he's been Wilfrid's most loyal and influential supporter in English Canada. Willison greets them with a broad grin, bowing to Zoë, clasping both Wilfrid's hands.

"What in heaven's name are *you* doing here?" Wilfrid's voice rings full of pleasure.

"I wouldn't miss it for the world. Your thoroughly deserved moment of triumph!"

"I'm rather enjoying it. But I was thankful to escape the crowd at the station with my skin intact."

Zoë knows how grateful Wilfrid feels for Willison's friendship. But since it's a political friendship, she wonders what Willison now expects in return. Men, even the most gentlemanly, always have a clear notion of their entitlements. Behind Willison she notices the inevitable presence of Alex "Silent" Smith, the party's chief bagman for Ontario. Tall and taciturn, Smith exercises excessive influence over party affairs and always seems to hover in the background wherever Willison goes. He raises his homburg to Zoë.

The Russell's owner, François-Xavier St-Jacques, tells Wilfrid of his very great delight at the election outcome. Zoë is sure St-Jacques would say the same thing to Tupper if the Conservatives had won, but she's forced to revise her opinion when he tells her, in French, "Imagine, Madame, a Prime Minister from Quebec! I never thought I'd live to see the day!"

Their suite is ready, St-Jacques assures her, and she relishes the thought of undressing and lying down. But the longed-for moment will have to wait: Willison is coming upstairs with them, although thankfully without Silent Smith. Escorting them through the cheerfully inebriated crowd up the staircase, St-Jacques lets them into number sixty-five, reputedly the largest and best-appointed suite in the hotel.

Once the door shuts behind them, everything is blessedly calm. A bundle of letters and another of telegrams, both neatly tied with string, wait on the writing desk. Beside them, a stack of newspapers and a beaded silver pitcher of ice water. Wilfrid goes straight for the telegrams. Tearing them open, he reads them aloud one after the other to Zoë and Willison: congratulations from an assortment of loyal supporters and blatant office-seekers.

Finally he comes to the one he's been waiting for. "Ah. Mowat is joining us."

Willison probably knows this already, may even have exerted some influence on the Ontario Premier's decision to enter the cabinet. Earlier in the campaign, Sir Oliver Mowat accepted a cabinet post in principle, but has been awaiting the official result before committing himself to resigning his office in Toronto.

"And to think Mowat was once Sir John A.'s law partner," Wilfrid says.

"He's expecting Justice," Willison comments dryly, "and *not* expecting to have to get himself elected."

"He'll have Justice and a Senate seat to go with it. We'll make Sir Oliver as comfortable as we possibly can."

"Ottawa not being the most comfortable city to live in," Willison adds, glancing sympathetically at Zoë.

Wilfrid telephones down to the front desk to dictate his reply to Mowat. Turning back to Willison and Zoë, he says, "Our team is nearly complete." A note of wonderment enters his voice.

"Things come to you more easily," Willison tells him, "now that you're in power."

Wilfrid looks intently at him. "Remember that speech I gave in Toronto years ago?"

"*That* one."

"Mowat was against it, Cartwright was against it, and Edgar and Mulock, all our great Ontario Liberals opposed it. Too risky, they said, too dangerous. A French Catholic telling Tory Toronto about equality and harmony would lead to violence. The Orange Order didn't want harmony—the Protestant Equal Rights Society didn't want equality. There would be riots! But I went ahead anyway and faced them in that hall you rented. They tried to drown me out, and I sweated under my clothes, but I got my point across. I told them I'd fight bigotry and extremism in Quebec as hard as I'd fight it in Ontario."

"It was a superb speech," Willison says. "A speech for the ages."

"And Premier Mowat was right there behind me on the platform, a man of our own party, with a secure hold on his province and a golden opportunity to stand up and endorse my views—but he said nothing. He did speak, as I recall, but said *absolutely nothing*. The next day he showered me with praise at our private luncheon, but nobody outside our inner circle ever heard him."

Zoë has been listening as the pitch of Wilfrid's emotion rises. She's heard this outburst before, almost word for word, but only in the privacy of their bedroom.

"I remember what you told me at that lunch," Willison says. "You leaned over and whispered, 'Damn him! Why didn't he say that last night?'"

Wilfrid sits back with a grin of satisfaction. "How things have changed. Now Sir Oliver Mowat is quite happy to join my cabinet."

Zoë admits the porter with their luggage. The men sip ice water and discuss the civil service, and she hangs up suits and dresses in the big oak wardrobe, listening closely. Willison expects Wilfrid to do a thorough housecleaning to rid Ottawa of Tories, from deputy ministers on down. The Undersecretary of State, Joseph Pope, was once Sir John A. Macdonald's personal secretary, for heaven's sake: it won't do. Wilfrid must be ruthless, must show people who think he's too much of a gentleman to be Prime Minister how mistaken they are.

Wilfrid isn't persuaded. Certain individuals may have to go, he concedes, but retirements should be on the basis of old age, and firings on the basis of incompetence, not politics. It's only natural, after eighteen years of Conservative rule, that senior officials are tinged with Toryism. But those not irredeemably disloyal to the new government deserve a chance.

"Men change, particularly when it's in their interests. We'll see how they adapt. In the British tradition, civil servants serve the government of the day impartially. I believe in British traditions. The good ones, anyway."

Willison is skeptical. "The civil servants may not be expecting your government to last. They'll bide their time before reverting to their old ways."

"Then we'll tell them we intend to remain in power a very long time."

They move on to the composition of the cabinet. It will contain no fewer than three provincial premiers: W.S. Fielding of Nova Scotia and A.G. Blair of New Brunswick, in addition to Mowat.

"You've done a masterful job of cabinet making," Willison says. "It's a college of experts, Wilfrid, a cabinet of all the talents."

"A cabinet of all the talents. May I use that?"

They're discussing the necessity of inserting Manitoba's Clifford Sifton into cabinet as soon as possible, speculating on how his astringent personality will clash with the astringent Tarte, when there's a sharp knock at the door. Zoë answers to a slim officer with a military moustache: Captain Sinclair, Lord Aberdeen's aide-de-camp. Wilfrid knows him well from private audiences with the Aberdeens, in which Sinclair was a discreet and invariable presence. He bows and announces he's come from His Excellency with a message for Mr. Laurier.

Willison excuses himself, and Captain Sinclair relaxes a little, apologizing for the lateness of the hour. "His Excellency told me I had better come in person, sir. We sent this morning's message by telegram, because you and Madame Laurier were still in transit. But as His Excellency says, there is no substitute for the Queen's messenger. He would like to see you at Rideau Hall at eleven in the morning."

Wilfrid smiles gravely and inclines his head.

When Captain Sinclair leaves, Zoë is alone with her husband for the first time since early morning. Immediately he excuses himself to sit at his desk and sort his correspondence—in case any of the letters is urgent, he explains. Realizing he's left her standing there, he turns back and asks if she's seen the cartoon in *The Globe*.

She has. He asks if she's read the caption. She hasn't. He hands her the newspaper from the top of the pile.

Zoë sits on the bed and adjusts her bifocal pince-nez. Even with their help, she has to hold the paper close to the bedside lamp to make out the caption. It quotes *The Times* of London: "Mr. Laurier counts warm friends on both sides in politics. Many Conservatives will be found to echo the remark, once made with regard to him by Sir John Macdonald: 'I can trust Laurier without the slightest fear. He is incapable of breaking his word even if he wished to.'"

"Do you think it's true?" she asks.

"About my keeping my word?"

"Of course not. About the Conservatives feeling friendly toward you."

"They may allow me a brief honeymoon, but it won't last. Old Tupper is furious I blocked him from filling the Senate with cronies before he left office."

"You can always blame Lord Aberdeen."

"Not really. I expressly asked him to refuse assent to Tupper's nominations."

"I don't like them comparing you to Macdonald."

"But why? It's a great compliment."

"Look what being Prime Minister did to *him*."

"What?"

"It killed him!"

Wilfrid laughs lightly. "My dear, Macdonald was twenty years older than I! And I haven't been in better health in years."

It's true, considering he's just been through a punishing election campaign: Wilfrid's resilience is increasing with age. For the moment his bronchitis is in abeyance, although it always returns in winter.

"I already miss the children." She's referring to their dogs and cats in Arthabaska.

Wilfrid comes to sit beside her on the bed. He takes her hand in his and kisses it. "I know you do. But as soon as we can, we'll find a house here—well, *you'll* find us one—and we can bring all the children to come and live with us. A house with a pretty garden where they can be happy. Especially Mademoiselle Topsy."

"It will be expensive."

"Remember Mulock's letter: there will be a trust fund. The party will look after everything. I know Silent Smith is too mixed up in it, but we'll never need to worry about the bills again."

"That was always the worst thing for you." It pains her to recall the times Wilfrid tried to resign as leader: his desperate letters to the party president explaining the precariousness of their finances, how he no longer had time to practise law, how he lacked the private wealth to underwrite obligations on the party's behalf. Even worse, he pleaded his personal inadequacy for the job: he actually felt unfit, a French Canadian in over his head in an English world. What if one of those resignation letters had succeeded? They wouldn't be here now, they'd be back home where they belong. But would it be enough for him? Enough to stay home in Arthabaska with the old practice, the old friends, the old marriage?

Of course not. Anyone can see he's infinitely happier now. Finally he feels the reins of power slipping into his hands. He vastly prefers power to being in opposition. When he lost the previous election to Macdonald five years ago, he erupted in expletives she's never heard him use before or since.

"Besides," he continues, "the Lavergnes will be moving their household here soon. You and Émilie will be able to reinvent a little of Arthabaska in Ottawa."

Zoë feels her entire body tense, even as her mind fights to stay clear. "The Lavergnes? *Both* of them?"

"Of course. Now that Joseph is an MP—"

"Joseph has been an MP for years."

"Yes, but now that he's a member of Her Majesty's government, he'll need Émilie to help him entertain, and such. You know how it is."

"Oh yes. I always have." She feels the old, old anger begin to churn her stomach. And she thought she'd put it behind her long ago, locked away in its vault, along with the humiliation.

"Please, my dear, I thought you'd learned to appreciate Émilie's friendship. You've said so yourself. It could get lonely for you here. Émilie will be good company in the long hours when I'm in Parliament."

"So she's coming for *my* benefit?"

Wilfrid kisses her cheek and squeezes her hand, kneads it slowly with his fingertips. "I have no illusions it's going to be easy, being in power. This is an impossible country to govern. I'll need a lot of help. I'll have to be careful and patient and forbearing. I'll need a strong cabinet, men I can trust. But I'll have something Macdonald never had in all his long, long years in power, something I need more than anything: *you*."

She lifts her gaze to those deep-set brown eyes flecked with yellow and green. They hold her fast.

3

August 1896

Émilie Lavergne moves swiftly about her room at the Russell House. It's a small confined space, and she covers it in a few strides. One more time she rearranges the showy white peonies, slightly past their prime, in the blue china vase. She approaches the open window as if expecting something new to materialize on the dust-streaked glass, something besides the dreadful heat, the endless overhead wires, the grinding streetcars of Sparks Street. She turns back to the double bed. The dowdy rose counterpane, shiny from the bottoms of prior occupants, distresses her: her sensibility demands finer things.

This dingy room is where Joseph has stayed since first being elected to Parliament. It's less than half the size of Wilfrid's sunny suite on the next floor down, and it simply won't do. Joseph's boiled white shirts and black suits hang in the narrow armoire like empty husks. There's scarcely any space left for dresses or hat boxes or shoes. It depresses Émilie to think how long they'll have to survive in this cell before they can afford a home of their own in Ottawa.

Never mind. She resolves to set the future aside, to dwell on the happy present. Wilfrid will be here at any moment. He wouldn't be specific about the time, saying only it would be after the luncheon following his first meeting with his new cabinet. Meanwhile

Joseph is spending the day across the river in Hull, putting his time to good use, sounding out legal acquaintances about his prospects for the bench.

Waiting for Wilfrid: the phrase sums up Émilie's existence. How agonizing it's always been to bring him to a new place, whether to bed or a belief in God. . . . Although it's two years old, she's chosen to wear the summer gown he likes so much, white peau de soie with short flounced sleeves and bare arms, several long strings of pearls draped loosely over the bodice. The neck square and deep, but not too—just enough to show off her shoulders. No earrings, since it's still early afternoon. An antique silver bracelet on her left wrist.

She swings past the armoire's oval mirror and doesn't entirely like what she sees. She can accept the deepening furrows under her eyes but not the slight droop under her chin, nor the matronly thickness beginning to envelop her middle. The dress clings gracefully until it reaches her waist, where it loses its way. It was absurd of the Parisian designer to add that extraneous thin strip of fabric encircling her hips. She'll have to have the gown remodelled as soon as she can find a stylish dressmaker in Ottawa. If such a thing exists.

"This dull, detested place," Wilfrid once called the city, in letters composed just down the stairs and along the corridor: "this commonplace, vulgar hotel." But, he also wrote, "*you* have the happy faculty of bringing sunshine wherever you go, of inspiring the flow of mind and soul, so the atmosphere of this awful place will be much improved by your arrival."

And now she's here.

In fact, Émilie finds the Russell rather charming in its old-fashioned way. She admires English style, if not the English themselves. It was so like Wilfrid to despise and denigrate his surroundings when he was feeling lonely or disappointed or depressed. It was the same for her, at home in Arthabaska. For years they exchanged two, three letters a week across the abyss, he here, she there—Joseph too off in the capital, the children away at school in Quebec City—and only Zoë, of all people, to keep her company. Wilfrid's letters, always so tender and thoughtful and solicitous, written in his fluent though stilted English so that Arthabaska's nosy postmistress couldn't read them, were all that kept her sane: even if he did make her jealous with his stories of women he'd met. Those days of mutual exile seemed to last forever.

Now all that has changed. With Wilfrid in power at last, and Joseph a member of his government, Émilie is determined to make Ottawa her home. Noticing an unfamiliar metallic taste in her mouth, she decides approvingly it must be the taste of Ottawa, caused perhaps by the drinking water, or the sulphurous air drifting up from the lumber mills that line both banks of the river beyond Parliament Hill. This city is their field of action. She'll advance upon it, embrace it, occupy it, populate it with her being and ideas and energy. Ottawa, with all its deficiencies, is where she and Wilfrid are fated to pursue their destiny—whatever form it may take.

For longer than she cares to remember, the obstacles to their being together have been insuperable. It's dizzying to see them swept away overnight. In his letters Wilfrid repeatedly referred to the "chains" of his political work, coiling ever more tightly about him as his career came into the ascendant. He portrayed himself as a Samson who could regain his strength only if he broke away from his duties long enough to spend a few precious hours in her presence. Soon they'll be in each other's presence almost daily. The irony is breathtaking: the chains that kept them apart so long have finally brought them together.

What other bonds might they snap? Not that she dares expect the ultimate union, but without question she can imagine it: can visualize it in vivid detail, taste its promise, its rightness. Men and women have done more outrageous things in history.

Can such things happen in Ottawa? She needs to understand this city better, has to learn how society here thinks, how it will receive the closeness of her friendship with the Prime Minister. The English, after all. But she and Wilfrid have never been secretive about that closeness, and they can't start now. Years ago they agreed not to dissemble or deceive, but to be as open as possible: open before family, neighbours, friends, above all before Zoë and Joseph. They've always behaved like people with nothing to hide. And they've been accepted as such, at least in friendly quarters, in spite of gossiping enemies. Of course, that was in Quebec City and sleepy, out-of-the-way Arthabaska, both tolerant places where Wilfrid is the favourite son and can do no wrong. . . .

Immersed in these thoughts, she almost misses the discreet but persistent knocking at her door.

She flings it open to Wilfrid standing in the corridor, courtly and perfect. He's wearing a pearl-grey summer suit and top hat, in one hand an extravagant bouquet of red roses, in the other a large parcel wrapped in plain brown paper.

"May I present these inadequate tokens?" He slips the parcel under one arm, removes his hat, offers the roses with a bow.

Émilie smiles broadly, completely forgetting her anxiety about exposing her irregular teeth. Seeing Wilfrid bow to her, however satirically, thrills her to the core.

At these moments of reunion, her doubts and misgivings dissolve in a flood of exquisite relief. She embraces him and takes the bouquet, drinking in its heady scent. He leaves his hat and parcel on the hall table beside the calling cards.

Leading him by the hand into the room, she removes the peonies from the china vase to make way for their more aristocratic cousins. She lays the peonies wetly to rest on top of yesterday's *L'Électeur*, the Quebec City newspaper loyal to Laurier and the Liberal Party.

"I trust Joseph won't mind," he says, his voice low.

"Of course not. He loves roses."

"I don't mean that. What have you been doing with yourself?"

"Waiting for you."

He smiles secretively. "Speak to me about the children. Tell me about your splendid little man and delightful girl. How are they?"

They sit facing each other on the uncomfortable blue settee, knees touching. The long sculpted slope above his upper lip is moist from the heat. She fingers a silky loop of his hair curling over the back of his high starched collar.

"As usual, the children are your first concern," she says with a mock pout, filled with simultaneous pride and regret. "Well, Gabrielle is over her summer cold. The last thing she told me when I left home was to give you her love."

"I hope she's enjoying her freedom from the convent."

"She's writing poetry again. Your praise encouraged her."

Wilfrid smiles boyishly. Glad she can give him pleasure this way, Émilie notices the hair at his temples is a little greyer than she remembers it: dusted with ash.

"I love to hear Gabrielle is writing verses. It shows what a lively imagination she has. It doesn't even matter whether they're good or bad as long as her mind is active."

"She's already eighteen. The marriageable age."

"*You* didn't marry at eighteen."

"True. I was waiting for the right man." She laughs, a little too loudly.

Wilfrid remains serious. "But Bielle mustn't rush. With all her gifts, she must wait until the right man comes along."

"The Sisters wanted her to consider a novitiate."

"Good Lord!"

She pats the back of his hand. "Don't worry, she wasn't interested. But Bielle received an excellent education at Jésus-Marie, thanks to you. We couldn't have managed without your help."

"Helping her has always given me joy."

"I know, my dear, I know. And now that stage in her life is over, and she must think about her future. For the moment she's fine at home. But if Joseph and I can buy a house in Ottawa, Bielle's marriage prospects will be greatly improved. She could—"

"Yes, and I would see much more of her. That would be delightful. Now what about Armand? He'll be returning to Quebec City before long."

"Armand is in good spirits, as always."

"Such a clever boy. I must show you his latest letter to me. It's filled with wonderful invective against the Tories: 'May you blow up Tupper, may you impale Foster,' and other provocations. He has a precocious interest in politics for a sixteen-year-old. Oh yes: 'And to destroy all that *cannaille*, you won't need bombs, only your famous eloquence.'"

"Really!" Émilie shakes her head in amused despair. "I don't know what to do with that boy."

"He must make you very proud. But he does have a tendency toward indolence. I wish you'd get him to exercise more. I know about indolence, I'm inclined that way myself. I've always been a lazy dog."

"Armand returns to the Séminaire in two weeks. I'm going to miss him."

"They'll be after him to join the priesthood too."

"He does have bouts of religious feeling, you know."

"What idealistic young man doesn't? It's natural at his age." Wilfrid rises from the settee, begins pacing. "I'm sure you don't want him to be a priest either, but it worries me there's even a possibility." He turns to face her. "The other day I went to hear the famous Father Plessis. He's a truly great sacred orator, his mind dwells in the loftiest spheres. But since I was sitting in the front row, I could observe his scrofulous shaved head and unclean robes, and it became obvious to me that far from refining a man, the priesthood does the very opposite. I thought of Armand's beautiful mind, and when I pictured him wearing those robes my heart rebelled. Far better to make him a man of the world who knows how to fight and love and do some good for his country than see him disappear into a life of empty piety."

Émilie winces at Wilfrid's impiety. "I'm sure he'll be pursuing the law. Like you and Joseph."

"At Laval, I suppose?"

She nods.

Wilfrid sighs in frustration. "Sometimes Armand's contempt for the English amuses me, but—"

"He's young, Wilfrid. Give him time."

"I know—he's in a rebellious phase. But if he'd cultivate his English, he could take law at McGill and he'd be far better off. The priests at the Séminaire put the most ridiculous notions into his head. They want to erect a little French-only stockade on the banks of the St. Lawrence. Well, it's 1896, and that's no longer possible!"

Émilie sits, waiting for the rest.

"Armand needs to understand: if he spoke English as fluently as French, it would advance his prospects immeasurably. Not only that, such a passionate French Canadian *needs* English if he's going to achieve anything for his people. I do wish you'd exercise your influence over him, my dear. It's still not too late."

Émilie wills herself to stay calm. She has her own anxieties about Armand, her own nagging fears, fragile hopes for his future. "Of course, of course, I agree with you. I'll do my best to persuade him. But you know as well as I, he's headstrong. It would do him a world of good to see you again, to hear all this from you in person. You know how he looks up to you."

"Sometimes I wonder."

"How can you doubt it?"

In her agitation Émilie abandons the settee for the roses, rearranging them absentmindedly. Wilfrid goes and sits in her place, staring moodily off to the side. This isn't the way she imagined their reunion. And all because he insists on dwelling on the children. "Please, Wilfrid, let's discuss something else."

He looks up sharply. "What could be more important than the young man?"

"Well, if you want more influence over him, he needs to see you more often! If Joseph and I were to move our household to Ottawa, Armand could be here every school holiday, every Christmas, all summer long—"

"Here we are again. Am I to arrange this too?"

"There's one thing you *could* arrange, and it wouldn't be so difficult."

"My dear Émilie, as knowledgeable as you are about the world, you greatly exaggerate my powers—"

"The *bench*."

He smiles in a way she doesn't especially like. "You want me to appoint my law partner to the Supreme Court."

"Of course not. Don't be ridiculous. Although I'm sure in time Joseph would make an excellent candidate."

"And I'm sure you realize I must tend to some other matters first."

"No doubt. But the sooner Joseph can earn something more than his pitiful parliamentary salary, the sooner we can move to Ottawa." She forges ahead, trying to ignore his impatient frown. "Once there was a time when you wanted that, Wilfrid, you wanted me near you more than anything. In your letters—"

"Yes, and I want it still. Clearly this hotel room is too small for both of you." He smiles again, but warmly.

She looks closely at him, verifying his sincerity. Unable to help herself, she returns to the settee, reaching for him with both arms. Wilfrid pulls her to him, and for a moment she treasures the rasp of his cheek against hers, the beloved friction. His hand brushes her bare throat and drops languorously to her left breast.

She stares at the contrast between the pale flesh of his fingers and the pale sheen of the silk. She feels shocked: not by the intimacy, which she craves, but because it's been so long.

He pulls his hand away. "I'll speak to some people about a judgeship," he says, startled. "You need to be here. *I* need you to be here."

She feels the entire surface of her skin flush under his gaze. "So you haven't forgotten the distant violin?"

"Never."

For an instant she sees a familiar gleam of desire creep over his features: the outer form of his longing for her, his love made visible. But the suggestion fades, and she wonders if she only glimpsed a memory. Banishing her doubts, she raises his hand in both of hers, presses it between moist palms, presses it to her heart.

They remain seated, drinking the iced lemonade Émilie ordered up for three o'clock. She asks Wilfrid about his cabinet meeting. Evidently Tarte and Cartwright are already crossing swords, full of mutual mistrust. Only Fielding and Mowat are behaving like statesmen. She tells Wilfrid *he'll* have to be the statesman. He replies that his election victory seems to have inspired everyone but him: he keeps feeling a surprising, irreducible sadness. He doesn't understand it, but he's heard of this happening to other politicians, discovering in victory more bitterness than joy.

She finds his ambivalence disappointing. Although she wants to pursue the matter, she can see he's wilting, exhausted from the heat. She feels tired herself, enervated from the excitement of being alone together after so long. Hoping a change of scene will revive them, she suggests a walk down in the streets.

"You know I adore strolling with you. But things are different now. I can't simply walk outside anytime I wish."

"Really? The company you keep must be restricted?"

"No, no, I just have to be prudent. My movements are watched far more closely now. You have no idea how the gossips scrutinize me. Every gesture, every expression is examined for political portents."

"You never cared about the gossips before. We used to have such lovely walks in Ottawa. Remember that pretty courtyard? It was so enchanting."

"This town positively dines on gossip. And with a new government coming in, everyone's nervous. There's great anxiety, a fear of losing prestige and position and privilege and all that. Not everyone wishes us well."

"What of it? You were elected by the people, not the gossips."

"Still, I can't present our enemies with a weapon to use against me. It's too early in the game."

Émilie shrinks from him against the end of the settee, feeling the oak armrest digging into her spine. "I've never thought of myself as a weapon." He smiles to disarm her, but she won't be put off. "Does this mean we can no longer be seen together?"

"There will be other ways. Other occasions. Just not strolling along Elgin Street *à deux* on a sleepy summer afternoon. People expect me to be hard at work on matters of state! This isn't Arthabaska, my dear."

Émilie feels her spirits sinking, but Wilfrid rouses himself, leaning confidingly toward her. "I've been rereading your letters. I do that from time to time. They're absolute gems, you know. I've always thought you should take up writing, you have such a flair for it. You have the sparkling mind and charming style of a Madame de Staël, a Madame de Sévigné—and your perceptions of people are just as acute."

"Stop it, Wilfrid."

He grins. "You always say that. You call me a flatterer and say you have no literary gifts, but you know I'm right. No need for false modesty. Your writing is like your conversation, gliding in delightful arabesques—"

"Enough!"

"If you allowed your pen free rein, there would be no limit to what you could do."

She can't help but smile at his extravagance. She shakes her head but lets him continue.

"I used to think if you took up writing, it would compensate for your loneliness. It would fill up your solitude and make it more appealing. But now I see grander possibilities. Here in the capital, you could actually *be* our Madame de Staël! Why not? Invite the famous to your *salon*, provoke them with audacious conversation, then write wickedly about them in the magazines. Why not see what you can do with your pen? Even Lady Macdonald wrote for the magazines in London and New York."

"Am I to be your Lady Macdonald?" The thought is out before she can suppress it.

Wilfrid hesitates. "Perhaps the wrong analogy, but you see my point—Ottawa needs you. My goodness, *Canada* needs you. . . ."

He settles back, and they regard each other with a flash of the old humour and avidity. At last they're rediscovering their special rapport and intimacy, their unique ability to poke fun without malice, to take unbounded pleasure in each other.

Wilfrid rises and goes to the hall table, returning with the parcel. He resumes his seat beside her. "I thought I'd bring these to you."

"My goodness. What are they?"

"Letters." He places the parcel between her hands, and she feels the weight of it, heavy as stone.

"*My* letters? *All* of them?"

"From all down the years. That's why I've been rereading them. I wanted to revisit you through your words, savour all their nuances—"

"Before getting rid of them."

"Before returning them to you for safekeeping. What you do with them, my dear, is your prerogative. You wrote them."

Émilie feels bewildered, frightened, unspeakably wounded. "Is that what you want? An *auto-da-fé*?"

"In any case," Wilfrid says patiently, as if what he's doing, as if the sacred trust he's in the process of betraying, is perfectly reasonable, "the letters are safer in your hands."

"Safer from what?"

"From prying eyes. I've had reason for some time to think my correspondence is being tampered with. Some letters I was waiting for didn't arrive. I don't want to take any further chances."

Émilie tries to think, to understand this. What is he saying, exactly? That her letters have been read by others? That she must no longer write to him? She struggles to absorb the fact that he's abandoning incalculable years of their lives. Every one of those pages is stained with her tears, her heart's blood, but all she can think to say is, "What do you want me to do with them?"

"Safeguard them, my dear. For both our sakes. And read them. You'll discover what a superb author you are."

"I didn't write them for publication."

"No, you wrote them for me, but also yourself. They'll reacquaint you with the woman you were."

"And who have *you* been?"

"You have my letters."

"They claim you want to be with me."

"They were—and are—correct."

"If that were true," she cries miserably, "you wouldn't be returning mine! You'd keep them, you'd cherish them. They won't curl up and die like, like these roses you've brought!" She feels an urge to pull his roses from the vase and dash them to the floor, deterred only by fear of tearing her fingers on the thorns.

"My dear," Wilfrid begins—

"What about 'My dearest, ever dearer'? What about St. Anne's Hill? What about the distant violin? *What has happened*, Wilfrid?"

She glances left and right, anywhere, as long as it's away from him. She wants to flee the room but has nowhere to go. Without warning she feels his hands hot on her skin, his fingers clamped on her bare upper arms. He brings his face up close to hers, a frantic anxiety playing about his eyes. "Please, Émilie, don't misunderstand me. Don't be unjust!"

"What *you're* doing is the most unjust thing I can imagine!" She wants to pull free of him but knows it will only send him into a panic. She allows him to continue holding onto her, even though it's beginning to hurt.

"I know how this must seem to you," he pleads, "how it must look, but believe me, I'd shout my love from the rooftops if I could. Try to understand: a Prime Minister's papers, even his private ones, are no longer his own. They become public property. Do we want the eyes of strangers prying into our most personal moments? Better to safeguard our privacy by putting it in your hands. That's all I ask, my dearest: take care of these precious letters of yours. And let me come and reread them now and then."

He's so desperate, so sincere, his request so reasonable. Slowly he releases his grip on her arms and subsides against the settee, waiting for her to concede.

She stares at the flesh of her arms, still showing the marks of his fingertips. She waits for the trembling to stop. "So you haven't given up on us?" she asks dully.

"Not in the least."

"St. Anne's Hill could still be ours?"

"If only you knew how much I want it."

"I'm sorry. I shouldn't have doubted you."

"I hate to see you distressed and sad. But I understand—all this waiting is painful."

"It's intolerable."

"You've had reason to doubt and distrust me in the past, but now, never. No matter how often I read them, those passages in St. Anne's Hill still bring our dream alive. It haunts me more than ever—especially in these labours I'm taking on."

"Yes. Labours that will keep you chained for years to come." She laughs ruefully, in spite of herself. "We'll be old and toothless by the time we reach St. Anne's Hill."

She feels calmer, her anger drained, released into the ocean of their mutual need for reassurance.

Impulsively he reaches for her hand, caressing her palm with his fingertips. "When people see us tottering along the sidewalk, they'll say, 'Just look at those two, what a delightful old couple. And so in love!'"

Wilfrid enfolds her in a farewell embrace ending in a kiss on the mouth, then leaves to collect Zoë. They're going to a garden party to which Émilie isn't invited.

Sitting on the edge of the bed, she drains an entire glass of lemonade. Her throat is parched, strained with unshed tears. She feels numb. Not quite there. The silence has a sinister quality.

The parcel full of her letters sits bulging, unopened, on the settee, a gift she never wanted. It repels her. She'll have to secrete it somewhere in the room, in her luggage perhaps. Joseph is returning soon. She must change into a more everyday dress.

Her hands haven't stopped shaking, faint tremors running up her wrists. Something has happened, something acknowledged, yet unacknowledged. Its meaning still isn't fully clear to her. What *is* clear is that the rest of her life remains to be lived: only not in the way she imagined.

In her mind she's kept alive the image of a country lane winding mysteriously into some gentle forest of the future, beckoning to her. All she had to do was follow that path. Now she sees it obstructed, barred by an ugly brick wall. Wilfrid put the wall there. He has the power to make her future possible or impossible, and she hates him for it: no one has a right to such power! Surely he's the most self-centred, capricious, unprincipled man alive, capable of fabricating the most treacherous illusions, communicating the most convoluted double meanings, which only he can interpret. She sees miserably that this is also one of the reasons why she loves him.

Is this how the end comes? Not the end: not yet. Émilie applies her mind to the problem. To know the truth of her position, she need only recall his words, written in his own hand. Having pored endlessly over his letters for clues to his real feelings and intentions, she knows them by heart:

"When you read the chapter 'St. Anne's Hill,' you will understand that when I read it, my heart grows full of images indulged in, never realized… ."

"Put the book aside. Keep it in readiness so that I may point out to you what has struck me about it, what would be my dream, what picture now haunts me. I would fondly dream of the repose of St. Anne's Hill, after the toils in which I am engaged… ."

"The wish you express, how often I have expressed it to myself! Yes, my dear, I will not forget it, even if I have to carry it with me to the spheres beyond… ."

"How gladly I would give my position to someone else, if someone else would take it. Unfortunately I feel the coils tighter every day around me. How I wish I could take you to the beach and rest there for hours. I would see you again as childishly happy as I once saw you in the little square here. But this is not and cannot be my lot… ."

"Time itself would be nothing if it brought our share of the blessings that are due to us, that are within sight, yet unattainable...."

Unattainable. He wrote the word himself, plain as day. For a long time she glossed over it, willfully overlooked it. But now she remembers it with appalling clarity.

What, then, *is* attainable?

When she first knew him in Arthabaska, Wilfrid was just a young country lawyer. He still had to learn which piece of silverware to pick up at her dinner parties, the proper way to eat an orange at table. She taught him all the etiquette that a gentleman of the world needs to know. She taught him how to eat, how to discriminate among wines, how to dress fashionably and with taste, how to conduct himself among the English elite with whom he must mingle to succeed in Ottawa. Along with elegance in dress and manner, she inspired him with her love of things English, nurtured by her days in London. Now, having arrived at the pinnacle, is he casting her aside because he no longer needs her?

Her immediate answer is no. Although his need for her tutelage is over, his need for her inspiration and ideas and vibrant conversation remains as pressing as ever. Wilfrid can talk to her in ways and on subjects that he can't talk to Zoë, or anyone else. When he's alone with his Émilie, he can be himself, without censure, without reproach. His spirit needs oxygen to breathe and soar and aspire to its limitless possibilities: she provides that oxygen. His mission requires help in steering a course through the perilous shoals of politics, especially among the English, above all among the Aberdeens and their household: she can provide him with that too. And his manhood demands the completion of a family. None of this can Zoë give him. In all these roles, the piano teacher is constitutionally, completely, hopelessly inadequate. Useless.

Now that she's in Ottawa, Émilie will find new ways to make herself indispensable to him. And in the process she'll grow closer to him: closer in ways they've never known before. She'll share his power.

She breathes deeply, rises from the edge of the bed, seats herself with dignity at the escritoire. She takes hotel stationery from the drawer and dips the hotel pen into the little inkwell and begins writing to him, her custom down through the years, her bridge across the abyss.

After two sentences she slowly puts the pen down. Finally she weeps.

4

December 1896

Like a courtier spreading his cloak before her feet, the caretaker scatters sand down the icy front steps of Notre-Dame. Zoë, snug in her sealskin coat, descends gingerly to Sussex Street, each stair melting into a sandy blur before her eyes. She reminds herself it's all right: she can see better at a distance.

Winter has arrived in Ottawa, and that much, at least, feels right, familiar. Zoë loves the exhilarating, ice-blue sky, the long sharp shadows thrown by a sun down low to the horizon. Safely arrived on the sidewalk lined with orderly snowbanks, she looks up at the cathedral. Its twin spires piercing the heavens are a grander version of St-Christophe, her own parish church high on the hill in Arthabaska.

Attending morning Mass has become her ritual since moving to the capital. Setting out for the cathedral lends purpose and comfort to her days, which yawn emptily ahead until Wilfrid returns from Parliament Hill at six. She misses Mass only on days when they're entertaining, and she has to oversee arrangements in the Russell's private dining room: they're still living at the hotel.

But she hasn't yet warmed to any of the Ottawa priests, much less to the austere Bishop Duhamel, known for his opposition to Wilfrid. She can't imagine confessing to them, as she did to Father

Suzor at St-Christophe, her shameful fantasies: gouging Émilie's eyes, breaking her nose so it spouts blood like a whale, knocking out her ugly teeth. Father Suzor, who heard her confession for years, took it all in stride, gently reassuring her that the Lord understands the nature of temptation and loves us all the more when we're tempted to sin but bravely resist. Courage, patience, acceptance, perseverance were Father Suzor's counsel: above all patience, for God blesses those who wait without complaining. While remaining steadfastly loyal to her husband, she must offer up her pain to Him who sees and understands. The greater her suffering, the more stars would gleam in her crown.

Zoë sets off on her frigid walk back to the hotel. A bitter wind stings her cheeks, floods her eyes with tears. She won't take a carriage. Wilfrid never exercises, and she has to get enough for both of them.

If the House of Commons was sitting, she'd go and occupy the seat reserved for her in the front row of the visitors' gallery, directly above Mr. Speaker—an office Wilfrid has awarded to the literary James Edgar, in lieu of a cabinet post. To her great surprise she actually enjoys the fractious, theatrical spectacle as it unfolds in the pit below her feet, she who once had no use for politics. Watching Wilfrid in command of the unruly House, and by extension the unruly country, allows her to be more useful to him in their bedtime conversations. She's forming opinions. Wilfrid says he finds her observations of men and motives helpful. But the first session of the new Parliament is over, its main purpose to vote the monies necessary for carrying on the public service, and in the process to display Wilfrid's new government to the nation. Like a peacock, Zoë thought at the time, displaying his feathers to the female.

Doggedly she proceeds along St. Patrick Street, up Parent and into the By Ward Market. Her gloved hands press her fur collar against her cheeks. The market streets are much quieter in winter. In warmer months they're crammed with the wagons of merchants and Jewish peddlers and market gardeners, the sidewalks crowded with customers lined up at fruit and vegetable stands shaded by giant umbrellas. Even now, with their doors closed against the cold, the little shops release their pungent smells of cheese and fish and freshly stuffed sausage into the air. The sidewalk is cluttered with discarded wooden crates. She has to squint to navigate around them.

Three sleighs stand side by side facing Lapointe's, steam rising from blankets on the horses' flanks, the occupants inside shopping for the day's catch. Zoë enters, quietly taking her place in line. She needs to order lobster and oysters for Saturday night's dinner party. Rather than let the Russell's chef order her meats and seafood, she buys them herself to ensure quality and freshness, and to get the best price.

She likes being inside the shop's sharp briny warmth. When M. Lapointe sees her, he makes the usual pleasant fuss, bypassing the other patrons to serve her first, and in French. His handlebar moustache reminds her of Émilie's husband, Joseph. Lapointe asks in a conspiratorial whisper who's on the guest list this time, and Zoë teases him by mentioning only the Clerk of the House and the Parliamentary Librarian. Lapointe's eyebrows narrow in disappointment until she relents, adding the names of prominent newspaper owners from Montreal, Quebec City and Ottawa, and several cabinet ministers, all with wives. He licks the tips of his moustache and orders his boys to crate up his best crustaceans for delivery to the Russell House, care of M. Desjardins, the chef. As she leaves, the other customers turn to stare.

Trekking across Sappers Bridge over the Rideau Canal, Zoë reaches the Russell a little after eleven. Upstairs in their suite, she removes three long pins from her hat, struggles out of her coat, unbuttons her high boots. She sits on the bed and sighs: fatigued not merely from her walk in the cold, but her never-absent longing to be elsewhere.

This is how it was for Wilfrid years ago, on first arriving in Ottawa. The poor dear wrote letter after letter home to tell her how desolate and out-of-place he felt: "The session has not even begun, and already I want to see it end. As far as I'm concerned, the best thing about being an MP is the salary." She knew back then his isolation was all the sadder for the memories it evoked: the boy of St-Lin being sent away to school after his mother had died, because his father wanted him to learn English from the Scots of New Glasgow.

Of course that doesn't explain her own misgivings. By now, after several months as Prime Minister's wife, she should be feeling confident in her role. But that's the trouble: it *is* a role, mere playacting. There's no school where she could learn the part, and even if she was bold enough to ask for her advice, the formidable Lady Macdonald, now a baroness, is living somewhere in the south of England, unreachable. Zoë simply has to do as Wilfrid did, learn from scratch. Yet there's a crucial difference: it wasn't *her* choice to live here.

She notices the enamelled pin lying on the dresser, white heather entwined with ivy, a gift to Wilfrid from Lady Aberdeen. The Governor General's lady is another conquest. Not that he has to work at winning these admirers. On the day he was sworn in, Lady Aberdeen presented him with a sprig of real heather, enclosing it in a note explaining the old Highland custom: if a girl meets a man and gives him a piece of white heather when he embarks on a quest, it brings him luck. For good measure she also enclosed the pin, to serve as a reminder after the heather had wilted.

At dinner at Rideau Hall the other night, Wilfrid wore the pin in place of his usual horseshoe stick pin. Lady Aberdeen looked transported when he took her in to dinner on his arm. Zoë was on Lord Aberdeen's arm, or rather one of them—on impulse the

Governor General offered the other to Émilie, explaining rather too loudly that Madame Lavergne looked lonely with her husband out of town on business. A very peculiar sort of gallantry, in Zoë's opinion.

All the same, Zoë trusts the Aberdeens, considers them friends and allies. Her Excellency has made up her mind that Madame Laurier is sad because she has no children: she herself has four. The concern is an extension of Lady Aberdeen's maternal approach to Canada. She's announced her intention of establishing a national order of nurses to provide home care for Canadians, in celebration of the Queen's Diamond Jubilee next year. She believes it will complement the National Council of Women, her vehicle for improving Canadian society by giving women more influence.

In fact, the Aberdeens have done more than anyone to make Zoë feel at home here: ironic, considering they're from Scotland. When Lady Aberdeen threw a mammoth fancy-dress ball in the Senate chamber, a revue of Canada's history since the time of Jacques Cartier, she assigned Zoë a starring role as wife of the Sieur de Maisonneuve, awarding only a small subordinate part to Émilie. When Lord Aberdeen read the Speech from the Throne in August, he gave it first in French, posting plainclothes officers around the Senate to insist on quiet, since English MPs always chat rudely during the French. And when the Toronto *Mail and Empire* greeted Wilfrid's election with a virulent diatribe against "French domination," claiming Quebec would now "demand its pound of flesh," the Aberdeens assured the Lauriers of their outrage.

It's a blessing such people occupy Rideau Hall. She must offer up a prayer of thanks tomorrow for the Aberdeens. And when she thinks what a great doer Lady Aberdeen is, despite the migraine headaches that periodically confine her to bed, she glimpses her own salvation. Zoë too will have to take action. Here in Ottawa she's going to stay, whether she likes it or not. She's fated to belong to everyone and no one, when all she wants is to be once more the simple wife of the small-town lawyer of Arthabaska. That was the best time of their lives. But Wilfrid has no intention of going back, so neither can she.

God has a purpose to everything, and she's beginning to discern His purpose for her. She's in a position now to *do* things: to exercise influence over people and events. There's no shortage of those who need her help. She can promote at the highest levels the clearly deserving, the unjustly ignored, the cruelly mistreated. She can advance the careers of gifted young musicians and artists, as she once did in the smaller sphere of Arthabaska. She can bring to Ottawa her mahogany grand piano, her menagerie of song-birds, her cats and dogs, even her dear nieces and nephews if she wants, as long as she can find a house big enough to hold them all. If only she'll act, she can do all this and more. She can even recreate, after a fashion, their old home life, carving out a warm and welcoming island in this frozen English place.

Imagining herself doing these things makes it all seem possible. Zoë's spirits begin to rise. In any case, it's entirely up to her: Wilfrid has no time. He's fully preoccupied with the exigencies and opportunities of the nation's young life, all the promise and peril. Gold has been discovered in the Yukon wilderness. Canadian and American prospectors have rushed north, and Wilfrid has sent the North-West Mounted Police after them to keep order. The world needs Canada's wheat, the prairies need more farmers. Immigrants will supply the necessary manpower, sturdy eastern Europeans, since English and French Canada can't produce settlers fast enough. Every railway promoter in the land is lobbying Wilfrid for the right to build lines across the prairies to transport the immigrants west, the wheat and gold east.

Wilfrid has brought Clifford Sifton into cabinet, a strange, abrupt, impatient man who is rapidly going deaf, to oversee the westward expansion. To Sifton the future is already here, it must be dealt with immediately. The border with Alaska remains in dispute, making both Wilfrid and Sifton anxious to reach a settlement with Washington before it decides the Yukon is simply too tempting, too empty, to leave in Canadian hands. Voices south of the border are already clamouring to swallow Canada whole. An organization called the Continental Union League favours annexation, and it isn't just a lunatic fringe: its headquarters are in New York, its members include Andrew Carnegie, Senator Henry Cabot Lodge, Theodore Roosevelt. The problems are vast and bewildering, yet Wilfrid is exhilarated. One of these days he'll worry himself sick over them, but for now he's transfixed by Canada's splendid and limitless future, and his own role in creating it.

For a woman of Quebec, it's enough to contend with the bitterness in her own province over Wilfrid's settlement of the Manitoba schools conflict. The bishops are outraged he didn't restore full French Catholic rights after the provincial government dissolved them, but he insists he's done all he can constitutionally, making the best of a bad job inherited from the Conservatives. With his gift for diplomacy—what the newspapers call his "sunny ways"—he's forged a compromise and prevented a religious civil war. But that isn't good enough for the bishops. They've denounced him to the Vatican as worse than liberal: as a free-thinker, anti-clerical, anti-Catholic. They've forbidden the faithful to vote Liberal on pain of being refused absolution. They've sent parish priests door to door to warn Liberals won't be buried in holy ground, and they've banned the writings of Laurent-Olivier David and *L'Électeur*.

These attacks make Wilfrid furious, yet he refuses to strike back. Holding himself in check is costing him enormous anguish. Only Zoë knows how painfully he bears the fury of the Church, *their* Church—only Zoë and one other person.

The muffled knocking of a gloved hand makes her realize she's forgotten all about her promise to go house hunting. Émilie lets herself into the room in a cascade of bright laughter scented with French cologne. She's wearing a long dark-green coat trimmed with mink and a matching mink hat, and is already talking about the houses she's picked out for them to visit.

Zoë falters. After her long morning walk, she's not sure her legs are up to inspecting houses: she definitely knows her spirits aren't. It's never easy to deny Émilie, but in the firmest tone she can muster she proposes they first take tea in the Russell House café. And Émilie, who isn't, after all, completely insensitive and inconsiderate, sees Zoë is tired and agrees.

They descend the grand staircase arm in arm into the lobby.

Sessional People, as parliamentarians and their staff are known, consider the Russell's café the place to see and be seen in Ottawa. It's done up with mirrors and gilt and dark wood panelling in homage to Paris and Vienna. During the lull between breakfast and lunch, the large room is nearly empty. Zoë and Émilie's coats are whisked away, they're shown to a corner table in its own little alcove. The tall, severely correct senior waiter takes their order for tea and *petites madeleines*, bearing it off to the kitchen like a royal decree.

Zoë fears she's becoming too comfortable in the care of the Russell's staff, acquiring a taste for being waited on. But since she dreads the prospect of poking into other people's homes, with Émilie fingering the draperies and asking embarrassing personal questions of the owners, she'd gladly remain in the café right through lunch. Émilie's colour is high, reflecting her excitement over their impending adventure. She sees tea as only a brief delay in her plans, a necessity to humour Zoë before plunging into the day's drama.

As Émilie chatters on, Zoë observes her. Émilie relishes giving descriptions of the three homes for sale, all conveniently within walking distance in Sandy Hill. She knows the virtues and drawbacks of each, the order in which they should be visited. Zoë nods from time to time in absentminded agreement.

Ever since Émilie Barthe, as she then was, descended on Arthabaska in the early years of the Laurier marriage and cut a swath through local society, having lived with her father in Paris and London, people have said how extraordinary she is, how witty and worldly and vivacious and cosmopolitan. And how remarkable that her high spirits and entrancing conversation make one completely overlook her plainness. The sharpness of her nose. The narrowness of her mouth. Her weak chin. Her oddly large, heavy-lidded eyes with their yellowish pupils, said to result from her habit of reading late into the night. *"Une jolie laide,"* people called her from the very first: an ugly beauty.

People were right, Zoë thinks. Not that it prevented Émilie from becoming an immediate threat to every wife in their circle. Silly, really: it was only Zoë who had anything to fear. From the very first she saw that Émilie had eyes for Wilfrid alone and, since he was already married, that she'd take the next best thing and marry his law partner. Even then Zoë was a step ahead of Émilie. It was just that she could do nothing to stop her.

Of course it was never Émilie's appearance but her knowledge of literature that Wilfrid admired. Their mutual love of reading is their self-described bond, and it's unbreakable. Certainly it's well beyond Zoë to share opinions about Madame de Staël or Victor Hugo (whom Émilie once actually met) or Byron or Mary Shelley. Once Joseph Lavergne married Émilie, changing her from a dangerous single woman into a supposedly safe wife, Wilfrid would rise from his desk in their small office every day, either at eleven in the morning or at English teatime, and announce: "Now, Joseph, if you will permit it, I will go and have a little chat with your wife." And he'd walk to the door with a book under his arm. Joseph's permission was always given, since in any case it was always taken for granted.

The Lavergnes' pretty home, Le Vert Logis, was the setting for this long-running literary salon of two. It's just four doors down the street from the law office, which in turn sits directly across the street from the Lauriers' house. The Lauriers and the Lavergnes lived within constant sight of each other in those days: a very narrow compass indeed. Everything happened in full view of everyone.

"You mustn't worry about the expense of buying another house," Émilie is telling her, "the party will cover the cost. Mr. Mulock will see to that."

"Oh—you know about his letter?" Zoë isn't sure whether to feel betrayed, angry or just irritated by the inevitable. Mr. Mulock's letter was a personal communication between the Liberal Party's richest MP and Wilfrid. There's no reason why Émilie should know about it. Or about the trust fund, or the promise to buy them a house. And if she does know, there's still less reason for her to tell Zoë—unless it's to flaunt her closeness to Wilfrid. And that too is unnecessary.

"I envy you the freedom to pick out any home you choose," Émilie declares. "How many women get that chance? Really, Zoë, you don't know how lucky you are."

"Oh, I think I do," she replies softly. She doesn't want anyone to overhear them discussing such private matters, even though no one is actually within earshot. "But won't you and Joseph be buying a house too?" She knows today's outing is as much for Émilie's benefit as her own.

"I certainly hope so. As long as he gets a judgeship."

"Wilfrid says he deserves it."

"Of course he does." Émilie puts on her bravest smile, her mask of supreme self-confidence that dares the world to contradict it. "Wilfrid won't fail us. He never fails either of us, my dear."

Zoë looks away across the dining room, grateful for the approach of the waiter carrying a silver tea service on a silver tray. She never ceases to wonder at Émilie's blithe assumption that all will be given her in time. Setting the plate of little cakes between them, the waiter asks the ladies' permission to pour the tea, which has already steeped, into frail china cups.

"I adore *le thé à l'anglaise*," Émile remarks.

This must be for the waiter's benefit, since it's hardly news to Zoë. She thinks how much more important this morning's rituals in the cathedral are to her than her friendship with Émilie. Or, for that matter, than the mock drama and hollow battles of politics, which consume Wilfrid's waking hours. Church, family, home: Zoë knows what matters. This morning she may make some progress toward a home, so Émilie is doing her a kindness after all. She should be thankful.

"The Americans have their White House," Zoë says, "so the President already has a place to live. Perhaps we should be like them."

Delicately Émilie inserts a *madeleine* between sharp front teeth and severs it in half. "Why would anyone want to be like the Americans?"

Zoë blows on the surface of her tea. "It's an insult to one's tea to blow on it," Wilfrid tells her, but nobody is looking except Émilie, and flouting Wilfrid's conception of good manners gives her a perverse satisfaction.

Émilie leans forward conspiratorially over the table. "What do you think about the knighthood?"

"What knighthood?"

Émilie leans back in her chair, grinning. She's trumped Zoë once again. "There's a rumour that the Queen is going to knight Wilfrid," she says gloatingly. "He'll be on her honours list for the Jubilee. You haven't heard? I'm astonished, my dear."

Zoë has never actually blushed in Émilie's presence before.

Émilie goes on: "Imagine, 'Sir Wilfrid.' What could be more splendid? And *you'll* be Lady Laurier!"

Émilie's grin is manic. Zoë suspects it conceals misery, jealous hostility: a conviction that Zoë doesn't appreciate such high royal favour, much less deserve it.

"Rumours are rumours," Zoë says. "I know for a fact Wilfrid doesn't want a knighthood. His supporters don't care for titles, and neither does he. He prefers to remain plain M. Laurier, the same as he's always been."

Émilie reaches into her pearl-embroidered purse for more surprises. "Here are the houses." Somehow she's obtained little photographs of all three homes for sale. She pushes aside the plate of *madeleines* to spread the black-and-white prints on the table-cloth in an arc, a croupier dealing cards. "There. Which one do you like best?"

Peering uncertainly at the grainy, indistinct images, Zoë fumbles in her purse for her pince-nez. "I'd need to see inside first."

"Of course you will. But from an architectural point of view, they're all quite distinguished, don't you think?"

Zoë studies the photographs. She doesn't know what to say. She hates being put on the spot.

The first house is built of brick in the French style, with a mansard roof and dormer windows. It has three storeys, and its elegance and symmetry appeal to her. The other two are of stone, more horizontal in design, with white, intricately carved verge boards and front verandahs and gabled windows on the top floor. One of them is evidently part of a terrace.

Émilie keeps up a running commentary. The brick house is on Theodore Street, the two stone ones on Daly, not far from Sanford Fleming's home. "Just think, you'd be walking along the sidewalk and Sir Sanford would step out of his garden and bow and present you with a long-stemmed rose. He's wonderfully gallant, a true gentleman of the old school. That terrace, by the way, is named Philomene, after the original owner's wife. Romantic, isn't it?"

"I like the first house best," Zoë offers.

"Oh, really? But stone is so much more distinguished than brick."

"I don't think I want to live in a terrace home. Too crowded."

"Of course. It lacks grandeur."

"There wouldn't be room for a garden. Or our pets."

"No, but the last occupant was the poet, Lampman."

"The brick one is the prettiest. It reminds me of our house at home."

"I suppose it does. But Zoë, at home you weren't a great Prime Minister's wife! Really, the nicest by far is the middle one. It has the most gracious lines *and* the largest rooms. You'd entertain splendidly there. You'll have ever so many obligations to fulfil now, you must think of that."

A brittle silence. "Since you like that house so well, Émilie, why don't *you* buy it? I'm sure you and Joseph will want to entertain splendidly too, once you're a great judge's wife."

Zoë stands up. An attentive young waiter rushes to pull out her chair, another hurries away to fetch their coats. She makes certain she exits the café first, as befits a Prime Minister's wife, great or otherwise.

5

Spring 1897

Émilie is jubilant. Joseph Lavergne's appointment as a judge of the Quebec Superior Court in Hull is finally confirmed. She's vindicated. She was absolutely right to persevere, to insist.

Her husband will no longer be merely a backbencher in Wilfrid's government, invisible within the Quebec Liberal caucus. Joseph finds parliamentary work disagreeable in any case. With his sensitive nature, he isn't cut out for the dirty work of politics. His talents and temperament suit him far better for the bench.

Of course the appointment, accompanied by a not incidental increase in salary, means they can finally begin looking for a home in the capital. Hull is out of the question, Émilie has assured Joseph: and in Ottawa there's only one possible location, Sandy Hill. Wilfrid and Zoë have chosen a yellow-brick Second Empire house at 335 Theodore Street, now being renovated at party expense. It previously belonged to an Ottawa jeweller, and Émilie finds it rather staid and out of fashion, but Zoë is thrilled, saying the floor plan reminds her of her home in Arthabaska. Émilie doesn't consider that a recommendation.

Joseph's ascension to the bench coincides with the coming of spring, and both arrive just in time to save Émilie's sanity. With Parliament recessed all winter, she's been spending tedious weeks in Arthabaska confined indoors because of the extreme cold. Joseph has been carrying on the law practice, training a junior partner to conduct the day-to-day business. For Émilie, the whole winter has been a dreary reprise of her old existence, the desperate stretches without Wilfrid. But this time, coming after the high hopes of the previous summer, it's been worse than ever. Wilfrid has practically disappeared into the fog of government.

When they return to the capital for the spring session, Émilie persuades Joseph to take a suite at the Russell in place of their old room. It has double the closet space and is located on the same floor as the Lauriers. It's definitely too expensive, but, she reminds Joseph, it won't be long before they'll be moving into their own home, and with his higher income they can almost afford the monthly rate. Besides, they need the extra space now that Gabrielle is with them full-time.

Émilie is determined to make the most of living at the Russell. She likes to imagine its five storeys surmounted by ramparts as a chateau on the Loire, and herself and Joseph and Bielle as guests of a benevolent count. The fantasy is difficult to maintain. Street-cars screech around the corner at all hours, and above the main entrance an electric sign has been installed, red, white and blue light bulbs picking out a garish Union Jack alongside the words, "Victoria Regina 1837–97." It's impossible to escape the excesses of imperialists mad to celebrate the Diamond Jubilee, equally impossible to avoid the barefoot urchins who swarm over the side-walk below the sign, offering to shine shoes or perform errands or Lord knows what else. They speak both languages fluently, which tells Émilie they must be poor French from Lower Town.

Still, the Russell has its advantages. Modern steam heat makes the rooms comfortable. Of the stores lining the ground level, the milliner's, men's wear and florist shops are convenient, although uninspiring. Joseph likes to patronize the cigar store. The café's menu is reliable, if repetitious. And so she makes a virtue out of necessity and decides to hold her first At Home at the Russell. It's most irregular to hold an At Home in a hotel, but that's the point: it will contribute a piquant novelty to the occasion. In any case, Émilie is too impatient to wait.

On the day of her At Home, Joseph has to be in Arthabaska to attend to the law practice. Émilie has seen him off on the train the night before, and now it's two hours until the grand event, and it feels like the dawn of her new life. As she dresses, she keeps glancing through the window to reassure herself the sky is still blue, the sidewalks still dry, the trees still leafing out: a perfect May afternoon.

The At Home already promises to become exactly what she desires, the social event of the season. She's had over six hundred invitation cards printed and hand-delivered across the city, saying simply, in flowing script:

Madame Lavergne
At Home at the Russell House
Saturday the 15th
4 to 7 o'clock

In her boldly declarative hand, Émilie has written the guests' names in blue ink across the top of each invitation. She's invited senators and judges, poets and cabinet ministers, high-ranking militia officers and senior civil servants, all the most prominent and interesting people in Ottawa, with wives. The majority have replied in the affirmative.

Émilie smiles with secret pleasure. Perhaps her guests suspect, or even know, that the Prime Minister will be coming. The more knowledgeable will have perceived his guiding hand in the arrangements. Perhaps they're curious about her, too: they've heard about this new arrival from Quebec, want to see for themselves what sort of woman has the Prime Minister's ear. Even, it's said, his heart.

It's her salvation to be organizing such a major event. During the long winter months Wilfrid's letters continued professing his adoration but rang hollow somehow, lacking the usual conviction and urgency. It all began to feel like a literary convention: his fulfillment of the forms of courtly romance, as if he was some medieval knight and she his unattainable lady locked away in her husband's castle. Their passion was in danger of becoming a house of words. They needed something real and substantial to revive it, something to give themselves to, some shared adventure in which they could collaborate as equal hearts and minds. Otherwise they'd be restricted to meeting ever more fleetingly in the Russell's lobby, or at formal dinner parties, or some Rideau Hall function, mouthing platitudes like mere acquaintances. What would it matter then that he'd once compared her to Josephine Bonaparte, invoking Napoléon's description, *"Elle était gracieuse en tout"*?

Rather than surrender to despair, Émilie listened to her own resourceful nature. It wasn't the same as listening to the distant violin, or dreaming of St. Ann's Hill, but infinitely more practical. After considering various possibilities, some quite outrageous, she seized on the At Home. It will be as much for Wilfrid as for herself. Imaginatively planned in every detail, consummately executed to ensure *un beau succès*, it must succeed on a scale to do credit to him: to his Quebec origins, his party, his administration, his circle of intimates, his own dearest Émilie, to whom he signs himself (even if only she knows it), "Of all your friends, the truest & sincerest & most devoted."

With all this in mind, Émilie has had a most satisfactory meeting with Wilfrid in his East Block office. It wasn't difficult to arrange: his private secretary, Ulric Barthe, is her cousin. She stood before Wilfrid, sharing his professional domain for the first time, hoping he wouldn't notice her hands were shaking, and admired the marble fireplace, the dark-green wooden blinds filtering sunlight from the Hill, the enormous baize-covered desk formerly occupied by Sir John A. Macdonald. After a slightly too formal and reserved greeting, she sat down across from him and energetically presented her plans for the At Home.

It would be held in the Russell's spacious double drawing room. It would be nothing like the ladies' teas so commonplace in Ottawa, but a massive and splendid celebration of society itself. Male guests would be as numerous as female. Mentioning the more eminent invitees on her list, she asked for Wilfrid's advice. Whom else should she invite? Whom should she avoid? There were gaps in her knowledge of Ottawa society, and she didn't want to make egregious gaffes.

Listening carefully, Wilfrid grew enthusiastic, animated, inspired. This was exactly the sort of occasion his Émilie excelled at. It would provide scope for her gifts as a consummate hostess. Ottawa's society matrons would realize an invigorating new spirit was among them, a free thinker in the best sense, a cultivated Québécoise who knew more about high style and fashion and good conversation than any of them. Wilfrid was so pleased with the boldness of her conception that he wrote a large cheque on the spot to underwrite the arrangements.

Émilie wasn't so much surprised by his generosity as relieved: in fact, she was counting on it, since Joseph's judgeship wouldn't take effect for several weeks. What gratified her most was Wilfrid's relaxing into his old warmth and affection, his eagerness to become once more her intimate companion and fellow conspirator. His spontaneous, irrepressible smile told her how happy he felt about her plans, how delighted he was by her presence, how impressed by her resolve to take the capital by storm. Instructing Ulric to provide her with a list of addresses for Members of Parliament, Senators and Supreme Court justices, he advised her to consult the Undersecretary of State, Joseph Pope. Pope knew absolutely everybody who mattered.

She'd met Pope socially with his wife, Minette, a Taschereau from Quebec City, her mother one of the Pacaud clan from Arthabaska and thus linked by long friendship to the Lauriers. Ulric took her upstairs to Pope's office. Although a touch pompous, Pope struck her as handsome, radiating a quiet sense of power derived from sitting for years at Sir John A.'s right hand, where he'd learned the precise location of men's secrets and vanities. Now, Émilie supposed, he'd know a little about Wilfrid's as well.

Pope understood exactly what she wanted. He rhymed off ladies and gentlemen in various walks of life who must on no account be omitted from her guest list. Political persuasion should be no barrier, he pointed out, and volunteered as many Conservative names as Liberals. He jotted them all down as he spoke, handing her at the end three sheets of stationery neatly covered with names, followed by full titles. He gave Émilie to understand it was important to observe the titles: "'Forms are things,' Sir John always said."

Stopping by Wilfrid's office on her way out, Émilie thanked him for his help. She composed her hands in front of her, as in prayer. "Until now I was becoming afraid," she told him quietly, "that you'd begun to forget about me. About us."

Wilfrid returned her gaze with equal seriousness. When his smile came, it was slow and sweet, almost feminine in its gentleness. "My dear, never believe such a thing is possible. You are always in my thoughts, do you understand? *Always*."

Armand is arriving soon from Quebec City, and Émilie has sent Gabrielle to the station to fetch him. With only two hours until her guests arrive, there's still much to do. She wants to know the hotel staff are carrying out her instructions to the letter. The Mulligan brothers, who have taken over the Russell from M. St-Jacques, have at least *some* sense of style: they've shown imagination and flair by opening the Russell Theatre next door. George Mulligan has assured her he's taking a keen interest in preparations for her event—and of course he's anxious to please Wilfrid—but, being a man, Mulligan will have overlooked important details.

Émilie hurries downstairs to the double drawing room on its second floor. It looks better than she expected. The burgundy velvet settees and easy chairs and circular banquettes have all been shampooed, almost freed of stale tobacco smells. The electric chandeliers glisten. The immense old rug has been cleaned, something it's needed for years: the red floral pattern bears an unfortunate resemblance to bloody footprints, but most of the rug has been covered with linen stretched flat for dancing, and the rest will soon be invisible under the feet of her guests.

Against the back wall, extravagant palms explode from gleaming brass pots, shielding the discoloured plaster. Ugly statues stand in the corner niches: nothing she can do about that. More palms flank the room's best feature, the marble fireplace, its mirror extending gracefully from floor to ceiling. Émilie is relieved to see one of her most critical demands has been met: the tall draped windows overlooking Parliament Hill have been cleaned and now admit a crystalline light.

Down a broad corridor where hotel staff will dispense dainties and teas, additional sofas and chairs are set out for the comfort of less ambulatory guests. Here the electric lighting strikes Émilie as too harsh: she summons an employee to dim the lights. An ensemble drawn from the Governor General's Foot Guards Band, supplemented by strings, is setting up in an alcove. Émilie introduces herself to Captain Gillmor, the music director, and asks about his repertoire. He's planned a mixture of airs from Victor Herbert's *The Wizard of the Nile*, a sprinkling of Gilbert and Sullivan and tunes from last season's Leicester Square musical *The Geisha*. She's glad Captain Gillmor has understood her request for music that is both gay and fashionable. She adds one more request: "Please ensure your musicians don't play too loudly. I want our guests to be able to hear themselves talk."

After a visit to the kitchen to deal with Chef Desjardins, who seems irked by the necessity to be agreeable, she returns to her room. She's relieved to find Gabrielle has returned with Armand. Émilie embraces her son warmly. Standing back to admire him, tall and debonair in his recently purchased frock coat, she compliments him on his flourishing new moustache. It doesn't make him look any older, as he undoubtedly hopes, but doesn't spoil his good looks either.

Armand stands impatiently for his mother's inspection, barely tolerating her adoring gaze, while his sister giggles beside him. "Mother," he demands, "would you please remind me why I'm here?" He can't avoid grinning at being the centre of so much worshipful attention.

"Why, to adorn my grand reception, of course. To crown my coming out in Ottawa society. It will be ever so successful thanks to your presence. And Gabrielle's, naturally."

"Thank you, *Maman*," Bielle says. "I'm honoured to attend with my little brother. Even if he's a brat with no manners."

"Not only to *attend*," Émilie replies, "but to assist me in welcoming our distinguished guests in the receiving line."

Armand grimaces. "*Please*, Mother. The place will be full of English!"

"Of course it will," Émilie says firmly, "and French too. You can be equally gracious to both."

"But I don't speak English well enough. I'll be an embarrassment to you and Papa and myself."

"And me," Gabrielle adds.

"Nonsense, my pets. You'll both be splendid. All you need to say is, 'Good afternoon, it's a pleasure to meet you. I hope you enjoy yourself.'"

"Good afternoon, it's a *plaisir* to meet you, please enjoy yourselfs," Armand mimics.

"Yourself. Besides, Papa can't be here, so you will be representing him, Armand, and upholding the family honour."

"And will our dear M. Laurier be attending too?" he asks slyly.

Émilie takes a deep breath. "Yes, yes, of course he will. M. Laurier wants us to succeed here in the capital. *All* of us."

The first to arrive are the society columnists from Ottawa's three English newspapers. With the musicians still tuning up, the ladies emerge as one into the drawing room. Émilie's nervousness vanishes at the droll sight of the rivals travelling together in a pack, each fearful of missing out on something or someone the others might see. The Three Graces, she thinks. Or Macbeth's witches.

Florence Randal of the *Journal* signs her columns "Kilmeny." Mrs. McIntyre of the *Citizen* styles herself "Frills." Their new competitor from the *Free Press*, whose office sits right beside the Russell, uses the *nom de plume* "The Marchioness." Émilie can't recall the young woman's real name, but covers her lapse by lavishing on her an especially warm smile. The poor girl needs it: she's the plainest of the three by far and knows it.

Émilie obliges the women by providing highlights of her guest list in advance. Miss Randal, with her cornflower-blue eyes and gracefully moulded mouth and chin, is the most attractive of them: chic and gracious, clearly a New Woman, to judge by her assertiveness. Mrs. McIntyre is sweetly vulgar, with a silly hat and too much plump décolletage. As Émilie sizes them up, they do the same with her.

Miss Randal declares she's never seen the Russell's prosaic old drawing room looking so elegant: "Why, it's been transformed into an artistic statement!" Mrs. McIntyre exclaims over Émilie's royal blue satin dress brocaded with lace and black velvet, the balloon sleeves flaring extravagantly, the square neckline revealing her still-youthful neck and throat and providing a tasteful glimpse of her "magnificent" (Wilfrid's word) shoulders. Émilie hopes the columnists will write not only about her dress, but her fashionably tilted white hat decorated with ostrich plumes. Her white gloves extend above the elbow.

Mrs. McIntyre is especially attentive toward Gabrielle, whose costume, a blue-and-white striped silk with a huge white picture hat, complements her mother's. Armand stares a little too obviously at Miss Randal, who seems to have bewitched him. Eventually the three women drift off into the drawing room to await events, trailing compliments. Armand gazes longingly after them.

She forgets all about the witches in her delight over the arrival of her first guest. Sir Henri Joly de Lotbinière is not only a minister in Wilfrid's cabinet and a former Premier of Quebec, but a seigneur who still collects rents from tenant farmers on his estate along the St. Lawrence. Émilie considers Sir Henri the most spectacular of the remaining aristocrats of her province. His snowy, wavy hair, drooping moustache and old-world courtliness make him the perfect knight. His glazed shirt front is dazzling. He bows and kisses her hand.

"Sir Henri, I can't tell you what a pleasure this is. I am honoured you've come to my little party."

"You do honour to *us*, Madame," he replies in a stentorian voice, adding more softly, "I feel proud that a countrywoman of mine should hold a magnificent *salon* in this dull place. You put me in mind of Madame Récamier."

This is the most shameless flattery, but Émilie adores being compared to Chateaubriand's beautiful lover. "Won't you have something to drink, Sir Henri?"

"As long as you are serving something more interesting than English tea."

"Champagne punch is offered at the buffet."

The old gentleman pauses to shower attention on Gabrielle and Armand, whom he's known since they were born, and moves on to introduce himself to the witches. They're fascinated by his august bearing, his aura of having stepped out of a novel by Dumas. In a few moments he's gracefully waltzing Miss Randal across the floor to a melody by Victor Herbert.

Émilie turns back to the spectacle of the Misses Ritchie, all four of them, sweeping down on her in a cloud of lilac water. Their charming, girlish high spirits fill the room as they announce themselves in turn: "Beatrice. Elsie. Grace. Amy." They act thrilled to see Gabrielle, whom they met while rehearsing for Lady Aberdeen's historical dress ball. Are the Ritchies sincere or pretending? So hard to tell with adolescent girls. They take turns flirting with Armand, who flushes with pleasure, Miss Randal forgotten. His English seems suddenly to have improved.

Several ladies of a certain age appear, all wearing enormous hats, feigning astonishment that they've arrived at the same place at the same time, when they were together only yesterday at the May Court Club: Mrs. Perley, Mrs. Sparks, Mrs. Southam, Mrs. Bronson. Émilie catches her breath, trying not to seem surprised or flattered that the wealthy dowagers are bestowing their presence on her.

The Misses Powell, Lola and Maude, arrive with their much older brother, the Chief of Police. Émilie can see why the sisters need chaperoning, especially Lola. Both wear their abundant auburn hair in pre-Raphaelite tresses, which cascade over romantic gowns of black and burgundy velvet hung with strings of oriental beads. She didn't realize Ottawa harboured such exotic creatures. Lola, with her amused air of self-possession and her commanding height, carries off this stylistic extravagance especially well. But she's excessively talkative, and Émilie has to interrupt her to receive the next set of arrivals.

Now she's worried her lady guests may feel bored without sufficient cavaliers to amuse them. Happily, at that moment she recognizes Nicholas Flood Davin, the voluble Irishman and Conservative MP known for his eloquence and wit, and man-about-town Agar Adamson, lean and handsomely clean-shaven. Adamson is still a bachelor, and they say Davin might as well be: his wife prefers to stay home in faraway Regina. Émilie finds Adamson attractive and Davin's flirtatious chatter amusing, and she resolves to get to know them better.

Soon the room is agreeably crowded, hot, noisy. Quite without warning, Wilfrid materializes at her side. Distracted by her duties, she hasn't seen him approach. He's alone.

Surreptitiously he squeezes her gloved hand while kissing her on both cheeks, mouthing an endearment no one else can hear. He holds out his arms to Gabrielle and Armand and embraces them in turn. "How splendid you look!" He steps back to study them. "Your mother must be so proud. Bielle, my compliments on your delightful outfit. Armand, it's wonderful you've come all the way to Ottawa. I swear you've grown a foot since I saw you last."

He inundates them with questions: Armand's studies, Gabrielle's poetry. He's careful not to prefer one over the other. The children glow under his affectionate gaze, giving him full and enthusiastic answers.

"Madame Laurier would have loved to see you all," he says finally.

"Oh, and where *is* Zoë?" Émilie pretends not to know.

"Unfortunately one of her ladies' musicales takes place this afternoon. It's been planned for weeks and couldn't be postponed. That young soprano she's taken up is leaving to study in Paris."

"Oh, another soprano. Is it true, then, what I read in a Toronto magazine? That Madame Laurier prefers the company of women to men?"

Wilfrid isn't sure how to respond, but it doesn't matter. Miss Gormully, the loveliest of the recent debutantes, is arriving with her older sister, Edith, married to Sanford Fleming's youngest son. The Gormully sisters are excited to be meeting the Prime Minister, but even as they bob and curtsey they keep glancing back and forth between Wilfrid and Armand, eager to see proof of the notorious rumour of a resemblance. Émilie realizes this explains her son's decision to grow a moustache at the first opportunity presented by nature: it partially covers his full upper lip, so like Wilfrid's. But the penetrating eyes and curling chestnut hair are practically identical, and he can't conceal those no matter how much he tries.

The Deputy Superintendent-General of Indian Affairs, Hayter Reed, known for his dim view of Indians, arrives with Mrs. Reed, striking in a bright red costume with black ruffled chiffon and black feathered hat. Mr. Reed's next-in-command, Duncan Campbell Scott, follows with his wife, the former Belle Warner Botsford of Boston, a well-to-do concert violinist. Joseph Pope has explained to Émilie that Scott is one of the two finest English poets in Ottawa. He's thought to have a better opinion of Indians than his superior, since he writes such inspiring, romantic verse about them. He's also great friends with the city's other poet, Archibald Lampman, but Pope has warned Émilie not to invite both the Scotts and the Lampmans: the wives detest each other.

She observes Mrs. Reed and Mrs. Scott chatting vivaciously with Wilfrid. Both women make indiscreet visual comparisons between him and Armand, and as they're moving on, she overhears Mrs. Reed saying, "My heavens! It could only be the finger of God."

"I've heard it called many things," Mrs. Scott replies, "but never that."

Should she really be putting Wilfrid and Armand in such close juxtaposition? Perhaps she should feel embarrassed for her son.

But in truth, Émilie feels the exact opposite: a hot, dizzying rush of pride. Guest after guest comes up the receiving line to be greeted by what appears to be, to all intents and purposes, a family. For the first time, she thinks. But not, God willing, the last.

These receiving arrangements remain in place for another half hour as guests continue pouring in. The band plays on, the music weaving its buoyant spell over the room. Keeping a close watch on Wilfrid's face, Émilie thinks he looks as happy as she's ever seen him. Bielle too is radiant, her inner beauty apparent to all. Even Armand is sociable, cheerful, outgoing, surprisingly comfortable with his role in the tableau. He's picked up a new English phrase from his sister, "How good of you to come," and is putting it to good use.

Émilie knows beyond a shadow of a doubt that this is exactly what Wilfrid needs: time away from his desk, his cabinet, his Zoë. Time to be himself, in a way he normally can't. Time with her.

The end comes in the person of Sir Oliver Mowat. His features grey, his sidewhiskers grey, his old grey eyes opaque behind wire-rimmed glasses, the Justice Minister shakes Émilie's hand with stiff English reserve and turns directly to Wilfrid, ignoring the children altogether. Mowat seems unaccountably excited about some new poem by Rudyard Kipling that has just appeared in *The Times*, "Our Lady of the Snows." Evidently, unbelievably, Kipling has composed the poem in homage to Wilfrid's new policy of preferential trade with the Mother Country. In an unmusical, high-pitched voice, Mowat begins reciting it, declaiming loudly above the music and the babble of voices. It puts Émilie's teeth on edge. She's relieved when he reaches the last verse:

A Nation spoke to a Nation,
 A Throne Sent Word to a Throne:
"Daughter am I in my mother's house,

But mistress in my own.
The gates are mine to open,
    As the gates are mine to close.
And I abide by my mother's house,"
    Said Our Lady of the Snows.

Mowat comes to a stop and looks about as if for applause. Whispering something in Wilfrid's ear, he makes to drag him off by the arm. Wilfrid disentangles himself long enough to say good-bye to Gabrielle and Armand, then turns to face Émilie, and in a low urgent voice tells her he'd much rather stay but has to go hear what Mowat insists on discussing. He embraces her: "*Au revoir,* my dear. Congratulations on a magnificent success."

Émilie savours his words and, even more, the public embrace. But the sight of Wilfrid's receding back pains her. She wishes her At Home could end then and there, at the abrupt close of its triumphant apex.

She's grateful for the distraction of a flamboyant new arrival. Miss Cissy Fitzgerald, the former West End Gaiety Girl currently starring in her own revue at the Russell Theatre, advances in a silk dress of expensive simplicity. Miss Fitzgerald is wearing numerous strings of pearls and carrying a small white dog. She's come directly from her Saturday matinee, and how wickedly worldly she looks, how unapologetically theatrical! Émilie doesn't even bother feeling jealous or resentful of God's unequal parcelling out of female beauty. Instead she gives Miss Fitzgerald a heartfelt welcome, telling her it was thrilling to see her dancing in her gorgeous costumes on Thursday night, fascinating to watch her sing and wink and have her way with the audience.

Miss Fitzgerald is charmed by Émilie's praise. In an arch English accent, she declares that she hopes Madame Lavergne doesn't mind her bringing along little Magic. He does like society, and he does like to lap milk from a saucer if there's any about. Cradled in its mistress's arms, the dog regards Émilie with deep-seated mistrust.

"Certainly! Of course!" Émilie replies with a high-pitched laugh. "My friend Zoë loves little dogs too!"

Looking beyond Miss Fitzgerald at the densely packed room, no longer able to see Wilfrid for the crush of bodies, she doesn't wonder if her event is a success: Wilfrid has pronounced it so. Like a sea at high tide, like a symphony building to a crescendo, her festivities have swollen inexorably, her guests celebrating, the music intoxicating, couples young and old dancing, the mingled roar of conversations deafening. She doubts Ottawa has seen anything like this in its entire existence. Never mind the society columnists, never mind the next day's papers, Canadians will be talking about Émilie Lavergne's At Home for a hundred years to come.

6

Summer 1897

From their Pullman compartment Zoë sees little that's alien about the American landscape, except the flag: and that, of course, is everything. All those martial rows of stars and stripes flaunted above public buildings and private homes. Finally the June dusk settles down over the flags and towns and green wooded hills of New England. Looking up from Carlyle's history of the French Revolution, Wilfrid lowers the blinds, and she feels comfortably at home, just the two of them, rocked by their progress toward the great metropolis.

They wake after dawn to a strange spectacle of New York tenements. She's never seen anything like it: row upon row of tall, weathered, rickety wooden structures, backing onto the railway tracks. The morning is already steaming. Negro men sit outside on wooden stoops smoking in their undershirts.

The atmosphere is so close that Wilfrid feels nauseated. She worries how his constitution will cope with seven days on the Atlantic. Neither of them has crossed the ocean before, and he isn't fond of travelling at the best of times, even though it's an inescapable part of his profession. He needs something in his stomach to settle him down. They take tea and toast in the dining car as the train pulls in to Grand Central, then walk along the platform to meet Joseph Mailhot.

Mailhot is Wilfrid's new valet. He'll accompany them to London, remaining with them throughout their travels to help with luggage and hotel arrangements and anything else of a practical nature. From the station they ride directly to the docks in a closed carriage, their steamer trunks strapped to the roof. Mailhot points out New York landmarks: astonishing skyscrapers, famous hotels. Although he comes from Arthabaska, Mailhot has seen the world. He's a man of good sense, and Wilfrid trusts him.

Walking up the gangplank to the deck of the *Lucania*, Zoë has a momentary attack of nerves. She feels overwhelmed by the immensity of the orange and black funnels, tall and fat as office buildings, already spouting oily smoke. She experiences revulsion against the monstrous, black-sided vessel that will transport them from the known world to a universe glimpsed only in books and magazines and dreams. Crossing the Atlantic suddenly seems a mad and dangerous thing to do, even if commanded by an Empress: unnatural. And Joseph Mailhot, now overseeing the porters delivering the trunks to their stateroom, will be unavailable to remind her it's all quite wonderful and normal and safe. He has to disappear below for the remainder of the voyage to a shared second-class cabin somewhere on a lower deck.

Surveying the stateroom's gold-plated fixtures and brass bedsteads, the adjoining sitting room with sofa, desk and reading lamp, Wilfrid pats her hand reassuringly: "We're going to be very comfortable here, you and I." One of their trunks contains a small library, books he's been accumulating for years—books Émilie has given him?—but hasn't had time to read. Zoë has packed two light French novels and her petit point and two sets of their own bedsheets, to protect Wilfrid from coming down with bronchitis. She hopes at least there will be some lively music from the ship's orchestra.

Picturing Wilfrid settling down on that sofa with his books and state papers for the rest of the voyage, not emerging until Liverpool, she urges him outside for a stroll on deck. They stand at the rail arm in arm, gazing at the Manhattan skyline as latecomers continue to board. A white-uniformed crew member tips his cap and introduces himself in a thick north-of-England accent as Purser Thomas Bagley. On behalf of Captain Glover, he welcomes the Lauriers aboard the *Lucania* and takes them on a tour of the first-class facilities.

Zoë remembers reading about the ship's maiden voyage in the *London Illustrated News*. Mr. Bagley is the article made flesh. The *Lucania* is one of the biggest and most powerful liners in the world, he declaims as they cross an empty dance floor in the enormous lounge—exactly the same in every respect as her sister ship, the *Campania*, which is travelling the same route in the opposite direction. Somewhere in mid-Atlantic, the sisters will pass and salute each other. They're the Cunard Line's first twin-screw vessels and the first to dispense completely with sail. Mind you, the Germans are building a bigger ship named after Kaiser Wilhelm, but she won't launch till September and then we'll see if she's really as fast as the Krauts claim. The *Lucania* has a top speed of twenty-one knots, breaking the old transatlantic barrier. . . .

They're standing in the dining room, a blinding sea of white tablecloths and gleaming glassware. Amid mingled odours of ironed linen and freshly baked buns, waiters idly await the passengers' arrival for lunch. Mr. Bagley has reached the end of his lecture. He tells the Lauriers they'll be taking their meals at the captain's table and rhymes off the other guests. Then he offers them sturdy wooden deck chairs in the sun on the rear deck, draping blankets across their knees.

Leaning back, Wilfrid turns his face lazily into the breeze blowing off the sea. "This is the life. I may actually become used to it."

Zoë is happy to see him so relaxed. The last parliamentary session has been exhausting. As usual he's worked too hard, immersed in correspondence from early in the morning, off at the House all afternoon, then back among his papers till late at night. She knows how much importance he attaches to this trip. Meeting the Queen and the great British statesmen, walking alongside royalty and world leaders, will bring international recognition to Canada. But if he isn't careful, it will also bring entrapment and capitulation and even dishonour in the eyes of his own people in Quebec.

As Lord Aberdeen has explained it, Wilfrid will play a prominent role in the military spectacle planned for the Jubilee, a procession involving thousands of troops in a great display of imperial power. Prime ministers and premiers from throughout the Empire, from all those far-flung splashes of red on the map containing a quarter of the world's population, will be there, but Canada's Prime Minister will be *primus inter pares*. Wilfrid is highly ambivalent about this. It's still on his mind, he tells Zoë, still bothering him. Military parades are all very well for show, but deeper schemes are in play.

For months he's been resisting the campaign conducted by telegram between London and Ottawa to award him a knighthood. The idea was cooked up by Joseph Chamberlain, the Colonial Secretary in Lord Salisbury's government. It's another little piece in Chamberlain's strategy to promote his obsession, Imperial Federation: a worldwide blood pact, as Wilfrid sees it, steeped in notions of Anglo-Saxon racial superiority. Chamberlain's fellow conspirators in the knighthood campaign are Sir Donald Smith, the Canadian Pacific Railway baron who is now Canada's High Commissioner to London, and dear Lord Aberdeen himself.

"But you've already turned down a knighthood," Zoë points out. "What more is there to say?"

"Oh, I doubt we've heard the last of it. What Chamberlain wants, he usually gets."

And what Chamberlain wants is to turn plain M. Laurier of Arthabaska and Quebec East into a titled English snob with an embarrassing string of initials after his name. Wilfrid can already hear the scorn pouring from the mouths of Quebeckers, starting with Henri Bourassa, the hot-tempered new MP from his own party.

Zoë sniffs. "I don't want to be Lady Laurier."

"And I," Wilfrid says, "am a democrat to the hilt!"

She's noticed he's beginning to quote himself, repeating lines from his speeches.

"In that case," she replies teasingly, using another of his epithets, "I'll follow your white plume."

Wilfrid's eyes narrow in a smile. "I'm speechifying, aren't I? Forgive me. But of course this is just a minor skirmish in a greater game."

The game is to draw Canada into Chamberlain's web of imperial entanglements. The Colonial Secretary wants all the colonies to join Great Britain in a new grand alliance: welding themselves into a common market, a common military, ultimately even a common parliament. He dreams of an invincible global juggernaut united in peace and indivisible in war, bound by imperishable ties of blood, steel and loyalty to the Crown. He wants the colonies to forget about their goal of national independence, an objective Wilfrid has described in another speech as "the polar star of our destiny."

"If I play into Chamberlain's hands, I lose Quebec." He looks down at his own hands, splaying out his fingers, turning them this way and that. "And if I don't play his game, I insult English Canada and our British hosts. But how can I tell Quebeckers to be loyal Canadians if it just means becoming second-class Englishmen? It goes against our nature. Everyone knows the people who want Imperial Federation are the same ones who want to stamp out French. They'd cut out our tongues if we let them."

"Well, then, a knighthood is out the question. It's good to have that settled."

Suddenly they're engulfed in a terrifying blast of sound. Zoë jumps in alarm, feeling the immensity of the noise vibrating in her organs.

"The ship's whistle," Wilfrid says with a knowing grin, as if it was his own idea.

He assists her out of her deck chair. They stroll to the foredeck to look down at the tugboats pulling the *Lucania* out to sea. After five minutes she's moving under her own steam, and Zoë feels a powerful thrumming in the soles of her feet, emanating from somewhere deep in the belly of the ship. The wind quickens and cools. A subtle rolling motion of the deck begins, giving rise to second thoughts about exactly where to place one's steps.

Rocking lightly on his feet, Wilfrid looks doubtful. "Is it I or the ship that's moving? Perhaps it's time we found our cabin."

He spends the rest of the day in their stateroom, commuting between the bed and the toilet. Zoë cradles his forehead with a damp cloth above the cold porcelain bowl, the pair of them swaying with the rolling of the ship, as his stomach empties itself of the excellent farewell dinner at Rideau Hall.

On their second evening at sea, they venture as far as the dining room. Zoë drinks a little consommé and nibbles at a piece of Dover sole. Wilfrid acts as graciously as ever with the captain and the other guests, but has nothing except a dry roll and some tea.

He graduates to their sitting room the next morning, passing several hours with government papers sealed in a black box. He concedes that, for all the visceral discomfort of being at sea, it's a blessing to be beyond reach of the House of Commons and the telephone. If there's an emergency, he can always be contacted by telegraph. "But apparently the country can get along perfectly well without me. I don't know whether to be pleased or not."

Finally they acclimatize themselves to the ship's movement and the bland English fare of the dining room and become fixtures of life on deck. Mr. Bagley is glad to see them again. He remarks that the seas are quite calm for this time of year. As long as it isn't raining, they find pleasure in bundling themselves up in their deck chairs and reading or conversing or watching the seagulls float motionless above the lifeboats, wings outstretched. Their fellow first-class passengers stop by to pay their respects: bankers, industrialists, lawyers, clergymen, others of unknown provenance. Begging the Prime Minister and his lady not to rise, they stand and chat about politics or business or the coming celebrations in London.

Zoë develops a relationship with the sea. At mid-morning she'll rise from her chair, leaving Wilfrid to his reading, and stand at the rail to commune with the endless, heaving expanse of water. It never bores her. The jade greens, emeralds, deep blues and menacing blacks are infinitely varied, constantly rearranging themselves like a troubled sleeper beneath blankets of foam. She loves the sting of the sharp salt air on her face. It's extraordinary: her landlocked existence back home has always been circumscribed by this fierce, God-like immensity, without her ever being aware of it. She imagines people she's never thought about, their ancestors, crossing this ocean from Normandy two centuries ago, clinging for weeks on end to their fragile wooden ships, sick and half-starved, as they awaited a glimpse of the promised land. She feels in awe of their courage.

Another discovery is almost as momentous. She and Wilfrid are completely free of Émilie. No Émilie to tell her what to think or feel. No Émilie to remind her what a fortunate and privileged and, by implication, undeserving woman she is. No Émilie to draw Wilfrid away for a cozy tête-à-tête over George Sand, or persuade him to share with her the confidences that properly belong to a wife.

Zoë delights in their exquisite privacy. It's a kind of freedom she and Wilfrid have never known, not even in their Arthabaska days, with friends and relatives and colleagues constantly about. They discover how to amuse themselves, how to live a simple everyday married life, how to find pleasure in each other. Even if it's only a temporary reprieve, taking place within the artificial confines of shipboard life, she can look forward to weeks without Émilie. And for that she's deeply, silently grateful.

On their last day at sea they feel as giddy as children. Their first sight of the English coast is thrilling: low, undulating landforms emerging ghostlike from the misty morning, coming into focus as green pastures daubed with sunlight. Gliding into the port of Liverpool, it's as if a storybook is coming to life and she one of the characters: not the most important, perhaps, but a character nonetheless.

Viewed from the deck of the *Lucania*, Liverpool is hardly a storybook city—entirely brown, its docks, warehouses and customs sheds worn from hard use, smudged with smoke, its skyline low and unambitious compared to New York's. A few people stand about on the quay admiring the liner's approach. Most go indifferently about their business as if it wasn't there. Tugs tie up to the ship, and a tender pulls alongside to deliver canvas bags bulging with mail. Thomas Bagley brings the Lauriers the correspondence that has been accumulating for them all week on this side of the Atlantic. Among the letters are several Jubilee invitations to add to those already received in Ottawa for receptions and balls, luncheons and dinners, ceremonies and country-house weekends. The Duke of Devonshire graciously requests the Lauriers' presence the very next day at a luncheon in Liverpool in celebration of imperial unity. There are official dispatches from Ottawa sent by Ulric Barthe, missives from Fielding and Tarte, heartfelt wishes from Lord and Lady Aberdeen for a marvellous sojourn in Great Britain and the Continent. And letters to both of them from Émilie. Zoë sets hers aside to read later. She doesn't see what Wilfrid does with his.

Forty-eight hours later they're travelling with Joseph Mailhot in a small, grubby, old-fashioned railway carriage from Liverpool to London. Mailhot seems to have enjoyed his voyage in company with a young American widow he met at his dining table. She allowed him, he confides, to escort her to shipboard entertainments.

On arrival at Paddington on a cool bright night—Zoë is struck by how late it stays light in England—they take a cab to the Hotel Cecil in the Strand. It's been open a year, the largest hotel in Europe, with eight hundred rooms on nine floors. Wilfrid is shocked by the size and luxury of the suite reserved for them by the British government. The manager shows them through, explaining unctuously it's the very largest he has, as if he doubts the Lauriers are quite entitled to it.

London isn't as Zoë has pictured it. But what did she imagine, exactly? Some child's idea of castles and royalty, pomp and chivalry. Instead she finds a dirty, cacophonous, teeming metropolis crammed with more carriages and carts and horses and excrement and human beings than a city should be expected to hold. The air is heavy with the sharp reek of coal smoke, worse even than Montreal. Among the faces crowding the sidewalks, many belong to other races: she's never seen such myriad skin colours and outlandish modes of dress. She constantly finds herself staring out of sheer fascination, having to pull her eyes reluctantly away out of politeness. The English themselves are as expected, black-clad and frosty, although clerks and cab drivers are more cheerful than at home. From the cabbies she learns the number of foreign visitors is abnormally high this summer "because of the Queen."

Because of the Queen, the face of London is being transformed. Historic buildings and heroic statues are having their granite and marble surfaces scraped and stripped and washed down, freed at last from the grime of the ages to emerge nakedly white in the Queen's honour. A vast web of scaffolding constructed of aromatic pine (probably from Quebec, Wilfrid says) is climbing over everything, defacing the façades of banks and shops and private clubs. Seats exactly eighteen inches wide are being sold off at a pound apiece. No vantage point along the procession route is exempt from becoming a perch for the masses. Churches are renting out their cemeteries, bleachers depriving the dead of a decent view. Someone, Wilfrid remarks, is getting rich from all this.

He and Zoë observe London's transformation through the windows of a special carriage, provided courtesy of Joseph Chamberlain's office, as they travel to and from the endless social functions that fill each day. They quickly learn the geography of Westminster and Mayfair and the City. Although Zoë would love to sightsee, Wilfrid tells her the situation demands they act like seasoned travellers, as familiar with London as those who have grown up here. Anything less will be deemed hopelessly colonial.

Everywhere they go, the talk is of Empire, Empire, Empire. And everywhere they go, the Prime Minister of Canada is politely asked to say a few words, which become more than a few once he gets started. Wilfrid's speaking style grows more effulgent than ever, inspired to new heights by the glittering ballrooms, the ever-flowing champagne, the stimulating company of richly gowned and jewelled hostesses and graciously condescending hosts in white tie and tails.

Seated in the audience during his addresses, Zoë sees him as the English must. She understands why they admire his romantic, clean-shaven features, his sensual yet sensitive mouth, his abundant wavy hair swept back from the temples, framing the high moulded forehead. His striking height. His dignified bearing. His sheer command of himself.

A shadow passes over these perceptions like a dark wing: this must be how Émilie perceives him too. Instantly Zoë dismisses the intruder, sends it flying on its way, as she's learned to do long ago.

The English are impressed to hear their language spoken with such mellifluous grace by a foreigner. Wilfrid's accent is elusive. The French-Canadian pronunciation is exotic enough, but aren't certain words receiving an unmistakably Scottish inflection? He repeatedly has to explain about learning English in New Glasgow. It's becoming conceivable for their hosts to accept this hybrid colonial, in spite of everything, as one of them. Zoë is of two minds about whether that's a good thing.

At a banquet in the Mansion House, the Lord Mayor remarks that all gathered here tonight are Englishmen. When Wilfrid rises to reply to the toast in his honour, he reminds his listeners that the blood of centuries of Frenchmen runs in his veins, and he's forever proud of it. Then he adds: "And still I am British to the core!" The audience gives him a standing ovation, led by the Lord Mayor himself.

At the National Liberal Club, where the mutton is barely edible, Wilfrid feels moved to say it would be the proudest moment of his life if a Canadian of French descent could affirm the principles of freedom in the Parliament of Great Britain. And if ever a day comes when British security is endangered, "let the bugle sound, let the fires be lit on the hills, and Canada will be the first to respond."

Afterwards Zoë tells him she worries when he abandons himself so completely to the imperial spirit. It's reaching the point where *The Daily Mail* describes him as "the strongest imperialist and one of the most clear-sighted statesmen of the Empire." But a few days later, in a wood-panelled House of Commons committee room, he speaks for an hour before an audience of British MPs and tells them, "Canada is a nation, and freedom is its nationality."

The granting of self-government alone has saved the Empire. All the proof one needs is the contrast between the United States and Canada. That sounds more like Laurier, Zoë thinks, settling back in her chair.

The next day, the Cobden Club presents him with its gold medal for distinguished service to free trade, and Wilfrid revives the theme of freedom. Raking the audience with his eyes, he declares that if the British Empire is to survive, it can only be upon the basis of the most absolute freedom, political and commercial. The freer the Empire is, the stronger it will be. He's cheered to the rafters. "Let Chamberlain take note of that," he tells Zoë.

Of course the real reason why British hearts are beating so warmly for Canada is the reduced tariff on British trade. What more tangible way for Canada to express its love for the Mother Country than through preferring her goods to American ones? This policy, offered without asking anything in return, has put the other colonies distinctly in the shade. The *New York Times* has predicted it will make Wilfrid the most popular of the visiting premiers, and it's right.

Every time Zoë watches him make a speech, she thinks of their time together on the ship. It makes her nostalgic: she misses those quiet, solitary pleasures, wonders if they'll ever return. What a jarringly sudden leap to the imperial stage, Wilfrid becoming a world statesman before her eyes, carving a new role for his country. Each morning when they sit down to breakfast in their suite, they scan the London papers for reviews of his latest pronouncements. In its coverage of the Cobden Club speech, *The Daily Mail* enthuses, without any awareness of condescension, "For the first time on record, a politician of our New World has been recognized as the equal of the great men of the Old Country."

Reading the article aloud, Wilfrid tosses the paper aside. "But we won't let any of this affect us, will we, my dear? Newspaper talk is cheap. It's far more difficult to stand up against the flattery of some gracious duchess. A weak man's head is turned in an evening."

Zoë appreciates his honesty. "And will they never stop feeding us? I'm putting on weight!"

"So am I. I'm not sure the Empire needs a new constitution, but every Jubilee guest will need one."

Everywhere the Lauriers go, people are talking about the Jameson Raid. It has deeply embarrassed Great Britain in South Africa and is now the subject of a parliamentary enquiry.

As far as Zoë can tell, the worst sin of Dr. Jameson and his Rhodesian cavalry wasn't invading the Transvaal Republic so much as bungling the job, failing to seize the Transvaal from the Boers and bring it under British rule. If they'd succeeded, people say, they'd have been welcomed by a joyful uprising of pro-British elements in the republic. And since President Kruger and his Boers are despicable reactionaries who enslave their African subjects, a successful invasion would have added moral virtue to financial reward: the gold mines of the Transvaal are worth a king's ransom. From there it would have been a simple step to unite the republic with the Queen's other possessions and create a greater British South Africa. But the raid didn't go as planned. Kruger captured Jameson and scornfully shipped him home to London, to be punished by his own country. The Boers' grip on the richest state in Africa is stronger than ever.

Neither Wilfrid nor Zoë paid much attention to the raid at the time, yet it's remarkable how much one learns about it. Everyone in London just assumes the plot was hatched by Cecil Rhodes, Premier of Britain's Cape Colony, working with his friends in the gold and diamond mining business who want a free hand in exploiting the Boers' resources. Even more damning are suspicions that the Colonial Secretary himself was complicit in the attempted coup.

Naturally Chamberlain denies it up and down. Conveniently for him, he's been appointed a member of the commission of enquiry. Even more conveniently, a scapegoat has been found at the Colonial Office, an official willing to sacrifice his career by swearing he kept information secret from his minister. Chamberlain has placed his hand on his heart and sworn to the enquiry he had no knowledge of any plan to invade the Transvaal. Englishmen in the know are calling it "Chamberlain's Lying-in-State at Westminster."

"This is the sort of man I'm dealing with," Wilfrid tells Zoë. "A man with no scruples. A man with the power to lie in public and get away with it."

He admits a certain qualified sympathy for the Boers. As unappetizing as Kruger is, his people are a beleaguered minority struggling to survive, to save their homeland from drowning in a rising Anglo-Saxon sea. Of course it's hardly politic to suggest such a thing—much less imply any parallel with French Canada—especially since British opinion has turned so savagely against the Boers. After Jameson's capture, Kaiser Wilhelm, whose own West African colony lies just north of the Cape, telegraphed congratulations to Kruger, unleashing a storm of jingoism in the British press. The Queen is said to be most displeased with her German grandson. The cheek! She will inflict on him the ultimate punishment, banning his participation in her Diamond Jubilee.

Already the popular cry, abetted by the more scurrilous newspapers, is for war against the Boers. The map must be painted red all the way from the Cape to Cairo. Suddenly the disgraced Jameson is a hero. Mass-produced statuettes of Dr. Jameson and his stallion are galloping across English mantelpieces, even as he languishes in prison.

This is the atmosphere in which Wilfrid addresses the Canada Club at the Cecil with two former Governors General, Lord Lorne and Lord Stanley, in attendance. Shortly before everyone sits down to dinner, Canada's High Commissioner, Sir Donald Smith, the man who drove in the last spike of the CPR, takes Wilfrid aside and tells him he's on the Jubilee honours list. In a few days he'll receive a knighthood.

"But that's impossible," Wilfrid says. "Out of the question. I've already declined."

Sir Donald strokes his long white beard and looks gloomy. "That may be, my dear Wilfrid"—his Highland accent is pitched so low, Wilfrid has to bend to hear him in the crowded dining room—"but what will Mr. Chamberlain say? What will the Queen say? What will *Ontario* say?"

They're good questions: especially the last one. Still, Wilfrid is irritated by Sir Donald's presumption that he has no choice in the matter. He knows Sir Donald himself has no difficulty accepting titles and is about to become Lord Strathcona. "And what will *Quebec* say?" Wilfrid replies.

The next day he pays an official visit to the Colonial Office. As he describes it to Zoë afterwards, he feels nervous and intimidated as he walks across the stone courtyard, past the forbidding Roman façade. Then he reminds himself he's the Prime Minister of a rising young nation, whereas Joseph Chamberlain is only a cabinet minister, a manufacturer of metal screws in Birmingham—even if universally regarded as the most successful man in England. Ushered deep into the maze of the Colonial Office by a succession of funereal officials, Wilfrid finds the Master, as Chamberlain is known to his underlings, seated at an enormous desk behind a blue baize door. A brown globe rests obediently beside him on a pedestal. He springs forward with a bound to grasp Wilfrid's hand, energetically pumping it while pouring out effusive greetings. Wilfrid barely has to speak.

Once they're settled into leather chairs in a corner, tea is served. Wilfrid observes the jet-black hair and elegant, youthfully handsome features of this man who is actually older than he, who believes he can pull the Empire together on invisible strings of loyalty like some grand puppeteer. Chamberlain's monocle dangles from a black ribbon. He wears an orchid in his lapel and a diamond pin in his cravat, hinting at the lavish rewards of his Birmingham career, and at the prizes waiting to be seized in South Africa.

Chamberlain seems prepared to listen as well as talk. He asks Wilfrid about Canadian political and economic affairs, on which he's been exceedingly well briefed by Lord Aberdeen. When inevitably the conversation turns to the knighthood, Chamberlain fixes his monocle in his left eye. He acknowledges the chilly reception a knighthood will receive in French Canada: undoubtedly unfortunate, but can't be helped. There is the Queen to think of. Her Jubilee celebrations will be the proudest moment of Her Majesty's long reign. She believes implicitly that the Empire under her rule is a benevolent creation, sanctioned by God, bringing to millions of subject peoples the blessings of British law and justice and parliamentary liberty.

To all this Wilfrid assents.

And so it follows that the Queen's honours are not given lightly. They are rare distinctions, bestowed only after much deliberation. Canada is the senior colony, the first Dominion, and thus the most representative member of the Empire as a whole: hence Her Majesty has chosen Wilfrid as the only Premier to receive a knighthood on this great occasion. She would be deeply hurt by his refusal. Insulted, humiliated. And if that weren't bad enough, it would leave the entire Jubilee honours scheme in utter disarray. If one couldn't simply—

Wilfrid holds up his hand. Chamberlain stops and waits, the monocle dropping onto his chest.

He too has reflected deeply on the matter, Wilfrid replies. For himself, he does not seek a title. He is a democrat to the hilt: his countrymen of both races know that. But at the same time, he has no desire to mar the harmony and joy of Jubilee week. If Her

Majesty wishes to knight him, he will regard it as the highest honour, extended not to him, but to Canada. A great many Canadians
want him to accept. On their behalf, and on Canada's, he will.

Just for a moment Chamberlain is startled into silence. "But
what about those Canadians who *don't* want you to accept?" he
asks suspiciously.

"I will explain to them why they should change their minds.
As I have changed mine."

Gradually the tension drains from Chamberlain's face, he begins to act more pleasantly. For the next half hour they have a stimulating discussion of Macaulay's *History of England*, which both
men have studied carefully and with great profit over the years.

On Wilfrid's last day as plain Mr. Laurier, Zoë finds him composed, philosophical. "Impossible not to be swept up in all this
Jubilee nonsense. One simply has to accept it."

The weather has turned warm. England has summer after all.
London is aflame with flowers, glowing like a theatrical garden.
The press is fond of reminding readers that every tree and shrub
and flower in the world grows somewhere in the Empire, and all
of them are now visible along the ceremonial route, sprouting
from ornamental beds and planters and flower boxes. Cables suspended above the streets are festooned with palm fronds and red,
white and blue bunting. Purple and gold draperies cascade down
the faces of buildings. The scaffolding now looks festive, draped
with scarlet cloth. Union Jacks bloom from balconies and rooftops.
Giant *VRI* emblems are everywhere. SIXTY GLORIOUS YEARS
A QUEEN, the headlines blare.

On Jubilee eve, Wilfrid and Zoë attend an enormous state banquet at Buckingham Palace. From their seats near the bottom of
the long horseshoe table, they peer like voyeurs over lighted candelabra at the tiny rotund monarch. She's seated far away, at the
exact centre of the head table, flanked by her descendants from

all the royal houses of Europe. The bosom of the Sovereign's black dress is decorated with gold embroidery specially worked in India. Diamonds sparkle in her enormous brooch and matronly white cap.

Everyone knows Victoria has stayed in mourning ever since Prince Albert died an eternity ago, but the no-longer-young Greek princess sitting between the Lauriers, somehow related to the Queen by marriage, believes it necessary to explain the reason for the black royal costume. Then, as if it's a great secret, she whispers that the dashing figures seated either side of Her Majesty are the Prince of Naples and the Archduke Franz Ferdinand of Austria-Hungary.

Zoë is getting used to the sight of royalty. They're just human beings, after all, who have been raised to think themselves grander than everyone else. And the aristocrats, both domestic and exotic, are getting used to the sight of her and Wilfrid. Tremors of recognition have begun passing between the Lauriers and all the princes and kinglets, dukes and duchesses, whom they're now encountering for a third or fourth time. The tall, heavily bearded Prime Minister, Lord Salisbury, has grown especially cordial toward them. Owning a villa on the Riviera, the Prime Minister speaks French fluently and enjoys practising it. One difference between Canadian and British politicians, Zoë has discovered, is that Salisbury and most of his ministers, titled or not, are unspeakably wealthy.

After dinner the guests are herded by footmen into the palace ballroom. The Queen Empress is wheeled in—she can't walk or stand for long periods—and installed in an ornate padded chair. The royal footstool is placed under her tiny arthritic feet. A brass band plays compositions that to Zoë's ears sound pompous, tuneless.

Three Indian princes are presented to the Queen. They hold out their curved swords to be touched by her, in some ritual obeisance that Zoë only vaguely understands, then it's the turn of the colonial premiers and their wives. The Prime Minister of Canada goes first.

Zoë scarcely feels complacent about meeting Queen Victoria, whom she regards as a quasi-sacred figure, but she's practised her curtsey to perfection and is grateful to have a non-speaking part, so she doesn't feel nervous. Wilfrid, tutored in the protocol for becoming a Knight Grand Cross of the Most Distinguished Order of St. Michael and St. George, bows deeply, going down on his right knee. When the process of sword and ribbon and seven-pointed star is complete, he rises to his feet as Sir Wilfrid. Well, Zoë thinks, he's still the same man I've always had.

Throughout the ceremony she's struck by the Queen's eyes: bright blue and bulbous, distinctly protuberant. Victoria's cheeks also bulge, above a weak double chin. Apart from the diamonds, she'd be perfectly at home as a well-fed, drowsy *grandmaman* in some Quebec parlour. She begins chatting with Wilfrid as if she's known him for years. Bending low to hear the Sovereign, he gently pulls Zoë closer.

"I have always regretted not visiting Canada," the Queen announces, inspecting Zoë with a glance. "But there are simply some places one cannot visit. Now it is too late, of course. The Prince of Wales went once, although he was very young at the time. He laid the cornerstone of your Parliament, I believe. Still, I have a strong affection for your country. Did you know that my father, the Duke of Kent, lived in Quebec City for two years? He was serving with the Seventh Royal Fusiliers. Extraordinary to think that was over a century ago. And of course I knew your Sir John A. Macdonald. He always reminded me of dear Mr. Disraeli. They looked so much alike, it was uncanny. Mr. Disraeli always spoke to me as one person to another, unlike Mr. Gladstone, who addressed me as if I were a public meeting. Lady Laurier," the Queen continues without pausing, "I see you wear spectacles. Does your eyesight give you trouble."

"Yes, Your Majesty. I'm afraid my eyes are very weak."

"I am sorry to hear that. Mine also. But I refuse to wear hideous spectacles in public. Ah well."

Weary and overheated, the Queen has run out of things to say. Wilfrid bows once more.

"You do great honour to Canada, Your Majesty. Permit me to assure you of the everlasting loyalty of your Canadian subjects."

On their return to the Cecil, Wilfrid is in a talkative mood. "It feels wrong being a 'Sir.' Rather like wearing somebody else's coat. Being at court is unsettling, didn't you find? You're never quite sure when to speak. Do you know what Disraeli said about dealing with the Queen? 'Remember, first of all, she is a woman.'"

Zoë wonders why he finds this comment so profound. "Of course she is, Sir Wilfrid."

On Jubilee morning, breakfast arrives early on a trolley. Joseph Mailhot comes promptly at six to dress Wilfrid, accompanied by Tillie, the practical Irish maid seconded to Zoë by their hosts. It seems Tillie and Joseph are getting along famously.

The night has been warm, filled with the sounds of people moving restlessly about down in the streets: loyal Britons determined to claim their two square feet of sidewalk, sleeping on them if necessary, to wake with a splendid view of the procession. Zoë herself slept only fitfully. Next to her in their enormous canopied bed, Wilfrid snored like an angel.

Bathing, preparing her face and hair with Tillie's help, Zoë feels the tension. It's a shame the morning is so dull and close. She keeps thinking of the plump old lady they met last night, no doubt going through these same early-morning rituals in her palace bathroom. For her sake, Zoë prays the weather will improve. Tillie squeezes her in stages into the pearl-grey silk gown Zoë bought in Montreal, fastening it up the back. She hopes she looks regal enough. The diamonds studding her necklace and entwined in her greying hair will help, as will the long grey gloves.

Wilfrid is in the sitting room, going over the day's protocol with his military attaché, Captain Bates, and one of Chamberlain's officials. When Tillie feels satisfied that nothing can be improved upon, Zoë emerges into the sitting room to greet the gentlemen. She practises her curtsey, and they all stand and admire. She blushes, giving a girlish laugh. She hasn't heard herself laugh like that for years.

"I hope I will do."

Wilfrid steps forward, kisses her cheek, embraces her with real ardour. "You look magnificent," he tells her, his voice hushed.

"And you too."

She can't take her eyes off him. He's wearing his Imperial Privy Councillor's uniform for the first time, as if born to it: dark-blue jacket heavily braided with gold lace, white breeches striped with gold, white silk stockings, gleaming black pointed shoes. Joseph brings him a plush velvet box, snaps it open with a flourish, and reveals the seven-pointed star of the Knight Grand Cross nestling on its purple cushion. Joseph removes the decoration, fixing it to the right breast of Wilfrid's jacket. Then he presents him with an enormous cocked hat and places it on his head at just the right angle. Wilfrid breaks into a sheepish grin.

The man from the Colonial Office notices Tillie is holding a full-length cloak for Zoë and informs Lady Laurier she won't be allowed to wear it in the ceremony at St. Paul's.

"I know," she says sweetly. "But I'm taking it with me in the carriage."

At exactly seven o'clock Captain Bates assists her into the open landau pulled by four chestnut horses and driven by two coachmen. Spectators stare from the sidewalk, greedy for the sight of royals or anyone else they think might be important. Several women giggle and wave, evidently recognizing Wilfrid, whose face has been appearing in the London papers all week.

Zoë shivers with excitement. She pulls her cloak more tightly around her shoulders and moves as close to Wilfrid on the seat as she decently can. The sky is murky, roiled by a wind that could mean rain. They move out into the street. Bobbies line the curb shoulder to shoulder, cordoning off dense masses of humanity stretching away down the side streets. London, a city accustomed for centuries to staging royal processions, mounting vast spectacles to display Britain's might and monarch to the world, is ready.

As Captain Bates has explained it, the order of march begins with the colonial troops. They will march the six-mile route to St. Paul's ahead of the royal procession, in which British regiments will escort the Queen. Deploying along the Embankment, the colonial procession will emerge into Whitehall and form up in the Horse Guards parade square.

The Lauriers' carriage turns into the immense stony space of the Horse Guards, where stands have been erected for visitors from the colonies. Zoë knows they have Canadian friends sitting there among the thousands of spectators. As each regiment arrives and shunts into place, she realizes what a massively orchestrated and exquisitely timed piece of theatre this is. Converging streams of soldiers—men trained to maim, kill and destroy—submit to a disciplined choreography, as if a lethal machine has been taught how to dance. The air is full of clashing sounds: clanking of sabres, thudding of leather boots, stamping of hooves, jingling of halter chains, sinister slapping of rifles spiked with bayonets. Fluttering pennants and excited horses are everywhere. Zoë has never seen so many horses, their bridles polished and gleaming. Officers shout orders to their men in different accents and languages. No one acts flustered or impatient. Everyone displays an implicit trust in the perfect organization of the Queen's day. Even the skies fall loyally into line: everyone has been wondering if the Queen's luck will hold—she's enjoyed splendid weather for every important ceremony of her reign—and just as church bells peal eight o'clock, the sun breaks through the clouds.

A bugle blast signals that the escort party is ready to lead the colonial forces to the palace. At its head is the Empire's most illustrious soldier, Field Marshall Lord Roberts of Kabul and Kandahar: "Bobs" as the English call him, riding a white Arab pony. He wears a flaring white moustache and white-plumed helmet, his scarlet tunic dripping with medals. To Zoë he looks as though he ought to be home with his grandchildren instead of playing at toy soldiers like a boy. The band of the Royal Horse Guards erupts into sound, each musician astride a black horse, and the blaring brass and thundering kettledrums make her heart lurch. She doesn't like martial music, yet the sheer sudden force of it is irresistible.

The first colonial troops to move out are the North-West Mounted Police, escorting the Prime Minister of Canada. With their long lances and red tunics, the Mounted are already crowd favourites. The Lauriers' coachmen flick the reins, and the four chestnuts move as one. Behind them march the Toronto Grenadiers, wearing tall busbies that must be growing more unbearable by the minute, and the Royal Canadian Highlanders, kilts and sporrans swaying.

Of the other units she saw in the parade square, Zoë likes the Australians best: big sunburnt troopers, their wide-brimmed slouch hats pinned up on one side by a black feather, carbines slung on their backs. Men on magnificent horses stretch back a mile, escorting Premiers from New South Wales and Victoria and Queensland and New Zealand and Newfoundland. Somewhere behind them rides the overstuffed Cecil Rhodes with his lancers from the Cape Colony and—questionably, in Wilfrid's eyes—the cocky troopers of the Rhodesian Horse, who rode on Jameson's Raid and are lustily cheered everywhere they go. Then come marchers from the more exotic reaches of the Empire: black-jacketed Zaptiehs from Cyprus wearing Turkish fezzes and riding Highland ponies, leathery-skinned Dyaks from Borneo famous, according to *The Times*, for their head-hunting proclivities, bearded and turbaned Sikhs, towering black Haussas from the Gold Coast, Jamaicans, Trinidadians, pigtailed Chinese policemen from Hong Kong, Malays and Maltese and Singhalese.

It takes the colonial procession nearly an hour to proceed up the Mall past tens of thousands in St. James's Park. When they arrive at Buckingham Palace, one of the Lauriers' coachmen leans back and shouts that the Queen is staring out her window. Zoë scans the windows but can see nothing. The colonial forces wind past the palace and continue up Constitution Hill, along Piccadilly, down St. James's Street.

Wilfrid waves with abandon to the cheering crowds, but Zoë feels too shy to join in. Who is *she*, after all? Instead she watches the watchers: young and old, parents and children, all fluttering their little Union Jacks, climbing lampposts wreathed with bunting, leaning out of upper-storey windows decorated with flowerboxes. Policemen on horseback keep a close watch, but the people look simply happy to be there because this celebration gives them joy. It's almost touching, the way the British have organized their society to make the ruled feel so adoring and grateful toward their rulers.

A cannon booms behind them in Hyde Park announcing the Queen is about to join the procession. Before leaving the palace, she presses an electric button transmitting her Jubilee message through five transcontinental cable routes to her subjects around the globe: "From my heart I thank my beloved people. May God bless them. Victoria, R.I."

The Lauriers' carriage rolls down Pall Mall, through Trafalgar Square under Nelson's squinting gaze, into the Strand. They pass a house where the grizzled survivors of the Charge of the Light Brigade are said to be gathered. At the entrance to the City, the soldiers reverse arms and march up Ludgate Hill into the square surrounding St. Paul's.

In the shadow of the great cathedral, Wilfrid and Zoë step down from their carriage. As surreptitiously as possible, not wanting to act like a tourist, she admires the immense dome, the sky blue except for a few fluffy clouds. She stretches her stiff legs inside her petticoat and leaves her cloak behind to be guarded by the coachmen.

An escort ushers the Lauriers to their seats on the cathedral steps. They have a perfect line of sight, shared by a man standing on a makeshift platform and peering through an ungainly contraption with spindly legs: the new art of cinematography on hand to capture the occasion. The first figure to appear in his lens is Captain Ames, the tallest officer in the British Army, towering above an enormous bay horse. He's followed by regiment after regiment of glistening, helmeted lancers, dragoons, hussars. Turbaned Indian cavalry wear brilliant tunics and gold rings in their ears, bluejackets pull polished brass naval guns, field marshals and generals and the Lord Mayor all ride on horseback, followed by the carriages of kings and queens, princes and princesses, bishops and archbishops, ambassadors and equerries, interspersed with bands playing fiercely, triumphally.

Her eyes straining into the light, Zoë pictures what the Queen will see when she arrives: a multicoloured blur of humanity rising up the steps of St. Paul's, a floating pyramid. At its base are lords of the Church of England, archbishops robed in purple and gold holding gilded croziers, bishops and lesser ecclesiastics in white. On the far side sit rows of black-robed judges wearing powdered wigs, and several rows of peers of the realm sweating terribly in their ermine-fringed robes. Some of the peers look as if they won't last the morning.

The colonial prime ministers are positioned halfway between Lord Salisbury and his cabinet, who sit below, and members of the diplomatic corps, seated directly above. The uniformed chests of the European diplomats are covered with jewelled orders. The Americans wear black evening dress. Most of the ladies are in summer white except the Orientals, whose green and blue silk dresses shimmer in the sun. Wilfrid points out to Zoë the aging Colonel John Hay, the United States ambassador, who as a young man was personal secretary to President Lincoln. Hay appears mildly bored.

Somewhat anticlimactically, the Queen arrives. She's seated in her open state landau pulled by eight cream horses, and she looks small and immobile, already sculpted in marble. She holds a black parasol against the sun. Facing her is her daughter-in-law, the Princess of Wales, whose husband Edward, the heir apparent, canters alongside.

When the royal carriage draws up before the ecclesiastics, it comes as a shock to see the Queen actually move. Taking the Princess's hand, she rises and, by stages, with apparent difficulty, descends to the ground. She climbs several steps, coming to rest on a dais before the Archbishop of Canterbury. He's flanked by Lord Salisbury, the First Lord of the Treasury, Mr. Balfour, and none other than Joseph Chamberlain.

Ecstatic cheering thunders across the square, washing up against the cathedral like waves battering a cliff. Zoë wonders if the assault will ever end. For the second time that morning, her heart stirs against her will.

The conductor raises his hands. The musicians and choir break into the *Te Deum*, giving thanks for a reign begun half a century before the choirboys were born. The Archbishop of Canterbury leads the chanting of the Lord's Prayer, in which the crowd joins. He then pronounces a special Jubilee prayer, asking God's blessings on the Queen and all her people. "God Save the Queen" is sung as fervently as a hymn, certainly more reverently than Zoë has ever heard it sung in Canada, and finally the Archbishop gives the doxology, "Praise God from Whom all Blessings Flow." Throwing orthodoxy to the winds, he cries, "Three cheers for the Queen!" The crowd responds with all its strength, and the service is over.

It has taken only twenty minutes. A longer, more strenuous service, everyone says, would have been beyond the Queen's powers. With a word to the Archbishop, Victoria Regina, Queen of Great Britain, Ireland and her Dominions beyond the Seas, Empress of India, returns to her carriage to go home. Zoë thinks she sees her wiping a tear from her eye but can't be sure. Perhaps it's only a speck of grit.

The procession re-forms, and Wilfrid and Zoë's carriage again leads the colonial forces on the return route. An elderly lord known as the Gold Stick for Scotland faints from the heat and falls off his horse. Fortunately he isn't badly hurt. Zoë feels sorry for him, but even sorrier for the little old lady who is the object of all the day's enormous fuss, its magnificent but preposterous excess.

"What a terrible burden it must be," she tells Wilfrid, "to be Queen. Having no choice about it, for your *entire life*."

"Yes, who would want it?" he replies, waving, smiling serenely at the massed Londoners. He leans close to the diamonds in her hair and says, "While we're here, I must meet Ambassador Hay."

Two days later the Colonial Conference begins within the gloomy confines of the Colonial Office. The protagonists are Joseph Chamberlain and the eleven premiers of the self-governing colonies. Government speaks to government: symbolic recognition, so the colonial leaders believe, of a new era of equality.

At the end of the first day, Chamberlain leads the premiers into the glare of afternoon to have their official photograph taken. It's posed to symbolize *his* conception of equality within the Empire. A junior official rushes outside with a single chair, positioning it directly in front of the steps. Chamberlain promptly sits down, cradling his silk top hat and gloves on his right knee. He wears a gorgeous cashmere suit with a large rosette in his lapel and a pair of exquisitely fitting high leather boots. The other leaders are arranged standing, slightly behind the Master.

Chamberlain places Wilfrid on his immediate right, turning his knees toward him so that their garments touch. Wilfrid stands with both feet firmly planted on the ground, hat in his left hand, a furled umbrella in his right. The other premiers remain stiffly at attention in their morning coats and watch chains. The photograph is taken and passes into history. Only Chamberlain and Wilfrid, Zoë notes, are without facial hair.

The Colonial Secretary has a sweeping mandate from Lord Salisbury to pursue Imperial Federation. But, as Wilfrid recounts to her over the two-week course of the conference, Chamberlain receives precious little encouragement from Canada.

The proposed Imperial Parliament is the grandest notion, yet the vaguest. Supposedly it would deal with issues concerning the Empire as a whole, its authority usurping Dominion Parliaments. To Chamberlain's shock and chagrin, Wilfrid is decidedly cool to the proposal, even disdainful. After all his banquet eloquence extolling British democracy, Chamberlain expected his support. But exactly what, Wilfrid asks, would be the status of colonial representatives in this hypothetical Parliament? And what would happen when British interests clashed with Canadian ones, as sooner or later they must? Chamberlain goes distinctly pale. Apparently the possibility hasn't occurred to him. Echoing Wilfrid, the Australian premiers also bristle over the threat to their autonomy. The South Africans agree. When only New Zealand and tiny Tasmania are sympathetic, the matter is tabled for consideration by a future conference.

As for an Imperial *Zollverein*, or customs union, in which Britain and the colonies would erect a common tariff barrier against the world, Canada has already given her answer. The Canadian preferential tariff on British goods is wildly popular in London. If the Mother Country reciprocates, as the British press is demanding, by giving Canadian goods privileged access to British markets, she will have to renounce certain treaties with her European neighbours. This Britain does. TRIUMPH FOR LAURIER, the headline reads.

A *Kriegsverein*, on the other hand, is something Wilfrid rejects as flatly as he can without appearing disloyal. The Australians can contribute monies to the Royal Navy if they wish, but Canada needs both her money and her troops for her own defense— against whom is patently obvious. How would it serve Canada's interests if her men were far from home, fighting in Britain's campaigns? How could Canadian autonomy be preserved if Canadians died at the command of a British general? Canada has no direct interest in distant imperial quarrels. If Britain herself became threatened, embroiled in some major emergency, it would of course be an entirely different matter. But how, in light of the display of military might the world has just seen, could one even imagine such a possibility?

In the privacy of their suite at the Cecil, Wilfrid says Britain fears her strength is waning, especially in relation to her imperial rivals, Germany, France, Russia and the United States. She wants to commandeer the colonies' youthful vitality, their natural resources and money and men, to secure and expand her possessions in Africa and Asia. Well, Canadians won't be turned into cannon fodder for rash military adventures. Wilfrid is well satisfied with the stand he's taken. He believes most Canadians, apart from the most jingoistic imperialists in Ontario, will support him.

Sir Charles Tupper arrives in London to fulminate against Laurier's stand, calling it "a declaration of independence, an insult rather than a compliment, an absurd scheme." Tupper's outburst is a badly timed attempt to air Canadian political grievances in the British press. After a day or two the novelty of his provocations wears off, and Zoë feels relieved when the silly old ass is ignored by the London papers, as he ought to be.

Wilfrid's most important coup isn't even public knowledge. In a private session with Chamberlain, he convinces the Colonial Secretary it's no longer practical for Britain to have full charge of Canada's relations with the U.S. Too many important and delicate issues must be negotiated between Ottawa and Washington, and inevitably these issues are intertwined. Resolving them requires a complex process of give and take, an intimate knowledge of—a commitment to—Canada's interests. Wilfrid insists on a freer hand. Chamberlain, distracted by bigger problems, agrees to give it to him.

Wilfrid then arranges an informal discussion with Ambassador Hay and asks him to convey to President McKinley his hopes for an early meeting. All affability and charm, bemused by this modest Canadian rebellion against the Mother Country, the venerable Hay enthusiastically agrees.

Zoë looks forward to the end of the conference: once it's over, she and Wilfrid are going to the Continent. In the meantime she attends concerts at the Royal Albert Hall and tours the South Kensington Museum and writes letters home to everyone she can think of. She writes to her old friend Emma Coutu about having her daughter Yvonne come to live with them in Ottawa as a helpmate. To Wilfrid's favourite niece, Louise Harvey, she describes the banquets and balls and garden parties and the odd ways of the English. She writes to Joseph Mailhot's mother in Arthabaska, assuring her that her son is well and continues to be of invaluable assistance to both the Lauriers. She writes to Lord and Lady Aberdeen, who would have loved to participate in the Jubilee celebrations but are obliged to remain in Canada while the Prime Minister is out of the country, letting them know Wilfrid has made a pilgrimage to their mutual idol, Mr. Gladstone, at Hawarden. Wilfrid and the Grand Old Man got along wonderfully. They had an inspiring conversation about political morality and the future of society, and Wilfrid says no other event during the Jubilee has given him so much pleasure.

And Zoë writes to Émilie Lavergne: not once but several times. After describing in detail for Émilie the Queen and the Palace and Windsor Castle and the court ladies' tight-waisted gowns and impossibly elaborate hats, the exciting journeys to Glasgow and Edinburgh, the pleasant trips to Oxford and Cambridge to receive honourary degrees, she tells her about the unspeakably lavish suite provided for them at the Cecil. Its view toward the Thames. Its luxurious chesterfields. Its gold-plated faucets and gilded mirrors. Its wide, canopied, extraordinarily comfortable bed.

Zoë assures Émilie she'll write again from various stops on their European tour. It will start in Paris, where Wilfrid is invited to speak. They'll be meeting President Faure and his wife, then they'll move on to the land of Wilfrid's ancestors in the Charente, as well as Switzerland, Rome and the Vatican, where they'll be received by His Holiness. Such a shame Émilie and Joseph can't be there to share it all. But no doubt they too are busy, looking for a new home in Ottawa.

They return to Canada in August on the *Labrador*, a Dominion Line ship considerably smaller and less comfortable than the *Lucania*. Wilfrid doesn't find the voyage particularly pleasant, but as they enter the Gulf of St. Lawrence, the water grows placid. Sailing upstream to Quebec City between the great river's forested, widely separated banks is a serene and dreamlike experience. They've been away from Canada nearly three months. They wonder how the country has changed, how it will receive them.

The answer comes that evening in a spectacle of immense bonfires blazing along the dark riverbank. Zoë draws Wilfrid away from his reading to stand at the rail and watch. They can see people silhouetted against the flames, some waving, others singing and dancing, but can barely hear them because of the distance to shore.

The ship's bearded Norwegian captain invites the Lauriers onto the bridge for a better view of the bonfires.

"How do they know it's us?" Wilfrid is grinning.

"We're in communication with every town by telegraph," the captain says. "They've all been asking what time we'd pass. They want to welcome you home, Sir Wilfrid."

The ship proceeds past a succession of villages and small towns, and the bonfires continue late into the night, lighting their way deeper into the country. "I adore this," Wilfrid tells Zoë, deeply moved. "There's something tribal about it. Something innocent and ancient."

In dense early-morning fog, they reach Quebec City. The fog disperses as they approach harbour, and the rising sun reveals the Aberdeens and thirty thousand others waiting to greet them on the dock at the foot of the cliff. Lord Aberdeen grasps Wilfrid's hand and holds on. "Your triumphs precede you," the Governor General says, admiration mingling with pleasure in his thin face. "Every day the papers were full of your travels. You're the lion of the hour."

The lion mounts a conveniently placed baggage cart and speaks off the cuff about his journey. He tells the crowd how proud he felt, as the Member of Parliament for Quebec East, and as both a Canadian and a *Canadien*, to be hailed in the halls of Westminster. He's not one who believes that God gave us Canada to fight the battles of our ancestors all over again. Today the nation can proudly take her rightful place among the nations of the world.

He knows very well, he tells Zoë, that calling Canada a nation will raise eyebrows, especially in imperialist circles. So be it.

Accompanied by the Aberdeens, they stroll through the festive mob, accepting handshakes, congratulations, flowers, stopping here and there to chat with the people. Joseph Mailhot has to hire a porter just to carry all the bouquets. In the afternoon they visit the Archbishop in his Basilica, a gesture intended to bind old wounds if not heal them. In the evening, the Mayor throws a reception and banquet at City Hall, and the ladies of Quebec present Zoë with a rosewood baby grand piano and many other gifts. There are so many, she exclaims, she'll need a new house to hold them all.

Lady Aberdeen beams at her. Lady Laurier needn't worry, she tells the crowded hall: the improvements to the Lauriers' new home in Ottawa have been finished in their absence. It's all ready and waiting for them.

7

August 1898

A suffocating humidity often spoils August in Arthabaska, but this morning is bright and fresh, fragrant with newly mown grass. As good a morning as any, Émilie supposes, for the novelty of a vice-regal visit.

The townsfolk are in a state: such excitement, such gossip, mixing anticipation with self-conscious anxiety. What are these English lords like? What will they think of us? How do they dress? Speak? Eat? Fornicate? (This from old M. Beaulieu, who has grown seriously demented.)

It's the first time a Governor General has ever set foot in Arthabaska. As the locals preen, they remind each other it's high time the Queen's representative paid them a courtesy call. The visit signifies overdue recognition of the town's many charms and attractions, its indubitable worthiness. You'd think Lord and Lady Aberdeen were coming expressly to meet *them*, Émilie thinks, and not simply because the Prime Minister happens to come from this provincial place.

Even those not invited to the intimate luncheon are certain what Madame (they can't bring themselves to call her Lady) Laurier will be serving. Most of the townspeople have already been inside the Lauriers' imposing red-brick home on the rue de l'Église, whether for a political meeting, a buffet supper, a picnic on the back lawn, or just to accompany their children to one of Zoë's *fêtes enfantines*. Surely she'll be serving the Aberdeens what she normally feeds *them*: tourtière, jellied salad, apple upside-down cake.

Wilfrid and Zoë have taken the larger of their two carriages to meet their guests at the Grand Trunk station, leaving Émilie briefly in charge of the household. Her Joseph has followed in a separate carriage to bring the Joseph Popes, who are arriving by the same train. Émilie finds it quite unnecessary to give instructions to the various Laurier friends and nieces serving the special meal. These women are so familiar with Zoë's tastes and habits that they know exactly how she likes things done. In this, as in other ways, Zoë is blessed. Of course she hasn't been blessed with children.

Émilie stands beside the sturdy walnut buffet watching Yvonne Coutu and the other girls bustling back and forth between dining room and kitchen. They're carrying little pots of *cretons*—Zoë's own version of the potted pork dish, famous throughout the town—and baskets of freshly baked *petits pains* covered with linen napkins. There's a deep tureen of *vichyssoise*, two enormous platters of lobster salad, plates of *cornichon* pickles and pickled beets and, yes, jellied salads. For dessert there are two maple sugar pies and, in case this Quebec specialty isn't to the Aberdeens' taste, plates loaded with lemon tarts and iced *petits-fours*, and a giant meringue topped with custard and wild blueberries. Fresh fruits are heaped into a pyramid in the centre of the oval mahogany table, laid with Zoë's finest lace tablecloth. An extra delivery of ice arrived yesterday from Tremblay's, and lemonade and iced tea have been made by the jugful. There's also chilled Chablis and, for later, Wilfrid's best port.

Everything is in readiness. There's really nothing for Émilie to do. She wanders through the front parlour, across the entrance hall and into the high-ceilinged drawing room, craving a moment's solitude.

As familiar to her as the drawing room is, she's never seen it empty of people till now. She feels oddly small and foreign in its subdued light. Nearly every piece of Louis-seize furniture is draped with a drowsing cat, observing her through half-lidded eyes. Every oriental cushion and fringed antimacassar is in place. A breeze ripples the lace curtains across the tall bay windows. Zoë's stereopticon sits on a small round table beside the grand piano.

On the mantel above the milky-white marble fireplace are little plaster busts of Alexander Mackenzie and Edward Blake, Wilfrid's predecessors as Liberal leader. How like him to honour these men, giving them pride of place in his own home. Blake was like a father to Wilfrid, in spite of—because of?—their political disagreements. On one occasion, Wilfrid relied on Émilie's subtle interventions to restore harmony between him and Blake, and she came through for him with flying colours.

That was several years ago. So much in their lives has changed. It's been a year since Wilfrid and Zoë moved into their house in Ottawa. They maintain two large and well-appointed residences now and, Émilie has to admit reluctantly, seem equally settled in both. Arthabaska has become Wilfrid's summer retreat, his beloved refuge from the pressures of politics. But only Émilie truly understands how crabbed and cramped and inadequate he once found living here, how desperately he longed to escape this artless little town, this narrow domestic life, to seek fulfillment in the wider world.

And what of her own fulfillment? She and Joseph also have two homes. They've found a small but fashionable—by Ottawa standards—brick house three blocks down Theodore Street from Wilfrid and Zoë. Its architecture is prim and proper, her scope for entertaining in its little parlour sadly limited. She still doesn't feel at home in Ottawa, doesn't quite belong. But at least the house provides her with a base for pursuing her social ambitions, for planning progressive euchre parties in aid of the city's favourite charities, its poor orphans and lost girls, and entertainments like her "Living Pictures" spectacle at the Russell Theatre. That lavishly costumed production took place in March in support of St. Luke's Hospital, starring, in its final tableau, Gabrielle Lavergne as "Our Lady of the Snows." Everyone agreed Bielle was utterly beguiling as the personification of an innocent young Canada— and Wilfrid smiled proudly down from his special box.

Émilie takes satisfaction in having become the hostess to whom Ottawa looks for originality and drama, not to mention the occasional *frisson* of the Prime Minister's presence. She knows this is the ultimate gift in her power to bestow, and a large part of the secret of her success. In return, she now receives invitations to all the season's events, important and unimportant, the most recent being a pleasantly indolent cruise on board the palace steamer *Empress*. While a band played light airs, the ship glided down the broad Ottawa all the way to Rockland, where passengers were disgorged onto the lawns of Mr. Edwards, the lumber baron. The guests played croquet, and under marquee tents the gracious Mrs. Edwards served a magnificent tea. . . .

Émilie feels her pleasure in these social successes rapidly reaching its limits. Something gnaws at her. To soothe the ache, she visualizes Wilfrid as he was in the old days: waking upstairs in the early morning, dressing, breakfasting, passing this drawing room on his way out of the house, crossing the street to the law office. At the appointed hour, he'd rise and speak to Joseph and stroll down the road with his languid gait to Le Vert Logis, where she sat waiting. The fire of small birch logs would be flickering in the grate, the tea water rising to a boil in the silver kettle above the spirit flame. There was always the delicious moment when she'd open the door to him, as to the man of the house, and he'd settle with a happy sigh into his favourite chair. The making and pouring of the best China tea, ordered from Montreal. The opening of the book whose pages they were sharing. And the rare, never-to-be-spoken-of moments when they went beyond literature, philosophy, tea, gossip, politics, to venture into more sublime and dangerous realms, which just now she can't even allow herself to picture.

How Émilie longs for those days. The longing is so painful she sometimes wishes she could forget them.

She's jarred by a commotion outside on the drive: the carriages arriving from the station. Hitching up the hem of her Parisian gown, she rushes to the front door, pulls it open, steps outside into the dazzling light of the pillared portico, the chatelaine making her grand entrance.

Lady Ishbel Maria Marjoribanks Gordon, Countess of Aberdeen, wants to see "the grounds."

Escorting Her Excellency by the arm over the lush lawn, Wilfrid relates in French how he and Zoë commissioned the home over twenty years ago from the brilliant young architect, Louis Caron. Lord Aberdeen walks behind them with Zoë on his arm, and the Popes and Lavergnes bring up the rear. They all listen to Wilfrid praising Caron's astonishing versatility. He scattered architectural gems up and down the street in a dazzling array of styles: Italianate and neo-Gothic, Queen Anne and Québécois. Wilfrid describes the master's penchant for richly decorated porches and dramatic balconies, his passion for turrets and round Roman windows, all of which make the rue de l'Église one of the most memorable streets in Canada.

Émilie is dying to point out that her house, too, is one of those gems, commissioned from Caron just a year after the Lauriers', but thinks better of it. Once again she notices how Ishbel—Émilie thinks of her that way, to bring the Countess down to earth—appropriates Wilfrid. The Governor General's lady has a way of heaving moistly at him, as if to swallow him whole. Her ringing syllables clatter everywhere in her dreadful accent, intimidating and silencing other voices. She's a handsome, full-hipped woman, big-boned rather than plump, at least forty, and wearing today a practical black travelling dress and bonnet instead of those ornate costumes she favours at her dinner parties.

Émilie assumes Ishbel has fallen in love with Wilfrid. How could she not? And Lord Aberdeen has simply followed suit, led by his wife in this, as in most other matters. The Governor General is a slight, soft-spoken Scot with a fastidiously trimmed beard and immaculately tailored clothing. Even on this warm summer's day, he's wearing a pale-grey vest under his suit jacket. Lord Aberdeen is renowned for his ability to imitate railway whistles. Émilie suspects it isn't he who is responsible for hanging portraits of Mr. Gladstone in every room at Rideau Hall: even, it's reported, in the master bedroom.

Since Governors General are constitutionally forbidden from attending the House of Commons, their consorts sometimes act as their eyes and ears in the visitors' gallery. Not content with this, Ishbel has insisted on a seat right down on the Commons floor—not in some inconspicuous spot, but directly between the Speaker and the front benches. There she sits every day when the House is in session, holding private chats about her pet projects and favourite causes with ministers and opposition members, even with Wilfrid himself. Émilie has yet to hear him complain.

The party rounds the house into the rear garden, and a tiny white dog bounds toward them. Brought up short by its leash, its foxy face swivelling rapidly from one human to another, it barks with comic ferocity and tries to leap into the Governor General's arms. Zoë calms the dog, apologizing for its bad manners, but Lord Aberdeen insists he doesn't mind: evidently this is the Pomeranian that the Aberdeens gave the Lauriers a year ago, knowing of Zoë's devotion to animals. They act delighted to see the creature again. Émilie reminds herself not to allow the children to persuade her to get a dog.

In a pool of sunlight between the rose bower and the vegetables, they pause to admire the elms and maples advancing up the hillside behind the house. Ishbel asks Wilfrid where he found the marvellous gardener to create all this.

"Oh, I made the garden myself," Zoë interjects shyly. "It took me years. I love working in my garden, but now we can't be here enough, so we hire a man to keep it up."

Émilie, who would never ruin her nails by plunging them into dirt, feels embarrassed for her friend.

"All this? Created by your own hand?" Ishbel replies. "More power to you!"

Completing the circuit of the house, they go inside, and Wilfrid leads them into the dining room. Armand is already waiting there with Gabrielle. Zoë has invited them to fill the remaining seats at table, a generous gesture that surprises and touches Émilie: Zoë could have invited any number of other guests.

Émilie thinks Armand is looking particularly grown-up and handsome today. But with an unnecessarily abrupt gesture, Joseph makes sure he and Gabrielle wait for the Aberdeens to be seated before sitting down themselves. She resolves to speak to her husband about embarrassing Armand by correcting him in public.

Yvonne Coutu and the girls serve the meal on royal-blue china edged with gold displaying a "WL" crest. While drinks are served, a verbal minuet takes place around which language to converse in. Wilfrid settles the matter by responding in English: a pity, since the vice-regal French is quite adequate. She supposes Wilfrid is acting out of consideration for Mr. Pope, the only guest apart from Armand who isn't fully bilingual. Although he affects disinterest in being in such illustrious company, Armand keeps stealing glances at both Aberdeens, as if, Émilie thinks with mixed amusement and concern, he's sizing them up for later retribution.

"I adore the landscape here," Ishbel announces, addressing Wilfrid. "The wooded countryside is so delightful. The hills remind Johnny and me of the fells in the Lake District, don't they? And the Nicolet winding down below the town—I felt I was travelling through a Suzor-Coté painting."

Wilfrid smiles at her mentioning the local artistic eminence, Marc-Aurèle de Foy Suzor-Coté.

"Does he still live here?" The question comes from Madame Pope, an attractive, modern young woman, not disposed to remain silent. She and her husband always act remarkably confident of Wilfrid's friendship.

"Yes, when he's not in France," Wilfrid replies. "He visits his dealer in Montreal but prefers to live and work here. I would too if I could."

Émilie smiles indulgently at this fantasy. "I understand Suzor is expanding the scope of his *oeuvre*," she puts in. "Moving into portraiture."

"As a matter of fact, he is," Wilfrid says. "I've commissioned him to paint Zoë's portrait."

"Really!" Ishbel erupts. "How splendid!"

Émilie looks across the table at Zoë, seated beside Lord Aberdeen. She's clearly pleased and flattered by Wilfrid's inexplicable tribute to her homeliness. For years Émilie has wanted a Suzor-Coté portrait—if not of herself, then of Gabrielle—but Joseph has insisted they can't afford it. Watching Bielle's lovely face and figure, she thinks what a superior subject her daughter would make for Suzor's talents.

As the conversation winds on, Émilie notes how the female voices conduct a dialogue with Wilfrid's. Sometimes he has that effect on mixed company: the men staying silent out of respect and admiration, the ladies becoming stimulated and drawn out by his warmth, intelligence, attentiveness. Unlike practically every other man she knows, Wilfrid actually enjoys female company, revels in it.

Once everyone is digging into the lobster salad, Ishbel clears her throat. "Now, everyone, we have some news. His Excellency thought this would be the best time and place to share it, here among friends. The world will know in due course."

She stares at her husband. The Governor General hesitates. His wife's prompting gaze withers him, makes him hesitate further. Émilie watches Minette Pope nearly gag on a crust of bread as she observes this silent struggle. It reminds Émilie of certain awkward moments during Lord Aberdeen's speeches, when his wife will pluck impatiently at his sleeve to make him speak up.

"Well, yes, indeed," he says finally. "As Lady Aberdeen intimates, we have some intelligence to report. The fact is—so it's been communicated to us privately, at any rate—the Queen has now appointed our successors. By November—the twelfth, to be precise—we will no longer hold the vice-regal office in Ottawa. We'll be sailing home a little earlier than expected, I'm afraid."

Wilfrid is visibly upset: Émilie has seldom seen his expression change so rapidly. But he keeps his voice steady. "I'm dreadfully sorry to hear this. We thought, we certainly hoped, you'd be with us another year at least."

"Ah yes, so did we." Lord Aberdeen's voice is hushed. "And it goes without saying, we will both miss Canada very, very much."

"The loss is ours, I assure you. And Canada's. May I ask the reason for your early departure?"

Ishbel can no longer restrain herself. "If it really *were* up to the Queen, I am sure we'd have remained for our full term. But no doubt Mr. Chamberlain"—she fends off a hard stare from her husband—"has his own good reasons for demanding our recall."

"No doubt he does, my dear."

"No doubt we have been insufficiently enthusiastic about his campaign for Imperial Federation. And perhaps as well we have too high an opinion of Canada."

As Lord Aberdeen searches for words, Wilfrid comes to his rescue. "May we know who your successor will be?"

It's Lord Aberdeen's prerogative to deliver this information too: his consort flushes brightly but remains silent. "In point of fact, it will be the Earl of Minto. Yes, Gilbert will be your man. Excellent chap, of course. Considerable experience. Good knowledge of Canada."

"I'm certain he and Lady Minto will do an absolutely *marvellous* job," Ishbel says under her breath.

Wilfrid looks doubtful. "I remember Lord Minto when he was Viscount Melgund—the military advisor at Rideau Hall. Afterwards he served as General Middleton's chief of staff in the North-West, fighting Riel. Not a name that goes down well in Quebec."

"Assuredly a military man," Lord Aberdeen says enigmatically.

Ishbel snorts. "A titled soldier. Riding to hounds. Hardly the sort of man needed here. What he's got to recommend him is, he's far more in line with Mr. Chamberlain's view of Empire."

"I may as well tell you," Lord Aberdeen adds darkly, "but for your ears only, if you please: Mr. Chamberlain has informed me that my 'resignation' will be announced tomorrow. In the London press."

"Resignation?" Wilfrid says. The table goes quiet. Everyone, no matter how powerful, shares a momentary feeling of powerlessness. Armand looks around the table at each person in turn, expecting someone to say something. His gaze comes to rest on Wilfrid and stays there, but Wilfrid remains as silent as everyone else. It's at that point, Émilie realizes later, that her sense of the good times ending begins.

During the remainder of lunch, conversation revolves around the Joint High Commission Wilfrid has created with President McKinley. Some months earlier, Wilfrid travelled to Washington to meet the President, as arranged by Ambassador Hay, now Secretary of State. Sitting together in the White House Blue Room, the two leaders hit it off famously. Wilfrid has described McKinley to Émilie as a bloated man physically, yet lacking a bloated sense of himself. Although Canadians see the President as a high priest of protectionism, Wilfrid found him welcoming, thoughtful, a moderately good listener for an American. He turned out to be surprisingly receptive to Wilfrid's proposal for a tribunal to settle the outstanding conflicts dividing their countries: not just one or two conflicts, but all of them at once.

Under the present arrangements, where Canada's interests are represented by the British ambassador to Washington, no progress whatever has been made on the lumber dispute or the Atlantic fishery or the all-important Alaska boundary, which determines whether Canada receives port access to the Yukon. Meanwhile new causes of friction arise all the time. The President and the Prime Minister agreed there's no reason why neighbours of good will can't solve their problems directly, without intermediaries. Acting on the assurance given him by a distracted Chamberlain, Wilfrid has bypassed the usual diplomatic channels. This marks progress toward his goal of Canada's conducting her own foreign relations. He wants to end the humiliating status quo, which he's described to Émilie as, "Miss Ottawa may have a voice, but etiquette forbids her speaking to Mr. Washington except through Papa London." McKinley may assume Mr. Washington will have an easy time seducing Miss Ottawa, but Miss Ottawa is learning to stand up for herself.

Perhaps, Wilfrid tells the Aberdeens, Chamberlain resents his initiative and is now taking it out on them. If so, he regrets it deeply. Lord Aberdeen can only smile in appreciation of the thought.

Wilfrid admits he's been counting on the Aberdeens' diplomatic skills during the Joint High Commission's work. The talks have been postponed by the outbreak of the Spanish-American War but are scheduled to begin soon in Quebec City: the first time an international negotiation will take place on Canadian soil.

"You mustn't worry," Ishbel tells him, "there's still enough time. We're already planning banquets and luncheons and receptions and tours of the Plains of Abraham. The American delegates will be so dizzy with champagne, they'll forget what they came for. His Excellency will do his usual wonderful job of charming them. You've had grand success with Americans, haven't you, dear?"

Lord Aberdeen's eyes are liquid, animated, reminding Émilie of a Gypsy's ferret she saw once in Montreal. "I do think we can make a *real* difference," he enthuses. "The Americans are full of swagger after defeating the Spaniards. We must show them Quebec City isn't Havana or Manila."

"Good heavens," Ishbel exclaims, "we don't want Teddy Roosevelt charging up Dufferin Terrace!"

Wilfrid says, "And now that the Americans have won their 'splendid little war,' as Secretary Hay calls it, they're finding it hasn't won them any friends. All of Europe sided with Spain, and only Great Britain is still friendly. A diplomat told me, 'The old pirate and the young pirate are joining forces for moral support.' By extension, Canada can offer the same friendship. All we seek is a reasonable settlement of differences before they become grievances."

"Which they already are, but you're too gracious to say so," Ishbel says.

"We shall have at least one advantage over the Americans," Wilfrid replies. "As secretary to the Canadian delegation, Mr. Pope knows the background to all these questions better than anyone."

Émilie looks at Pope to see how he takes this compliment. His eyes remain turned toward his chief.

"Mr. Pope," Wilfrid continues, "was in Paris for the arbitration of our dispute over the Bering Sea. He performed valuable research and became *the* authority on fishing rights and boundary claims. The Americans didn't get everything they wanted then, did they? And I'm certain they won't now."

"In Paris," Pope says, "we worked under very trying conditions. Quill pens instead of steel nibs. Yes, honestly! No blotting paper—one had to spread sand lightly over the paper to dry the ink on official documents. Best of all, each of the American delegates was flanked by a large spittoon. Whenever the stately old arbitrator, the Marquis Venosta, heard warning sounds of the impending use of these conveniences, he ducked for cover."

Ishbel: "We must order up a brace of spittoons for Quebec City."

Wilfrid: "They will be our first line of defense. I should also mention that Mr. Pope, in addition to learning to write with a quill pen, has taken up cycling."

"My wife is always telling me I should be more in fashion, Sir Wilfrid. For once, I am."

"Joseph goes *everywhere* on his new bicycle" —Minette Pope is as much amused as proud— "even when it's snowing."

"We look forward to seeing your prowess in Quebec City," Wilfrid says. "Better your bicycle than Colonel Roosevelt's stallion. But I can tell you now, Mr. Pope, you're going to have a colleague as secretary to the Canadian delegation. A co-secretary, as it were." He pauses, enjoying the suspense around the table: "Henri Bourassa."

Someone gasps. Émilie knows it's Armand. As a law student at Laval's Montreal campus, Armand has switched political loyalties. Henri Bourassa is now his inspiration and ideal: the principled, pure-hearted, uncompromising defender of Quebec's interests in Ottawa. Émilie sees the disbelief in Armand's face. Surely his hero would never accept such a position from Wilfrid? She also sees why acceptance of this assignment is irresistible to Bourassa's ego.

Wilfrid addresses his listeners' incredulity. "Of course you're wondering why I chose M. Bourassa for such a sensitive task. First, he's a young man of great intellect and ability. As Tarte says, the trick is to channel his brilliance in the right direction. Second, like any idealistic young Quebecker, including myself at his age"— and here he looks straight at Armand—"Bourassa regards English Canada with a great deal of suspicion, even hostility. I myself once opposed Confederation, for heaven's sake! But such feelings are rooted in fear, not reality, bred by isolation and ignorance. The more our M. Bourassa comes to know Canada, the more difficult it will be to maintain his suspicions. The more he becomes personally involved in our great questions of national development, the more he'll see things from a Canadian point of view. He'll realize Canada has enormous potential to benefit *all* its people."

"Allow me to play devil's advocate," Lord Aberdeen replies. "Don't you worry M. Bourassa will try to undermine Canada's interests?"

"Not at all, Your Excellency, I won't give him the opportunity. But I'm also certain his sense of honour is too strong. His grandfather may have been a rebel, but the Papineaus have always been men of principle."

"I'm surprised you were able to persuade M. Bourassa to join us."

"Let me share the argument I used with him. Canada now has an opportunity to conduct foreign relations in a new way. Instead of the resorts to force that other nations use, or threats of force, we'll put our faith in diplomacy. We won't win everything we seek—after all, what the Americans have, they keep, and what they don't have, they want. But we'll demonstrate our faith in peaceful dialogue and constructive negotiation. That approach is infinitely preferable to war, real or threatened. And God knows, the Americans have threatened us with annexation often enough. I want to create a new model for resolving differences. That's why I'm leading our delegation in person."

The Aberdeens smile as one. "Admirable, Sir Wilfrid," the Governor General says. "And highly optimistic. But I heartily agree, we must do everything possible to encourage peaceful methods."

"We can only hope Colonel Roosevelt never becomes President," Ishbel adds. "They say he wants to give Britain the Philippines in exchange for Canada. It's cheaper than invading."

Émilie sees Armand opening his mouth to say something, probably about preferring American rule. She cuts him off with a withering glare.

Once the desserts have been sampled and praised, the party moves outside to the verandah overlooking the back garden where a low table is set with coffee, tea and port. It's a pleasant place, brightened with bunches of cut gladioli and zinnias and asters: the only part of the house where Zoë allows smoking. Wilfrid passes a wooden box of slim, fragrant Havanas to his gentlemen guests, not including Armand. The two Josephs, Lavergne and Pope, accept.

M. Lévesque, the photographer, arrives at the appointed hour, his assistant carrying the camera on a tripod. The Popes and Lavergnes step aside to allow the Aberdeens and Lauriers to be photographed together as a souvenir of the occasion. Émilie studies Zoë. She's looking older: a bareheaded peasant, her dull grey hair pulled back into an unkempt bun, as if this was just another day, another visit from the locals. Although the puff sleeves of her flowered print dress are becoming, Émilie finds the lace embroidery down the front too reminiscent of an apron.

At last Lévesque finishes fussing with his subjects and equipment and gets under the hood to take his pictures. When he and his assistant leave, Ishbel turns the conversation to her favourite causes. Émilie resigns herself to a long stretch of listening.

Ishbel is thrilled that her Victorian Order of Nurses is finally, if grudgingly, receiving the respect of the medical profession. For months now the less enlightened doctors have been speaking out bitterly against the very idea of trained nurses going into people's homes. The doctors are all men, of course, and afraid these female nurses, however qualified, will lower medical standards, by which they mean do them out of jobs. But now that the VON is operating in a small way in Ottawa, Toronto and Kingston, the doctors see it doesn't usurp their power and admit it's not such a bad thing after all.

She's less optimistic about prospects for the Ottawa Improvement Commission. Its purpose is to transform the capital from a drab, muddy lumber town into a Washington of the north. With the nursing body and the National Council of Women, the commission was to be part of her legacy for the betterment of Canada. But now, Ishbel says solemnly, due to her unexpectedly early departure, she must count on Wilfrid to keep it alive.

He assures her he will. He's spoken to Tarte, who as Minister of Public Works is fully in support. He too wants to create a stately esplanade out of tumbledown Sussex Street, extending from Rideau Hall all the way to Parliament Hill and across the river at Chaudière Falls. Carriages and streetcars will be able to make a complete circuit of the Ontario and Quebec sides of the capital, symbolizing the union of the two founding races.

Ishbel positively glows. It must be the port, Émilie thinks. "We must all look fifty years ahead!" Ishbel exhorts, then falls silent. A shadow passes across her face, and Émilie wonders if she's suffering from one of the severe headaches said to plague the Countess under stress. But apparently she's only feeling regret over leaving Canada—even Ottawa—too soon.

Ishbel admits to a sneaking fondness for the capital. She realizes no one present is a native of Ottawa—everyone forced to live there arrives and leaves with serious doubts about its attractiveness—but for herself, she'll take home vivid memories of the place. One stands out above all others.

She proceeds to tell the story about nearly drowning in the Ottawa River. Everyone present, except possibly Armand, knows about the incident, but Émilie doubts anyone but the Governor General has ever heard it recounted in such intimate detail by the heroine herself.

Two years ago, Ishbel begins, having nothing pressing on an early spring afternoon, she and Captain "Boy" Sinclair, the Aberdeens' trusted aide-de-camp, decided to take the pony carriage for a ride up the Gatineau Road. Boy harnessed Ishbel's favourite ponies, Cowslip and Buttercup, and they boarded the old plank ferry that crosses the Ottawa. On the Quebec side they had a little chat in French with the curé, who was strolling up and down in front of his church, preparing his Sunday sermon. Then they started up the road. It passed between a row of houses on the right and the river to the left, terribly swollen from the spring floods. Water spilled over the banks and across the road, but Ishbel told Boy it would be all right, since other carriages and wagons were going the same way.

They got safely through one drowned section of road and found the water wasn't so deep after all. When they came to the next flooded section, a man was loading his cart with firewood. At the sharp slap of logs hitting logs, Cowslip gave a nervous swerve to the left. It was no more than a foot or two, but it was a foot or two too much. Losing his footing, Cowslip plunged into the water, dragging Buttercup in after him. In an instant, both ponies disappeared under the surface. The half-overturned carriage followed, and in an oddly graceful motion, Ishbel and Boy were dumped into the bone-chilling current.

She found herself treading water, Boy beside her trying to smile reassuringly, his moustaches pouring like faucets. She heard him say, "Don't worry, it's all right," and she tried to smile back.

She remembered hearing one ought to float in such circum-stances, so she stretched out her legs and lay back. Boy got onto the landward side of her to avoid being dragged by the current, tucked one arm around her waist, and began swimming to shore. She tried to go limp, so as not to fight his manoeuvre, but her whole head went under, which was not at all pleasant.

Boy was out of his depth and struggling. Later he'd say he feared things looked very nasty right then. Ishbel wondered how long one could remain conscious under water, and whether any-one on shore would see them in time to help.

Somehow Boy found the strength to keep stroking at right angles to the current. At last he reached a shallower spot where he found his footing. As he hoisted her to a standing position, Ishbel saw Buttercup's head resurface just for a moment, surprisingly far away, then vanish forever.

Two men came alongside in a flat-bottomed boat. Dragged down by her waterlogged dress, Ishbel clambered on board, feel-ing herself being pulled upwards by the arms and pushed uncere-moniously from below by Boy. In a moment they were all standing on shore. The two men offered to take them to a house to warm up, explaining that this was a notoriously dangerous spot: the road had been shored up last year at great cost, but the floods had un-done all the work, and now there was an invisible drop of twenty-five feet from the roadway to the riverbed. But all Ishbel could think about was her beloved ponies, gone to a horrible death.

It was a miracle the same thing hadn't happened to her and Boy. How they'd been expelled clear of the carriage, how they hadn't been swept into the river and sucked down by the current, were mysteries for which she could only thank God. Or Boy. Who was very distressed and insisted on blaming himself, since he'd been driving. But in fact, she pointed out, that was foolish of him: it was her idea, after all, to take the Gatineau Road.

After visiting the curé to ask him to prevent sensational reports being sent by the telegraph operator, they recrossed the river by ferry and returned to Rideau Hall on foot. Ishbel ordered them both to take hot baths. She told His Excellency about the accident, and although he was of course beside himself at the news, he rallied to send all the necessary telegrams in Canada and overseas to prevent people from becoming alarmed, just in case they heard silly rumours. She had her bath and went straight to bed. At six she rose and dressed for dinner.

That evening's dinner party was a small one: only the Lauriers and three Liberal Senators, with wives. Lord Aberdeen had wanted to cancel, but Ishbel wouldn't hear of it. The dinner conversation naturally turned to the incident on the river. The Lauriers and the senatorial party had already heard about it.

It was Sir Wilfrid himself—of course he wasn't *Sir* yet, Ishbel says, beginning to flush bright pink—who showed the greatest comprehension of her situation. The senators' wives just made things worse by bemoaning the ponies' deaths and going on and on, but Sir Wilfrid simply sat very still, listening intently. He realized it was actually Lord Aberdeen who was the most distressed by the whole affair. He turned to Johnny and, quietly but very firmly, told him how well Lady Aberdeen looked despite the unfortunate accident, how calm and resilient she was, what courage it had taken for her to manage such a frightening turn of events. Knowing him as she did, Ishbel saw her husband becoming genuinely comforted and reassured by Sir Wilfrid's words. All his burden of responsibility was lifted—something she herself had been unable to accomplish. Meanwhile Madame Laurier, sitting next to her husband, smiled warmly and nodded at each of his remarks, adding the weight of her unspoken sympathy.

It was then that she saw clearly, months before he was elected Prime Minister, that Wilfrid Laurier had the gifts to lead a divided and anxious nation. He had such an unerring sense of the emotional logic of a situation, the precise action required to resolve it, and so, she realized, yes, yes, yes: he would listen sensitively to Canada's tremulous heart, would observe calmly its endless agitations, would move swiftly to address them, like a wise physician—much as Sir John A. Macdonald was said to have done. Of all Canada's leading men, only Laurier had the intellect and compassion, the sheer mental stamina and emotional capacity, to bring a fractured nation together. Even his mastery of the principles of British liberalism, indeed of the English language itself, far exceeded that of his countrymen. ...

Out of breath, Ishbel flutters to the end of her paean to Wilfrid. She looks around the table as if waking from a dream, belatedly realizing she's in company. Thank heaven, Émilie thinks, she didn't go any further.

A new voice breaks the silence on the verandah.

"But why," Armand asks logically in French, "since Her Excellency cared so much about her ponies, did she risk their lives during the spring floods? The river is always dangerous at that time of year. Anyone who knows the slightest thing about conditions on the Quebec side could have told her that."

Émilie has forgotten all about Armand's presence. Before she can move to silence her son, Wilfrid simply changes the subject. "Excellencies, we must introduce you to one of our Quebec delicacies. You haven't lived until you've tasted roast young suckling pig *fermière*, cooked in the French-Canadian manner. Before you leave Ottawa, Lady Laurier and I will serve it to you."

Everyone follows Wilfrid's lead, tacitly ignoring Armand's interruption. It hasn't occurred.

Armand reddens, glares furiously into his coffee cup. Émilie steals a glance at the Aberdeens. They appear completely unflustered as they respond gratefully to Wilfrid's invitation.

Émilie turns to her husband, and Joseph meets her gaze with a stricken expression of abject helplessness.

So like Joseph. His tongue-tied shamefacedness is the very picture of her dissatisfaction with her marriage. It makes her think of his ineffectual response, reported to her years ago, when his brother challenged him to do something about the persistent rumours concerning her and Wilfrid: "What do you want me to do?" Joseph told his brother then. "I have a good wife. Why humiliate her unnecessarily? She admires him, as I admire him myself. I prefer to live in peace and let people talk."

Too shaken to pay further attention to the conversation, Émilie tries to think what good has come of attending this luncheon. Finally she remembers: learning that the Aberdeens will be leaving the country. That, at least, is something to be thankful for.

8

October 1899

Surrounded by grooming cats and caged canaries, Zoë sits at a
card table in the morning room doing the household accounts. It's
her favourite part of the house on Theodore Street. Brightened
by two walls of windows, it contains her player piano and indoor
plant collection and is perfect for receiving her card-playing
friends—the current games of choice are bridge and poker—and
the steady stream of visitors seeking her assistance with a musical
career, a charitable cause, a nephew down on his luck, in need of a
government job.

Wilfrid comes storming downstairs. She looks up, one eye still
on her column of figures. He's swearing. Throttling a newspaper in his fist. Very unusual. She hasn't seen him this angry since
the winter, when the Americans on the Joint High Commission
reneged on their promises. She's just about to chide him for hir-
ing too many carriages instead of taking the streetcar, which stops
right outside their door, but sees this is hardly the time. She never
fears one of Wilfrid's bad moods, only wants to know the cause so
she can help him through it.

He flings the paper to the floor, startling the cats. He picks up
her latest acquisition, a grey Persian, and gently resettles it on the

rug so he can sit down. "My good dear Zoë, I thought we agreed on a moratorium on new pussycats. I've never seen this one before."

"That's because she's new."

"What's her name?"

"Blossom. *En anglais*. A gift from Lady Minto, so I could hardly refuse. Something is upsetting you."

"General Hutton."

"That dreadful man."

His anger doesn't surprise her: it's been mounting for days, stoked by the public's seething obsession with the approach of war. Wilfrid can't abide reading the newspapers anymore. The *Montreal Star* leads the pack in baying for Boer blood. The *Star*'s Conservative publisher, Hugh Graham, bent on becoming Canada's William Randolph Hearst, is whipping up the public's thirst for war in South Africa. At the other extreme, the French dailies thumb their noses at the imperialists: *La Presse* and Tarte's own paper, *La Patrie*, are virulently opposed to any suggestion that Canada send troops. Quebeckers see the Boers, in their rustic hats and sunbonnets, as a threatened minority, a religious agrarian people like themselves. But in Toronto, even the moderates now consider war necessary. They speak of advancing the cause of civilization and rescuing South African blacks from Boer "terrorism."

Zoë has seen all the headlines, read all the articles, trying to spare Wilfrid the aggravation: THE EMPIRE'S CAUSE. AWAITING THE CALL. RUMOURS OF WAR. Today's *Globe* has sunk to repeating rumours going around the London clubs. Boer military units are said to be on the move. Boer soldiers are persecuting British citizens in the Transvaal, threatening Britain's colonies in southern Africa. New Zealand and the Australians have already committed troops, superseding Canada as the leading member of the Empire. Wilfrid is feeling beleaguered, abandoned by his friends. He needs to speak to John Willison.

But the paper he's flung to the floor isn't *The Globe*. He picks it up, hands it to Zoë with a dismissive gesture. It's the latest issue of the *Canadian Military Gazette*, a journal occasionally useful to Wilfrid as a source for whatever intelligence Frederick Borden, his Minister of Militia, has neglected to share with him.

"The *Military Gazette* isn't always reliable," Wilfrid says, "but *this* story is preposterous."

Zoë scans it quickly. Purporting to draw on official sources, it claims the government of Canada will immediately send troops to South Africa in the event of war. It describes the strength, composition and military capabilities of the Canadian contingent, names its commander, identifies its embarkation point.

"Complete rubbish. There could only be one source," Wilfrid says contemptuously.

General Edward Hutton arrived last year with the Mintos when they replaced the Aberdeens. He was appointed Canada's new commander of the militia by the British Ministry of War and is known to be close to Joseph Chamberlain, who wants his own man keeping an eye on things in Ottawa. Hutton affects an overbearing air of authority: he bristles and swaggers and snarls. Unlike Lord Minto, whom Wilfrid has begun to like and trust, General Hutton calls the Boers "infamous blackguards" and "detestable scum." He also feels free to criticize Canadian defense policy. All of this, to Wilfrid's immense annoyance, makes Hutton inordinately popular with his men. He clearly views his appointment as a mandate to prepare Canada for war. The full extent of his pretensions was revealed when he and his society wife, said to have connections at Court, rented Earnscliffe, Sir John A. Macdonald's former home, from Lady Macdonald.

Wilfrid begins pacing the room, watched warily by the cats. "Hutton has a contingency plan for sending troops. That's normal. I've known about it for months but never paid it much attention. It's the sort of thing generals do to amuse themselves when there's no war. But now that he's leaked his little plan, he's circumventing Parliament and undermining my authority."

"You can't have that," Zoë says.

Wilfrid unburdens himself. He advocates, as if he was back in court. There's no reason why Britain must actually use massive force to crush a small nation of farmers—and even less reason to drag Canada into it. True, Kruger and his government have denied citizenship to the Outlanders, as the British gold seekers in the Transvaal are called: the Outlanders aren't allowed to participate in politics or even vote. But does that mean blood must flow? Just to teach the Boers a lesson in democracy? Surely a more civilized solution lies within the grasp of a civilized empire.

In any case, Wilfrid stands firmly by the resolution he presented to Parliament. Canada sympathizes with attempts by Her Majesty's government to seek justice for the Outlanders, but at the same time Canada hopes that expression of sympathy, "of universal sympathy extending from continent to continent and encircling the globe, will cause wiser and more humane counsels to prevail in the Transvaal and avert the awful arbitrament of war."

"*That* is Canada's position," Wilfrid says, slamming his fist into his palm. "It's as far as I can go without a change of policy debated and approved by the House. The sovereign will of Parliament can't be overridden by some tin-pot general, no matter how popular in Whitehall."

"Well then, you must explain all this to the public," Zoë tells him. "Especially the English public."

Wilfrid says Alexander Graham Bell was doing the devil's work when he invented the telephone: it invades a man's privacy, ruins his peace of mind. But he has to admit, it comes in handy sometimes. Ulric Barthe waves to signal that the operator has found John Willison. He hands the earpiece to Wilfrid, who presents his mouth to the speaker mounted on the wall.

"Is that you, John? Good. I'm giving this to you on an exclusive basis."

Zoë picks up her knitting. The telephone is just around the corner in the front hall, and if she leans back, she can see Wilfrid, hear his every word. His voice becomes deep, confident, expansive: he gestures with his free hand as if addressing an audience. "John, there is a great deal of misunderstanding in the country about the government's wartime powers. Our volunteer soldiers are to be used only in defense of the Dominion. They are *Canadian* troops, under control of our government."

Wilfrid pauses. "Are you getting this down, John? Then let us postulate Spain attacks Great Britain. Spain also attacks Canada's coastal territories, because we are part of the Empire. In this hypothesis, we use our troops not only to defend ourselves, but can also send them over to Spain or England to join in the British war effort. But you see, the case of South Africa is *not* analogous. The Transvaal Republic presents no direct threat to Canada. And although we may be entirely on Britain's side, and willing to help, I don't see how we can. The Militia Act doesn't permit it. And so it is that we haven't offered a contingent."

Zoë hears him pause again while Willison says something. When Wilfrid replies, he's adamant. "No, no, no, not a word of it! That statement in the *Military Gazette* is sheer invention. Imaginative, but dead wrong."

Willison argues a point.

"It may very well mirror Ontario's convictions. But I am not the Prime Minister of Ontario, any more than I'm the Prime Minister of Quebec. By the way, I haven't noticed many signs of war fever in the Maritimes, have you? There are some parts of the country where war isn't a cause for jubilation."

The next day's *Globe* publishes Wilfrid's analysis almost word for word under the headline THE PREMIER'S STATEMENT. He hopes it will calm public hysteria about the coming of war.

That hope is dashed when a cable arrives from Joseph Chamberlain. Addressed to the Canadian government, the telegram disingenuously acknowledges a patriotic offer of troops by "the people of Canada"—an offer that hasn't been made. Apparently Chamberlain has been reading the *Military Gazette*. With remarkable precision, he spells out his wishes: eight companies of one hundred and twenty-five men each, drawn from units of the Canadian militia, preferably the infantry, to be armed with .303 rifles and equipped and transported at Canada's expense. Once they arrive in Cape Town, the British government will assume the cost of supplying and paying them. They should embark for South Africa no later than October 31.

When Wilfrid hears about the cable over the telephone, his voice goes grave and low. Zoë waits until he hangs up and joins him in the hallway. He goes into the drawing room and sits down suddenly, as if pushed. "The cable is bad enough," he mutters, "but it's already in all the papers."

"The fires are being lit on the hills," she observes, standing beside him, resting her hand on his shoulder.

Meanwhile there's Quebec to consider. It has given Wilfrid more MPs than any other province. He can't ignore French Canada by caving in to the imperialists, but the pro-war press is already making Quebec into the issue. The *Montreal Star* has launched a propaganda campaign masquerading as a public opinion survey, sending telegrams to mayors, militia officers, clergymen and other notables, complete with prepaid replies. By printing only replies supporting the sending of troops, the paper makes it appear Canadians are virtually unanimous. The *Star* reports the very few opposed all have French surnames and charges them with sympathy for the enemy. It runs a headline that Wilfrid finds contemptible, unforgivable: COWARDS IN OTTAWA.

He also receives a letter from Senator Sir John Carling, the rich brewer and former Macdonald cabinet minister. "French Canadian loyalty is now on trial," Carling tells him. "I hope it won't be found lacking."

Wilfrid still thinks the whole wretched affair will blow over somehow. Britain will achieve her ends in South Africa without committing mass murder. Kruger will come to his senses and realize he doesn't stand a chance against the world's mightiest military power. In the end, the only thing that overwhelming power is good for is to resolve disputes peaceably. The awful arbitrament of war isn't only immoral, he believes: it's out of date.

Later that day Émilie drops by. It isn't at all unusual for her to be in and out of the Lauriers' house, but as Zoë serves her a cup of tea, she senses the visit has some special purpose.

Émilie works up to her point gradually, surreptitiously. "Have you seen the afternoon papers? The British government is chartering sixty-seven steamers for South Africa. Sixty-seven! What are they planning to do? Lock up every Boer man, woman and child?"

"It does sound like a lot."

"The British are planning to send a *massive* force. It's the Spanish Armada all over again."

"The Boers seem quite capable of defending themselves. The papers say they've assaulted British women and children. There's a rally in Toronto to protest the atrocities—"

Émilie's brittle laugh interrupts her. "Don't believe everything you read! The press is making excuses for an invasion."

"I don't believe everything I read. Wilfrid makes sure of that."

"Ah, Wilfrid. Is he home by any chance?"

"Yes, but he's working on his speech for our trip to Chicago. We're not to disturb him."

Émilie pauses as she lifts her teacup to her lips, striking a pensive pose. "I wonder how the meeting will go with President McKinley. Wilfrid will need some support, don't you think? Advisors. A retinue."

"Retinue?" Zoë isn't entirely sure what Émilie is getting at, but she has her suspicions. "Mr. Mulock and Mr. Willison are coming with us. They know the Americans well."

"And they know English Canada, but not Quebec. Everything Wilfrid says in Chicago will be reported back home. He needs to keep French-Canadian interests in mind. Wouldn't it be useful to have a compatriot along?"

"Mayor Préfontaine is coming from Montreal. And Laurent-Olivier David."

"Préfontaine? Too parochial. He'll be useless. Wilfrid needs someone with a stronger grasp of international affairs. I suggest Joseph."

"*Your* Joseph?"

"Of course. Who better? He knows Wilfrid's mind and political objectives. Who better to anticipate hidden dangers?"

"Yes, but—"

"Look at the years they've spent discussing politics. Joseph understands how Wilfrid thinks. He'll provide him with sound advice. He always has Wilfrid's best interests at heart."

"But why—"

"Zoë, it's a perfect fit! I mentioned it to Wilfrid at one of your musicales. He promised to think about it, but he must have forgotten."

"It's not up to me to tell Wilfrid how to run his affairs."

Émilie smiles knowingly. "Nonsense, my dear, you do it all the time. Come now, just this once, for an old friend. Remind him there's a Quebec immigrant population in Chicago. Joseph knows their leading men. Joseph can be infinitely useful to him."

"And of course he'd need to be accompanied by his infinitely charming and useful wife."

"We all want Canada to make a success, don't we? A social as well as a political success? Zoë, just think of the fun we'll have, you and I! Think of making grand with Mrs. McKinley!"

It's a relief to get out of Ottawa. Both Zoë and Wilfrid feel it. He's determined to make a favourable impression in Chicago. Although the Joint High Commission ended in deadlock, he still hopes for a settlement. If he can turn American sympathies toward Canada, he could yet sway Congress to allow port access to the Yukon through the Alaska Panhandle.

But wooing America in its current mood will be difficult. Lately the United States has been more interested in seizing its neighbours' territory. Hawaii, Puerto Rico and Cuba have all been occupied, not to mention the Philippines. The U.S. now has 75,000 soldiers stationed in those islands, putting down the bloody insurrection that followed their "liberation" from the Spaniards. Wilfrid says the Filipinos are the first to realize that America is the new Spain. More thoughtful Americans are asking what has become of the Republic's founding principles: Thomas Jefferson's vision of a nation that renounced militarism, conquest and all the other evils of the Old World. Meanwhile American newspapers casually advocate invading Canada as the logical extension of America's right to the continent.

Zoë doesn't want to hear any more troubles. On the train to Chicago, she finds it agreeable to chat with the wives in the party, especially Madame David. The Lavergnes aren't included. She forgot to remind Wilfrid of Émilie's generous offer to accompany them.

On arrival in Illinois Central Station, they're greeted by brass bands and noisy crowds, Chicagoans determined to give a rousing welcome to the foreign visitors. The Mayor shakes hands with everyone in the Canadian party, including the ladies, and conducts them through the crowd to a line of waiting carriages. Around the Lauriers' carriage, a sizeable group has formed: reporters clutching pads and pencils, eager for a few words from the exotic visitor with the manners of a French aristocrat. Not knowing what else to ask, they seek his views on American politics. After the disappointing failure of the Joint High Commission, how are his relations with President McKinley?

Relations remain most cordial and constructive, Wilfrid replies with a disarming smile. He holds the President in the highest esteem, considering him a true friend of Canada. The visit will only strengthen the bonds of friendship between neighbours.

And what does he think of President McKinley's Democratic challenger, William Jennings Bryan?

Wilfrid pauses. Zoë senses him weighing some inoffensive, neutral response—it could be fatal, after all, to stray into the host country's imminent election campaign—but he forges ahead with a reply she knows reflects his honest opinion: "Mr. Bryan's speech at the party convention in 1896 was sophomoric. Since that time, he has redeemed himself. I believe Mr. Bryan to be a thinker and a philosopher."

Zoë hopes the newspapers won't make Wilfrid regret his words the next morning.

Another questioner strikes closer to home: "Mr. Prime Minister, back in July the State Department was very unhappy with you. You told the Canadian Parliament that if the U.S. and Canada couldn't compromise on Alaska, there were only two ways left to settle the dispute, binding arbitration or war. Could you please explain?"

"Most certainly," Wilfrid replies. "I will explain by quoting the very next sentence I spoke in our House of Commons: 'And I am sure *no one* would think of war.' War between such good neighbours is unthinkable."

As the reporters scribble down his words, Wilfrid gives a little wave and turns toward the carriage, but shouts coming from the rear of the crowd make him hesitate. They're in French. He turns back.

"Are my compatriots here?" he asks eagerly. "I didn't expect to hear my mother tongue in this city."

Looking over the reporters' heads, he switches into French. He addresses the little knot of men at the back about the struggle to preserve the French language and culture in an English-speaking country, whether Canada or the United States. Frustrated at not understanding, the reporters urge him to speak English.

"Forgive me, gentlemen, I simply couldn't leave my countrymen without a few words in our language. But permit me to tell you a little story. Recently I conversed with a justice of the United States Supreme Court, who explained to me at length the superiority of the American system of governance. Well, is it not one of the prime tenets of your system that freedom of speech prevails? I will be speaking in English tomorrow, if you wish to come and hear me then." And to cheers from his countrymen, he completes his remarks in French.

"I'd better stop while I'm ahead," he mutters under his breath, and he and Zoë climb hastily into the carriage.

When they reach their hotel, word comes that Chamberlain has issued an ultimatum to President Kruger: Britain is demanding an immediate grant of citizenship to the Outlanders. If Britons in the Transvaal receive their political rights, there will be no war.

Wilfrid sighs. "The ultimatum is designed to fail. The Outlanders will soon be a majority in the Transvaal. Why should the Boers surrender their country? They don't accept the law of nature that Britons must be masters of the earth."

The streets around the hotel are mobbed the next morning. It's Chicago Day, the city's annual celebration of its resurrection from the Great Fire that nearly destroyed it twenty-eight years earlier. President McKinley never misses the occasion. This year he'll lay the cornerstone for a grand new federal building.

The Lauriers' carriage makes its way through the crowds to the building site at the corner of Jackson Boulevard and Dearborn Avenue. Mounted policemen are keeping people away from a reviewing stand erected for the President and his guests in front of the Union League Club. Mounting the steps, Wilfrid and Zoë are introduced to Mexico's Vice-President Mariscal—the Mexican President being too ill to travel—and to various members of the McKinley cabinet and Washington diplomatic corps.

Seated after the blur of introductions, Zoë admires a recently completed skyscraper soaring alongside the newer building's steel skeleton. Festooned with bunting and an enormous Stars and Stripes, the skyscraper climbs the heavens like some gigantic, gaudily dressed stilt walker. Spectators lean out of its windows, adding to the circus spirit, but they're outdone by daredevil construction workers sitting high on the girders of the unfinished structure, waving down at gawkers below. Zoë can't bear to look at them. One false move and they'll topple to their deaths.

Roars down Jackson Boulevard herald the President's arrival. His carriage makes stately progress through the mob, allowing Mr. McKinley frequent opportunities to rise and remove his top hat to salute the voters. He ascends the reviewing stand with portly grace, and when he reaches Wilfrid, tells him it's enormously gratifying to see him on American soil again, and what a pleasure to meet Lady Laurier at last. The President fixes her with an extraordinarily luminous stare, as if she's the only one in the crowd who matters.

People say McKinley's strongest conviction is to be liked. Zoë does find him likeable: in his morning coat and striped trousers, he resembles a vegetable marrow on legs, surmounted by a smiling pumpkin head. His clean-shaven face is kindly and unexpectedly handsome, his signature bright pink carnation flaring from his lapel.

McKinley crosses the street surrounded by his police bodyguard and accompanied by an Episcopalian clergyman and a Roman Catholic prelate. Mounting a dais before the future entrance to the new building, he gazes reverently at the massive cornerstone of Illinois limestone suspended like a pagan deity from wire cables. He silences the crowd with a sweep of his arm. Welcoming the foreign leaders, his cabinet members and the public, the President introduces the two clergymen, who pronounce blessings on the ceremony. He then declares that this new building will symbolize the greatness, the dignity, the ever-increasing power of the United States. He cites the Republic's recent gains in wealth and territory and observes that the population has doubled over the past thirty years, not counting the new possessions. He draws the loudest cheers when he declares that the American flag now flies over a greater land mass than ever before in its history.

The President steps forward for the pièce de résistance. Bowing to the brawny labourers working on the new structure, a gesture Zoë finds rather charming, he accepts a trowel from the building's architect, loads it up with wet cement from a mortarboard held by a workman, and deftly, from frequent practice, throws mortar onto the base. The band right beside Zoë explodes into a martial version of "The Star-Spangled Banner." The workmen quickly ease the cornerstone into place. The President returns across the street, and his guests follow him inside the Union League Club for a celebratory lunch.

At the head table, Zoë is seated next to Ida McKinley, who has been waiting in the club all this time. It's widely known Mrs. McKinley suffers from epilepsy and has a low tolerance for the endless official functions her husband must attend. But she's exerted herself to make an exception for this occasion.

As Wilfrid chats with the President, Zoë finds herself drawn to this gaunt, pale, fragile-looking woman. Mrs. McKinley must have been very pretty once, her eyebrows thick above large eyes. She makes a striking figure in her high-necked green silk dress. "I always sit next to the President at banquets," she tells Zoë, gesturing clumsily toward her husband on her right. "That way, if I take a seizure, William can cover my face with his handkerchief. He always carries a clean one, just in case."

Nodding as if this was perfectly normal, Zoë casts about for another topic of conversation. She falls back on the tried-and-true gambit that never fails her in every kind of social situation, at home or abroad: asking about the children.

"Well now, Lady Laurier, I have something sad to tell you. Both our sweet daughters passed away in infancy."

Zoë is mortified: no one has told her.

"Oh now, please don't be upset. The second one went to heaven right after she was born. Then my dear mother died, who I could ill afford to lose at the time, and that's when my illness began. I suppose it's not so surprising, really. And two years later our lovely Katie went from typhoid fever. She was only three."

Zoë is startled by how quickly she feels tears stirring.

"There, there. It was all a long time ago. Now tell me about your family, I do like to hear about people's children."

Zoë makes a gesture of helplessness. "I'm afraid I have nothing to tell." She tries to smile, searches for the words in English. "Wilfrid and I love children. But we have to make do with our nieces and nephews, and our dogs and cats. And our friends."

"Oh. I see. So we are both childless, you and I."

With that bond established, the women slip easily into a long and sympathetic conversation about their travels and loneliness and mutual impatience with politics, chatting happily until the coffee course arrives. Regrettably they have to stop to listen to their husbands speak. It seems President McKinley's handker-chief won't be needed after all.

The Mayor of Chicago proposes florid toasts to the United States and the President, and McKinley rises to his feet. Zoë observes the cavernous depth of his cleft chin, deciding it accounts for at least some of his handsomeness. In manner he has the calm, self-assured mastery of occasion that seems to mark all great lead-ers. Or is that gift, she wonders, bestowed by the office itself? In Wilfrid's case it's always been there.

The President's speech dwells on the destiny of great nations, mentioning only one in particular. The United States has been blessed by God to win every war it has ever fought, he declares with solemn satisfaction. On every occasion, the Republic has emerged from the conflict with its honour intact and without stain. It has annexed every type of territory, from the coral reefs and coconut groves of Key West to the icy wastes of Alaska. Now it has extended its jurisdiction to the faraway jungles of the Philippines. (Lusty cheers.) Yet the United States has never struck a blow in combat but for the cause of its civilizing mission—and it has never struck its colours, either. Most recently, loyal Americans have shown their patriotism by volunteering to fight against the tyranny of Spain, not for the glory of arms and conquest, no indeed, but for the love of peace and freedom.

McKinley's language, although uttered in a soothing and benev-olent tone, strikes Zoë as remarkably belligerent. She doesn't remember hearing anything similar in London or Paris. It gives the lie to the notorious description of the President by the hero of San Juan Hill, Theodore Roosevelt, that he has no more back-bone than a chocolate éclair. And it provides a cautionary backdrop to the speeches by the Mexican and Canadian leaders.

Vice-President Mariscal, speaking after the toast to Mexico, keeps his remarks brief and innocuous. Following the toast to Canada, it's Wilfrid's turn. He's glowingly introduced by Senator Shelby M. Cullom, Republican of Illinois. This is mildly ironic, as Wilfrid has told Zoë: the good Senator once contended that the United States should own the whole of the northern hemisphere. But now Cullom is the epitome of hospitality and graciousness, paying his guest the ultimate compliment. "I do not desire to embarrass Sir Wilfrid, but he has seemed to me in his association with our people to be almost an American."

As Wilfrid rises, a warm wave of applause rolls out of the cigar haze to greet him. He proceeds to speak with as much heartfelt feeling as Zoë has ever heard him use. He salutes Chicagoans' courage and heroism in rebuilding their city after the Great Fire, praises the President, expresses his admiration for the many extraordinary achievements of the United States, past and present. Canadians and Americans share a continent, he says, and much, much more. And yet, he must admit, recently they have met obstacles coming to agreement on certain questions, among them the Alaska boundary.

Theatrically, Wilfrid surveys his listeners for a moment: "Shall I speak my mind?"

"Yes, yes!" they cry, warmed by his oratory and the Mayor of Chicago's brandy.

"Then permit me to say, Mr. President, that we citizens of Canada and the United States are sometimes too prone to stand by the full conceptions of our rights. We try to exact all our rights to the last pound of flesh. Permit me to say also that Canada does not desire one extra inch of American territory. But if I state that we want to hold on to the land we have, what will be America's response? Will we have your sympathy?

"I am here today, above all, to say that we do not intend to stand upon the extreme limits of our rights. Rather, in our dealings with the United States, we are ready to give and take. We can afford to be just. We can afford to be generous, because we are a strong and generous nation—just as you are."

Applause interrupts him. It's quieter and more formal than the applause for the President, but respectful. Wilfrid's candour has gained his audience's full attention.

"Now, I am the first to admit that relations between our two countries today are not as good, as brotherly, as satisfactory, as they ought to be. Yet why? We Canadians and Americans are of the same stock. We spring from the same races on one side of the border as on the other. We speak the same language. We have the same literature, and for more than a thousand years we have had a common history. When we go down to the very bottom of our hearts, Mr. President, we find that there is between our peoples a true, a genuine friendship."

Loud hurrahs: now he has them. The President himself looks up, smiling, and applauds Wilfrid with hands held high. Zoë exhales before she remembers to applaud too.

After another full day of speech making, highlighted by Wilfrid's address to two thousand leading businessmen at the Chicago Board of Trade, the Canadian party boards the train to go home. Before leaving, Wilfrid pauses to dash off a note to Gabrielle Lavergne, wishing her a happy twenty-first birthday.

The ragged outskirts of the city slip by. He stretches his long legs into the aisle of the parlour car and tells Zoë he's satisfied with the trip. He's done what he could to contribute to a friendlier understanding of Canada by Americans. Now it's their turn to reciprocate.

"Personally, I like Americans," he says offhandedly. "Of course I'd like them even better if they weren't so selfish and grasping.

They were certainly in the wrong on the Joint High Commission. But now I've shown I won't be bullied, and it just makes me more popular at home."

After the border crossing, John Willison strolls up the aisle to join them. Wilfrid is ready for him. "Have you seen this editorial, John?" He brandishes the *Chicago Tribune*. "We heard plenty of sympathy for the Boers in Chicago. Now the *Tribune* compares their cause to the American Revolution."

"Yes," Willison replies cheerfully, "aren't you glad our papers don't go in for such hyperbole? We prefer to report things as they are." He hands Wilfrid a copy of that day's *Globe*, delivered to him at the border station.

Zoë leans over to peer through her pince-nez. WAR INEVIT-ABLE, she reads.

Wilfrid bristles. "Why the headline? War is never inevitable. Among men of good will, there's always an alternative."

Willison sits down across from them. "You must tell it to the Boers. Read about *their* ultimatum."

Wilfrid runs his eyes down the story, shaking his head. "The Boers want Britain," he explains to Zoë, "to withdraw all troops from the Transvaal border and agree to arbitration. If Britain doesn't accept within forty-eight hours, there will be war." He sets the paper aside. "Between Kruger and Chamberlain there's no trust whatever. But don't you see, John—it was *Chamberlain's* ultimatum that began this process. He merely provoked another."

"With all respect, the Boers are now the belligerents. They talk of 'putting our faith in God and the Mauser.'"

"Yes, why should they give up without a fight?"

Willison chews nervously on his knuckle. "I hope you're not planning to say that in public."

"John, we're having an honest debate, you and I. Let us, at least, face facts. Public opinion is another matter."

"Canadian public opinion is a fact *you* must face."

"If opinion in English Canada is against me, I have the newspapers to thank!"

"That may be. But at *The Globe* we continue defending you against unfounded attacks. For now, at least."

"What are you saying?"

"In yesterday's editorial we condemned the argument that because you're French, you're preventing the country from doing its duty. We called it an argument unworthy of serious reply."

"And so it is. But please understand: if there were a *real* emergency, I'd ask Parliament for thousands of men and millions of dollars. I just don't see why Canada must participate in all the minor wars in which England is constantly engaged."

The next stop is London, Ontario, and among the boarding passengers is a junior *Globe* reporter. He's been dispatched from Toronto to meet Willison, who comes back looking unusually excited.

"You have news?" Wilfrid asks uneasily.

"I'm afraid so. Boer troops have crossed the frontier and invaded British territory. War has begun."

Zoë doesn't like the triumphant expression on Willison's face, but likes even less the look on Wilfrid's: shock mixed with incredulity.

"I didn't think it would come so soon. If at all."

"War always comes too soon," Willison says. "But now it's a reality, and the Boers have fired the first shot."

"That makes it all right, then."

"You'll have to act now, Sir Wilfrid."

"Don't 'Sir' me, John. I'm not a creature of Empire."

"We're all creatures of Empire, one way or another. It's inescapable."

"Nonsense."

"Canada expects a decision. You'll either send troops or be forced to resign."

Wilfrid glares at him. "Your thinking is much too black and white for me. I remain unconvinced." He falls into a sober silence: his mask for anger, and the signal for Willison to withdraw to his chair.

Wilfrid remains silent all the rest of the way to Toronto. Zoë knits and stares out the window at the southern Ontario landscape. The colour of the maples has reached its height, but not as brilliantly as she remembers it in Quebec. Acutely, painfully, she sees how isolated he is, stranded between worlds. Everyone else has the luxury of holding passionate convictions, opinions to live and die for, rooted in tribe and race and blood: but not he. He must fight for the good. He must unite what refuses to be united. It's a lonely place to be. He put himself there, as he put himself between her hearth and Émilie's.

In Ottawa Tarte is waiting for them at the station, eyes flashing, goatee thrusting, yet still gallant toward Zoë. No doubt he's upset Wilfrid has been spending so much time in Willison's company. Tarte sounds all the alarms at once. They aren't off the platform before he's telling Wilfrid of battles raging in his absence between the pro-war and anti-war factions in cabinet: battles Tarte won, of course. He's certain General Hutton is conspiring with Lord Minto. He has evidence of ministerial disloyalty. Frederick Borden is telling the newspapers the government will send troops. This has overexcited the military men, which has in turn enflamed resistance in Quebec.

"A protest rally is taking place tonight in Montreal. Many in our own party are going to be there. They'll denounce the jingoists' attempts to force Quebeckers to fight Zulus and barbarians."

This provokes a shout of laughter from Wilfrid. "And what does *La Patrie* say about fighting Zulus?"

"Why, *La Patrie*—"

"Yes, my friend, it's all right. I don't have to read *La Patrie* to know what it thinks."

"I warn you, Wilfrid, we've reached the breaking point. Our Quebec caucus is digging in its heels. Opposition to this Anglo-Saxon war has hardened, and you can't afford to ignore it."

"Undoubtedly. As I can't ignore the hardening views in Ontario in *favour* of war. Joseph, do one thing for me, please. Bring the leading men of our Quebec caucus to my house tomorrow night. You know the ones I mean. Be sure to include the most vociferous opponents of war—besides yourself, of course. We must have all this out before cabinet meets."

To prepare for the MPs' arrival, Zoë is assisted by the cook and Yvonne Coutu. Émilie rushes over "to make herself useful" but only wants to talk about Chicago and the President and Mrs. McKinley. Seeing her disappointment at being left out, Zoë feels a little guilty.

Émilie looks strained, even cross. "And why isn't Joseph invited to the meeting tonight? I don't understand."

Zoë makes an effort at sympathy. "You're forgetting he's no longer a member of caucus." But sympathy is followed by its opposite. She's in a rush and just wants Émilie out of the way, out of her sight. Rather than say anything she might regret, she busies herself setting out linen napkins and freshly polished silverware. Émilie walks out in a sulk.

The gentlemen begin arriving slightly before eight. Tea, coffee and cakes to sweeten their disposition are spread across the buffet. The leaded French doors between the dining and drawing rooms are opened. On Wilfrid's instructions, no wine or sherry is to be offered: discussion will be heated enough as it is.

He ushers each arrival into the drawing room on his arm, settling him into a chair in the gentle ambience of pale rose and soft green, chatting warmly, asking after the man's health and wife and children, regardless of his opinion on the war. Despite Tarte's assertions, he knows the Quebec caucus is far from unanimous.

Zoë stands in the opening to the dining room behind her baby grand piano, inviting the visitors to help themselves from the buffet. A small fire burns in the grate. Wilfrid seats his guests in a circle so that the factions are mixed together, not arrayed face to face like hostile armies. Two avowed opponents of war are present, Jean-Lomer Gouin and Rodolphe Lemieux. Two others, Napoléon Champagne and Napoléon-Antoine Belcourt, favour sending troops—perhaps because of their names, Wilfrid has joked to Zoë. A pair of venerable members arrives together, Sir Henri Joly de Lotbinière, the old seigneur, and Charles Fitzpatrick, an Irish Catholic who acted for Louis Riel at his trial. Neither is enthusiastic about going to war, but Wilfrid knows both will abide by whatever decision cabinet makes tomorrow.

The last to arrive are Tarte and his protégé, Henri Bourassa. Wilfrid expects Bourassa to create the most trouble, yet can't help being drawn to the young man, feeling an instinctive kinship with him: he's the man of the future. With his closely trimmed dark hair and beard, Bourassa looks superficially unlike his rebel grandfather but has the same burning gaze Wilfrid remembers in Louis-Joseph Papineau, the same unshakable belief in his mission as the self-appointed champion of French Canada. Bourassa has an aristocratic bearing and another quality setting him apart from ordinary politicians, an acute and penetrating intelligence. Zoë knows that Wilfrid wishes he, not Tarte, was Bourassa's mentor.

Legs elegantly crossed, Wilfrid settles before the fireplace, surrounded by men who owe him much. "Gentlemen," he begins, "in the last session of Parliament I expressed Canada's sympathy for the Outlanders in the Transvaal. They are, after all, our fellow British subjects and are being denied their civil rights. But I also supported a peaceful solution to the crisis. For my views, as you know, I've been vilified in some quarters, and I've stood my ground. But now that war has broken out, the ground has shifted. We're being called upon to stand and be counted. We all have our private views, but we must go beyond personal opinion and take a stand as a party, as a government, as a country. It must be a principled position, a position we can all live with, whether as Frenchmen of Quebec or Englishmen of Ontario."

Wriggling impatiently in his chair, Tarte jumps in. "For us, Wilfrid, the front line in this battle is-is-is Montreal, not the Transvaal. Yesterday's headline in the *Montreal Star* said everything: 'Our Country Must Be Kept B-B-British.' It shows how the English really feel at the bottom of their hearts. They want to keep the *Canadiens* subservient. They don't care about our views and they don't give a damn about our scruples. They want to shut us out of decisions about our own destiny."

"My dear Tarte," Wilfrid replies, "I apologize for saying this since you're a journalist yourself, but we should never judge a people by its newspapers."

"That's all very well, but the rest of Canada outside Quebec sees only its own shadow. The English must be made to understand where Quebec stands and why. Quebec will not support a war in which she has no i-i-interest. I've said this in cabinet, and I've told my followers, 'Not a man, not a cent, for South Africa.' That's what we're all waiting to hear from you. When will Quebec's voice *ever* be heard in this country, if not when we have a Prime Minister from Quebec?"

Hanging back in the shadows, Zoë feels the truth of Tarte's argument. She hopes Wilfrid will reply with equal conviction.

His voice remains calm. "I understand your position. But I am Prime Minister of *all* the people, and I can no more accede fully to Quebec's desires—assuming we knew what they were—than to the bigotry of the *Montreal Star*. Mark my words, gentlemen: Canada is in danger of splitting apart along racial lines. If we fail to act wisely, we will do irreparable harm. And let me assure you, I haven't worked to achieve power in this country in order to oversee its demise. We must find a middle way through the crisis, a path allowing us to emerge whole and united. That must be our paramount goal."

Like a counsel for the prosecution, Tarte ignores Wilfrid's plea. "Chamberlain said last week he gratefully accepts Canada's offer of troops. But *who* made such an offer, and on what authority, and through what channels? I submit there was a clandestine attempt to undermine our democracy and force our hand. I submit General Hutton and Lord Minto and Minister Borden have a lot to answer for!"

"My dear Tarte, if you please!" Wilfrid pauses, trying to recover his equilibrium. "This morning I met with the Governor General. I told him these kinds of suspicions exist, that they only make it more difficult to arrive at a satisfactory solution. Lord Minto understands—"

This is too much for Henri Bourassa. "Understands!" Zoë manoeuvres into a position where she can observe Bourassa sitting on the far side of the circle, his feet squarely on the ground, palms planted flat on his knees. "Sir, do you ever take account of public opinion in Quebec?"

Wilfrid smiles wearily, but not unkindly. "My dear Henri, the province of Quebec does not have opinions. It has only sentiments."

Bourassa stiffens. "I want no part of your 'middle way.' There is a far more vital principle at stake, and that is the democratic principle of no taxation without representation. Why should the Quebec people bother to vote for Laurier and the Liberal Party if their wishes are ignored on such a vital issue?"

"Their wishes are not ignored. But theirs aren't the *only* wishes in this country. Sentiments in Ontario are as real as sentiments in Quebec."

"More so, I fear, in your mind. You gave your word, sir. You stated in public that not a single Canadian would go to war without the consent of Parliament."

"No, I didn't say that. I said I didn't see *how* it could be done without the consent of Parliament. Nonetheless, a way must be found."

Bourassa's mouth clenches with indignation. "You mean to say you won't even recall Parliament?"

"Given the mood of the country, no, absolutely not. A debate in Parliament at this time is the last thing we need. It would only reopen our racial wounds. Besides, our government would be defeated. Your opponents are not only the Conservatives, Henri. I've asked the Whip to count our own members according to their views on the war, and we simply wouldn't have the votes." Suddenly the room goes dead silent. "So you see, gentlemen. The circumstances are extremely difficult."

Bourassa draws himself up to the full height of his dignity. "It is because they are difficult that I'm asking you to remain faithful to your word. To govern, sir, is to have the courage to risk losing power for the sake of principle!"

Zoë hears the intake of breath around the room, and suddenly Wilfrid is on his feet. He takes two strides until he's standing directly in front of Bourassa. Hesitating, he places a hand on Bourassa's shoulder. "Ah, my friend. You have an impractical mind."

The shoulder twitches impatiently under his hand, yet Wilfrid remains there, towering over the younger man.

Bourassa stares grimly ahead. "If you decide on war, Prime Minister, you leave me two choices. To speak against your ministry or resign outright."

Rodolphe Lemieux looks back and forth between Wilfrid and his inquisitor. Seeing them both pale and immovable, he tries to break the impasse with a bad pun. "Well, Henri, since the wine is evidently poured, there is nothing to do but drink." He says *Boer* instead of *boire*.

As the MPs are leaving, Zoë wishes them all a good night, while Wilfrid draws Tarte aside. When she returns to the drawing room,

Wilfrid is saying, "Now listen, old friend: I don't want your resignation too. One tonight will be quite enough."

"But what do you plan to *do*?" Tarte asks vehemently. "You still haven't told us. How do you propose to keep the votes of our English MPs without leaving me no choice but to resign?"

"We have to compromise, you and I. There's no alternative."

"But why should *we* be the only ones to compromise? Bourassa believes this war is unjust, and so do I. Do you?"

"It may not be the most just war Britain has ever fought, but far more important is what's at stake here at home. The interests of Canada *and* Quebec demand we keep the country together. Emotions in the English provinces are running too high to be denied. We can't afford to fight them. And we don't need to."

"What about Quebec?"

"Quebec can be placated. You know as well as I, most Quebeckers will accept Canadian participation as long as military service is purely voluntary. The Mayor of Montreal is on our side, so is *Le Soleil*. But it's still not a popular war, I admit, and that's why I need you: I need you at my side in the next election. Quebec must stay with us or we'll lose power. We'll lose everything you and I have worked for over the years. That is the greater evil, Joseph. If you resign now, you'll only be accused of disloyalty, and Quebec along with you."

"I'll think it over," Tarte mutters.

"Thank you. I'll see you in cabinet in the morning. Think of the minimum you can live with."

The next day is Friday, October 13, and it puts Zoë in mind of a funeral. A chill implacable rain pelts down from a bleak sky. Wilfrid leaves for Parliament Hill early in the morning and returns by streetcar after six. It's dark when he leaves, darker when he arrives home.

As he kisses her cheek, she tries to read in his face how the cabinet meeting went but sees nothing but grey exhaustion. His winter cough has already begun. He places his dripping umbrella in the stand, hands her his wet overcoat and silk hat. He goes straight into the drawing room to warm himself by the fire. On the streetcar coming home, he tells her, two militia officers plied him with questions about the makeup of the force going to South Africa. They were so obnoxious that he had to find another seat.

Cook serves them a hot supper in the dining room, but Zoë only picks at her food, too intent on listening as Wilfrid reconstructs the day's events.

Seated at the head of the cabinet table in the East Block, he surveyed his tense, suspicious ministers, remembering how elated they were on first meeting three years ago, flushed with victory, brimming with optimism. They were brothers then. Now they're splintering into resentful cliques, as ready to attack each other as fight the Conservatives, and all over their separate conceptions of a country they share and love. Yesterday's observation by *La Presse* is painfully accurate: "We French Canadians belong to one country, Canada. Canada is for us the whole world. But the English Canadians have two countries, one here and one across the sea."

Wilfrid gives each of his dozen ministers a turn to speak, but from the start they aren't prepared to let each other finish. The interruptions grow angrier and noisier, less a reasoned debate than a parliamentary brawl, and for a sickening moment Wilfrid has a vision of presiding over first his government's dissolution, then the nation's.

If Tarte is prepared to compromise, he's hiding it well. His stabbing finger and infernal stutter, worse when he speaks English, irritate and infuriate his colleagues. Wilfrid keeps picturing Bourassa looming behind Tarte's shoulder, egging him on, but Tarte isn't alone. The Secretary of State, Sir Richard Scott, an irascible, white-bearded Catholic, presses the anti-war case with equal ferocity. Scott has the Irish mistrust of England: he's convinced he's battling an imperialist conspiracy to coerce the government. General Hutton has boasted that when he served in Australia, he toppled a government that ignored his advice. Hutton represents a subversive element within Canada, Scott says indignantly, and Lord Minto is no better.

Bringing the Governor General into it is Scott's mistake. William Mulock leaps to Minto's defense. Speaking with the power of Toronto's commercial class behind him, Mulock argues that Canada needs Britain's support to have any chance of winning the Alaska boundary dispute, and therefore had better stand by the Mother Country now. Moreover, Mulock insists, his great bearded head turning left and right, the Liberals are courting disaster by letting the Conservatives become the party of patriotism. Tupper is winning hearts and minds by alleging the Prime Minister was first in the Jubilee procession but last in the Empire's hour of need.

Rather than reply to this provocation, Wilfrid lets Frederick Borden speak. Everyone knows where Borden stands. As Minister of Militia, he's been unabashedly pushing for a military role in South Africa, the bigger the better. Borden is closer to General Hutton than he ought to be, but like Mulock, he's clever enough to clothe his views in Canada's self-interest. He argues from a paradox: the national destiny, the road to full nationhood, ultimately lies in embracing Mother Britain, becoming her partner in the great imperial quest. This argument has never made any sense to Wilfrid.

"We've been presented with a golden opportunity," Borden enthuses, speaking directly to his leader, "to show we are no longer a colony but a mature nation of the Empire. Let us take a position befitting our size and prosperity and importance. This is a rare chance to prove the mettle of our fighting men. We must not let it pass. This country has needed a national mission: now we have one."

Tarte can barely contain himself. The little man rises as high in his chair as he can. "My d-d-dear colleagues, you forget Canada already *has* a mission, and that is to be an independent nation that thinks for itself! You also forget where the real strength of our government c-c-comes from. You like to think you can govern without Quebec but you can't. And in Quebec we refuse to march to your immoral imperialist wars. Since we have no say in imperial war councils, we refuse to pay an English tax in money and b-b-blood!"

Mulock springs to his feet. "That's enough!" he bellows. "If what we've just heard is the position of this government, I can serve it no longer. I'm writing my letter of resignation. You shall have it, Sir Wilfrid, within the half-hour." And pushing past Sifton's restraining arm, Mulock storms out of the room.

At this point in his narrative, Wilfrid stops to offer Zoë a wintry smile.

"Well? What did you do then?"

He gives a hard, dry cough. "I did what any sensible statesman would do: I declared a recess. I told them all to go and eat a good lunch and return after food had calmed their stomachs. In the meantime I took the Quebec ministers down the hall into my office."

With his Quebec colleagues, Wilfrid is unapologetically blunt: Mulock's anger shows how the land lies. In light of public opinion in Toronto, even *The Globe* finds it impossible to defend the government's inaction any longer. And once *The Globe* defects, desertions by Ontario MPs are inevitable. The Liberals will lose their majority in the House.

No, English Canada won't be denied its own splendid little war. The Boers on their dusty farms half a world away might have our sympathy, Wilfrid tells his compatriots, but the English Canadians are our partners. They must be listened to. It's like a marriage, he says, eliciting rueful smiles and knowing nods around the room: neither party gets its way all the time. Sometimes pride has to be sacrificed for the sake of domestic peace. Total resistance is futile.

His real audience is Tarte. Without Tarte's co-operation, the game is lost. Tarte has the power to keep Quebec in the fold or cut it adrift from the rest of the country, especially if the war comes to a vote in Parliament. Wilfrid is determined it never will.

It's Tarte, and only Tarte, who replies. As opposed as he is to this wretched war, there's only one reason he would ever agree to sending troops, and the Prime Minister has expounded it: the country is in a horribly fragile state. And yet there's one point on which he must insist. The British want Canada to commit itself irrevocably whenever they decide to fight another of their endless wars. That is where Canada must draw the line. Even if Canada supports Britain this time, it must refuse to set a precedent for the future.

As Wilfrid repeats the gist of Tarte's words, Zoë can see a faint smile relieving the tightness around his mouth. She can picture what happens next: the two old schoolmates take up their pens to draft a compromise resolution.

When cabinet reconvenes to discuss the draft, Mulock's letter of resignation sticks provocatively out of his breast pocket. He and Borden want Canada to foot the entire bill for recruiting, equipping and shipping a full-fledged regiment, based on the Hutton plan, but Sifton and Fielding take a more moderate stance. They urge that the cost in money and lives be kept to a minimum: cabinet should limit the contribution to a modest force of volunteers, no larger than Chamberlain's request. By the end of the afternoon, shepherded by Wilfrid's patient prodding, the moderate position triumphs. Tarte's essential proviso binds the fragile compromise together like a gaudy ribbon.

Wilfrid addresses the newspapermen who have been milling impatiently about the East Block entrance. He stresses that his government isn't sending an official contingent—a unit of the militia—but simply providing an opportunity for Canadians who wish to volunteer with the British in South Africa. Thus the Militia Act is being respected. Only a thousand volunteers will be taken. The cost to Canada will be so minimal, it isn't even necessary to summon Parliament.

How, Zoë asks him, does he think the country will react?

"In Ontario I'll be accused of delay and half measures—to which I'll reply we've taken action on the war's third day, exactly as Chamberlain requested. In Quebec I'll be accused of betrayal. I'll reply that since so many English want to fight for the British, we're merely giving them the chance."

"Meanwhile you've kept your government together."

"As you know better than anyone, I don't get carried away by passion and so I refuse to be stampeded by the passions of others. I have to look at right and wrong, to see the effect of any decision on the unity of the country. In the end the country will support me, whatever the yellow press may say."

"I agree," she says. "You've done the right thing, the necessary thing. Still, I wonder about Tarte's question. Are the British in the right?"

Wilfrid's expression turns from weariness to sadness. "Even if they are, war is war. I despise the suffering it will cause. The British are saying it will soon be over, they'll eat their Christmas dinner in Pretoria. I hope to God they're right."

The ink is barely dry on the cabinet resolution when recruiting offices open in twelve cities across the country. Wilfrid remarks dryly that his mind must have been known by others long before he knew it: Borden has even displayed the foresight to order new supplies of military clothing. Still, it's a major task to raise, organize, equip, arm and transport a force equal to Canada's standing militia, with a preparation time of only sixteen days. The embarkation date is set for one day before Chamberlain's deadline. Training will have to take place on board ship during the thirty-day voyage to Cape Town.

Borden and Mulock appeal to Wilfrid's belief that Canada must grow more independent of Great Britain, arguing it would be a great shame to allow the Canadian volunteers to disappear anonymously into British regiments. Far better to create a separate Canadian unit that will keep its identity and integrity. It should resemble General Hutton's idea of a balanced force, comprising not only infantry but cavalry and artillery.

Preparations for this enhanced force go forward without any grand pronouncements, but with Wilfrid's blessing. Once committed to the mission, he tells Zoë, it's best to conduct it in a way that does Canada the most good, gives her the greatest credit. So Borden's department takes certain liberties, to which he turns a blind eye. When Tarte and members of the Quebec caucus become suspicious, he assures them they have nothing to fear. Tarte has already been burned in effigy in several Ontario towns.

The only available vessel large enough to carry the First Canadian Contingent, as it becomes known, is the Allan Line's *Sardinian*. In record time it's refitted as a troopship, with extra bunks, hammocks, galleys, mess tables, latrines, rifle ranges, horse stalls, dog kennels. It has to be repainted and equipped with electric lights and ventilation fans before it embarks from Quebec City. People joke that the ship is aptly named: a thousand men, two hundred horses and four nursing sisters will be squeezed aboard a vessel built to hold half as many passengers.

Donations to the contingent pour in from businesses. Patriotism in time of war is good advertising. Companies boast that Canada's fighting men will be eating their beef, smoking their tobacco, writing home to loved ones on their paper. George Fulford of Brockville, the wealthy manufacturer of Dr. Williams' Pink Pills for Pale People, contributes a huge quantity of his product to enrich the soldiers' blood. Boxing gloves and punching bags will prepare them to face the enemy. Canadian rye whisky will ease their minds. A harmonium will accompany their singsongs. But when clergymen complain that too much tobacco and spirits are being donated, and too few Bibles, the Soldiers' Wives League procures a shipment of New Testaments, and the Methodist Book and Publishing House sends quantities of inspirational Christian literature.

Ottawa's D Company is departing for Quebec City late in the afternoon, and the Lauriers make an appearance at the official send-off. The march past takes place in chill autumn sunlight along Wellington Street. A crowd forty deep watches in giddy excitement in front of the Parliament Buildings while Wilfrid and Zoë shiver on a makeshift reviewing stand.

The regimental bands of the Governor General's Foot Guards and the Forty-Third Battalion file past playing "Soldiers of the Queen." Surging spectators accidentally push a well-known society matron into the fast-stepping ranks of the band, and she clings precariously to the bass drum until able to escape through a break in the crowd. When the men of D Company appear in their white pith helmets and new green serge uniforms, bearing rifles and marching smartly in unison, the people cheer deliriously. Zoë is startled to hear such guttural sounds erupting from human throats.

Down Wellington Street at the Union railway depot, fifteen thousand people sing "The Maple Leaf Forever" and damn the Boers. The police provide Wilfrid and Zoë with a mounted escort for their carriage. They watch as a police cordon guarding the train breaks under the pressure of bodies. People lunge through to mob the boarding soldiers, desperate to shake their hands before they set off for the other side of the world.

The bands strike up "The Girl I Left Behind Me." Zoë feels like a spectator at a riot. People are so obsessed with the soldiers that they don't notice the Prime Minister's carriage in their midst. Lord Minto has descended to the platform to see the soldiers off personally, and now the Governor General is struggling to keep his footing and not get swept away by the crowd, a swimmer caught in the undertow.

Amid the chaos Zoë notices an extraordinary sight. Boarding the train with the men is a differently uniformed figure, indubitably female. Her close-fitting khaki skirt and belted jacket and graceful hat sporting a red cockade can't hide her attractive features, her pinned-up hair. She's wearing an armband with the Red Cross symbol, waving to someone in the crowd. As if not wanting to prolong the farewell, she disappears quickly inside the train.

Zoë catches sight of Agar Adamson, the young society beau, all alone and looking bereft. Wilfrid motions to him to climb up into the carriage. At first Adamson is reticent, but Wilfrid insists. The three of them sit smiling and shaking their heads, unable to hear each other speak. Zoë admires Adamson's bright blue eyes, his fine Roman nose. As the train pulls out of the station, pursued by savage screaming, much of it female, she wonders if the soldiers will be safer on the battlefield. At last the noise dies down, and Adamson tells them how badly he wanted to be on that train.

"I applied, of course, along with the rest of the Foot Guards, but only a hundred and twenty-five got picked, and I wasn't one of them."

"Luckily for you," Wilfrid says.

Adamson flushes. "Luckily, sir? Oh no, if you don't mind my saying. It was my big chance."

"To. . . ?"

"To prove my mettle. As something more than a summer soldier, I mean. I'm to be married next month, and my fiancé was pulling for me to go. Now Mabel says I should keep volunteering and hope to get on with the next contingent. There will be one, I hope?"

"But what a terrible start that would be to your marriage," Zoë exclaims.

"If Mabel could, Lady Laurier, she'd come with me all the way to the battlefield. She says we should go to South Africa on our honeymoon. If there are any Canadian casualties, I might get signed up on the spot. We don't go to war every day."

Adamson thanks them and hops down into the gathering dusk.

As they proceed home, Zoë sees another familiar figure in the dispersing crowd, Joseph Pope walking back to his office, an abstracted expression on his face. Wilfrid orders the driver to stop.

"Why so glum?" he asks Pope as he climbs aboard. "Not filled with pride on this glorious day?"

Pope manages a smile. "It's a grand day, Sir Wilfrid. But one of the passengers on that train is my sister Georgina."

Zoë remembers. "Good heavens, the nursing sister. Such a beautiful lady."

"And the only woman on the train, Lady Laurier. She's sailing to South Africa against my wishes."

"I suppose a modern woman can do as she likes," Wilfrid remarks.

"Yes, sir. Although with our father long dead, I tend to see myself as head of the family. But of course Georgina is free to do as she wants."

"You can be proud of her," Zoë says. "She's a—how do you say it—a pioneer."

"Indeed, and very well trained in her duties. But I'm afraid for her. A war is no place for a woman."

"Think of the suffering she'll alleviate," Wilfrid says. "The comfort she'll bring to the wounded."

Zoë looks closely at Pope. She's touched by the anxiety and fear in his face.

"On the other hand," Wilfrid says, "I understand your distress. I wouldn't say this to just anyone, but I'm not happy with our decision to go to war. I doubt any good will come of it."

Pope watches the crowd before responding. "Sir John Macdonald would have agreed with you entirely."

"Would he?"

"You may recall that in '85, Britain asked him to send troops to relieve General Gordon in the Sudan. Sir John refused. Privately he told me, 'Why should Canada pay for the mistakes of Britain's foreign policy?'"

"But in today's world, even Sir John couldn't have held out. And it's doubly impossible for a French Canadian. Of course war never solves anything, does it? Except to decide who is stronger. The rule of the jungle."

Wilfrid looks upset, shaken: as if he's seen the future, or witnessed a murder.

9

Winter 1900

As far as Émilie is concerned, the twentieth century has already begun. Joseph insists on correcting her, pointing out the mathematical fallacy of considering oneself in the new century until next year. He explains the calculation in tedious detail, but Émilie sticks to her guns. In any case it *feels* like a new century, she tells her husband over the scattered remains of a Saturday breakfast. Suddenly and ominously the world has changed.

Using the tip of his white linen napkin to dislodge toast crumbs from his moustache, Joseph tries to counter his wife's pessimism. "Look how prosperous the country's becoming! All this expansion out west, all the ranching and mining—prosperity makes people confident. Canadians are finally taking pride in our accomplishments."

Émile grunts. These days, it seems, they disagree more often than not. In some ways she doesn't like Joseph's greater self-assurance since rising to the bench. "This pride you talk about, what is it? The English are proud to die for the British Empire. But what pride can *we* take? What do you think those riots were about?" Staring at the snow piled deep in the yard, Émilie shudders. The Montreal flag riots, as the press is calling them, took place earlier in the week. Armand recklessly threw himself into the thick of the demonstrations, putting his life at risk. "To think there were gunshots! He could have been killed."

"There now," Joseph murmurs, "the boy is perfectly fine, isn't he? Nothing to worry about."

"But what about next time?"

"Why should there be a next time?"

Émilie feels deeply irritated. Under his veneer of patience and reason, Joseph is so naive. No matter the subject—the riots, the English, Wilfrid and she—he simply refuses to open his eyes, to see what's happening in front of his nose. And the riots have brought the war in South Africa home.

At first the conflict proved more difficult for the British than expected. General Buller didn't eat his Christmas dinner in Pretoria after all. The Boer farmers have won the world's admiration and sympathy with their bravery and horsemanship and commando raids, their consummate skill at the new style of guerrilla warfare. But now the British are beginning to turn the tide, and English Canada smells victory as a hyena smells blood. The Montreal riots were triggered by the British victory at Paardeberg, from which the Canadians emerged as heroes. Are English Canadians going to use every triumph, Émilie wonders, as an excuse to attack French Canadians?

On the coldest day of the winter, McGill students poured into the streets to celebrate. Drinking toasts and singing "Rule Britannia," they converged on Dominion Square, where the *Montreal Star* had erected a board to post the latest news. The students lit fires on the snow and drank the *Star's* beer while cheering every report from the front. Reinforced by gangs of local toughs, two thousand marched on the offices of *La Presse*, *Le Journal* and Tarte's *La Patrie*, in Place d'Armes. At each French-language newspaper, the marchers forcibly hoisted the Union Jack. At City Hall, they so intimidated Mayor Préfontaine that he raised the flag himself, making a speech about the glories of Empire and giving civic employees the afternoon off. Finally someone incited the crowd to march on l'Université Laval de Montréal.

In the Laval building at Ste-Catherine and St-Denis, Armand stood at a window, watching in disbelief as the mob marched toward him. They broke down the front doors and entered the building, smashing furniture, tearing pictures off walls. They shouted anti-Catholic insults and demanded the flag be raised in honour of victory. The Union Jack was no sooner run up the pole than a Laval student shinnied up and cut it down. It became the prize in a free-for-all on the front steps until the McGill students recovered it and retreated.

The next day, remembering his mother's forebears who had fought with Papineau, Armand marched in the front ranks of the counter demonstration. Laval students, joined by angry workers carrying the Tricolour of France, went to each of the three French newspapers in turn and unceremoniously lowered the Union Jack. Filling the streets for half a mile, they halted in front of the *Montreal Star* building to yell slogans and sing "La Marseillaise," then tore down the flag and trampled it underfoot.

After that act of treason, the militia was called out to defend the armoury: there were fears Laval students would raid it for weapons. But the militia didn't defend Laval itself, where McGill students returned that evening with their own citizen vigilantes carrying clubs, iron bars, frozen potatoes and at least one revolver. Shots were fired. Several young men were wounded. Laval professors and a few policemen turned water hoses on the mob and dispersed it into the freezing dark, encrusted in ice.

The next day's newspapers hurled accusatory headlines in both languages, while community leaders demanded an end to the violence. At Wilfrid's request Monseigneur Bruchési, Vice-Rector of Laval, ordered his students not to retaliate. McGill's Principal Peterson apologized for his students' behaviour and offered to pay for damages. Every last window at Laval had been shattered.

But the real damage was greater. The rioting students had acted out the bitterness and mistrust spoken every day at home by their elders. Canadians were shocked to see their raw emotions exposed to the world. American and British commentators expressed surprise at the violence emanating from normally placid Canada. At a Rideau Hall dinner, Émilie overheard Lord Minto saying it would take only another small spark to set the whole country aflame.

Émilie is as disturbed by the riots as anyone. Yet even as she worries for Armand's safety, she feels a fierce, secret pride in him. He has the backbone to defend his faith, his people's good name. He's already a man: a man of character.

Soon after Wilfrid announced the sending of troops, Bourassa resigned from the government, and in the ensuing by-election recaptured his seat as an independent candidate. Wilfrid let him stand unopposed. He saw the wisdom of not running anyone against such a popular figure: "If I were twenty," he admitted to Émilie, "I would be cheering him too."

In fact, she knows, Bourassa is extremely useful to him. He can speak the mind of Quebec to English Canadians as Wilfrid never could, reminding them of a starkly different reality existing within the country, a conception of honour the obverse of their own. Meanwhile the English carry on in an orgy of patriotic sentiment. Émilie finds it embarrassingly gauche as well as repugnant, yet it's impossible to express what she feels to anyone, not even Joseph: certainly not Wilfrid. Armand is the only one who understands, as she understands him.

With Wilfrid, Zoë and Joseph, she occupies the Prime Minister's box at the Russell Theatre one evening when some socialites present a *tableau vivant*, "Britannia and Her Colonies Defending Liberty." Lord Minto's niece, Lady Victoria Grey, plays a militant Britannia accepting homage from her colonial acolytes. These include Miss Lola Powell as Australia. Ever so gracefully, Britannia vanquishes her brutish foes, thrilling the audience in the final scene by holding aloft the literally blazing torch of liberty and passing it dangerously close to her cascading hair. For all its dramatic flourish, Émilie doesn't think the evening equals her own "Living Pictures" tableau of the previous year. Nor does Lady Grey come even close to outshining Gabrielle Lavergne.

The emotions of the Russell's audience are pitched higher than usual that night: the names of more Canadian war dead have been released. Émilie finds the sadness people feel entirely natural, but her sympathy is overshadowed by pious pronouncements about the fallen. Every one of the dead soldiers, apparently, was of unimpeachable character, a sterling example of the purest manhood Canada can offer. Perversely, recitations of their nobility and selflessness make a virtue of their deaths. Instead of recognizing a tragedy, it becomes more unthinkable than ever to question the cause they died for.

After an earlier British debacle known as "Black Week," Chamberlain asked Canada for more troops, and Wilfrid has offered another twelve hundred. Young English Canadians are rushing to sign up. It's considered a badge of honour to at least try to enlist, and a mark of shame not to. "Where is the son of the Minister of Militia?" a newspaper headline shouts, accusing Frederick Borden's son of humiliating his father by studying medicine at McGill instead of killing Boers. Young Borden immediately volunteers with the Second Canadian Contingent.

Émilie is deeply grateful Armand isn't subjected to such pressure. She's also glad he doesn't play team sports: a mania to plunge into battle seems to be running through teams like a fever. Hockey and lacrosse clubs are losing their men in droves. The Ottawa Rough Riders football club, named after Teddy Roosevelt's fighters in Cuba, has sent five of its best players to the war. At charity events one can't escape paeans to "Lords of the Northland" responding to the call of Christian patriotism, assuming the burden of bringing civilization and progress to darkest Africa. At a recital in aid of the Red Cross Relief Fund, Émilie can barely suppress a guffaw when the master of ceremonies calls the soldiers "pure as the air of the sunlit North." She suspects they're anything but. Most have enlisted out of boredom and a sensible desire to avoid marriage.

The other prevailing motive is the romance of heroism. This is the case with Agar Adamson, whose longing to enlist has finally been fulfilled. Adamson is preparing to leave his new bride for the veldt, and Émilie for one will be sad to see him go. She hopes he won't come to harm. Ottawa will be even less amusing without him. Adamson is joining Strathcona's Horse, a regiment raised in the west and funded out of his own fortune by the immensely wealthy Lord Strathcona. As an easterner, Adamson is an exception in its ranks: he's caught on through his political connections, aided, Émilie happens to know, by his wife's willingness to flirt with Borden.

"The Horse," as everyone calls them, have been recruited to beat the mounted Boer guerrillas at their own game. Who better than our own hard-riding men of the plains? They arrive in Ottawa at the end of February en route to South Africa, five hundred expert horsemen and marksmen, all supposedly single (by order of Lord Strathcona), all bivouacked in the Aberdeen Pavilion at Lansdowne Park for two weeks of training. The elite regiment is commanded by the legendary Colonel Sam Steele of the North-West Mounted Police. It consists mainly of Steele's fellow Mounties, supplemented by cowboys and ranchers, prospectors and hunters.

Inevitably, these westerners in their Stetsons, riding boots and dress uniforms make a big impression on the capital. Women admire them, men envy them. Émilie has to admit they're an eye-catching lot, but she finds it laughable when Ottawa debutantes and society columnists gush over them at teas and dances. Her amusement grows when she hears about the Horse fighting lumberjacks in the Bank Street bars and entertaining ladies of the night in the cattle barns that serve as their stables.

One young lady who doesn't need to be squired by an officer of the Horse is Lola Powell. Since their meeting at the At Home, Émilie has been following Miss Powell's career with mounting interest. Miss Powell lives with her widowed mother and sister in a stone house opposite the gates of Rideau Hall. She's quickly identifiable at balls and parties by her flowing auburn hair as she chatters and laughs uninhibitedly, never caring how silly she might sound, ever ready to lead singsongs from the piano. Miss Powell knows all the latest "coon songs." People called her "gay" and "larky."

Since the Mintos' arrival, Miss Powell has become a favourite at Rideau Hall: or rather, a favourite of Lord Minto's—Lady Minto barely tolerates her. Everyone knows the Governor General squires Miss Powell on picnics and canoe excursions, sometimes as part of a larger party down the Ottawa, sometimes alone, just the two of them, up the less-travelled Gatineau. Everyone knows she's his favourite dancing and skating and skiing partner. The pair spend afternoons tramping or skiing through the Rockcliffe woods, and the rest is all too easy to imagine. Meanwhile the regally beautiful, superbly tailored Lady Minto consoles herself with trips to New York and London in company with one or another of the young military officers who serve as aides-de-camp. It's all a far cry from the Presbyterian idealism and earnest good works of the Aberdeens.

Émilie tries not to be shocked but can't help it. The Mintos are the only people in Ottawa who have ever made her feel like a prudish Victorian. How, she'd like to know, are they able to conduct their affairs so publicly, yet with such impunity? It's the title, of course: their exalted position affords them the privilege to do exactly as they like, and everyone else be damned.

Émilie burns with jealousy and resentment. She's beginning to feel ridiculous: still yearning for Wilfrid like a lovesick schoolgirl, still pining for the fulfillment of long-rehearsed, long-postponed dreams. Her hopes, predicated on a fading past, are receding ever farther into an impossible future. For the first time in her life, she's beginning to feel old. Past her prime. Undesired.

She knows she ought to accept things as they are. Wilfrid seems to have done so quite successfully. He's accepted Zoë, that fat pig, slow as she is. Why can't *she* accept too—accept time and destiny and marriage and Joseph? God has willed it. She must obey.

But God forgive her, she can't bring herself to that place. It feels too much like capitulation. Like death.

A ceremonial parade bids farewell to Strathcona's Horse. The Mintos preside alongside the Lauriers. Standing with Joseph on Parliament Hill, Émilie catches sight of Lola Powell in the crowd, positioned as usual not far from the Governor General. The only person wearing a white coat, Miss Powell can't be missed. Her hair is captured by a dramatic hat with veil, her eyes fastened insolently on her lover, not caring who notices. Lord Minto, looking somehow diminished by his uniform, stands rigidly at attention as the cavalry passes by, flanked on one side by his wife, on the other by Wilfrid and Zoë.

Émilie feels a stab of kinship with Miss Powell. Both are victims of the same mocking fate: to have fallen in love with a man who is already married. Both are forced to watch their beloved from afar, separated from him by indifferent bystanders and outdated social conventions, while he fulfils his obligations to his office, his public and his wife.

Émilie finds it unbearable to live so completely apart from Wilfrid. She craves his gaze, his touch, his recognition. For the life of her, she has to invent *some* way to be with him, if only for a moment.

She hears Zoë is confined to bed and can't attend Parliament. It comes to her that the House of Commons is one place where she can draw close to Wilfrid, sharing his company in plain sight, without anyone's taking it amiss. She knows he'll be speaking that day. Bourassa is addressing the House about the war, his first major speech since being re-elected, and Wilfrid will have no choice but to reply. Canada expects it of him.

At mid-afternoon, wearing a favourite dress of dark burgundy satin trimmed with tulle, she slips into the front row of the visitors' gallery where Zoë usually sits. She likes the way her dress spreads around her like a fan. She has a good angle from which to observe Wilfrid, watch his every gesture, follow the shadow of every thought crossing his features. He's seated in the centre of the front bench to her right. Some routine business is being conducted, and he looks politely bored. The gallery is low enough to create the illusion that she could reach out and touch him.

Abstracting herself from her surroundings, Émilie wanders within the confines of her mind. She stares at Wilfrid's neck, the smooth, pale upper part barely visible above his high collar. She remembers stroking the bare, sensitive nape. She had her way of comforting him with a slow, gentle but persistent motion he described as irresistible. He said no woman had ever touched him that way except his long-dead mother. The stroking seemed to soothe and move him, giving him entry into some place of child-like wonder, some reservoir of tenderness, that brought him close to tears. Delicately she'd probe the hollows of his skull behind his earlobes. Gently she'd stretch his ears outward from his head, an act that always made him smile. She'd massage his temples with her thumbs, moving her fingertips laterally to meet in the centre of his broad forehead. Finally she'd trace slow circular patterns over the nearly bald area covering the top of his skull: the seat, as she imagined it, of his genius.

By this time, his eyes would be closed, he'd have drifted off into a dreamy, trancelike state. It would seem, then, that she had him in her power. Once she'd seen a conjurer hypnotize people on stage, and she wondered if Wilfrid could possibly come under her command. Would he be suggestible enough to do as she ordered? But she could never work up the courage to try. Still, she found the idea delicious. She still does. The thought of being able to make him do her bidding arouses her.

Visiting her at Le Vert Logis, he'd sometimes lie back on the settee, his beautiful head resting in her lap. Her fingers would caress his cheeks, first one, then the other. She focuses on those cheeks now, their delicate pallor. At a certain point, when her touch had melted him, he'd turn his head compulsively to one side and kiss her fingertips, a moment that always thrilled her even when she knew it was coming. His hot breath on the sensitive flesh of her palm. His very evident desire. On one occasion, she became so stirred by his excitement that she urged him toward her bedroom—the room where she slept alone—but he gripped her wrist and held her back with a peremptory glance, a sharp cautionary word, afraid someone was arriving at the door.

One afternoon Armand and his cousin Renaud did burst in on them, startled to see M. Laurier with his head in *Maman*'s lap, his lips on *Maman*'s hand. She had to concoct an excuse about his having a severe headache: it was the only interruption they ever suffered. One person she knew would never disturb them was Joseph. But Wilfrid wasn't willing to take the risk, not then, even though when younger he'd felt free enough.

Henri Bourassa has risen to speak. Drowsily, against her will, Émilie pulls away from her memories and pays attention.

Bourassa speaks in the only way he'll ever be understood by the majority of his fellow MPs, in his second language. Not long ago, when he tried to address the House in French, Honourable Members drowned him out with shouts of "Speak English!" Fortunately his English is immaculate: clear, idiomatic, without the thick accent that makes Tarte's unintelligible at times. She looks for Tarte and finds his seat empty, then remembers he's just left for Paris. Wilfrid has appointed him Canada's High Commissioner to the Great Exposition, no doubt hoping for an interval of peace.

But clearly Bourassa intends to fill the void. He says he knows his position on the war is unpopular: cries of "Hear, hear" from both sides of the aisle. Ignoring them, he launches into a denunciation of Chamberlain. It's Chamberlain who lies behind Canada's slide into war, Chamberlain who had the audacity to welcome an offer of troops that was never made, and the Prime Minister capitulated. Worse, he didn't even consult Parliament.

Émilie watches Wilfrid to see how he responds. His eyes are fixed on some invisible point midway between the aisles. Outwardly calm and unconcerned, he leans forward to jot a note on the back of an envelope.

Bourassa mocks the claim that Canada hasn't "officially" sent troops. He derides the notion that there's any real difference between calling for volunteers and sending the standing militia. He even scorns the "no precedent" clause in the original cabinet decision. Everyone, including General Hutton and the English-language press, now sees Canada as assuming the burdens of Empire indefinitely, far into the future, clause or no clause. "The precedent, sir," Bourassa says, looking directly at Wilfrid, "is the accomplished fact."

At least the country is finally free of General Hutton: "Fortunately that bellicose gentleman is now exercising his military talents against the Boers." It's just as well that applause from the galleries is forbidden, since Émile feels like applauding: she detests Hutton. And she feels like cheering when Bourassa scorns "the jingo articles in the Chamberlain press" and "the policy of government by newspaper headlines." Laurier's capitulation to the yellow press, he thunders, has reduced Parliament to "something like a smoking contest."

Émilie is startled and embarrassed by her own gleeful reaction to these provocations. After all, Bourassa is attacking Wilfrid. Yet she agrees with him.

Setting aside her conflict of loyalties, she continues watching Wilfrid's face. His bemused expression seldom changes, except once when his forehead wrinkles in irritation. He signals a page to refill his water glass. The House, meanwhile, listens to Bourassa in grudging silence. Parliamentarians have to respect him as a man of principle. Here is another rebel Papineau, but one who swears by his loyalty to the foundations of British parliamentary democracy and justice. "I am a liberal of the British school," Bourassa asserts, "a disciple of Burke, Fox, Bright, of Gladstone." How often Émilie has heard Wilfrid say exactly the same thing.

The Speaker rises: it's time for the dinner recess. The House will reconvene in an hour and a half, when Bourassa will conclude his remarks. The time has flown swiftly. Émilie is expected at home, but Wilfrid hasn't spoken yet, and she still hasn't fulfilled her purpose in coming here.

Wilfrid is about to leave for dinner with some colleagues when he glances up at the gallery and sees her for the first time. He looks surprised, then smiles, saluting her with a little bow. His smile is tinged, she thinks, with pleasure. What a pity they can't dine together! She makes up her mind: she'll stay as long as required.

She puts on her coat, crosses Wellington Street in the wintry darkness, walks the two blocks to the Russell House. At the front desk, a clerk dials home for her and hands her the telephone. Joseph answers.

"I'm attending the House of Commons this evening," she tells him. "There's a fascinating debate on the war. I'll be home when it's over."

Although this is highly unusual, Joseph knows better than to argue with her, to ask for an explanation. Stiffly he thanks her for letting him know. Now the cook can go ahead and serve dinner to him and Gabrielle.

In the Russell café, Émilie orders lightly. She really isn't hungry. After a moment's hesitation, she requests a glass of claret.

It feels oddly luxurious to be sitting in the café again. Being on her own gives the old place a glamorous aura, as if she was back in Paris, a single woman with the city at her feet. The waiters recognize her. She doesn't care if some of the patrons are shocked to see her there alone. One or two men she knows nod and smile, and she knows what they're thinking: what sort of woman dines alone at a hotel? But she has her reasons.

The claret sits extremely well on her stomach. She scarcely touches her chicken. Instead she savours her wine and thinks of Wilfrid: the youthful Wilfrid, the reckless Wilfrid of years ago, the youthful and reckless Émilie. She orders a small carafe. When will she get this chance again? Joseph always disapproves when she wants more wine.

Back in the Commons gallery, she feels elated. Such a rare and exalted sensation of freedom: to be without constraints, nowhere one has to be, no one to please!

Bourassa has already resumed his speech. Wilfrid sits half-turned toward him, at an angle that allows him also to look up at the gallery now and then and meet her eyes. It's perfect.

Émilie feels the pleasurable inner glow spread from her stomach to her extremities. She smiles at Bourassa's choice phrases: "this new imperialist military policy," "this megalomaniac frenzy."

He demands that the war question be put to the people. As for himself, "A Liberal I was born, and a Liberal I will die!"

"It's time to die!" some inebriated MP yells.

Émilie wonders if Bourassa is overdoing it, becoming self-righteous and bombastic. But his next point finds its way straight to her heart. From a purely materialistic point of view, he declares, French Canadians are well aware they'd have been better off in 1776 to join the United States, but instead chose to remain loyal to Canada and the Crown. Now it's time to honour that loyalty: time to accept the compact between English and French as a union of equals, binding on both sides. If Confederation is a union of two free peoples, one side must not expect submission from the other.

"I do not ask for total independence from Britain," Bourassa declares, staring defiantly at Tories who accuse him of exactly that. "Then what do I wish? I wish that the constitution of my country be respected. Mr. Chamberlain and his frantic disciples, and his unconscious followers both English and Canadian, are leading us toward a constitutional revolution, the consequences of which no man can calculate. If new policies are going to govern this country, neither the Colonial Secretary nor any representative of the imperial government has the right to say what they shall be. It is *our* duty, as a free Parliament representing the free opinion of the people, to say what is going to be the policy of the people."

Bourassa proceeds to his motion. Asserting Parliament's natural sovereignty, it resolves that the House refuse to consider the government's actions in South Africa as a precedent committing Canada to any future military involvements. And further, that the House oppose any change in Canada's political and military policies in relation to Great Britain, unless initiated by the sovereign will of Parliament and sanctioned by the people.

As Bourassa sits down, a scattering of MPs pound their desks. Some are Liberal, some Tory: all, Émilie notes, are from Quebec.

Wilfrid rises and addresses the Speaker. She feels he's address-ing her, too. She notices a ringing in her ears. She's beginning to feel a little dizzy. Perhaps she didn't eat enough. The sight of him, his full mouth, his fine hands, so near yet so distant, is almost unbearable. She shuts her eyes, concentrates on his words.

Wilfrid is adamant that sending troops to South Africa was the right thing to do: a decision supported by the great majority of Canadians. This is democracy in action. "What state would the country be in today if the government had refused to obey the voice of public opinion? The result would have been a cleavage of the population along racial lines. A greater calamity could never take place in Canada."

Cheers sweep through the chamber, and Émilie nods behind closed eyes. Of course he's right. Wilfrid is always right when it comes to keeping the country together. Wise and just.

He repudiates Bourassa's claim that Canada's actions have been dictated by the British. It was the Boers, not the British, who pre-pared for war, who instigated war. Émilie opens her eyes briefly, testing to see if the dizziness returns, then closes them again. Wil-frid's line of reasoning is making her skeptical.

He wins her back when he says his government's actions haven't committed Canada to participating in future wars. In future, as in the present, Canadian participation will be decided by public opin-ion. "And if it is the will of the people of Canada at a future time to take part in a war for England, the people of Canada will have their way."

For a moment she forgets about the content of Wilfrid's speech and surrenders to his voice, letting its richness wash over her in waves. Such a sound: velvety and sensuous, robust and voluptuous, reassuring and healing. She feels it reverberate in her heart, her very muscles. It caresses and stirs her.

But what is he saying?

That on the day last month when Canadians fought so valiantly to defeat the enemy at Paardeberg, some of them dying in the process, "on that day it was revealed to the world that a new power had arisen in the West."

This strikes Émilie as both momentous and preposterous. She focuses on his words again. He declares he has dedicated his political life to promoting unity, harmony and amity among the diverse elements of the country.

That's certainly true. He's sacrificed his personal happiness—and hers—on the altar of Canada.

"But that work of unity and harmony between the chief races of the country is not yet complete."

Oh God.

"We know by the unfortunate occurrences that took place only last week in Montreal that there is still much to do. But there is no bond of union so strong as the bond of common dangers faced in common. Today there are men in South Africa representing the two branches of the Canadian family, fighting side by side for the honour of Canada. Already some of them have fallen, giving to their country the full measure of their devotion. Their remains have been laid in the same grave, there to rest to the end of time in a last fraternal embrace. Can we not hope that in that grave shall be buried also the last vestiges of our former antagonism?"

The cheers are massive, rebounding off the ceiling, the echoes absorbed by more cheers. Émilie reopens her eyes. She must see Wilfrid at the triumphant climax of his speech. He sits down, his face transfigured.

Exhausted yet inspired, she too sits, half-listening to several short speeches from Quebec MPs who support Bourassa's motion. Finally, just before midnight, it comes to a vote. Members rise in their places as their riding is named.

Yeas, ten, the Speaker reads out. Nays, one hundred and nineteen.

Papers fly into the air like carrier pigeons. Members of both parties leap to congratulate Wilfrid, flocking around his desk, pumping his hand. Still seated, he accepts their tributes with grace.

The night is almost over. Émilie too rises and moves as quickly as she can, heavy with purpose, toward the exit. Only one thing remains.

She descends the stairs among the other visitors, holding onto the railing to steady herself. She finds the members' corridor that runs behind the curtain leading to the government side of the House. Slipping behind a uniformed parliamentary guard whose back is turned, she edges along the wall and waits.

For several minutes MPs keep coming out of the chamber through a gap in the curtain, looking at her in surprise. Several recognize and greet her. She feels horribly exposed. She's anxious, short of breath. In an agony of waiting, she nearly loses her resolve and decides to go home. Then Wilfrid emerges. He's with Mulock, listening to him dispense advice. Once again Émilie's nerve nearly fails her. But she stands her ground and waits, until finally Wilfrid sees her.

Instead of giving her the gorgeous smile she anticipates, his face darkens. Realizing her error, she wants to turn and flee, but it's too late. She's here, she has to go through with it, she expects it of herself.

"Your speech was magnificent!" she cries. And embraces him with all her strength.

Even before she touches him, Wilfrid's shoulders have stiffened. "Why, Madame Lavergne." His tone is icy, his manner English. Disentangling himself, he takes a step away from her. "Whatever are *you* doing here?"

Nicholas Flood Davin happens by. The florid MP evidently means to engage Wilfrid in conversation but, seeing Émilie standing there like a woman struck, he takes in the situation and changes his mind.

"Ah, there you are," Davin says brightly. Addressing Wilfrid and Mulock: "If you will permit us, gentlemen, I've offered to escort Madame Lavergne home in my new motor car. Are you ready, Madame? Sir Wilfrid, you must let me give you a ride one of these days. It's most exhilarating!"

10

Spring 1900

Some of this Zoë sees with her own eyes. The rest she pieces together by reading the papers, asking questions, listening.

It's nearing the end of April, and the last of Ottawa's snow is gone. Trees are leafing out early in the exotically warm, dry weather. Across the river in Hull, in the low-ceilinged kitchen that serves as her dining and sitting room, Marie-Ange Kirouac builds up the fire under the soup kettle. Her husband left for work before seven. Their little frame house in the congested heart of Hull is a few blocks from the E.B. Eddy mills on the river, where Antoine Kirouac runs a paper-making machine.

Marie-Ange scrimps constantly to make Antoine's pay stretch far enough to feed the family. Of the four children, the two eldest are at school. Three-year-old Elzéar is outside in the street playing with his friends, and Henriette is asleep in her cradle in a corner. Another baby is coming: Marie-Ange is grateful it's still a few months away. Once again she couldn't afford the dollar to pay the chimney sweep. She keeps her open fireplace as neat and tidy as possible and burns mostly scrap pine, which is cheaper than coal or hardwood.

This morning the residue of pine pitch in the flue catches fire. It burns surreptitiously for a few minutes, spreading silently up to the broken chimney pot, then an ember floats through the opening and lands on the roof. Like every other home in the neighbourhood, the Kirouacs' roof is covered with weathered wooden shingles.

Old Mr. Dorion notices the fire and hammers on the front door. Promising Marie-Ange he'll go straight to the fire hall for help, he assures her chimney fires are nothing to worry about, they happen every day. She's well aware of that: Hull's little fire department seems to put out one every week, and as far as she knows, nobody ever gets hurt.

When the firemen still haven't arrived after five minutes, Marie-Ange gathers up Henriette, carrying her into the street, and calls loudly for little Elzéar. She can see flames rippling along the roof's peak. They remind her of the colour, size and shape of autumn leaves. She's relieved when Elzéar finally appears. Clinging to her skirts, he becomes tearful as his friends run around him in circles, shrieking with excitement. Their mothers come outside to see what all the fuss is about and try to reassure Marie-Ange, glancing up at their own roofs now and then. A brisk wind is blowing.

A fire wagon arrives with four men. The driver explains he got lost: "It's like a maze around here!" The blinkered horses are calm, not seeming to know anything is wrong. Suddenly there's an odd swooshing sound, and the Beauchemins' outhouse next door, which is insulated with old hay, erupts in flames.

By the time the firemen are climbing their ladders, a full water bucket in each hand, fire is licking at the eaves of both the Kirouac and Beauchemin homes. The firemen refuse to allow Marie-Ange to go back inside to rescue her belongings. With her children in tow, she couldn't have carried much anyway. She notices neighbours down the street are hastily nailing sacred pictures to their doors in hope of divine protection.

The devil of it isn't so much the fire as the wind, getting stronger all the time, driving the flames from roof to roof: first in a line due south, then sideways, as gusts whip the fire around to feed on whatever it can find. The wind rips burning shingles into the air and flings them onto neighbouring roofs, starting the process of contagion all over again.

Like their neighbours, Marie-Ange and her children find refuge in the stone cathedral. She only hopes her other two are safe inside their school, then remembers it's built entirely of wood.

Chief Benoit of the Hull fire brigade assigns all available men to go wherever buildings are burning. He's rescinded his standing order not to pump any water until his arrival on the scene, but still isn't sure it has reached all hands. He telephones across the river for help. Ottawa's Chief Provost dispatches his department's pride and joy, the steam engine "Conqueror," famous for its pumping capacity of fourteen hundred gallons per minute, across the Chaudière Bridge.

Reaching the Hull side, the Ottawa men don't know which fire to attack first. The familiar stench of smoke is far stronger and more pervasive than they've ever known it. Right in front of them, thick black clouds billow from the upper storey of the Imperial Hotel, its patrons and staff outside on the street staring helplessly upwards. Beyond the hotel entire streets are ablaze. The post office building, the court house and a row of stores are on fire. Panic-stricken people are rushing home to see if home still exists. Wagons veer in every direction, dragged by terrified horses.

Since the Eddy pulp and paper mills are the largest and most important assets in Hull, the Ottawa firemen decide to take "Conqueror" there. On arrival, they find Antoine Kirouac and his co-workers, who don't realize their homes are lost, wetting down stacks of timber in a desperate attempt to save their livelihoods. E.B. Eddy has triumphed over lesser calamities on his way to becoming the largest match manufacturer in the British Empire. Now he stands at a window in the attic of his biggest mill, watching the flames swirl closer. Later he'll tell Zoë, "If you can imagine a snowstorm of particles of fire, Lady Laurier, it will give you some idea of the inferno."

The best efforts of Eddy's employees and Ottawa's firemen won't be enough to save his mills. The best efforts of the Hull fire brigade won't be enough to save Hull. As the tinder-dry houses flare up one by one, flaming shingles land like cannon shot among vast pyramids of Eddy's best Ottawa Valley timber. The logs were destined to provide North America with newsprint and matches and clothes pegs and washboards and wooden buckets: to supply Torontonians and Chicagoans with their daily diet of news, to light Cuban cigars in New York clubs. Now they go up like giant matchsticks.

The fire generates its own wind. Rushing downhill toward the river, it leapfrogs the channel between Hull and Victoria Island. Before their escape route can be blocked, the Ottawa firefighters throw down hundreds of yards of hose and retreat across the Chaudière Bridge. They succeed in saving their horses but have to leave "Conqueror" behind, to be consumed by the fire it was meant to extinguish.

On the Ottawa side, residents and shopkeepers stand in the streets of Le Breton Flats, watching the black clouds thicken as they boil in their direction. Workers in the J.R. Booth and H.F. Bronson lumber mills smell smoke before they see it. They look across the river at a Hull enveloped entirely in darkness, the smoke-filled sky lit garishly here and there by leaping spires of red. Everyone on the Flats knows the fire is coming for them. They're relieved to see the Ottawa firemen returning off the bridge, their wild-eyed faces blackened with ash, then realize they're not bringing their equipment.

Chief Provost knows his fifty-one men are no match for the biggest fire he's ever seen. He telephones Mayor Payment to request reinforcements, and the Mayor telegraphs Montreal, Smiths Falls, Brockville, Peterborough, even distant Toronto. Buglers run through the streets sounding the call-out to militiamen of the Governor General's Foot Guards and the Forty-Third Battalion. Meanwhile the chief orders his men to concentrate on saving the waterworks on the Flats near Pooley's Bridge, right next to No. 1 Fire Station. The works supply Ottawa with clean drinking water, and Provost's duty is to ensure the city doesn't fall victim to epidemic as well as fire.

Everyone in the fire's path hopes for a miracle. Most deem a miracle unlikely and decide it's best to leave while they can. Some calculate there's still time to pile clothing, bedding, valuables, children and pets onto wagons or carts, pulling them by horse or hand over Pooley's Bridge, and from there to higher ground on the limestone escarpment overlooking the Flats. Soon the air is full of the rumbling of wagon wheels. But those who act too slowly, or hesitate over which possessions to save, are surprised by the swiftness of the flames eating their way across the wooden bridge. They have no choice but to abandon their homes and flee.

As soon as the firestorm slams into the Booth lumber yard, the Flats are doomed. Booth's mill has its own built-in water system, installed after a previous fire, and the pumps save the building but can do little for the millions of board feet of lumber out in the yard. Workers sweating feverishly at the pumps and hoses watch the moving wall of flame bypass the mill, sweeping past them with a terrific roar to advance on their homes.

The fire bowls up Duke Street. Champlain the portrait photographer escapes from his studio with his two most expensive cameras, just before bottles of developing fluid explode into multicoloured fireworks. Bullets and gunpowder inside the hardware store erupt in reply. Outside on the street, men shout and women cry out, confused by firebrands flying through the fog of smoke.

The noise and heat are overpowering. Panicking, they drop their valuables and run, carrying or dragging their screaming children.

The last building on Victoria Island to burn is the largest: the stone-walled generating station of the Ottawa Electric Company. Before power to half the city goes out, Zoë is sitting in the visitors' gallery of the House of Commons, knitting. She's keeping an eye on Wilfrid, an ear on a desultory debate about the awarding of post office jobs to deserving Liberals, including Wilfrid's half-brother, Charlemagne. The Conservatives are self-righteously protesting the Liberal patronage appointments, even though Sir John A. Macdonald himself practised the same system—in fact perfected it—when all the lights in the chamber flicker and die.

In the dimness Zoë makes out Mr. Speaker rising in his place. He interrupts a Conservative MP to suggest a recess until the lights return. A page hurries to Wilfrid's side and speaks into his ear. Immediately he rises on a point of order: he's informed a disastrous fire is at this moment consuming Hull and endangering neighbourhoods on the Ottawa shore, and in light of the emergency moves an immediate adjournment of the House. The motion is seconded, passing unanimously. Zoë packs away her knitting and walks down the darkened stairway to meet her husband.

In the lobby, much speculation about whether the fire will reach Parliament Hill. Wilfrid and Zoë follow the curious to the western edge of the Hill, accompanied by Ulric Barthe and two nervous parliamentary guards. Standing at the railing where the cliff drops to the river, they watch horizontal smoke clouds speeding across the water from Hull to Ottawa. The sun still shines through the wind and smoke, casting a ghastly sheen on the river's surface: the unnatural light reminds Zoë of a solar eclipse she once witnessed. Two women standing near her are fascinated by the sight, leaning close together under a large black umbrella as if to protect their flowered hats from showers of sparks. When they realize the Prime Minister is beside them, they look at each other and bob simultaneously.

"Look over there." Zoë follows Wilfrid's finger pointing toward Wellington. A line of dishevelled refugees is straggling onto the Hill, some carrying children swaddled in blankets, others with their arms wrapped around bundles that look like children until they spread them out on the lawn, revealing pathetic odds and ends of clothing or kitchenware. A fat young man strains between the traces of a cart piled high with furniture, proud of himself for having saved—or looted—so many valuables. Another man carries a rocking chair. He looks dazed and bewildered, searching for the right place to set it down.

Filthy and exhausted people throw themselves onto the grass beside their possessions. Zoë's first thought is to go over and speak with them: "Those poor souls have lost everything!" Wilfrid takes her by the arm, and they hurry across the lawn. The first person they reach is a smudge-faced girl of four or five sitting on a straw mattress, weeping inconsolably over a broken doll.

Many bold and brave acts are performed during the afternoon, some more successful than others. Farmers drive their wagons into the fire zone and carry people to safety. An undertaker puts his hearse to similar use. A mother drops her baby out of a second-storey window into the arms of her husband, before escaping herself. Despite the best efforts of the principal and his teachers to throw water on the flames, Wellington Street Public School is destroyed. Somebody rescues a small black bear from a shed.

A decision to use dynamite to cut off the blazing Flats from the fine homes of Rochesterville turns out disastrously. The explosions heave flaming debris skyward, where it catches the wind and flies south to ignite other buildings. Soon the palatial stone home of J.R. Booth is ablaze, its gabled windows a lurid yellow, its chimneys spouting flame like fountains. The Booth mansion is democratically destroyed along with more humble homes and the boarding houses of artisans, mechanics, labourers. The Victoria Brewery and the Martin and Warnock flour mills burn magnificently. Erskine Presbyterian Church is lost, although Reverend Dr. Campbell saves the Communion pitcher.

Inside Woods' Tailors on Queen Street, men busy themselves stuffing their pockets with underwear and socks and shirts, until police detectives arrive in response to Mr. Woods' frantic phone call. The officers block the exits and frisk the looters on their way out. Practically everyone is caught with stolen goods. There are too many to arrest, so the officers give them a kicking.

Police Chief Powell, Lola's brother, mobilizes the volunteer militiamen of the Guards and the Forty-Third into a bucket brigade. Lined up on Nanny Goat Hill, men who have been unsuccessful in enlisting for South Africa wet down buildings on the east side of Booth Street, drawing water from the fire department's surviving steam engine, "La France." They save that side of the street, the one closer to Parliament Hill. The other side is completely gutted.

By half-past three the first detachment of firemen from Montreal arrives by train, bringing a pump engine, hoses and horses. They have to disembark before reaching the CPR station, since it no longer exists. A second detachment arrives on a later train, and the Montreal firemen stand shoulder to shoulder with the Ottawa men, the escarpment at their back, to beat the flames away from Upper Town. The escarpment provides a natural protective barrier that funnels the fire southward. Roaring like a hurricane, the flames cut a swath of devastation half a mile wide and three miles long until they reach Dow's Lake, where they run out of houses for fuel. The fire tries to leap across the macadamized road to the

Dominion Experimental Farm buildings, but the Farm workers fight back valiantly and put an end to its progress.

Up on Parliament Hill, Wilfrid and Zoë spend hours comforting the stricken, the suddenly homeless, the speechless. Together and separately, they go from place to place on the lawn, expressing their sympathies to people who can only sit and stare into space with paralyzed faces or reply in monosyllables.

Zoë asks after their children. She holds out to them the certain hope of food and shelter for the night. Wilfrid instructs Ulric Barthe to telephone the Mayor to find out exactly what sort of measures are being taken. He tells Ulric to pledge the Dominion government's aid in whatever form is most urgently needed: no request is to be refused. Finance Minister Fielding is to issue a cheque for relief purposes immediately, the bigger the better.

Zoë is listening to a distraught woman who doesn't know where her children are, wondering all the while how God could allow such a tragedy to befall so many, when she sees her maid Tillie running toward her. Tillie is the Irish servant she had in London, such a jewel that Zoë arranged to bring her to Ottawa a few months later. When Tillie arrived, she was accompanied by a dependent father who took lodgings on Le Breton Flats, and now she's in a tearful panic: she's looked among the survivors on the Hill and can't find him. She's afraid the old man has perished in the flames.

Tillie is so close to hysteria, Zoë has to break off trying to comfort the weeping mother. Tillie is desperate to go searching for her father on the Flats, but Wilfrid says the most they can do is hire a carriage and look for him among the crowds trudging up Wellington Street.

The three of them climb into the carriage of Albert Kilrea, who drives Wilfrid when he doesn't take the streetcar, and they enter the river of refugees flowing toward them: people with nothing left but the clothes on their backs. Zoë's eyes burn, her cheeks feel on fire, the air is full of stinging cinders. The haze of smoke with its acrid stench of burnt lives is sickening. She covers her nose and mouth with her handkerchief and urges Wilfrid to do the same.

Tillie is calmer now that something is being done. She scans the faces in the crowd, her eyes following Wilfrid's and Zoë's gestures as they point out men who might be her father. None is.

Albert stops the carriage at the approach to Pooley's Bridge: this is as far as they can go. By now the flow of evacuees from the Flats has stopped. Zoë is afraid that whoever was going to escape has already fled. She watches roofless structures burning, timbers crashing to the ground in showers of sparks, whole walls falling into the street. From the dying buildings come strange sounds of whistling and sucking and popping. Even tall trees are aflame, their sap sizzling: for some reason, the burning trees seem particularly horrible. Through the thick smoke to her left, Zoë makes out the silhouettes of the bucket brigade, figures moving like ghostly dancers on a stage.

A policeman respectfully tells Wilfrid that no traffic is allowed to cross the bridge into the Flats. When Wilfrid mentions Tillie's father's name, the policeman grins knowingly. Oh yes, he's familiar with Mr. O'Grady. "See those buildings on the right, sir? The only ones left? One's the fire station, so you can bet the firemen saved *that*. Another's the waterworks, and beside it is Couillard's Hotel. The bar's full of lads celebrating their salvation. Mr. O'Grady is one of them."

The policeman dispatches a handy boy to fetch Mr. O'Grady from the bar, and soon he's sitting in the carriage, unsteadily but quite cheerfully, beside his daughter. Tillie weeps with relief. Mr. O'Grady is a man about sixty, crimson cheeks, very little hair, reeking of liquor and sweat. After her joy at his survival, Tillie is embarrassed by her father's condition.

"Don't fret," Zoë whispers in her ear, "just be thankful he's alive." Wilfrid invites Mr. O'Grady to stay at their house with his daughter until he can find lodgings.

On their way home they pass the Drill Hall on Cartier Square, where police have sent the homeless. Already masses of people are huddled on the parade ground with their children, others lined up to receive canteens of water and some army biscuits. They all look so orderly, so peaceable, but really, Zoë thinks, they're just stunned into obedience, shattered and helpless. The pitiful sight quickens her resolve.

She can picture the immensity of the challenge ahead: feeding and clothing and sheltering thousands of adults and children, not only here but on the Hull side, until new homes can be built for them. It will take vast amounts of money and organization, even imagination, if these people are going to be looked after properly. Someone will have to head up a public campaign: someone capable of raising large donations of food and clothing as well as money, someone with the determination and prestige to ensure the authorities do the right thing.

The wind dies down that evening. The remaining fires in Hull and the Flats and Rochesterville flicker sullenly but harmlessly, with nothing left to burn. Through a glorious cloud bank of orange and pink, the sun sets behind the Gatineau Hills. Zoë watches it from her carriage on her way to see Lady Minto at Rideau Hall.

At first she considers the sunset a cruel mockery of all the citizens whose homes are a glowing red hell. Then a strange certainty: this sky is the very image of a stained-glass window, a divine signal of redemption and hope. It promises healing and rebirth for the shocked inhabitants of two cities still without electricity, still shrouded in a pall of deathly and nauseating smoke.

The next morning it's announced that Lady Minto and Lady

Laurier are president and vice-president, respectively, of a relief committee under the auspices of the National Council of Women. Its mission is to collect and distribute food, clothing, bedding and other provisions for every homeless person in Ottawa and Hull.

The Governor General's consort and the Prime Minister's wife often act as patrons of charitable causes, but this time, as far as Zoë is concerned, it isn't a figurehead position but a job, assigned her by the Lord. He expects great things of her. She rolls up her sleeves and gets to work. First she turns, for practical reasons, to Wilfrid. His full support is necessary to make her more effective. Before he leaves for his cabinet meeting, they hold their own meeting at the breakfast table.

Wilfrid listens to Zoë's plans, nodding repeatedly. "Yes, yes indeed. This is exactly what's needed. You're taking the bull by the horns, my dear. It will get everyone pulling together."

"I've told Lady Minto I'll approach all your friends—the wives of your ministers and wealthiest supporters. If they're going to be generous, they need to know they won't be alone."

"I'll have Ulric place calls for you."

"That's all right. I'll do it myself."

"At least tell them you're speaking on my behalf, as well as your own. Let them know we expect them to do their part."

"No doubt they'll ask what the government is going to do."

"Fielding has sent ten thousand to the City. When the House reconvenes next week, I'll move a hundred thousand more and see it passes the same day. But we don't want people thinking the government is taking care of everything. They have to do their part ."

"Food and clothing are the most important things. Some of your rich friends have a change of dress for every day of the year— think of Mr. Fulford and his Pink Pills for Pale People. Surely he and Mrs. Fulford can spare some. Clothes, I mean."

She begins by telephoning the wives she knows best, women whose good will she can count on. To those without the devil's instrument in their homes, she sends notes by messenger. Their generosity, even their willingness to work in a clothing depot or soup kitchen, is impressive. It gives her the courage to move on to wealthier and more formidable ladies. She writes down a lengthy list.

Zoë's is startled by her own forwardness. Knowing they don't dare refuse her, she eggs the ladies on to make the biggest donations they can, to ransack their closets and those of their husbands, to obtain from their cooks whatever excess flour, beans, oats, sugar, bacon, potatoes and other foodstuffs aren't immediately required in the kitchen. When someone responds less generously than she can afford to, Zoë doesn't hesitate to push: "Well, Mrs. Perley is giving *two* hundred." Or, when she can get away with it, "The Mulocks have pledged *five* hundred." Or, "Madame Lavergne is donating four men's coats and ten blouses and skirts and a trunk full of quilts and undergarments."

In fact Émilie is anxious not only to donate, but to participate in the relief committee. Zoë puts her in charge of sorting donations of clothing into men's, women's and children's, by size, at the Drill Hall. Émilie actually seems grateful to be given work and responsibility.

Zoë realizes her campaign will proceed much faster if she delegates some of the work. She asks certain women to approach ten other people. While soliciting contributions, they should ask each woman to call on ten of *her* friends, and so on, until donations snowball into a mountain. If some people are asked more than once, so much the better. After all, fifteen thousand people have lost their homes. And seven, it's now reported, have died.

After spending a full day and much of the evening on relief work, knowing it's only the beginning, Zoë prepares for bed. She feels utterly exhausted, yet satisfied the Lord's work is being done. She knows the collecting and sorting and distributing of donations throughout Ottawa and Hull are in good hands. The National

Council of Women can call on an army of experienced, hardworking volunteers who know how to organize these sorts of missions and execute them successfully. All thanks to Lady Aberdeen.

Wilfrid removes the pins from Zoë's hair as she sits at her dressing table before the oval mirror. Watching the silvery bun loosen and fall to her shoulders, she thinks how she's among the fortunate, the blessed. She tells herself not to mourn the thick black hair of her youth, nor her slim face and figure, but to thank God for everything she has. She undoes the ribbon of her coral-pink nightgown just below her throat, so it doesn't pull on her neck, and sits very still as Wilfrid draws the pearl-handled brush through her hair with firm, measured strokes. Afterwards she lies back on their bed. He brings a cool damp towel and, arranging it over her eyes, turns off the electric lamp and climbs in beside her.

Wilfrid wants to know the exact extent of the fire damage. On Saturday morning Albert Kilrea drives them to Le Breton Flats, and from the edge of the escarpment they look down onto the vast plain of devastation.

Bright sunlight cuts through the haze of smoke still rising from the debris. The sheer completeness of the destruction is appalling. The street grid is still apparent, some roads lined with charred, skeletal trees or electricity poles. But there are no houses or shops, only stone foundations filled with mounds of scattered bricks and blackened timbers. Here and there a spectral wall rises out of the drifts of ash. Zoë tries to discern by what logic these phantom walls have survived while others haven't. She looks south, where she can see the occasional empty shell of a building lording it over the surrounding flatness. Wilfrid says he's heard about such incongruous situations. Wooden shanties survive while stately homes nearby are completely destroyed. A little smithy goes unscathed while the stone shop next door is levelled. There's no explaining it.

They see people down on the Flats, dozens of them, wandering slowly, aimlessly, among the ruins of their homes, bending to examine something, trying to comprehend what has happened. Zoë exerts her mind to imagine how they must feel. She remarks that all these people must be in shock, and Wilfrid responds, "This is what war looks like. It's what we're doing to the Boers."

He has insisted government aid must be divided fairly between Ottawa and Hull. "The river must not be a line of demarcation," he's told Fielding. "To each according to his need." Now he wants to inspect the damage on the other side and tells Albert to drive them to the water's edge.

The Chaudière Bridge is a nightmare of twisted girders. In some places the bridge's sagging metal superstructure is still visible, in others nothing remains above the water line but stone piers. Until the bridge can be rebuilt, the Ottawa Transportation Company has donated a steamer ferry and barge to deliver supplies to Hull. Someone has organized a taxi service consisting of sturdy rowboats. Already it's doing a brisk business, picking up passengers and dropping them off at an improvised wharf below the ruined bridge.

When the man in charge of the service sees the Lauriers, he places his largest rowboat at their disposal. Albert, still wearing his bowler hat, takes one set of oars and the manager the other, saying in French how honoured he is to have the Prime Minister and Madame Laurier as passengers. Of course there will be no charge.

The current is strong, the two men have to strain at the oars. As they draw close to the Quebec side, Zoë finds the sight overwhelming. Few walls remain in the centre of Hull, apart from the gaunt remains of the Eddy mills: a smokestack soaring above the eyeless exterior, "E.B. Eddy Co., Washboards" still legible on one of the walls. An Italianate tower resembling a relic of Florence is all that's left of the post office. The courthouse is completely gutted, but the jail is intact: its inmates were grateful to be rescued from their cells and transferred to the prison in Ottawa.

Once they're on land, the vile smell of burnt wood is overpowering. Wilfrid begins striding in the direction of what was once rue Principale, ashes blackening his grey trouser cuffs, and Zoë, escorted by Albert, hurries to keep up. A young priest approaches them. Introducing himself as Père Martin, he volunteers to guide them through the ruins.

Half of Hull's thirteen thousand people are destitute, Père Martin says as they pick their way up the street, circling around charred timbers. Over two hundred acres are destroyed on this side of the river. Nobody knows the extent of the financial loss, but most people are uninsured. Some survivors have taken refuge on the shores of Minnow and Flora lakes, where they've spent the past two nights camped out. Luckily the temperatures have stayed mild. Food supplies have begun arriving from Ottawa. The clergy has taken charge of distributing them, so that everyone receives something. Zoë is pleased to know the Church is doing its part. It's the best hope for Hull, which doesn't have the advantages of the capital.

After the desolate walk, it's shocking to see Hull's cathedral rising up intact and apparently undamaged, surrounded by chaos. Zoë reminds herself it's impious to wonder why the building was spared. In the presbytery, she and Wilfrid meet with the priests. Praising their dedication to helping the victims, Wilfrid describes the steps his government is taking, then explains the work of Zoë's women's committee and its liaison with the Ottawa and Hull Fire Relief Fund, created the day before by Ottawa City Council.

If they can get the dispossessed through the weekend, Wilfrid tells the priests, government help will soon be here. He stresses the importance of giving people hope for the future: hope in *this* world as well as the next. Families mustn't be allowed to despair and feel they have to move away.

Wilfrid and Zoë are ushered into the nave. Hundreds of adults and children are packed tightly among the pews, some sleeping, some standing and talking in subdued groups, some sitting with bowed heads. Eyes turn in their direction. It seems to Zoë the entire population of Hull is looking expectantly at them, seeking some cause for encouragement, some shred of good news. A few smile at their arrival, a few break into applause. Most continue to look haggard and hopeless.

Zoë steels herself as she and Wilfrid plunge into the crowd. She feels like a fraud for having nothing to offer them beyond her attention and sympathy. After two hours of circulating through the aisles, listening to terrible and moving stories, they have to leave. Père Martin and several other priests escort them down to the river, where the rowboat manager is waiting for them as promised.

Back on the Ottawa side, Albert Kilrea drives them around the Flats, stopping now and then so that Wilfrid can speak to people wandering in the rubble. He assures them help is coming, but as he and Zoë discover, they're already helping themselves. Parents and their children are combing through the smoking ruins of their homes, searching for iron nails: they pick them up swiftly and delicately by their fingertips, drop them into tin cans.

"If you don't mind my asking," Wilfrid asks a red-faced man in a worker's cap, "why are you doing that?"

"Oh, the nails are still perfectly good, sir," he replies, "'specially now they've been tempered by the fire. We'll need them to build new places."

By the time Albert gets them home, both Zoë and Wilfrid are in tears.

The Ottawa fire victims are apportioned among several shelters: the Drill Hall, the Exhibition Grounds, the Amateur Athletic Club, the Salvation Army barracks. These also accommodate the overflow from Hull. Although the homeless are encouraged to take refuge with family and friends, Zoë's committee still feeds thousands daily. The relief effort becomes her life. She sees even less of Wilfrid than usual.

Working tirelessly at her side, Émilie proves invaluable. She has a talent for organization and hard work that Zoë knew about, but has never seen put to good use. She had no idea they'd make such a good team.

One day at the Drill Hall, they welcome a carriage from Rideau Hall: it's full of toys. Four of the Governor General's children—Lord Melgund, Lady Violet, Lady Eileen, Lady Ruby—arrive in a separate carriage like little Santa Clauses, chaperoned by an aide-de-camp, Captain Mann. The homeless boys and girls are lined up on the parade ground to receive their dolls and toy trains and wooden soldiers from the vice-regal offspring, and their shy, stumbling thank-yous are heartbreaking. Afterwards Captain Mann leads them in three cheers for their benefactors. The Captain, considered the outstanding skater among the ADCs, gallantly pours tea for the evening meal. He cuts an anomalous figure, gripping a blue tin teapot in one hand, holding his silk hat and lavender gloves in the other.

Handling money makes Zoë nervous. As quickly as possible she turns cheques over to Mr. Perley, the Relief Fund chairman, who has arranged with the Bank of Ottawa to receive donations. Since the fire has been a big news story across the country and around the world, money is pouring in from everywhere. Individuals and families subscribe a dollar or two through their banks. The Chinese Benevolent Association of Victoria, B.C., contributes the handsome sum of five hundred dollars. The Queen and the Lord Mayor of London send two hundred thousand. Donations arrive from the United States and France and a Mrs. Walters of Valparaiso, Chile, who mails a pound sterling.

Benefit concerts and church suppers and rummage sales to aid the victims take place in large and small communities. Quantities of food and clothing arrive from all over the country, transported by the railways free of charge. The T. Eaton Company of Toronto sends a train car full of clothing and dishes. Someone in Wilfrid's cabinet gets the idea of exempting foreign donations from customs duty, and the Swift Company of Chicago, where people know something about fires, ships twenty barrels of pork, ten barrels of beef, six hundred pounds of ham and a thousand pounds of bacon to Ottawa.

When Mr. Perley announces the fund has reached a million dollars, Zoë worries people will think it's enough and stop giving. The new objective is to keep the homeless from moving away to find jobs: the money is put to work buying building materials, tools and home furnishings. Soon hundreds of houses are under construction in both cities, and hundreds of men employed in building them. The CPR rebuilds its station and freight sheds on the Flats. Shops reopen in a matter of weeks, operating on generous credit terms from their suppliers.

Over in Hull, Mr. Eddy overcomes another challenge. A year earlier, disgusted with iniquitous insurance rates, he negotiated a cheaper policy that paid out only a hundred thousand per fire, far from enough to rebuild his plant. But Eddy's businesses are so profitable that he soon attracts the necessary investment capital to refit his mills with the latest pulp-and-paper machinery. Antoine Kirouac gets his job back. On Le Breton Flats, the Booth and Bronson sawmills donate lumber for rebuilding homes and businesses, but J.R. Booth and his former neighbours in Rochesterville, wary of living too close to the source of their wealth, construct new homes in Upper Town.

Lady Macdonald is selling Earnscliffe and everything in it. For her first social outing since the fire, Zoë can't resist attending the gigantic auction sale.

In the nine years since Sir John A.'s death, his widow has been summering in the south of England, wintering on the Italian Riviera. She's shown little interest in revisiting Ottawa, much less returning to live, and now she's severing ties completely. For years Lady Macdonald ruled over the capital's society with an iron fist, her disapproving gaze casting a shadow over public attempts at frivolity. She grew into a near-mythic creature, more respected than loved, and not in the least missed. Still, everyone is insatiably curious to peek inside Earnscliffe and take this opportunity to examine the famous couple's possessions over the three days of the auction.

Zoë worries it will be considered vulgar of her to make an appearance, even as a spectator. Émilie assures her that her presence will attract little notice on the third day. Already the house has gone under the hammer. Earnscliffe's new owners are Dr. and Mrs. Charles Harriss—he the English composer, she the rich heiress.

"I have to admit," Zoë says, "I feel a little closer to Lady Macdonald now. After all, we've done the same job. Mr. Pope stays in touch with her. Apparently she's a great admirer of Wilfrid. She thinks he resembles Sir John, not only in policy but personality."

"Dear God, I hope not," Émilie replies.

Earnscliffe's lawn and gardens, shaded by tall maples, are more imposing than the property on Theodore Street. The auctioneer's podium is set up in the drawing room, the sale already in progress, standing room only. Zoë and Émilie squeeze inside the French doors. Émilie says it's *de rigueur* for Ottawans with social aspirations to purchase *something* at the sale, no matter how expensive. People have been paying ridiculous sums for the bed in which Sir John slept and died, his oak wardrobe, his extensive library. At the moment his rather baroque secretary desk is on the block: inlaid with various native woods, it's inscribed "Dominion SecreTORY" and was originally presented to him by his political supporters.

Zoë finds the desk ungainly. She wouldn't have it in the house. A wild flurry of bidding pushes up the price, until finally the desk goes to someone seated near the front.

As vases and silverware are knocked down, Émilie notices something amusing. She whispers to Zoë that Dr. and Mrs. Harriss are seated on opposite sides of the room and can't see each other for the crowd. Without realizing it, they've been raising their cards in competition, bidding up the price of articles they want for their new home. In this fashion they've paid far more than necessary for Lady Macdonald's favourite chesterfield, as well as marble busts of both Macdonalds, before discovering their mistake—which of course the auctioneer has failed to point out.

Zoë finds something repulsive in the whole display of greed, the lust to appropriate the Macdonalds' lives. The profligate spending is especially distasteful so soon after the fire. People should be using their money for the benefit of the hungry and dispossessed. She's glad when they can take advantage of a break in the proceedings to slip away.

As she and Émilie cross the lawn, a young man in a straw boater comes hurrying up the pebbled path behind them. He draws alongside, carrying a peculiar lamp with a twisted iron base, which Émilie later describes as art nouveau. The young man is smiling in satisfaction, evidently pleased with his new acquisition. He has a pudgy face and full lips and hair parted down the middle. Awkwardly he tips his hat to Zoë and Émilie, gripping the iron lamp in the crook of his arm.

"Please excuse me, Lady Laurier, I was hoping to make your acquaintance," he blurts, plump cheeks reddening. "I've been a lifelong admirer of your husband. My earliest political experience came when my father and I heard Sir Wilfrid speak at Massey Hall and now I have the privilege of working in his government. I've just arrived in Ottawa to take up my post and need to furnish my new digs, so I thought, 'What better way to start than to own something once owned by our first Prime Minister?' Of course *he* wasn't of the right party, but—"

"And you are. . . ?" Zoë enquires.

"I'm terribly sorry, William Lyon Mackenzie King. My father is John King, barrister, of Toronto."

"How do you do, Mr. King. And this is Madame Joseph Lavergne, whose husband is Justice Lavergne of the Quebec Superior Court."

Émilie smiles briefly and inclines her head.

"I'm so honoured to meet you both. I believe this is a very, very lucky day!"

"I hope so too," Zoë says. "For everyone's sake."

"Luck is on my mind, Lady Laurier. On Monday I begin my duties editing the *Labour Gazette,* so I'm anxious for all to go well. Mr. Mulock has hired me personally and I don't want to disappoint him."

"I'm sure you won't disappoint anyone, Mr. King. Mr. Mulock is well known as a generous man and a fine judge of character. Well, it is very nice to have met you."

"And you, Lady Laurier. Likewise, Madame Lavergne. I hope to meet the Prime Minister too, before long." And he scurries off with his prized lamp.

"What a peculiar young man," Émilie murmurs. "Something slightly off about him."

"Just another seeker after Wilfrid," Zoë says with a sigh. "I meet them every day."

11

Autumn 1900

Since the night Wilfrid cut her in the parliamentary corridor, a night she tries to remember as seldom as possible, Émilie has seen almost nothing of him. The exceptions are dinner parties chez Laurier, where she and Joseph continue to be invited, along with many others. On those occasions Wilfrid has been unfailingly cordial and kind toward her, asking after the children, asking after her health. But then he's unfailingly cordial and kind to everyone.

Perhaps she prefers the absence of contact. Perhaps it's for the best. She's beginning to see Wilfrid differently now. While immersed in the myriad details of fire-relief work, she's thought about his behaviour toward her over the years, understanding it in a new light.

Love isn't words, she's concluded. Love isn't even some finished, immutable *thing*, some composition played on a distant violin. Love is doing. She pictures it as an accumulation of a thousand acts, passionate, devoted, constant, building to a crescendo, then levelling off into tender and sustained intimacy. By that measure, Wilfrid is scarcely loving at all. His actions certainly aren't constant. They're the actions of a divided and unreliable man. On occasion he might risk some thrilling act of love, some stirring declaration, only to annul it immediately afterwards, alarmed by his own boldness, and wall himself up within his power.

Sadly, this has happened so often that Émilie somehow missed it—just as she'd miss the pattern in some old familiar carpet. In fact it's been as predictable as a dance: forward and back, sideways and back. She and Wilfrid have danced their parts all too well.

In the meantime she's been seeing something of Mr. Davin.

She has to admire Nicholas Flood Davin: an exceptionally enterprising man, if a touch mad. That night on Parliament Hill, it turned out the motor car wasn't his after all but belonged to his friend Thomas Ahearn, the businessman who introduced the telephone and horseless streetcar to Ottawa, and has now bought its first automobile. The two Irishmen share an off-colour sense of humour and a taste for fat Cuban cigars, as well as Mr. Ahearn's electric car. Ahearn has taught Davin how to drive it up to its top speed of fifteen miles per hour without overly menacing pedestrians. Several times the MP has contrived to borrow the machine and offer Émilie a lift: once, to demonstrate he meant no disrespect to the Lavergne marriage, extending the invitation to her and Joseph when the three of them were invited to a Rideau Hall theatrical. Émilie has been working in the evenings at Cartier Square when Davin has arrived in the wheezing, dark-green auto, wearing driving cap and goggles, to see if she needs an escort home. After assuring him she can manage very well on her own, she always accepts.

With insinuating smiles, ladies on the committee have told Émilie of other evenings when she wasn't there and Davin came by the Drill Hall looking for her. It seems he's often at loose ends when the House isn't sitting. He always smells, not unpleasantly, of shaving lotion and Irish whisky. It's just that Mrs. Davin won't join him in Ottawa, he explains—she prefers to stay home in Regina, to be near her friends—and a man naturally gets lonesome for a little companionship of an evening. And, he'll add teasingly, as if it's her fault, Madame Lavergne is not only a most congenial conversationalist, but the best-read, most widely travelled, most fascinating lady in Ottawa.

Émilie doesn't object to Davin's flattery. There's nothing wrong with flattery, as long as you don't believe it. And Davin has a lively wit, has written books, poetry. He's famous for his speeches in the House, even if they're more memorable for oratorical style than substance. Bourassa calls him "Almighty Voice."

Davin is a born raconteur, full of stories from his days in Cork and London and the wild North-West, where he founded the first newspaper and is now the only surviving Conservative MP. It impresses Émilie that he also advocates the vote for women. As for his flirtatious attentions to her, they're entertaining at best, harmless at worst. He really means nothing by them. She's told he has at least two illegitimate children back in Regina. Émilie has always been a woman who rises above petty conventions.

One morning at the end of September, she's in her room when her maid, Thérèse, tells her the Prime Minister is waiting downstairs. Émilie catches her breath. Why has Wilfrid come now? Why *here*?

She calms herself by spending a full minute in front of her mirror, adjusting her dress, tucking wisps of hair into her chignon. She wishes it wasn't turning grey like Zoë's. She wishes she was wearing something more interesting than her old russet taffeta with the long sleeves, but there isn't time to change: Wilfrid might have only a few minutes to spare, and she wants to make the most of them. Hastily she adds a pair of pearl-drop earrings, then goes down the stairs with measured steps.

He's seated on a chair in the parlour, his gloves perched on his top hat, the hat perched on his knees. The yellow and white gladioli in the black Chinese vase are wilting, their lower blossoms turning brown. She should have replaced them yesterday.

"Why, Wilfrid, what a lovely surprise."

He rises and kisses her on both cheeks. "You've been well, I hope?"

"As well as can be expected." She pauses. "Considering I haven't seen you in ages."

"It's difficult to lead a double life when one is Prime Minister."

"So I've noticed."

"That's partly why I've come."

"Really? Now, I'm curious about *that*. Please, Wilfrid, sit." She goes to the chesterfield and pats the seat beside her, but he resumes his place on the chair.

He clears his throat. "I've often thought about how I treated you that night in the House."

"So have I." How clipped her voice sounds, snapping shut at the end of her sentence.

"I don't blame you for being angry. I'm not sure, exactly, how to explain it. Or whether I should have to. Your own behaviour was distinctly odd."

He pauses: waiting, in fact, for *her* explanation.

"I embarrassed you," she admits grudgingly.

"You put me on the spot. In front of one of my most important ministers."

"I should have known better. I should have held my feelings back. But I'd been despairing about us, Wilfrid—with good reason, I must say. I needed some sort of closeness, some recognition from you. Was that too much to ask?"

"Of course not, but—"

"It's true I chose a peculiar moment." She realizes she's almost not sorry.

He studies her. "But why would you choose the worst possible *place*?"

"Now you're angry."

"I also wonder why you accepted Davin's offer of a ride home."

"Is it just that Mr. Davin is a Conservative?"

"Please be serious."

"I'd have thought you'd be grateful to Mr. Davin. He provided an escape from the awful position I'd put you in."

"That hasn't been your only drive with him. It's all over town. Really, Émilie—how must Joseph be feeling?"

She nearly laughs in his face. "How noble of you to be concerned for Joseph!"

"How much do you know about Davin? Everyone else is quite familiar with his adventures. His *ménage* with a certain lady not his wife is legendary. What do you suppose people think of you for being his friend?"

This time she does laugh, although not unkindly. "It wouldn't be the first time!"

When Wilfrid blushes, she takes the opportunity to ring for Thérèse and order tea.

"So you've come to reprimand me about Mr. Davin. And remind me of my wifely duties." It gratifies her that Wilfrid does at least this.

He sighs, shaking his head. His expression softens. "No, I suppose I've come for the same reason you came to the House that night. I feel desperate too sometimes. I long for the old days together. Just your serving me tea takes me back."

"Ah, back then I served you with my own hands."

"Shows how you've risen in the world." He smiles faintly. "I have to admit, my life lacks a dimension when you're not in it. There's no colour, only blacks and whites. At best, greys. No brilliant shadings, no delicious nuances, only the tiresome facts. The crude demands of the moment."

"But Wilfrid, that's the life you've *chosen*. You've been living it for years. What more do you want?"

"Something more enduring. Something that will matter when I'm no longer in politics."

"Surely your work in government will endure."

An uncomfortable silence falls between them. The grandfather clock Joseph inherited from his parents ticks more obtrusively than usual. Émilie is puzzled why Wilfrid has interrupted his busy morning to come and tell her these things. Is he just following some sentimental impulse to pay homage to the past? Yet he never says anything he hasn't thought deeply about—

He changes the subject. "Tell me about the children." Safer ground. Just as well.

"Bielle is radiant, as always, enjoying being in society. At the moment she's in Quebec City visiting her brother. Armand is doing extremely well at Laval since he moved there. He's turned twenty, of course."

"Of course. I sent him my congratulations. Still cheering for Bourassa, I suppose."

"Oh yes. But he parts his hair like Laurier."

Wilfrid grins with pleasure. "He knows what's important, at least."

She doesn't tell him Armand is in charge of distributing the pro-Bourassa newspaper, *Les Débats*, in the halls of Laval. Or that he ends his letters to her with the cry, "*Vive Kruger! Vivent les Boers! Mort aux Anglais!*"

She's feeling wary. Wilfrid's claiming to long for the old times makes her skeptical. Still she asks, more out of curiosity than need, "Why do you suppose you were feeling desperate, as you put it?"

"At times I wonder about the wisdom of my choices."

"Really? I'm surprised."

"Nothing is ever as it seems, you must know that. To others I appear completely wrapped up in dedication to my work. But my mind and heart are often elsewhere."

"You do appear wrapped up in your work. And your dear Zoë."

Wilfrid stands, moving to the mantelpiece, which now strikes her as unacceptably cluttered. "So you still doubt my devotion?"

She shrugs and says nothing.

"After all these years? We've been over that ground so often."

"Yes, we have. You forgot my birthday last March."

"Only under pressure of the House sitting all night. I sent you a book afterwards. Have you forgotten?"

"Of course not. I'm only teasing you. Can you remember the title?"

"Stop it! You're cruel. See how distracted and weighed down I am by the burdens of office? If only I could throw them off. . . ."

"Good heavens, and do what?"

"Go back to my original profession." He says it with seeming conviction. She makes a face of disbelief. "Oh, I know, it wouldn't be easy resuming the law. It would take courage. But I find the idea infinitely desirable. Rolling up my sleeves, re-entering the battle for my daily bread—the old familiar battle of the ordinary man—how satisfying that would be."

"Would it?"

"And finally I'd be in a position to prove how I feel about you."

"Oh come, Wilfrid."

"What do you mean? Our dream has never died. I've never abandoned it."

Émilie can't allow herself to believe his words: in the end that's all they are.

"You're talking as if it were five years ago. Or ten. We have to live in the present."

"I'm living in the damned present, believe me! That's all I ever do. I'm all too aware of today's demands, *and* of what's coming tomorrow. The blasted election campaign is going to swallow me whole, the way it always does. I'll be completely unable to live any sort of life. And then what? More of the same, ad infinitum. It's a lonely existence, my dear."

She waits in silence. She won't collude in this, won't rejoin the dance. He can dance alone if he wishes.

"But you know," he says, a dreamy expression coming over his features, "it's entirely possible I'll lose this election. In fact it's beginning to seem quite likely. Ontario will reject my 'disloyal' approach to the war. The west will follow suit, and I'll be back in opposition. Then I'll have no choice but to resign, and the party will have no choice but to accept it. I'll be rid of politics at last. And you and I will finally have our chance."

In the not so distant past, Émilie would have been transported by this declaration, won over instantly. Instead, her jaw tenses, she feels in danger of being trapped. She does love having him near, but she's discovered you have to create your own life: you can't wait for someone to do it for you.

"You're very good at dreaming our old dream, Wilfrid. And of course it's a beautiful, entrancing, intoxicating dream, it always was. But you know, I think we've learned something, you and I: we can live without it."

His features go rigid. The creases around his mouth deepen, making him look suddenly older.

Alarmed by the transformation, she adds, "I've watched *you* do it for years! You can live without your Émilie—except as a loyal friend who's never far away, always ready to be at your side, and listen, and respond."

"How can you turn your back on *us*?" he whispers.

She goes to him in a great rustling of taffeta, reaching to enfold his head in her arms. "Don't be upset," she croons. "Don't be sad. I'm not turning my back. Everything will turn out all right. For both of us. You'll see."

Afterwards Émilie is furious: with herself, not with Wilfrid. What has she done? How could she be so careless, so stupid, so destructive?

After sipping his tea and talking distractedly about nothing, he said goodbye and left for Parliament Hill. She watched through the window as he crossed the road in the sunshine to board his streetcar. With his top hat and walking stick, he looked as elegant and indomitable as ever. But she knows he went away feeling abandoned and unconsoled. She's made him sad. Far worse: she's killed their dream. Now she's truly lost.

In another ten days the election is called, and the campaign swallows Wilfrid whole, just as he said it would. Émilie follows it from a distance through newspaper reports, political chat at dinner parties, gossip that Joseph brings home from the courts. Paradoxically, following Wilfrid from afar makes her feel closer to him. She's used to this from her Arthabaska days, when he was away for long periods in Ottawa. It feels normal: whereas being in the same city yet not together left her feeling farther apart from him, their separateness made explicit, undeniable.

She also sees less of Zoë now. The need for the women's committee is over, fortunately for the fire victims, and their paths don't cross as often. In any case Zoë seems to be keeping her distance. This is almost as bad as Wilfrid's absence on the hustings. Conversation with Zoë has often—too often—been the next best thing to being with him, as if they were both widows of the same husband.

Guiltily Émilie finds herself wishing she still had the relief work. The committee supplied an urgency to her days, an abiding sense of satisfaction that nothing, apart from motherhood and Wilfrid, has ever given her: the feeling that her life is consequential.

But the homeless have moved back into their old neighbourhoods, into the thousand new homes that have risen on the ashes on both sides of the river. Citizens of the capital know something they didn't know before: when disaster strikes, their community will rally to help them and their families, regardless of race or religion. At least the fire, Émilie thinks, has taught us that much.

The election campaign is less conducive to racial harmony, despite Wilfrid's efforts to build bridges across the divide. Émilie admires his never-ending sense of mission, explaining the French to the English, and vice versa. He never ceases trying to make Canadians understand they're Canadians, no matter where they live or which language they speak or who their ancestors were, or, for that matter, how grievously they've suffered at each other's hands. His oratory reaches new heights in a speech to the much-persecuted Acadians. It's Wilfrid at his best, and Émilie clips the account from the newspaper. He tells his audience in Arichat, Nova Scotia, about being in England for the Queen's Jubilee:

"I had the privilege of visiting one of those marvels of Gothic architecture, which the hand of genius, guided by an unerring faith, has made a harmonious whole. In it, granite, marble, oak and other materials are blended. That cathedral is the image of the nation that I hope to see Canada become. As long as I live, as long as I have the power to labour in the service of my country, I shall repel the idea of changing the nature of its different elements. I want the marble to remain the marble; I want the granite to remain the granite; I want the oak to remain the oak; I want the sturdy Scotchman to remain the Scotchman; I want the brainy Englishman to remain the Englishman; I want the warm-hearted Irishman to remain the Irishman; I want the proud Frenchman to remain French. I want to take all these elements and build a nation that will be foremost amongst the great powers of the world."

Wilfrid is beginning to tell Canadians a new story, and it's a romantic one: that this twentieth century belongs to them. He offers them a version of their future beyond anything they've ever heard or imagined. Will they be big enough to embrace his vision? Émilie doubts it. There's simply too much small-mindedness everywhere, too much bigotry and extremism.

The small men opposing Wilfrid live by the sterile philosophy of divide and conquer. Sir Charles Tupper, still hanging on as Conservative leader, goes to Quebec City to flatter local prejudices.

Absurdly, he denounces Wilfrid as an imperialist for sending troops to South Africa, proclaiming, "Laurier is too English for me." In Ontario, the Conservatives say the exact opposite: Laurier and his government are too beholden to Quebec, too uncommitted to the Empire, too bent on threatening Canada with "French domination." Émilie can't comprehend why so many in Ontario are obsessed with this fear. The English are in the majority, after all, and the immigrants flooding onto the prairies all speak English, or are learning it as fast as they can.

One day during the campaign, Joseph brings home a copy of the *Toronto News*. Shaking with indignation, he reads aloud the inflammatory, racist editorial. British Canadians will find ways, the paper threatens, whether through the ballot box or otherwise, to "emancipate themselves from the dominance of an inferior people that peculiar circumstances have placed in authority in the Dominion."

At times the race cry overwhelms the war as the campaign's main issue. Underlying all the hysteria is a simple question: can a French-Canadian Roman Catholic be allowed to lead the country? Of course even Wilfrid's worst enemies know better than to attack him personally. He's too admired, too popular. Instead they try to discredit him through their favourite bogeyman, Joseph-Israël Tarte. Tarte's speeches in French can easily be mistranslated and misinterpreted to prove Quebec's "disloyalty." Émilie knows how badly Wilfrid needs Tarte's organizational genius in Quebec, but he's a serious liability in Ontario. Conservatives of the Orange Lodge persuasion have published a pamphlet attacking him, and Wilfrid is forced to speak in his defense. Tarte has even gone to the extreme of publicly pledging loyalty to the British flag. Émilie is disgusted. The only thing that gives her any hope for Toronto is Joseph Atkinson's new paper, *The Star*. On its front page it quotes Protestant clergymen praising Wilfrid's leadership and statesmanship and denouncing those who use his religion against him.

Wilfrid's friend President McKinley is simultaneously fighting his own battle against William Jennings Bryan. Although she isn't naive enough to think they're any more principled, Émilie finds American politics blessedly free of Canada's sectarian prejudices. Luckily for both leaders, their countries are revelling in prosperity at the moment: the voters aren't hungry for change.

One day after McKinley's decisive victory at the polls, the Canadian election is held. Long before the final results roll in, it's clear Wilfrid's persuasion and eloquence and charm have triumphed once again. He's sufficiently loved to win another majority. His notion that the voters would liberate him from the chains of office was, of course, a pipe dream, as she knew it would be: another of his fine flights of fancy.

It does appear the Conservatives' anti-Tarte, anti-French campaign has succeeded to some extent. Liberal seats in Ontario are reduced. On the other hand, Wilfrid has won all Quebec ridings but seven, and the Maritime provinces have gone strongly Liberal. More surprisingly, Sir Charles Tupper has been defeated in his own riding in Cape Breton, his political career finished at last. The Conservatives are headless. If they hoped for another Macdonald to lead them, they're sadly disappointed: Sir John A.'s son, Hugh John, who resigned the premiership of Manitoba to run against Clifford Sifton, has lost badly. The Conservative rout extends across the west. Of less interest to the newspapers, but far greater interest to Émilie, Nicholas Flood Davin has gone down to defeat in Regina.

Not one of Wilfrid's ministers has lost his seat. His own margin of victory in Quebec East is the largest in the country. He bestrides the nation, virtually unchallenged. He must, Émilie thinks, be happy now.

Wondering if she'll ever see him again alone, she busies herself with social life. Her real, everyday companion is the ghost of their love. It looms over her shoulder as she watches some entertainment at the Russell Theatre, reads Lamartine or Baudelaire in her bedroom, strolls alongside the Rideau Canal under bare branches on chill late-autumn afternoons.

When the post-election invitation arrives to dine with the Lauriers, she and Joseph naturally accept. It's a celebratory occasion, attended by the usual guests, the Fieldings and the Mulocks and the Blairs and the Siftons and the Popes. Émilie knows she ought to feel privileged that she and Joseph are included in such company, but seeing Wilfrid in his dining room with the crimson wallpaper and mahogany furniture, peering down the long table at him over dazzling candelabra, turning aside to hear something Zoë wants to tell her in French, isn't the life she wants. She feels false and defeated, pretending to enjoy herself.

During the fish course, the telephone rings in the front hall. Yvonne Coutu answers, slipping into the dining room to whisper something in Wilfrid's ear. He excuses himself, returns five minutes later. Crossing the room to his chair, he glances apprehensively at Émilie. He seems to want to say something to her: a disturbing sensation.

He remains standing, and his guests break off their conversations and look up. "I'm afraid I've some unhappy news." His eyes scan the table. "I hate to disturb our festive mood, but there's been, as it were, a death in the family. Evidently our friend Davin has been found dead in a hotel room in Winnipeg. He put a bullet through his brain."

Émilie gasps. Everyone at the table hears her. She feels a dark shock of puzzled astonishment, a sadness mixed with fear. Yet there's no real pain. Wilfrid's eyes are locked onto hers as if they were alone. That delicious communion, consummated despite the presence of Zoë and Joseph and all the other startled, vividly candlelit faces, is enough to make her feel, momentarily, content.

1 2

December 1900

Zoë detects signs of contentment: at least when he's not thinking about the war. The election over, Wilfrid is home more. On
evenings when they aren't entertaining, they sit for an hour or two
in the drawing room, he reading, she knitting, a fire taking the
edge off the December chill, until he excuses himself to go upstairs
with his papers. He no longer complains about her fussing. When
she rises to make them a cup of tea, it's a delightful idea. When she
brings him a small crocheted rug for his legs because there's always
the danger of his bronchitis returning, he's touched, appreciative
beyond politeness. When she suggests they invite that nice young
man from the Labour department, Mr. King, with his colleague
and friend Mr. Harper and several debutantes—both men being
conspicuously in need of a wife—Wilfrid agrees, as long as it's on
a weekend when he hasn't too much to do. And when she asks him
about the state of things in cabinet, he discourses optimistically
about the domestic political situation, then asks her advice. She
doesn't hesitate to give it.

The time is promising to attempt something more ambitious.

By now seven thousand Canadians have gone to South Africa.
Wilfrid is increasingly troubled by the seemingly endless war,
over which he has absolutely no control. He's told her about the

dreams. A corpse lying in filth, eyes open, watching him, tracking his every move. The enemy attacking Ottawa, killing children, assaulting women, he and the other men powerless. Shells bursting in the street, their own house taking a direct hit, the roof collapsing, Zoë pinned under blazing timbers.

He's never been told the truth about the war, not by Lord Minto, not by Frederick Borden, certainly not by the newspapers. Even Borden, he suspects, receives no special intelligence as Minister of Militia. They all hear only what Chamberlain and his allies in the press want them to hear. It drags on and on: an unbelievable narrative of "overwhelming" British victories, punctuated at irregular intervals by more Canadians killed and wounded. Although he speaks in public about a war for justice and liberty, privately Wilfrid has concluded the British cause is entirely trumped up, greed for diamonds and gold masquerading as lofty principles.

Zoë watches him grieving over every casualty report. He insists Borden inform him of the name and age of each dead Canadian. They sound so ordinary, most of them barely men: Burns, Burtch, Donergan, Findlay, Goodfellow, Jackson, Larue, Leblanc, Lester, Lewis, Maundrell, Manion, McQueen, Patenaude, Scott, Smith, Somers, Taylor, Todd, White. Each was somebody's son, his body now irretrievably smashed, sacrificed to the government's will. The destruction of each young life makes him mourn his decision to go to war all over again, no matter how unavoidable it was politically. When Borden forwards without comment the name of his own son, a lieutenant in the Royal Canadian Dragoons, Wilfrid feels physically ill.

It remains unclear what "victory" against the Boers will look like. They hang back in the hills, refusing to fight a pitched battle against vastly greater British forces, then materializing on horseback at will to ambush slow-moving supply lines, riding hard, shooting with deadly accuracy, vanishing across the veldt. They know every gully and bush and stunted tree. They're prepared to outwait and outwit the invader, to continue inflicting damage until he goes home. Fighting to protect their farms and families makes them fierce and implacable enemies, and most of the world has rallied to their cause.

Rather than dumbly endure the conflict, Zoë's instinct is to face it head-on. The more Wilfrid knows about it, the more possible for him to understand and deal with it, personally and politically. She's heard Agar Adamson is home on Christmas leave. Happily, Lieutenant Adamson has escaped being wounded but, like many of his fellow soldiers, contracted typhoid fever, which kept him in bed for weeks in Durban. Now he's recovered and receiving a hero's welcome. Other veterans have also returned—Ottawa's D Company has been treated to a rousing street parade—but Adamson is in a class by himself. As an officer in Strathcona's Horse, he's part of an elite unit that the British have taken to their hearts. He's been in the thick of the fighting, and Zoë hopes he'll be willing to speak in private about his experiences.

Miss Georgina Pope, one of the four nurses who accompanied the First Canadian Contingent, is also back in Ottawa. Having Miss Pope to the house together with Lieutenant Adamson will make for an interesting afternoon. Each can encourage the other to speak frankly about the brutal campaign that's costing Britain, and ultimately Wilfrid, allies and moral authority and peace of mind. At least that is Zoë's hope and prayer.

If Miss Pope and Lieutenant Adamson are the least bit shy about sitting in their Prime Minister's drawing room, they don't show it. Both act calm and self-assured, in the way of modern young people just returned from seeing the world. Settled by the fire with scones, crème fraîche and raspberry jam, they seem to find it natural that Wilfrid would want to talk with them. Both have arrived, to Zoë's surprise, in uniform. Both expect to return to South Africa as soon as possible—unless, as Adamson cheerfully puts it, the long-awaited set-to with the Boers happens while he's home and brings the whole show to an end.

Miss Pope defers to Adamson but watches him intently, and Zoë senses she'll speak up when the time comes. Although attractive, her face is strong, without feminine softness. Under the rakish brim of a khaki sailor hat, her eyes have the high vigilance of someone accustomed to danger, a woman who has seen things normally denied her sex. Adamson looks older, more drawn, less handsome than the last time Zoë saw him, his Roman nose compromised by a military moustache. He's suffered some loss of weight from his illness, but his eyes shine and his spirits are as ebullient as ever: he seems a man whom nothing could discourage.

Surveying his guests benignly, Wilfrid commends them on their bravery and thanks them for their service to the country. He enquires after Miss Pope's health, learning she escaped the typhoid epidemic. He asks Adamson what it feels like to come under enemy fire, and Adamson replies he's quite sure the Prime Minister is familiar with the sensation. Wilfrid grins. Adamson adds that the Boers are using expanding bullets, which spray lethal bits of metal in all directions: "The brutes have no conception of fair play."

When Wilfrid mentions hearing that the Boers will raise a white flag, then open fire on our troops when they come to take the surrender, Adamson admits he's never seen it happen. But he's seen plenty of subterfuge and deceit: "A Boer is a peaceful farmer one day, a commando fighter the next, a spy always. They snipe at us from behind every rock. It's said one Boer sniper is worth a hundred trying to catch him. And forgive me, ladies, but the women are no better."

"Oh?" Wilfrid's curiosity is piqued. "Tell us more."

Adamson describes the day he and his men arrived at a very tidy, smart-looking farm, finding only the wife and her two daughters home. They wore beautiful clothes, as is the custom with old

Dutch families. The Canadians commandeered their horses and mules and a good lunch, and drank their health in an excellent cup of tea. When Adamson asked where the menfolk were, he was told they'd gone to tend the cattle up north. "Poor women," he says with a tight smile, "the war is hard on them, but it's impossible to believe a word they say. We found a cache of weapons in the root cellar and more in some freshly dug graves behind the barn. The crosses were inscribed with their grandparents' names."

Adamson concedes there are times in war when you see the enemy as entirely human, just as human as yourself, and you can easily imagine being in their place. At other times, you're filled with such hatred that you want nothing but revenge. "I'm afraid revenge is what makes fighting a war tolerable."

He describes one of the more tolerable moments. A man under his command won Canada's first Victoria Cross. No doubt Adamson has regaled many listeners with this tale, Zoë thinks, his delivery as polished and dramatic as an actor's. Trying to lead the Boers into a trap but coming under heavy crossfire. Dismounting and taking shelter behind some trees. Sergeant Richardson seeing Private McArthur lying badly wounded in open country without a horse, riding under withering fire to pick him up, bringing him back to safety. "I've seen many an act of courage, sir, but none like that. I forwarded an account of Richardson's action to headquarters, thinking it would be a great thing to get a V.C. for Canada."

"That's wonderful," Wilfrid says. "I understand you were mentioned in dispatches yourself."

"So I believe, sir."

In August the big push north into the Transvaal began, with most of the British forces taking part. Adamson's group took several towns. They charged Amersfoort from three sides and rode very hard with bullets raining down and took the town.

"Once Amersfoort was ours, it was given over to loot. Yes, I know, it was a terrible mistake. Homes were sacked, and the

Tommies found women's underclothes to replace their own dirty things. One shop was looted for everything from bicycles to baby carriages. Houses were smashed to pieces to provide fuel for bonfires, since the nights were bitterly cold."

"I understood our troops were under orders not to loot."

"So did I, sir. But the high command made no attempt to prevent it. Two days later we entered Ermelo. I rushed to the town hall and pulled down the Transvaal flag and have it still, folded in perfect condition in my luggage. This time the orders were no looting. I commandeered the largest house in town and made arrangements to sleep a dozen officers there."

"Whose home was it?" Zoë asks, putting herself in the place of the mistress of the house.

"It belonged to a wealthy Hungarian merchant, who turned out to be a Mason like myself. He'd been out fighting with the commandos but wished to surrender. I promised I'd do my best for him. His wife was *most* charming. They did us very well— served an excellent Chateau Margaux with our dinner, and some sweet champagne—and are now living peacefully with a *laissez-passer*."

"Agar," Miss Pope says, "tell the Prime Minister what happened that night."

Adamson looks uncomfortable and purses his lips. "Well, assuming the Prime Minister and Lady Laurier wish to hear about that sort of thing. . . ."

"We'd prefer to hear everything, if you don't mind," Wilfrid says.

"All right. These things happen in war. About three in the morning, I heard a racket at the front door. I went downstairs and was met by a young woman on the verandah who spoke to me in Afrikaans. She was dreadfully upset. My brother Mason appeared in his night robe and translated while I stood there in my shirt-tails, legs positively freezing. It seemed three soldiers had entered her house and were in bed with her sisters, trying to rape them. I realized I had to tackle the job myself, once I had my breeches on. Being without them would have been most compromising! So I did what I could, but the brutes made their escape in double quick time. I fear they were our men."

Wilfrid doesn't comment. "I hear a lot about your Colonel Sam Steele. What do you think of him?"

Adamson looks even more discomfited. "Colonel Steele is my commanding officer, Sir Wilfrid. If I have any complaints, I should really address them to him."

"I understand. I'm not looking for complaints. Just tell me: is he a good leader of men?"

"Since you are my Prime Minister, and asking the question in confidence—to be honest, not always. He can be callous in command. Just to give one small example, some of our men were suffering terribly from ill-fitting boots, and Colonel Steele refused to allow them to ride in the wagons."

Miss Pope adds, "Perhaps I can speak more freely, since Colonel Steele isn't my C.O. Everyone knows he's far too fond of the bottle. We all have first-hand experience of it."

"True," Adamson says quickly, "although he's not the only one, of course. The pot shouldn't be calling the kettle black. But he does get beastly drunk with his officers, even with his batman. On the other hand, to give the Colonel credit, he objected vigorously to the last assignment we were given. Said it wasn't fitting. Not the sort of thing Lord Strathcona raised the unit to do."

"And what assignment was that?"

"For lack of a better term, sir, a scorched-earth campaign. Searching homes for armed men. Confiscating chickens and cattle and pigs. And when necessary, burning down farmhouses and outbuildings. That's the hardest thing for our prairie boys who grew up on farms themselves. It upsets them. Personally, I consider the worst job to be rounding up the women and children and herding them off to concentration camps—"

"Concentration camps," Wilfrid repeats, his brow furrowing. "I'm not familiar with the term."

"It's a new policy, considered necessary by the high command. They're being built all over the veldt. Vast enclosures of barbed wire anchored by blockhouses at each corner. The guards in the blockhouses keep an eye on the inmates and repel raiders, in case the Boers try to rescue their families."

"The inmates are families? Women and children?"

"Because they provide sustenance to the guerrillas. So we simultaneously deprive the Boers of their families and animals and food, while giving them a good reason to come in off the veldt and surrender."

"But how are the families being cared for? Surely they don't sleep out in the open."

"No, sir, they have army tents. But to be honest, their rations are pretty thin."

"Their rations are *dreadful*," Miss Pope interjects. "No meat, scarcely any vegetables or fruit, no milk for the children. It's such a poor diet that disease is already spreading through the camps. There aren't enough doctors and nurses to treat it."

"What kind of disease?"

"Mostly typhoid," Adamson replies. "The same as we get in our encampments. War is war, I'm afraid, it affects everyone pretty much the same. General Kitchener believes the camp policy will finally bring this one to an end. He's frustrated by the guerrillas' refusal to play the game and fight a pitched battle. The enemy will be in such drastic straits, he'll either have to give battle or throw in the towel."

There's a silence in the room, during which Wilfrid stares unblinkingly at Adamson. "Yes," he says at last. "War is war. But this is a kind of war I've never head of. Good Lord, women and children! Why must *they* suffer for Kruger's obstinacy? And Chamberlain's?"

Zoë has never seen these camps mentioned in the press. She tries to picture starving mothers and children penned up like cattle inside barbed wire. Adamson seems to read her thoughts: "I must admit, some things leave a bitter taste in the mouth. And people here at home talk such maudlin rot about South Africa. I suppose they mean well—"

He stops himself, and Zoë glimpses a bitterness in the man, a darkness she hasn't seen before.

"People may mean well," Wilfrid replies, "but most of them have no conception of war. You should tell them, Adamson. Go on a speaking tour, like young Mr. Churchill. Give the public the unvarnished truth."

Adamson shakes his head. "I'm afraid I don't have Churchill's dramatic speaking style. Nor his thrilling tales of espionage."

"Nonsense. You've seen a side of war that's invisible to the rest of us."

"I doubt people would pay to hear me talk about going unfed and unwashed for days. Or sucking on stones because there's no clean water. Better still, making campfires out of cattle droppings."

"Oh, I don't know," Wilfrid says, "anything can sound heroic if you make it so."

Adamson's face remains serious. "There's nothing heroic about catching typhoid, sir. And when you hear about the women and children in the camps getting it, you sympathize. But then you hear about Gat Howard—"

"Ah yes, the famous Major Howard. I was sorry to hear he'd been killed. A friend of yours?"

"I met him once. We had dinner in Pretoria before I got sick. He tried to recruit me, but I wasn't keen to be an irregular."

"A reckless character. Is that fair?"

"Perfectly fair, sir: not a cautious bone in his body. His men are like that too, they all try to live up to his reputation—'Howard's Canadian Scouts,' as they're called. That recklessness did him in finally. When they found his body riddled with bullets, his men decided he'd been killed in cold blood—the Boers laughed over his corpse, so the story goes. They raised their right hands and swore on the spot they'd never take another prisoner alive."

Wilfrid lunges forward in his chair. "That's against the rules of war!"

"Howard's Scouts don't care a fig for the rules of war. They've sworn to make the Boers pay—they wear black feathers in their Stetsons as a symbol of their oath. It gives you some idea why I didn't join up."

Wilfrid stands. He paces between his chair and Zoë's piano, before which so many of her musical protégés have tremulously sung. "Please excuse me. I need to stretch my legs." Her senses go on alert: it's unheard-of for him to show agitation before others.

He stares at the pattern in the Persian rug. "Killing prisoners is shameful," he mutters, almost to himself. "Godless. And they'll do it in Canada's name." He glances up suddenly at his visitors. "There's a movement in London to draft me as a peace negotiator."

"We heard about that before we sailed home," Miss Pope says. "Will you agree?"

"Difficult, I imagine," Adamson adds, "to get either side to accept anything less than complete victory."

"Very difficult indeed. I've been thinking it over, trying to decide whether negotiation has any hope of success. Another question is whether both sides would accept me: Canada is a combatant, after all. But your stories prove how urgently we need to end this war. A ceasefire would be a start."

Zoë watches his face. He's mentioned the peace broker role to her, and she's heard it mooted in the press, but until now she didn't know he was taking it seriously. She's unwilling to see him assume more responsibilities, fearing damage to his health. But if he takes it on she'll support him.

Adamson says, "Your reputation as a mediator makes you the ideal candidate, sir."

Wilfrid looks skeptical. "The people who put my name forward say Canada is an example to the warring parties—a model of political harmony between two former enemies. Never tell a soul, but I have my doubts about that." He hesitates. "Let me be frank with you: I need to say this to somebody who's been in the war. If I had my way, I'd bring every last soldier and nurse and batman home immediately—all our Canadians. I'd see all wounds healed, all families reunited. If I had the power to send you to war, I should have the power to bring you home too. But I don't, and it grieves me very much."

"Sir Wilfrid," Adamson begins, "I'm sure no one holds you personally responsible for—"

"But I am, you see." Zoë notices how the flesh either side of his mouth is sagging, his left eyelid drooping. "I've allowed Canada to be dragged into this mess, this vortex of militarism, which is the curse and blight of Europe." He's strangely moved. For some reason she wants him to stop, not to show weakness, but when he continues, his voice is strong and clear: "I'd dearly welcome the chance to bring about peace. I never again want to see Canadians suffering and dying in some godforsaken part of the world for no good reason. *Never* again."

A more famous protagonist of the South African war comes to Ottawa. Travelling on his North American speaking tour, Winston Spencer Churchill is receiving a mixed reception: American audiences are at best dubious about Britain's war, at worst hostile. Residual Dutch feelings in New York and Irish sympathies in Boston have given young Mr. Churchill a rough ride. The Boers are seen as fighting their own version of the War of Independence.

Zoë reads the newspaper coverage of the New York speech. Introducing Churchill, Mark Twain said, "Mr. Churchill is by his father an Englishman, by his mother an American, no doubt a blend that makes the perfect man. England and America, we are kin. And now that we are also kin in sin, there is nothing more to be desired."

Zoë puzzles over Mr. Twain's meaning: especially "kin in sin." Wilfrid explains Twain believes Britain shouldn't be fighting in South Africa, any more than the U.S. in the Philippines. But in the end, apparently, most of Churchill's listeners were swept up by his romantic tale of capture and harrowing escape. He went to South Africa a war correspondent, burst out of a Boer prison and came home a hero, publishing all the way, producing a torrent of newspaper dispatches and books in which his personal exploits assume equal importance with the actions of 150,000 British soldiers in the field.

Wilfrid is curious about the man. Recently Churchill was elected to the House of Commons. He's expected, like his late father, Lord Randolph, to play an important role in British politics. He left on his speaking tour before taking his seat in Parliament, hoping to exploit his fame and amass the fortune without which no British politician can rise to the top. Unable to attend Churchill's Ottawa performance, Wilfrid asks Zoë if she'd mind going. When Émilie catches wind of it, she succeeds in inviting herself along.

The manager of the Russell Theatre escorts the two ladies to their seats in the Prime Minister's box. Zoë is surprised to find it draped in a giant Union Jack. The theatre is packed, decorated fore and aft with bunting. She and Émilie catch sight of Macken-zie King, recently appointed Deputy Minister of Labour, sitting below alongside Bert Harper, second row centre. It amuses Zoë how Harper defers to King, who is his roommate but also his boss, and calls him "Rex."

The red curtain rises, revealing the young Englishman onstage in a cutaway coat, standing beside a podium, magic lantern and screen. Immediately Churchill bursts out with, "Thank God, to be once more on British soil!" The applause is deafening.

He isn't bad-looking, Zoë thinks: athletically built, a polo player apparently. Despite a sturdy voice that makes people com-pare his oratory to his father's, he speaks with a lisp. This boyish impression is accentuated by his clean-shaven face, full lips, apple cheeks, a slight curl to his hair. Yet he has the self-confidence and self-regard of a much older man.

Churchill dispenses with introductory remarks. Plunging into his announced topic, "The War as I Saw It," he assumes, quite correctly, that his audience knows all about him. He puts one hand on his hip, the other grasping a slim wooden pointer. The first lantern slide thrown up on the screen is a map.

"This is South Africa," Churchill declares, aiming the pointer like a rapier squarely at Pretoria. "It belongs to us."

Through the triumphal cheering, Zoë can hear Émilie's voice, disgusted: *"Mon Dieu!"*

The next few slides show photographs of Boer guerrillas, bearded farmers in battered civilian clothes with bandoliers across their chests, about whom Churchill makes cutting comments. Nonetheless, he assures his audience, the Boers are a formidable and terrible adversary. He proceeds to recount the story of his cap-ture after a British armoured train was derailed by guerrillas, pref-acing the tale by saying, "Of course, I have also told this story in a book, which it would be unbecoming of me to advertise here. But I earnestly hope each one of you will procure and read it."

Zoë enjoys Churchill's breezy, almost lighthearted description of his escape from prison: scaling the fence, jumping the freight train at night, leaping into a ditch before dawn, his miraculous luck in knocking on the door of the only British citizen for miles around, who hid him in an unused mine pit before smuggling him onto a wool train headed for the Portuguese coast. These heroics are far more interesting than the young man's theories about the justice of Britain's cause, or the political arrangements that should be made after the war.

Churchill doesn't refer to the idea of Wilfrid's acting as mediator. But he has admiring words for Canada's military contribution, no doubt wanting to shore up any sagging local support for the war: "The assistance Canada and the other self-governing dependencies of the Empire have rendered can never be overestimated. Canada's part in the war has not been taken in vain. Through her soldiers in Africa, she has won for herself a dignity and a name among nations which otherwise she might not have attained in many years." Predictably, these remarks go down well with the audience.

"There is, moreover, a sense of unity throughout the Empire today, a common feeling between the rancher of the Alberta plains and the English farmer, that each belongs to the great British Empire, and the Empire belongs to him. Let us hope the time is not far distant when the Union Jack will wave over a free and united South Africa."

In a show of democracy, Churchill permits a few questions afterwards. An earnest Protestant clergyman of liberal persuasion asks when this terrible conflict will be over. "I was often asked the same question in the States," Churchill replies with a smugly knowing smile. "I always asked in turn, 'When will the campaign in the Philippines be over?' My American questioner would answer, 'Just as soon as the Filipinos realize we are there to stay, and further resistance to our forces is useless.' And that is exactly the situation in South Africa."

At the end of the performance, the ovation rocks the theatre. While most of the audience rises to its feet, Zoë and Émilie remain seated.

An usher brings their fur coats, and they prepare to leave. Not caring if she's overheard in the neighbouring box, Émilie declares loudly, "Mr. Churchill certainly has a high opinion of himself. I've never heard so much self-congratulation in a public speaker. I hope you'll tell that to Wilfrid." Of course she says it in French, not expecting the audience members nearby to understand.

Snowflakes drift through the dark looming elms as Albert Kilrea's carriage, fitted with runners, sweeps up the winding drive to Rideau Hall. The Mintos have planned a small informal Christmas party, twenty or so guests to meet and mingle with visitors from abroad staying with them over the holidays.

The Lauriers and the Lavergnes face each other on the carriage seats. It's an old tradition of theirs, dating back to early times in Arthabaska, to do something together on Christmas Eve. In years past they attended midnight Mass with family and friends at St-Christophe, sharing a hearty full-course meal afterwards at one or another of their homes. In Ottawa the customs are sadly different, Zoë thinks.

Mr. Churchill is among the vice-regal house guests, and Émilie insists he'll be the least interesting. She's looking forward to meeting the Mintos' other visitors, especially the American artist Charles Dana Gibson, whose Gibson Girls appear in *Life*, and the rising young Scottish MP Ian Malcolm, surely destined to become a far more important politician than Churchill.

To Zoë's mind it's very like Émilie to admire the Gibson Girls: those impossibly haughty, imperious visions of the New Woman, whose wasp waists and long necks and casually piled hair make them look as superior as they are beautiful. They're what Émilie would aspire to be if she were a generation younger.

"My dear," Wilfrid says, inclining his head toward Zoë, "tell Émilie and Joseph what you heard this afternoon."

She's glad of the chance to relay her prize piece of gossip. "Well, it's no secret why Mr. Churchill is staying with the Mintos. Mrs. Chadwick told me over cards. It seems one of the guests is a young Englishwoman named Pamela Plowden. Churchill has been pursuing her for ages, and now he's pursued her all the way here. According to Mrs. Chadwick, he's already proposed unsuccessfully, but he's not giving up."

"Perhaps he'll have better luck in Our Lady of the Snows," Wilfrid remarks. "Miss Plowden may be feeling homesick and give in."

Émilie remains silent. Joseph chuckles: "You don't approve of these aristocrats, do you, dear?"

Émilie's hands stir impatiently inside her fox-fur muff. "I couldn't care less what aristocrats do with each other when they're alone. It's their condescension I don't like. I can't tolerate the way the Mintos invite their rich friends to visit, then have the locals over as an afterthought. It's no way to treat the Prime Minister of Canada."

Wilfrid smiles into the darkness. Zoë doesn't need to turn and see his face: she can sense it.

The Mintos' idea of informality is liveried footmen, ballroom gowns, black tie and tails. They're great believers in adherence to protocol. Gone is the Aberdeens' custom of inviting large sections of the citizenry to Rideau Hall for levees or skating parties, even buffet dinners. But from the moment Zoë steps out of the carriage, she can see tonight's affair will be more festive than usual. Enormous holly wreaths imported from England hang from the brightly lit portico. She can hear female laughter—Lady Minto herself?—and the sharp scrape of ice skates from the outdoor rink around the corner. Lady Minto is a superb skater, better at figures than most Ottawans.

"We should have brought our skates," Wilfrid says lightheartedly, forgetting that he likes skating as much as he likes walking.

As the maids take their coats, Zoë sees Émilie is wearing a stunning new gown, black crêpe de chine over cerise satin. It makes her wish she'd overcome her frugal instincts and bought something new for the occasion.

Informed the Lauriers have arrived, Lord Minto strides out to greet them personally: something he'd normally never do. The Governor General looks flushed, exhilarated. He wipes his waxed military moustache with the back of his hand. In place of his customary punctilious manner, the high spirits of a younger and freer man reign.

His Excellency grabs Zoë by the arm, as if it's a great lark, and escorts her down the long corridor, inquiring how she likes the new décor. He and Polly have recently redecorated, adding a new wing at the rear. With all their children and constant house guests, they simply had to have more bedrooms. At the moment Polly is out on the rink with her teacher, the world skating champion Mr. Meagher, but she'll be anxious to come in now that the Prime Minister has arrived. This rings true to Zoë: Lady Minto is clearly taken with Wilfrid, given to seeking his views on every subject.

Minto continues on the subject of the renovations. "We couldn't have left the place the way we found it, good heavens, no. The establishment was too awful, all dreary chintz and mournful colours. Polly had to redo everything, including the flowerbeds. We even found a portrait of Gladstone in one of the bedrooms! I kept having visions of Lady Aberdeen emerging from under a sofa."

His latest brainchild, Minto confides to Zoë, is for a much grander official residence to be built on Nepean Point, near Parliament Hill, with a splendid view of the Ottawa. Rideau Hall, meanwhile, could be converted into a National Portrait Gallery. Zoë has to restrain herself from telling him how close this comes to Lady Aberdeen's own vision.

"Of course we had to get rid of the Aberdeens' Haddo Club"—
he pronounces it with great distaste—"a glorified debating society where the cook and the butler were the equal of their master
and encouraged to best him in argument. I assure you, Lady Laurier, the servants at Rideau Hall now know their place!"

They arrive at the Large Drawing Room. Attentive waiters
weave their way among the guests, offering trays of delicacies and
champagne. Three enormous pine trees lit from top to bottom
with candles stand before the tall windows overlooking the snow-
covered terrace and gardens. Skaters in toques glide past outside.
The ADCs are out there too, Minto says mischievously, so Polly
and Mr. Meagher won't get lonesome.

Zoë sees another reason, besides the champagne, why His
Excellency is acting so boyish. Lola Powell is at the piano, hair
streaming over the shoulders of her black velvet dress. She's surrounded by the Minto children—a juxtaposition Zoë finds distinctly odd—as well as three of the Ritchie sisters, the young lady
who writes a social column for the *Ottawa Free Press*, and the ubiq-
uitous Messrs. King and Harper. To Miss Powell's heavy-handed
accompaniment, the group is singing "O Come All Ye Faithful."

A waiter equips the Lauriers and Lavergnes with champagne
while the Governor General launches them on a round of introductions. Mr. Reuter, scion of the European telegraph empire, is
pleasantly ingratiating. Mr. Baring, of the great London banking
family, is supercilious. Mabel Evans, a young heiress from Buffalo
whose husband is nowhere to be seen, is touchingly earnest and
idealistic, eager to use her fortune to become a patroness of the
arts. Zoë approves: she likes Mrs. Evans and says she herself has
found it immensely gratifying to launch aspiring artists into the
world. Mr. Gibson, an artist who needs no such assistance, is gallant and handsome, as befits his creations. Zoë is sorry to learn
he's not accompanied by his wife, the celebrated Irene Langhorne

of Virginia, said to be his favourite model, whom Wilfrid was eager to meet.

Eventually they come to Pamela Plowden, reclining on a sofa and cradling a glass of champagne in gloved fingers. She's conversing not with Mr. Churchill but his fellow MP, Mr. Malcolm. Miss Plowden is exquisitely slim in a gown of rich white satin embroidered with diamond sequins, and she smiles vivaciously at the Lauriers and Lavergnes in turn. Mr. Malcolm jumps to his feet: charming and clever, he begins making spirited conversation with Wilfrid about the Queen's illness and the German naval build-up.

But Zoë and Émilie have eyes only for Miss Plowden. Her reputation as one of the most beautiful young women in England is amply justified. Émilie quizzes Miss Plowden about her impressions of Canada. Like so many well-born English visitors, she's enchanted by winter. Not that she can skate or ski like the Mintos, but she absolutely adores watching others do it in the woods of Rockcliffe Park. If it weren't for the extreme cold, she could easily picture living in Canada, at least for a year. Such a marvellous contrast to India, where she grew up.

"Where, if I may ask, is Mr. Churchill?" The vehemence behind Émilie's question makes Zoë nervous.

"Just over there," Miss Plowden says lightly, with a graceful nod of her head. "Winston seems to prefer his own company this evening."

Zoë glances in the direction of the nod. Young Churchill is sitting by himself in a corner near one of the Christmas trees, gloomily smoking a cigarette in a long ivory holder.

Mackenzie King abruptly materializes in their midst, without Mr. Harper for once, his round face beaming like a puppy's. He's already put himself on conversational terms with Miss Plowden and eyes her hungrily, although Zoë understands he has a crush

on young Lady Ruby, the Mintos' dewy-eyed middle daughter—
an impossible match.

King has overheard them mentioning Churchill. "His address
last night made a great impression." There's a fawning note of awe
in his voice. "I went backstage to meet him and found him tallying
the box office receipts with the manager. He seemed very pleased
with 'the take,' as he called it. And he was very genial toward *me*. We
made an appointment to meet this morning at the Russell House.
When I got there, he was sitting in the café drinking—not coffee
or tea, ladies—*champagne*. At eleven in the morning! I can tell you,
I was taken aback. Not exactly our custom here, Miss Plowden."

Zoë, who has become quite fond of Mr. King, doesn't want
him to appear too much the callow colonial. And she wishes he
would take his eyes off Miss Plowden's shimmering bosom.

Zoë starts to say something, but Émilie interrupts. "Well,
Mr. King, since you and Mr. Churchill have met, perhaps you'll
introduce us to him."

Anxious to be of service, King leads them to Churchill's corner
where he's communing with a snifter of brandy and soda. With
glowering reluctance he rises, stubbing out his cigarette in an
ebony ashtray. King makes the introductions, and Zoë wonders
at Churchill's manners: he could certainly act more like a gentleman. Noting that Miss Plowden has remained behind, she intuits
what has happened between the two of them.

Churchill becomes cordial on realizing he's being introduced
to the Prime Minister's wife. Smiling with his mouth only, he
looks down at Zoë from hooded, slightly bloodshot eyes. She has
the impression he'd bolt from the room if given half a chance. His
nod to Émilie, accompanied by the word "Charmed," is dismissive.

King is pleased to announce he and Churchill have something
in common. "When Mr. Churchill was in South Africa, the Boers
put a price on his head. And after the rebellion in Upper Canada,
the Crown put a price of a thousand pounds on the head of my

grandfather, William Lyon Mackenzie." He grins like the Cheshire Cat.

"Is that so?" Churchill says, mildly amused. "Then your grand-father must have been a far more important chap. The Boers only put twenty-five quid on *my* head."

To a question from Zoë about his tour, Churchill gives a revealing reply: in America the houses have been far less lucrative than on his tour of Britain. Zoë is surprised by his frankness but likes his willingness to poke fun at himself: "One night in the States, there was no public lecture at all. Instead I was hired out for forty pounds to perform at a party, like a conjuror." He was also invited to dinner at the State Mansion in Albany by Vice-President-elect Roosevelt, "an overbearing man, of obnoxiously pro-Boer sentiments."

Churchill much prefers Canada. He looks forward to Montreal and Toronto and the last leg of his visit, a journey by train through the frozen wilderness to Winnipeg. He intends to go to the Hudson's Bay Company and buy one of those marvellous raccoon coats with an enormous collar before returning to England.

Émilie clears her throat, drawing everyone's attention. "We all enjoyed your lecture last night, Mr. Churchill, but I've been wanting to ask: what, in your opinion, gives Britain the right to be fighting in South Africa in the first place?"

Churchill fixes her with a cold reptilian stare, and Zoë feels an uncomfortable tightness in her chest. "The right, madame? Not the right, surely—the *obligation*."

"You feel an obligation to steal the Boers' land?"

"As long as the Boers feel an obligation to persecute our citizens, we have no choice. By the way, I don't regard it as theft. How did the Boers get their territory in the first place? And how is that any different from what you did in Canada? You 'stole' the place from the Indians, did you not?"

"That was the doing of the British."

"Oh? I was under the impression it was the doing of the French, originally."

So far Churchill has kept his good humour, relatively speaking: easier, perhaps, since he's scored a point or two. But Émilie refuses to drop her argument.

"As hard as I tried, I didn't hear a single reason last night why we Canadians should be sacrificing our sons in South Africa."

"Madame, that's not for me to comment on. It was a decision by your government and your Prime Minister, who I notice is standing nearby. Perhaps you should ask *him*. I'm just glad the Canadians are there."

"When we agreed to send troops, we didn't know about your concentration camps. We had no idea you intended to persecute the innocent. To treat Boer women and children like animals."

"Good heavens," Churchill retorts, no longer masking his irritation, "Boer women and children are scarcely innocent: they're enemy combatants. They feed and shelter and aid and abet their husbands and fathers, so they can go back out on the veldt and kill British soldiers—and Canadians too, while they're at it."

"Needless to say, they wouldn't have to if you weren't invading their country."

"See here, madame. Those Boer families are far safer under the protection of the British Army. Their own men use them as decoys and shields. I'm afraid you have no knowledge whereof you speak." Émilie tries to reply, but Churchill cuts her off. "Moreover, Boer children in the camps are now going to be educated by qualified teachers from throughout the Empire, including Canada. We shall do our enemies the favour of teaching their children the glories of the English language. We shall raise their level of education and instill in them a few decent, civilized notions, so they can take their place in the modern world instead of living in dark realms of moral ignorance and religious superstition."

The rising anger in Churchill's voice makes Zoë extremely uncomfortable. It also attracts Wilfrid's attention: immediately he comes over to join them. She sees the alarm and annoyance in his eyes, which move between Churchill and Émilie. King introduces the two men, and Churchill declares he's honoured to meet the Prime Minister.

"A pleasure, Mr. Churchill. And how have you been enjoying our Canadian hospitality?"

"Enormously, Prime Minister, thank you." Churchill's eyes are hooded once more. "Until just a moment ago, actually. You have a splendid land, a great Dominion. But I'm afraid I'm beginning to weary of the sound of my own voice. Madame Lavergne has kindly given me another reason to do so."

There's a commotion at the side entrance. Lady Minto enters with rosy cheeks from the terrace, chatting brightly, trailing an assortment of handsome young men. She's enveloped in a simple, full-length mink coat, her hair piled like a Gibson Girl's under a fashionable mink hat fastened with a diamond brooch. Lady Minto halts abruptly to survey the room. Her retinue stops behind her, awaiting her pleasure. She nods brusquely to her husband, who has joined the carollers around Miss Powell, but when her eyes settle on Wilfrid, her severely beautiful face lights up, transformed.

Feeling all the room's energy shift to this new focus, Zoë is devoutly grateful. Wilfrid's arm encircles hers as he leads her away from Émilie to pay their respects to Her Excellency.

13

Winter - Spring 1901

The Queen is dead.

Émilie feels shaken. Her response surprises her: she's never felt any particular admiration for Victoria, much less affection. Yet a fundamental part of her existence has vanished. All her life she's known no other sovereign on the throne of the Empire of which, for better or worse, she's a citizen. She doubts she'll like singing "God Save the King."

Victoria's era closes twenty-one days after the official start of the new century, as if Her Majesty had decreed she wanted nothing more to do with it. In Ottawa the Parliament Buildings are draped in swags of black, creating a grim contrast with the surrounding expanse of fresh snow. Stores and homes immediately follow suit, setting a bust or portrait of the Queen in their windows, framing it against a backdrop of black crepe.

The mourning period lasts well into February, casting a pall over the social season. The balls and teas and skating parties that make the long Ottawa winter bearable have to be suspended. At the opening of the new Parliament, ladies are expected to follow Zoë's example and wear black, including a thick veil to hide the face as completely as some follower of Mohammed. The only place where merriment prevails, ironically, is Rideau Hall: the Mintos continue inviting the usual stream of aristocratic or merely rich house guests from London and New York, ushering them outside to go skiing and skating, while the rest of society sits gloomily indoors.

Just as mourning ends, Joseph's promotion arrives. It's a far more devastating blow. The fact that he insists on regarding it as a piece of rare good fortune makes it all the more intolerable.

Returning from his chambers in a state of elation, Joseph calls Émilie into the parlour to announce he's being transferred to the Provincial Court in Montreal. He takes up his position in three months. It's a signal honour, if somewhat overdue, in his opinion: belated recognition of his years of faithful service in Hull. As he starts to enumerate the advantages of moving to Montreal, his usually sad and subdued face is positively radiant. But he has a struggle to remain enthusiastic, confronted by his wife's increasingly obvious distress.

Just think of it, he says, voice straining, their income will go up considerably, along with their social standing. They'll be able to live in a French-speaking milieu, enjoy a more sophisticated and congenial society. For Émilie there will be new realms to conquer: at last she'll be able to host a genuine literary *salon*, since all the authors of any consequence are in Montreal. Gabrielle will be able to choose from a wider pool of eligible young men. They'll be nearer Armand: surely that will make her happy. And they owe it all to Wilfrid, dear Wilfrid, who never ceases looking out for their interests. . . .

Excusing herself, Émilie rushes upstairs to the bathroom. She locks the door and weeps uncontrollably.

Oh yes! Dear Wilfrid looking out for their interests! As always he's only looking out for his own. And as always he has a sadly mistaken idea of what they are.

Pulling her handkerchief from her sleeve, Émilie dabs at her nose, examines her eyes in the mirror. The lower rims are an angry red. After the shock comes rage: it infuriates her to think of all she's done for him over the years. Without her devoted efforts, where would he be today? But he won't admit that, won't accept that his rise to power isn't entirely of his own making, that at one time he simply lacked the ambition to succeed so brilliantly, lacked even the imagination. She gave him both. He was happy enough then to take her offerings and appropriate them, adopting them as his own. She asked nothing in return. And now this. This is how he shows his so-called love.

Reluctantly she realizes that if she's going to avert complete disaster, she must set her anger aside, must calm herself and think clearly. Her future depends on it. She returns to the parlour. Joseph is pacing anxiously, tugging at the ends of his moustache.

He rushes to her side. "Are you unwell, my dear?"

"Perfectly fine, thank you. Just cramps." She sits down. "Joseph, we must discuss this matter, you and I, must think it through together. Your appointment is marvellous, of course, a great tribute, a feather in your cap. But let us ask ourselves: is moving to Montreal the right thing to do? For us and our family?"

His expression turns from concern to bewilderment. "I can't imagine why it wouldn't be. . . ." Émilie hates it when he looks like that: befuddled, thick. How could anyone ever attribute to him the wisdom of a judge?

"You mentioned Bielle. Don't forget, she's being courted by that nice civil servant, what's his name—he has a good job in the Senate. When he receives that promotion he's expecting, he'll ask for her hand, I'm sure of it. If we leave Ottawa now, we'll ruin her prospects. How can we do that to her?"

Joseph raises his eyebrows. "I admit, I hadn't thought of that. But my goodness, there are plenty of other promising young men. And if M. Prudhomme is serious in his intentions, he won't let this stop them. He'll get on the train to Montreal and propose to her there."

Émilie ignores this, racing on, not even sure what argument she'll make next. "And what of Armand? It doesn't matter to him whether we're in Montreal or Ottawa, we're still far from Quebec City. As for you and me, Joseph—I don't know." She pauses pensively: a dramatic touch. "What makes you think we'd even be happy in Montreal? We're so nicely settled here. We have this charming little home, this pleasant life. We have good friends, and all the prestige we need, really: invitations to Rideau Hall, the opening of Parliament, the Prime Minister's residence. Does Montreal offer anything better than that?"

Joseph stares at her. "But my dear, you're always saying we haven't enough money. Not enough to live as we should, at any rate. Now we will. The extra thousand will make all the difference."

"Really, Joseph! Do you actually think money is so important to me? It's scarcely worth turning our lives upside down for another thousand."

Joseph falls silent. The light has vanished from his eyes. He looks at the floor and coughs, but not to clear his throat in order to speak. He has nothing further to say, no more arguments to offer. He knows very well what his wife really means.

Émilie hasn't visited Zoë in weeks, but as it happens they've planned to have tea the next day, and she resolves to make the most of it. She wonders what her reception will be.

She finds her friend in the morning room, feeding soft-centred chocolates to the Pomeranians. There are two of them now: Zoë considers them good company for each other amid all the cats and birds. The newer dog barks incessantly at Émilie. She wants to strangle it.

Now that the days are growing longer, the sun rising higher in the sky, the cluttered room is flooded with light even at three in the afternoon. The canaries serenade each other noisily from their cages. Zoë calms the dog, shoos it into the hallway, shuts the door, compliments Émilie on her dress. The maid brings tea and sugar biscuits, setting the tray on the little round table between their chairs.

Zoë knows all about Joseph's appointment, of course. She's even anticipated this is what Émilie wants to discuss. She brings it up without prompting, and with seemingly genuine sympathy: "You must be terribly upset. Is it very strange, preparing to leave for Montreal?"

"To be honest, I haven't even begun to prepare. I haven't offered the house for sale. I don't want to think about it. I simply dread the idea."

"But as you've said before, Montreal is a wonderful city! Don't you think you'll be happy, you and Joseph, once you've moved?"

Émilie glares at her. "Try putting yourself in my place. If you had to go and live there now, how would you feel, leaving your home and familiar surroundings and all your old friends?"

Zoë gives a delicate shrug. "I did that when I left Arthabaska to come here."

"Yes, but now? We've become creatures of the capital, you and I. We belong here."

"I always think we belong wherever our husbands are."

Despairing, Émilie adopts a different tack. "Gabrielle isn't getting any younger. She's become very fond of that young M. Prudhomme, you know, and their courtship is going so well, but now this move will *ruin* it. Why don't men stop and think about the others in their family!"

"I've often thought the same thing."

Émilie broaches a question that has nagged her for weeks. "Zoë, tell me honestly. You know Wilfrid better than anyone—"

"Oh. You think so?"

"—and truly I need to know: is he doing this because he's angry with me?"

Zoë looks mystified. "Angry? About what?"

"Because I embarrassed him."

"When?"

"When I—when we were at Rideau Hall, at Christmas. In front of the Mintos. When I made my little assault on Churchill."

"Oh, that." Zoë frowns. "It's true Wilfrid was upset at the time. But you know how he is, he gets over things."

Émilie isn't sure how to take this. "I can't help feeling I'm being punished."

"Sometimes we think we're the cause of things when we aren't. Sometimes things happen for other reasons."

"And in this case?"

"Wilfrid and the cabinet believe Joseph is an outstanding judge. They think he deserves the promotion."

Émilie has to blink back tears of frustration. "It can't be *that* simple! And how important is some court appointment compared to the friendship among us four? Zoë, we've *always* been together. Now we're going to lose everything we've had all these years, everything we've known and shared. I'll be separated forever from the two dearest friends I've ever had. It's unjust. Horrible!"

Zoë reaches across the table, taking Émilie's slim hard hand in her plump soft one. "There, now, it's not so bad. We'll still have our friendship. We'll still see each other when we can, won't we? You'll be like our other old friends in Montreal—like the Davids."

We'll be *nothing whatsoever* like the Davids, Émilie wants to cry out. But she knows she shouldn't be expecting help from Zoë, shouldn't be expecting anything. She's mad to look for sympathy from a woman whose interests are diametrically opposed to her own. Who, when it comes right down to it, is her enemy. And yet there's no one else.

"Zoë, I know we've had our differences over the years, you and I. You've certainly earned the right to hate me—"

"Émilie! I've never—hated you."

"No, you're above hatred, aren't you? I wonder why." She falls into a miserable silence, then rallies her remaining strength. "I have just one request. Please tell me you'll consider it. As an old friend."

Still pressing her hand, Zoë says, "Of course."

"Will you ask Wilfrid, for all our sakes, to reconsider Joseph's appointment? Try and find him some other position? So we can remain here?"

Although Zoë nods, her expression is doubtful. "Yes. All right. It won't hurt to ask."

Émilie feels numb with humiliation. "I shouldn't be asking you this, I know. I just can't bear to be sent away. To be exiled."

Zoë's pupils dilate, glittering with what Émilie at first takes for tears of sympathy—or is it only her bad eyesight? Or something more malevolent. "It's a shame you can't just stay here and let Joseph go to Montreal by himself. He could return home on weekends to be with you. Oh, but such possibilities aren't given to us, are they, my dear?"

If Zoë intervenes on her behalf, Émilie never knows it. A week goes by, then another, and spring shows signs of arriving. The imposing snowbanks along the sidewalk outside her door melt down to low, blackened ridges flecked with grit. Finally only one court of appeal remains.

She takes the streetcar to Parliament Hill, the same route Wilfrid takes every day. Walking up the pavement to the East Block entrance, she arrives shortly before eleven o'clock. She's wearing a new dress from Paris and a feathered hat that always makes her feel special, powerful. She hasn't made an appointment because she doesn't want him to be forearmed: she needs the advantage of surprise.

The uniformed guard has no idea who she is and asks if she has an appointment. She says yes. He telephones the Prime Minister's office, and when cousin Ulric comes out, he acts amused to see her, the young fool. Using all the tact and charm she can muster, she asks for a few minutes of the Prime Minister's time.

Ulric goes to inquire if Sir Wilfrid has room in his schedule. While Émilie waits on a bench, the guard, realizing he's been lied to, glowers and plays irritably with his pencil. If Wilfrid refuses to see her, she'll simply stay here, wait him out. He mustn't underestimate her determination. She no longer cares about propriety, about embarrassing him again. Too much is at stake.

After an agonizing delay, Ulric returns to say the Prime Minister will see her now. She's startled: she expected to be turned down. Ulric escorts her along the high-ceilinged corridor with its distressing odour of floor wax and opens the last door, stepping aside to let her enter.

Looking up from his desk, Wilfrid is unsmiling, unhurried, unsurprised. He tells Ulric to leave them. He rises slowly, coming around the desk to stand before her. No kiss on the cheek, no touching of hands, only a bow of the head.

"I've been expecting you. I thought you'd seek me out at home."

"There's more privacy here."

"Émilie, judicial appointments are a cabinet decision—"

"Oh come, Wilfrid! Don't take me for a fool! Your cabinet won't overrule you. You get what you want."

"The recommendation for Joseph's appointment came from the entire Quebec caucus. It was unanimous. Everyone thinks he's the ideal candidate to fill the vacancy in Montreal."

"Surely there were other deserving candidates."

"None as deserving as he."

"That's absurd!" She's surprised by her own ferocity.

Wilfrid looks grimly at her. "You underestimate Joseph. You always have. He has many fine qualities. I'm told by those who have studied the matter that his legal judgments are impeccable, his reasoning irreproachable. He's a good man and a good Liberal. He's served his country in Parliament and on the bench, and his time has come."

"And mine along with it?"

"A man has only one career. If he makes the best of it, he deserves to be rewarded."

Émilie feels her knees quaking. She's afraid they're going to buckle under her. "Excuse me, I must sit." She lowers herself into a green leather chair, which must be Ulric's when he takes dictation.

"There's something else," Wilfrid says. He doesn't move but remains towering above her, and she realizes he's more thoroughly prepared for this conversation than she. "When a man in public life is honoured with a promotion, when his country shows its esteem by giving him new responsibilities, his wife's duty is to be by his side. To rejoice in his distinction and share in his happiness."

"Her *duty*? You have a cheek, instructing me on my obligations! Was I obliged to tutor you in the ways of the world when you were a greenhorn lawyer? Was it my duty to improve your table manners and your English conversation? My God, Wilfrid, if we all did nothing but our duty, the world would never change! We'd all just mind our manners and keep our places and be swept along by the will of others, the way *Zoë* is. Is that what you expect of me? To be an obedient little Zoë, grateful for whatever you decree?"

His expression becomes even colder. "You have no right to insult Zoë. She acts of her own free will. She does what she believes is right."

"Which is what you believe is right."

"Zoë has a mind of her own. You underestimate *her*, too."

"I'm glad to hear it."

He leans down to drive his words home, and it feels like an assault: "As you know better than anyone, I speak with some authority about obeying the claims of duty. I've sacrificed much to duty, even more than you realize, but I've gained more in the bargain. And I have *no regrets.*"

The last statement hurts her more than anything he's said. Meanwhile she hasn't even made her case. She stands again, to be closer to his level. "Never mind these high-flown principles, Wilfrid, what about ordinary consideration? Simple decency? Did you think you could discard me without even speaking to me?"

"I'm not discarding you."

"Why do you *hate* me? What harm have I ever done to you?"

He takes her hands in his, squeezing them hard. His voice drops, turns rich with feeling: "Émilie, how could I ever hate you? You've been my dearest, most important friend. As I've been yours."

"Then why are you casting me out?"

"Your question is based on a false assumption."

"Stop talking like a lawyer, Wilfrid. This isn't a test of logic, it's about two hearts, two souls. You're fond of Shakespeare: 'Love is not love Which alters when it alterations finds.'"

Hesitating, he replies: "'O no! it is an ever-fixed mark That looks on tempests and is never shaken.'"

She sees from his eyes that she's reached him. "'Love alters not with his brief hours and weeks, But bears it out even to the edge of doom.'"

"The edge of doom. Is that where we've arrived?"

"What else can I think?"

"Montreal is hardly doom. It's only a couple of hours away. I'll be going there, you'll be coming here, it will be a new arrangement, that's all. In time it will seem normal."

"Arrangement? Normal? The arrangements are bad enough now, they've been bad for years—always seeing each other from a distance, through the wrong end of the telescope. But this is far worse. Montreal isn't even visible from here." Saying this fills her with despair. Speaking the truth makes it undeniable. She's taken a scalpel, exposed the cancer that's been there all the time, underneath the skin. "If you don't hate me, why are you sending me away? What are you gaining?"

"Personally, I gain nothing. Quite the opposite: I lose. But Montreal gains a first-rate justice. And you, my dear, I'm sure you'll gain something too, in time."

"Don't mock me, Wilfrid. It's cruel."

"It's not mockery, it's fate. We have to accept it. Come now, think of all your dear friends in Montreal who will be delighted to have you back. Think of the Pacauds, the Davids—"

There they are again: the bloody Davids. She sees it clearly now. He and Zoë have colluded in this, have united against her, and now they're retreating together in triumph into the fortress of their marriage, laughing.

With a swift, efficient motion, she removes her right glove and slaps him hard across the cheek. It produces a satisfying *crack*. The sound of snapping a dry limb from a tree that's already dead.

A story is making the rounds, a kind of joke. A man desperate for employment travels to Ottawa to see the Prime Minister. He reminds him of the government job Wilfrid promised him a year ago, and the previous year, and the year before that. "Oh, did I promise you?" Wilfrid asks. "Well, then, I promise it still."

Only, as Émilie happens to know, it's not a joke.

She's going through her closets, weeding out dresses and hats and shoes and petticoats she no longer wants, candidates for the St. Luke's rummage sale. She still manages to fill three steamer trunks with clothes worth taking to Montreal. As she folds them and packs them away, she contemplates another story she's just heard, an even less humorous one: a bizarre incident, astonishing for Ottawa, or anywhere.

It seems a certain Member of Parliament, a bachelor who fancies himself a Beau Brummell, has had his career as a ladies' man cut grievously short. At one time, the MP's reputation was so notorious that some injured husbands put up money to print a pamphlet exposing him as a skirt chaser and adulterer. Émilie has to admit, she can find nothing particularly criminal in his behaviour. After all, if the gentlemen's wives hadn't been so compliant, they'd have had nothing to complain about. Nor is there anything unusual about the MP's habit of pursuing all the young women he can find at Russell House receptions: he only succeeds in making himself look ridiculous. He's no longer young, after all, even if he does dance with exuberance and style.

But recently the MP made the mistake of fancying the beautiful, bored young wife of a prominent society doctor. Evidently he was successful in pressing his attentions on the lady, whose husband too often left her home alone during his travels. Growing suspicious of his wife, the doctor announced he was going away to Toronto for several days, but instead returned home late at night, carrying surgical instruments in his leather bag. Letting himself silently into the house, he crept upstairs in the darkness.

In her imagination, Émilie dwells lingeringly on what happened next. The amorous couple caught in the bedroom *in flagrante delicto*. The quick and unexpected application of the chloroform-soaked cloth. The merciless *snip snip*, followed by the highly professional stitching operation, the hygienic mopping up. She pictures the wife conveniently exiting the scene by fainting.

The MP is so devastated that his confidence is completely destroyed, his career shattered. He disappears from Parliament and creeps away from the capital overnight. Émilie wonders why Justice Joseph Lavergne could never have felt strongly enough about his own wife or marriage or male honour to commit some equivalent act of outrage and vengeance, some parallel crime of passion, which the world would surely have considered amply justified. If only he'd had the courage, the self-respect—what a victory could have been his.

14

Autumn 1901

Zoë watches for him at the front window, opening the door as the streetcar rattles off down the tracks. From the moment he climbs the steps, leaning heavily on his walking stick, she knows something is wrong. His cheeks are pale, his lips. His eyes have an unaccustomed look: lowered. First they seek hers, then desperately evade them.

"What is it? What's happened?"

He shakes his head. "Very sad."

"Is it someone we love?"

"It's the President. Shot. This afternoon."

"My God." She crosses herself three times. "Poor dear Mrs. McKinley. How will she ever manage now?"

He goes slowly past her into the drawing room and drops into a chair. He's hatless, sweating. Summer is hanging on into September. "Why do the Americans keep doing this?" His voice is faint and hoarse, coming from far away. "Always their best. This makes three Presidents in our lifetime, and I've admired them all. McKinley is no Lincoln, but he's an honourable man, a good man at heart."

"And a good husband. I pray Mrs. McKinley wasn't there to see it."

"Apparently she was ill in bed."

"Thank the Lord. At least she didn't watch him die."

Wilfrid, who has been staring into space, swivels his gaze around. "He's not dead. The doctors are doing their best for him."

There were two shots, it seems, one bullet grazing the President's ribs. The other is lodged somewhere within the enormous frame. He was shaking hands with a lineup of well-wishers at the Pan-American Exposition in Buffalo, and the gunman lined up patiently with the rest of them: an immigrant of some sort, an admirer of Emma Goldman, who has come under suspicion as author of an anarchist plot to kill the President.

"The man had his right hand bandaged, hiding a pistol." Zoë feels sick, imagining all the hands extended toward *him* over the years, and all the hands to come, groping for him, clutching at his flesh, greedy with presumed innocence and secret desire, eager to invade his being. "Teddy Roosevelt has rushed from the Adirondacks to be at the President's side. So," Wilfrid adds, with a sigh of resignation, "let us pray he survives."

For a moment Zoë does pray, even though she knows Wilfrid intends the phrase metaphorically.

"I've been counting on McKinley, believing in his good will and sense of fair play. I was sure he and I could reach agreement on Alaska, if only we were left alone by Congress and the Foreign Office. Lord Minto is right: if this dispute were a private affair, two reasonable men could settle it in five minutes. And the President and I are reasonable men. We'd get a Pacific port and a corridor to the Yukon and it would put an end to all the rumours of an American coup up there. You realize what happens if the President dies?"

"Mr. Roosevelt succeeds him."

"And Mr. Roosevelt will simply negotiate by means of the U.S. Navy. A civilized friendship will be out of the question."

Zoë considers the black-and-white nature of this scenario. "It's natural to fear the worst. But perhaps you're being hasty. Perhaps Roosevelt isn't as crude as he pretends. Your sunny ways work well here, with all our religious and racial problems—why shouldn't they work with Washington too? No matter who the President is?"

He smiles wanly. "I appreciate your faith in me. And your optimism."

"I don't think I'm unduly optimistic. In the meantime I'll pray for President McKinley's soul and his complete recovery."

"Both at the same time? Just to be on the safe side?"

"Yes. And for Mrs. McKinley's happiness."

Eight days later the President dies of complications from gangrene, and Theodore Roosevelt is sworn in. The fatal bullet is never found. Although Thomas Edison sends one of his inventions, an X-ray machine, from his workshop in New Jersey, it isn't employed to locate the bullet. When she hears about this, Zoë is puzzled: perhaps the doctors didn't understand how to use it.

Emma Goldman is arrested but released for lack of evidence. The conspiracy talk widens to include Spanish Cubans enraged by America's victory in Cuba, and disgruntled Filipinos unable to accept progress, out to avenge the loss of their country. Surely there was some foreign involvement in the President's murder, some sinister breach of America's frontiers. Surely the hideously successful plot couldn't have sprung from the mind of a lone gunman, some deranged immigrant once welcomed to America's shores. . . .

Wary of the flailing of a wounded America's limbs, Wilfrid instructs his officials to conduct a discreet investigation. He wants to know if the assassin, a Russian Pole named Leon Czolgosz, ever spent time in Canada. The inquiry comes back negative. It emerges

Czolgosz was actually born in Michigan, grew up in Detroit. Zoë sees his photograph on the cover of a popular weekly magazine: Czolgosz peering like a wild animal between the bars of his cell, his face disfigured by a beating from the police. She finds it very like President McKinley that, as he fell, he cried out to his guards, "Don't let them hurt him!"

Czolgosz expresses no regret for his actions. Soon he will be put on trial, found guilty, executed in the electric chair. His coffin will be filled with sulfuric acid to speed his body's decomposition. Zoë tries to imagine whether people with such crazed notions exist in Canada. She banishes the thought: there's no space in her mind for it, particularly now, when Wilfrid is about to leave on a cross-country tour without her. He'll be exposed to large crowds every day for weeks.

The Duke and Duchess of Cornwall and York are coming for a much-anticipated royal visit. Both Wilfrid and Lord Minto have major roles to play in the heir to the throne's elaborately planned progress across the nation: Quebec City to Victoria, then back to Halifax. Wilfrid is upset that this means he can't attend President McKinley's funeral. He wants to pay his respects in person.

He also worries how the unintended slight will be perceived in Washington. He and the Governor General compose a long and eloquent letter of sympathy addressed to President Roosevelt, regretting America's tragic loss, explaining why imperial protocol demands their presence at home: some day, after all, the Duke will be King. They ask Joseph Pope for help in drafting the letter to ensure all the diplomatic nuances are captured. Wilfrid gladly adopts Lord Minto's suggestion to declare a national day of mourning for the slain President.

On the eve of his departure to meet the royals in Quebec City, Wilfrid unburdens himself of a different problem. Zoë can see it weighs heavily on his heart: as heavily, almost, as McKinley's death.

"Tarte has turned against me. I fear he badly misunderstands the state of things. Sooner or later I'll have to put an end to his scheming."

"What is Israël scheming now?"

Wilfrid's inner conflict distorts his features. He looks pained yet coldly adamant.

"He's been sounding the waters to test his popularity—among the English, oddly enough. Measuring his support in Ontario against the day I'm not around."

"I'm sure he's not the only one."

"He's one who should know better. But he thinks he knows something about me that others don't. All through our school years he watched me cough blood, saw my handkerchief run red with it. Ever since, he's believed my days are numbered."

"Really? Who has fought harder for you? Who delivered Quebec in two elections?"

Wilfrid sniffs dismissively. "You're right, he's been invaluable. But before that, who fought more fiercely *against* me? Don't forget, Israël Tarte was once the most rabid, dyed-in-the-wool Bleu in the province. Switching allegiance comes naturally to him. He has more colours than a chameleon. He likes to say, 'The man who never changed his mind never used his mind.'"

"But plotting against you? What proof do you have?"

A cynical smile plays briefly about his lips. "No big incontrovertible proof. Only small ones. They add up." She sees he enjoys playing this cat-and-mouse game: one of his less endearing traits. "Exhibit A—Israël has come to resent our program of settling the west. According to him, we're filling Manitoba and the Territories with 'worthless foreigners.' He's jealous of Sifton, angry he won't do more to encourage colonization from Quebec. Exhibit B—Israël uses his portfolio at Public Works to go around the country giving speeches and interviews in favour of protectionism, a new National Policy, knowing full well it runs counter to our position.

He's had the manufacturers in Toronto cheering him to the rafters. Now they're willing to forgive him everything, even his heresies during the war. It's pocketbook over principle. He thinks he can win over Ontario by appealing to industry, combine it with Quebec, and take the country. Let the west and the Maritimes lick their wounds, they haven't enough seats to make a difference."

Zoë doesn't entirely see the harm. "What if Israël is right? Wouldn't that give you another majority?"

"I haven't finished. Exhibit C—and this is the most damning—he's heard the same rumours about my medical symptoms as everyone else."

"Of course he has. Because you insist on exaggerating your symptoms and discussing them with every doctor you meet at a dinner party."

Wilfrid now believes he's contracted cancer. So far no physician agrees with him. It's strangely reminiscent of his insistence years ago on having consumption.

"You can't be too careful. In any case, physicians are supposed to keep their patients' information confidential. But Tarte has had his son-in-law, who studies medicine under Dr. Tessier, sound out the good doctor's opinion of my health and prospects, even though it's in violation of—"

Zoë interrupts. "Yes, Wilfrid—perhaps because Israël *cares* about you. He hopes to hear those nasty rumours proved wrong."

"Perhaps. And if they aren't, then he hopes to replace me. In the last campaign the Conservative newspapers asked, 'If Laurier wins, shall Tarte rule?' He's ready to rule."

He presents her with a look of zealous vindication, the advocate summing up his case before the bar. But she refuses to give him his guilty verdict. "I think you should wait and see, Wilfrid, before condemning Israël. Be careful before cutting off your own right hand."

He nods solemnly. "You're right, my dear. I couldn't agree more. As you know, I always proceed with caution. Even in cabinet I never play the dictator. People used to think I was too tolerant to run a government. They mistook my lack of personal resentments for a lack of will. Well, I won't rush to judgment this time either. And having reached my conclusion, I won't hesitate to act."

Wilfrid takes Joseph Pope with him to Quebec City. Pope has been labouring assiduously alongside Lord Minto's secretary, Major Maude, scheduling the arrangements for the royal tour. In the delicate matter of travelling with royals, Wilfrid considers Pope as indispensable as Sir John A. Macdonald did in other matters.

In company with Their Royal Highnesses and Lord and Lady Minto, Wilfrid and Pope share a special train equipped with every comfort, laid on by the CPR president, Lord Shaughnessy. Day after day they proceed across the nation, reviewing guards of honour at every stop, saluting military processions, visiting local beauty spots. Invariably they're welcomed by flower-decked triumphal arches and blaring brass bands, the speeches floridly loyal, the dinners hearty and indigestible.

Zoë is happy to remain home. She's spared the tedium of speechifying and the agony of having to be constantly gracious with complete strangers. All the same, she never stops worrying about Wilfrid: his safety, his stomach, his lungs. She's provided Joseph Mailhot with a satchel of powders, syrups and cordials to ward off every conceivable malady, as well as a trunk filled with Wilfrid's best clothing and ceremonial uniforms, and another trunk containing nothing but changes of bed linen, washed and aired at home, to defend his constitution against mould.

Meanwhile she gets on with doing good. Wilfrid calls her his Minister of Public Charity. Her methods are simple, eminently practical. If a recently bereaved widow needs a position as postmistress in a Quebec village, Zoë calls on the Postmaster General, Mr. Mulock, and the appointment is arranged. If a promising young soprano is invited to sing in Boston but lacks a passport, Zoë visits the appropriate deputy minister, and bureaucratic obstructions are removed. When one of Wilfrid's nieces or nephews requires tuition money or dental work or train fare, she takes care of the bill. When some deserving poet or painter, or the head of the Salvation Army Rescue Home, needs a wealthy patron, she arranges the necessary introductions.

Mackenzie King promises to attend her next musicale. She'll make sure he meets several young ladies of good family, any one of whom would make him an excellent wife. Mr. King is effusively grateful, as always, but so far hasn't followed up with any of the estimable girls Zoë has introduced to him. He never seems to take the next step. Zoë suspects the problem has something to do with Bert Harper. They go everywhere together, openly discussing how they delight in their evenings by the fire in their apartment, reading aloud from Emerson, Browning, Matthew Arnold and works of social betterment: above all, from Tennyson's *Idylls of the King*. They're fond of quoting Galahad's sublime pronouncement, "If I lose myself, I save myself!" Zoë must find a way to separate the devoted pair, to get Mr. King alone in a room with some irresistible female. There's so much to be done that sometimes she wishes Wilfrid would travel more often, freeing her from the time-consuming obligation of holding his dinner parties every week, and let her get on with the Lord's work.

Concurrently with the royal tour, Tarte is conducting his own tour of Ontario. The little man dashes from one industrial town to another, from Welland to Hamilton, Stratford to Berlin, North Bay to Peterborough, investigating cotton and woollen mills, inspecting foundries and carriage works, touring sausage and shoe factories. Before the workers at each stop, he extols in his heavily accented English the virtues and benefits of high tariffs. His stutter has almost vanished now. He receives municipal deputations, hearing to his great gratification echoes of his own hymns to protectionism as the high road to wealth.

In the small towns Tarte paints a rosy picture of a protected home market for farmers. In Toronto and Montreal he professes with the zeal of a convert his faith, and the faith of the Manufacturers' Association, in protectionism. In Bowmanville he drops all pretence of caution and admits his real ambition: jutting out his narrow chest, he declares that if he really *were* Master of the Administration, as the Conservatives love to call him, he would "take the tariff item by item and raise it, so as to keep for Canada the profits from her labour and resources, and in this way build up a real nation in this country."

English Canadians begin taking another look at Tarte. Apparently the talkative Frenchman isn't as black as he was painted. Just two years ago they were hanging and burning him in effigy. Now he seems to have smart ideas about improving their lives: more ideas, in fact, than the Prime Minister and his cabinet.

Wilfrid returns from the royal tour thoroughly exhausted. All across the continent he's been reading newspaper accounts of Tarte's one-man pilgrimage, supplemented by indignant letters: Sifton, Cartwright, Fielding and Mulock, free traders all, have penned their outrage over Tarte's self-serving, renegade pronouncements. Sifton has threatened to resign: if the party adopts Macdonald's discredited policy of protectionism, he warns, every Liberal west of Lake Superior will fight it, even at the cost of bringing down the government.

Wilfrid's mind is made up. The next morning, waving aside Zoë's entreaties to remain in bed, he goes directly to his office, summons his old friend and ally and demands his resignation. When Tarte tries to argue the political soundness of his proposals,

Wilfrid cuts him off. He says flatly he doesn't care: the issue isn't protectionism versus free trade, it's cabinet solidarity, loyalty to the leader, respect for the government of which Tarte is a member. If he'd wanted to change Liberal policy while remaining a minister, he should have persuaded his colleagues behind closed doors. As it is, he's championed a cause that deviates sharply from the government's position: a disloyal and unpardonable course. He has no choice but to leave the ministry.

Wilfrid doesn't mention that someone has reported overhearing Tarte make a fatal admission: "Laurier may be better loved, but I have the great interests behind me."

The letter of resignation is on Wilfrid's desk the next morning. The cabinet regroups, weakened in Quebec, but satisfied its integrity has been restored. The ministers clap each other on the back, heartened to be once again united and glad to be rid of the sharp-tongued little man with all his ideas and arrogance and moral superiority.

Wilfrid comes home grim-faced at losing Tarte, yet convinced it was necessary. Zoë takes his coat. She hugs him longer than usual.

"Politics is a strange business," she says softly. "Remember you told me once, 'So long as I have Tarte and Sifton with me, I shall be master of Canada.' And you're still master."

"Well," he replies, his tongue dry with fatigue, "I only have Sifton now."

Afterwards the phrase echoes in her mind. She applies it to their life: he only has Zoë now.

From time to time she wonders how Wilfrid feels about losing his Émilie. Even if it was by his own choice, he's lost her as surely as he's lost Tarte. It must be terribly hard for him. But she never asks.

To Zoë, Émilie's absence from Ottawa feels as tangible and overbearing as her presence: a perpetual, governing condition of her existence. At any moment, absence could be magically transformed into presence, and Émilie could be back from Montreal, as unavoidable as ever, renewing her claims on Wilfrid. And on her.

But one morning she wakes and realizes she hasn't thought of Émilie for days. She finds herself breathing more easily, sleeping more soundly. She gives up chocolates after dinner. With admiration and pleasure, Wilfrid observes that her English has improved, thanks to the constant practice that results from her willingness to go everywhere in society.

He too doesn't mention Émilie. Perhaps he's distracted by arguments with Britain. The Americans want Britain to agree to let them build a canal connecting the Atlantic to the Pacific through Panama. For months Wilfrid has been telling London that, as a condition for allowing the canal to proceed, there should first be a favourable settlement of the Alaska dispute. But now the British, anxious for good relations with Roosevelt, have ignored Wilfrid and signed a Panama Canal agreement with Washington. The Alaska boundary issue will go instead to a tribunal of "independent" jurists: a body stacked blatantly in Roosevelt's favour. The President not only carries a big stick, Wilfrid observes, but uses it on every possible occasion, on friend and foe alike.

For days he remains in a funk. But when his birthday arrives on November 20, he brightens, embracing life again: the life they share.

"Here I am at sixty!" he proclaims as they're dressing. An early snow dusts the maple branches outside their bedroom window. "For now I have my health, the best I've ever had, and there probably remain to me some worthwhile years. Wouldn't you say, my dear?"

"Oh, probably."

"Although clearly it's the beginning of the end." He grins boyishly under the whitening waves either side of his forehead. "Who knows, eventually I may regret having lived so long."

"You have to live long enough to read Willison's book about you."

The old Toronto ally insists on writing his biography now, while Wilfrid is still in office, rather than waiting until the story is complete. Willison wants to capture a sitting Prime Minister at the very height of his powers.

"He believes it will help the party win the next election. Writers are so vain, they always exaggerate their influence." Wilfrid knots his tie. "He thinks he's made me. All because I had to 'follow' his advice on South Africa."

"*His* advice?"

"I know, it's nonsense. Willison has such a talent for rubbing me the wrong way. He sent a note wishing me 'a good old age.' I replied I have no earthly desire to live to a good old age. As long as my health continues and I can work, I'm quite willing to live as long as Methuselah, but at the first sign of weakness, let Providence whisk me away! Nothing so sad as to survive oneself."

Zoë feels pleasure at hearing him talk this way: confident, self-assured, fearless. Émilie's ghost may not be exorcised, but it remains outside the room, outside the house even, shuddering in the gathering cold of another winter.

When she goes into his study to do a cursory tidying up of all the books and newspapers and documents lying about, she comes across a letter. Unlike his official letters, it's written in his own hand, not his secretary's, and on plain vellum paper instead of the stationery stamped "Office of the Prime Minister of Canada" encircling the coat of arms.

It appears to be a draft. He's scribbled it hastily, occasionally crossing out and replacing words. It's written in English. The fact that there's no salutation catches her eye. She reads on:

Though there is now a long distance between us, my dear friend, I do not, one single day, forget you. The friendship of the past has been too close to be followed by an absolute separation.

Separation there may be in one sense, and it is certainly one of the great misfortunes of my life. But in another sense, one can easily cross that space. Last month in Montreal I thought I saw you in the throng on that balcony at the Windsor Hotel. My eyes aren't what they used to be, so I wasn't sure. I hope they didn't deceive me.

The thought that preoccupies me now is how you are feeling in the new atmosphere that you breathe. May you be happy in that place! Many things will tend toward that end, above all your own admirable spirit. In one particular, at least, Montreal must be congenial to you. It is the city in which our country has reached its highest degree of intellectual development. I am sure you must find there a mental satisfaction that would not be obtainable anywhere else.

I was in Quebec City a week or so ago and sent word to your boy to come see me, which he did. I had a very pleasant interview with him. He is a fine boy, remarkably well informed about everything. I was surprised by the intellectual development he has already attained. But on certain things, his ideas are very much stuck. He is ready, should the opportunity occur, to throw the whole English population into the St. Lawrence.

I am not much concerned by those ferocious designs. Time and maturity will moderate them. But his anglophobia becomes more serious when he systematically refuses to speak or study English. The opportunity, once lost, will not recur, and some day he will be the first to deplore the narrow views he holds today. I have said this before, and hope you will not mind if I say it again: might you not change his mind and make him take up the study of English literature, which you yourself so admire?

I did not think it advisable to argue with him on that subject. He was in a contentious mood, and would have met all my arguments with increased fury. His soul is oppressed by the wrongs inflicted on his people by a race that, as he put it, has no business being here. I thought it just as well, at that moment, to let all his great indignation blow off. I felt the best thing was to call your attention to the problem, so that you may use your persuasive powers to show him the error of his ways. He can easily reach the top of his profession; this, however, he cannot do absolutely successfully unless he learns to jump indifferently from one language to the other, and to speak both with the same ease and accuracy.

Now what about your daughter? I saw her here just for an instant some weeks ago. She has simply developed into a full-blossomed rose. She must be great company for her mother, and it must cause you pain to reflect that, in time, daughters will be taken from their mother's side. It seems to me that I understand your grief—almost as you feel it yourself. I am aware that the wound is there, that nothing will heal it. Will you at least reconcile yourself to that unavoidable end, or will you fight it with all your energy and strength? My anxiety is to see you reach a place where the pain will be, if possible, less acute.

I have this great advantage: my life is a constant struggle and worry; all my energies have to be concentrated to perform the tasks before me, the difficulties of which increase every day.

Are you aware that I am now an old man? I have just crossed the last limit. The next one will be the end. It may be near, it may be far—probably far—but there it is, almost in sight: it is the law of nature. I should not complain, and I do not. I have every reason to be thankful to Providence. But I cannot help missing the good old times!

Goodbye, my ever dear friend. All blessings to you and your own.

Yours faithfully, W.L.

Zoë has been reading standing up, not holding the pages in her hand but leaning forward over the desk, staring down at the sheets filled with Wilfrid's fluid scrawl, his tall verticals. Now she sits, releasing her breath slowly. Sitting in his chair helps her to see and feel as he does.

Viewed from this angle, nothing in the letter really surprises her. The feelings all seem perfectly natural. What's jarring is reading exactly how he puts it into words for her. This is new.

The words are like a secret language, shared only by them. A code, signifying something mysterious, something else, something more: something different from what it appears to be. Even her improved English can't unlock it.

She hopes he's sent the final version.

1 5

December 1933

I promised I would return: as it happens, feeling considerably more sanguine now than when I began this narrative. More *alive*. Relating Zoë's and Émilie's stories, rather than my own, has helped restore some balance and coherence and meaning to a less than satisfactory life. If I lose myself, I save myself.

Those words are now carved on the statue of Sir Galahad erected to commemorate the "heroism" of hapless Bert Harper. The statue stands on Wellington Street directly in front of Parliament, erected at the instigation of Mackenzie King—with the approval of Sir Wilfrid Laurier—after Harper foolishly drowned under the ice of the Ottawa River, trying to rescue some doomed maiden.

According to the latest prognosis from my doctor, I too am doomed. It's a pity: but aren't we all? And at least I've outlived the others.

What does it matter, finally, if my health remains abysmal? What do I care if Hitler and Mussolini are dragging civilization down to wallow in the pigpen of history? Last night made up for all that. It was the crowning moment of my career, filling me with a giddy, secret pleasure, a fragile hope that we *Canadiens*, in our own corner of the New World, might yet build a society of light worthy of the God who put us here.

I still don't know how the tribute evening came about, whose idea it was. No one in "the movement" wants to tell me. At least they hope it will become a movement some day—at the moment it's only a small group of exuberant Quebec nationalists spontaneously assembled under the banner of "Jeune-Canada." Why they insist on using that debased name is beyond me, they who see themselves as the spiritual children of Papineau and Bourassa. Another paradox of this infuriating country.

But never mind. It touches me deeply that they also see themselves, if only a little, as the children of Lavergne.

One who has no children of his own can only feel grateful for this recognition of paternity. Last night, in the restaurant they'd reserved in Montreal's *vieux port*, the beef was tough but the wine plentiful and the speeches magnificent. Those young men were so passionate and eager, so full of energy and ambition and invention, so eloquently thoughtful and kind, that I couldn't believe what I was hearing. I had no idea the battles of my youth are still remembered, my ideals still held dear and worth fighting for. I experienced a kind of ecstasy.

The young lads, some just beginning their careers as lawyers and journalists, the rest still students or seminarians, have the good old *Patriote* blood flowing in their veins. They believe in the principles for which Bourassa and I fought so fiercely all our political lives. If they can't have their own country, they demand, as a bare minimum, a country where their language and religion are accepted and respected, where the government cannot send them or their sons to war at the command of a foreign power. They understand that these liberties aren't concessions from our English "masters" but God-given rights, prerogatives of a normal country, a real country, not a colony pretending to be a country.

As speaker after speaker praised the battles I fought for those rights, I almost wept. It was the wine, of course. I had to struggle to keep my eyes dry.

The most difficult part was being unable to speak more than a few words in thankful reply. These damned polyps on my vocal cords have made it impossible to talk much above a whisper. Among my Conservative colleagues in the House, I've become known as the silent MP: a contradiction in terms. So the days of my political life are numbered, no matter what happens to my natural life. But I managed to get this much out, loudly enough that everyone near me could hear: "If the years have passed, if I have grown old and my head has grown bald, the heart remains young, the soul serene, and the doctrine has not changed. I entrust to you young men tonight the ship I launched thirty years ago. May you bring it safely to port with the wind in its sails, saluted by cannon from the enemy's citadel!"

I doubt this old-fashioned homily adequately conveyed my gratitude, but it didn't matter. The young men know what I stand for.

What they don't know, can't know, is all the rest of it. And why writing it down now has provided me with a measure of salvation, of redemption for all the years of waste, unfulfilled promise, unachieved goals. The outright failure.

They can't know how, after doing everything I could to expose and torment Laurier over the years—condemning his hypocrisy on the language issue, unmasking his carnival of the corrupt and the corrupted, rejoicing in his government's defeat, mocking him as *"le vieux coq"*—I went to see him late one night in 1917, when practically all his English supporters had betrayed and deserted him.

Of course Laurier had been wrong in 1914 to support the Conservative government's declaration of war. He'd joined Robert Borden in obediently jumping into the trenches alongside the British, forgetting what he'd said years earlier about the vortex of militarism being the curse and blight of Europe. But three years of war and millions of unforgivable deaths later, Laurier finally remembered he had principles. He pulled himself onto his weary old legs and stood up in Parliament to defy Borden on conscription, flatly refusing to compel the sons of Quebec, or any province, to fight a war they don't believe in. The fact that he knew his principled stand would cost him most of his English-speaking MPs, who immediately flocked to Borden to share in the spoils of coalition government, made him, in my eyes, all the more doomed and courageous and admirable and truly heroic.

So on that bitterly cold December night shortly after his defeat in the conscription election, I went to the Lauriers' home in Ottawa unannounced. Lady Laurier opened the door, seeming unsurprised to see me. As warm and maternal toward me as ever, she showed me upstairs to the great man's study, where I found him sifting through the newspaper accounts of his election disaster.

The English papers were gloating over the landslide victory of Borden's Union government: for Laurier, a defeat of staggering proportions. In Quebec, on the other hand, he'd won all seats but three. Naturally he was exhausted, utterly spent. His cheeks were ashen and lined. At that point I hadn't seen him in a couple of years, and I was shocked by how much he'd aged. His face, although still formidable, had acquired a stiffness resembling the death mask that would be taken from it two years later.

"They cheered for me," he said, "but they didn't vote for me." He actually seemed glad I was there.

I didn't apologize for the years of attacking him verbally and in print. But I told him in no uncertain terms how much I admired him for fighting the imposition of conscription. He nodded: "The racial chasm this has opened may not be closed for generations." He told me that Bourassa, who by this time was editing our superb newspaper, *Le Devoir*, had sat exactly where I was sitting, just before the election, and assured him of his gratitude and full support. Of course, he remarked with irony but no apparent bitterness, that support had been used in English Canada to discredit and destroy him.

I didn't see Laurier again until he lay in his coffin. He rested at home for three days, as prescribed by Church tradition, until the massive state funeral attended by tens of thousands of Canadians and *Canadiens*.

I was the first to arrive at his house. Hot on my heels was Mackenzie King. I couldn't help feeling King was being presumptuous, as usual, pushing in as if he belonged to the family.

Side by side we leaned over the edge of the bronze casket. I'd have vastly preferred to be alone at that moment, so I tried to ignore King and concentrate on Laurier's dear familiar features, now palely and eternally altered, frighteningly inert. The embalmers hadn't entirely succeeded in hiding the discoloured bruise where he'd struck his forehead on his desk as he'd fallen in his office. I tried to tell myself his soul was at peace. It was difficult. He was dressed in his Windsor court uniform bulging with gold braid, which created an unnatural impression of Britishness.

"I wish he'd worn his plain black coat, the one he wore in Parliament," King said, as if talking to himself. And as if Laurier had had any choice in the matter.

Not content with succeeding him as leader of the Liberal Party, King moved into the Lauriers' home just four years later, completely changing the décor, sleeping in their bedroom, disturbing their ghosts. But before he could push in, Zoë, who had bequeathed the house to him in lieu of an heir, had to live out her remaining time there.

"*C'est fini,*" Laurier had whispered to her, his final words. She'd held his hand, gripping it fiercely, trying to keep him alive. For her it wasn't quite finished, except in her mind. She told me she didn't see much point to life without Wilfrid. She was practically blind, practically eighty.

I visited her at Theodore Street twice a week, reading aloud to her from newspapers and magazines so she could keep up with politics, and with social events in Ottawa and Arthabaska. My reading amused her, kept her distracted. We'd sit in the morning room surrounded by the surviving dogs, cats, parakeets. If she didn't doze off, she'd reminisce about the old days, her memory jogged by some name in an article I was reading. That habit of hers provided me with many of the stories I've recounted here.

Her death, two years after Wilfrid's, was followed a year later by Joseph Lavergne's. To Mother's black disappointment, Father had never attained the exalted position of Chief Justice of Quebec, which she'd coveted and considered his by right: the final fruit of her love for Wilfrid. Father's best and only chance at the appointment came while Laurier was still Prime Minister. But when the post went to another candidate, Mother was beside herself with heartbreak and grief. I wrote a livid letter of protest on the family's behalf, denouncing the humiliation done to our poor father.

With both Laurier and Lavergne gone, Mother became another person. Although she could have remained in the family home in Montreal, she chose to enter a convent on Drummond Street. I saw her seldom after that. She preferred to keep to herself, shut away from the world, shielded by the safety of high stone walls and the gentle mutters of praying nuns: a strange reversal for a woman who had once gloried in her social and amorous triumphs.

I wasn't especially sorry. The Sisters protected her from a recently acquired habit of overindulging in the household supplies of sherry and wine. Besides, Mother's melancholy and moroseness made her bad company. Her intellectual sparkle, her *joie de vivre*, had vanished.

One day she emerged from the convent for an hour to join Zoë for tea in a Montreal café. The two old "friends," one nearly sightless, the other nearly speechless, didn't have a great deal to say to each other. Apparently they passed most of their meeting in silence.

Like Zoë, Mother found no pleasure in life without Laurier. But unlike Zoë, she also felt deeply, unforgivingly angry: as though his death was yet another bitter betrayal, another desertion, his ultimate stratagem to escape her.

In her final testament, Mother left her letters from Laurier to my cousin, Louis-Renaud Lavergne. She trusted Renaud, rather than me, to preserve them for posterity. This was understandable, I suppose, given my long-standing opposition to Laurier: I accepted her wish without acrimony. And since we've remained friends since childhood, Renaud let me read and copy the letters. He agreed it was better for historical purposes that the letters, written mostly in English, which I'd taken such agonizing pains to learn, should exist in duplicate. Fire, after all, is a constant threat to records of all kinds.

Mother's own letters to Laurier—the ones he'd returned to her in the brown paper parcel—were a different matter entirely. These Mother entrusted to my sister Gabrielle for "safekeeping," with instructions they should be suppressed.

It soon proved Bielle and I had conflicting interpretations of that edict. I saw it as meaning that only the family could have access to the letters, that they should never be released to the outside world. But when I asked to read them, Bielle denied me. She claimed Mother had told her I was never even to set eyes on them. Being a dutiful daughter, she had to obey: she adamantly refused to consider my legitimate rights in the matter, which were certainly moral if not legal. When I continued to insist on those rights, Bielle became alarmed. One night, suspecting I'd break into her house to ransack the place in search of the letters, she fed them to the flames in her fireplace.

I felt devastated, utterly bereaved. Over and over I asked myself why Mother had trusted Bielle to read her words to Laurier, to share her most intimate thoughts and candid confessions, the deepest secrets of her heart, yet had refused the same confidence to me. It drove me mad. I became convinced the letters contained the keys to my existence.

Bielle herself tried to comfort me: an impossible task. She assured me she hadn't even read the letters. I refused to believe her. She, who had every right to ask the same questions about her paternity as I, couldn't possibly have been so obedient and passive, so devoid of natural curiosity. But she told me there were things Mother didn't want either of us to see or know, and she was sure Mother had been right. Our lives, and Mother's and Father's, had been difficult enough. Some secrets need to remain secret.

I could never accept these well-meaning fabrications. The only way I could replace the lost letters, even partially, was to reconstruct fragments of the lives they'd contained. Hence the narrative you hold in your hands. Without Bielle's fiery act of destruction, this book wouldn't exist.

On one occasion, and one only, I allowed my own curiosity to get the better of me. It was in that last encounter with Laurier, during the dreadful days of the war, when we talked late into the night about the election result and the grim prospects for the future—not so much his future, since he knew he was nearing the end, not even Canada's, but the world's.

After a discussion of the global crisis, he offered me a glass of port and, rare for him, poured one for himself. With the port warming my belly, I took a deep lungful of air and let my words out on the exhalation: "Are you my father?"

He looked steadily at me from under his thick brows, which hadn't turned white like his hair. Without altering his expression, he said, "You know old Judge Plamondon? The gentleman who lived next door to me in Arthabaska? He had the soundest judgment of any man I know. Pressed by a mutual acquaintance about your parentage, he exclaimed, 'Nonsense! Everyone knows Laurier is impotent!'"

He continued staring at me, smiled serenely and refilled my glass.

I emptied it in one long draft. Before I spoke, I paused, composing my words carefully in my mind. "During all our political disagreements over the years, only one thing has pained me. It's that you should believe I love you any the less when I oppose you, and the past doesn't count for me. It's actually when I fight you that I feel this most strongly. As God is my witness, I love you. But forgive me, I love my country too."

Laurier simply nodded, a gesture I took for complete acceptance. "Love is stronger than hate," he said. "And who can choose his own father?"

Ever since that night, I've believed, whether the son of Laurier or Lavergne, I have reason to be proud.

Author's Note

This is a work of fiction. I've written about historical figures as I imagine them to have been. For readers who would like to return to the "known" world, I've posted some historical background on the main characters, including photographs, on my website, *www.roymacskimming.com*.

Walking in Laurier's footsteps was an essential part of my research. Laurier House in Ottawa is the former 335 Theodore Street; under the heavy overlay of Mackenzie King's later occupation, it's still possible to detect Wilfrid and Zoë's gentler and subtler presence. The Laurier National Historic Site is located in Laurier's birthplace of St-Lin, Quebec, north of Montreal. And the Musée Laurier in Arthabaska (now part of Victoriaville, Quebec), situated in the airy Italianate house where Wilfrid and Zoë lived before moving to Ottawa, is preserved much as the Lauriers left it. A few doors down, on the other side of the street, stands Le Vert Logis, the private home originally occupied by the Lavergne family.

Many books were helpful in imagining the story. My starting point was *Dearest Émilie: The Love Letters of Sir Wilfrid Laurier to Madame Émilie Lavergne*, edited by Charles

Fisher (NC Press, 1989). With the help of archivist Maureen Hoogenraad, I found additional letters from Laurier to Émilie in the Émilie Barthe Lavergne collection at Library and Archives Canada. In quoting the letters here, I've taken the occasional liberty.

Laurier in Love would not exist in its present form without Sandra Gwyn's superb study, *The Private Capital: Ambition and Love in the Age of Macdonald and Laurier* (McClelland & Stewart, 1984). We all owe thanks to Ms. Gwyn for rediscovering the romance in Canadian political history. Another memorable rendering of the Wilfrid–Zoë–Émilie triangle appears in Heather Robertson's *More than a Rose: Prime Ministers, Wives and Other Women* (Seal Books, 1991). I found valuable information in *Armand Lavergne*, edited by Marc La Terreur (Collection classiques canadiens, Fides, 1968).

I'm greatly indebted to several Laurier biographers, however much my interpretations differ from theirs. J.S. Willison's *Sir Wilfrid Laurier and the Liberal Party* (George N. Morang, 1903) captures Laurier at the height of his political success. O.D. Skelton's *Life and Letters of Sir Wilfrid Laurier* (The Century Co., 1922) still conveys a clear sense of Laurier's political values. Joseph Schull's *Laurier: The First Canadian* (Macmillan of Canada, 1965) is imbued with a strong sense of the man's psyche. A penetrating Québécois viewpoint appears in *Wilfrid Laurier: Quand la politique devient passion* by Réal Bélanger (Presses de l'Université Laval, 1986). A more personal version of Laurier's life, as one might expect from a writer named after him, is found in *Sir Wilfrid Laurier and the Romance of Canada* by Laurier L. LaPierre (Stoddart, 1996). *Laurier: His Life and World* by Richard Clippingdale (McGraw-Hill Ryerson, 1979) was helpful for insights into the times through which my characters moved.

Laurier's conduct of Canada–U.S. relations is described in Lawrence Martin's *The Presidents and the Prime Ministers* (Doubleday Canada, 1982). For Lord and Lady Aberdeen's relations with the Lauriers, I read *The Canadian Journal of Lady Aberdeen* (The Champlain Society, 1960). A source for Lord and Lady Minto is *The Canadian Career of the Fourth Earl of Minto* by Carman Miller (Wilfrid Laurier University Press, 1980).

For Great Britain's war in South Africa, I consulted Thomas Pakenham's *The Boer War* (Futura, 1982). The authority on Canada's role in the war is Carman Miller in his *Painting the Map Red: Canada and the South African War, 1899–1902* (McGill-Queen's University Press, 1993) and *Canada's Little War* (James Lorimer, 2003). For background on the end of the Victorian age, I drew on *The Proud Tower: A Portrait of the World before the War, 1890–1914* (Macmillan, 1966) by Barbara W. Tuchman. At the Victoria and Albert Museum in London, I viewed a wonderful, grainy film clip of Queen Victoria in her Diamond Jubilee procession.

I'm indebted to Phil Jenkins's *An Acre of Time* (Macfarlane Walter & Ross, 2001) for details of the Great Ottawa Fire of 1900. Also helpful were *Ottawa: The Capital of Canada* by Shirley E. Woods, Jr. (Doubleday Canada, 1980) and *Ottawa: An Illustrated History* by John H. Taylor (James Lorimer, 1986). In the City of Ottawa Archives I benefited from finding textual and photographic materials on the Russell House Hotel and the 1900 fire.

Being able to access newspaper collections on microfilm at Library and Archives Canada was invaluable. I consulted especially *The Globe*, *The Toronto Star*, *The Ottawa Citizen* and *The Ottawa Journal*. *The New York Times* online was helpful regarding President McKinley, as was Gore Vidal's novel

Empire (Ballantine, 1987). John Kalbfleisch, historian of Montreal, kindly provided me with columns about Laurier from *The Gazette* written by his predecessor, Edgar Andrew Collard.

With the novel's public events, I've tried to be faithful to the historical record. Exceptions are several cases where I've changed the timing slightly for narrative convenience. For instance, I've placed Émilie's At Home in May 1897 instead of December; Lieutenant Agar Adamson returns home from the war four months early; and Major "Gat" Howard's death is hastened by three months.

I would like to thank my publisher, Patrick Crean of Thomas Allen Publishers, for believing in this novel; my editor, Janice Zawerbny, and copy-editor, Edna Barker, for pointing me in the right direction; Lisa Zaritzky of Thomas Allen for getting me on the road; my literary agent, Dean Cooke, for his wise counsel; my friends John Bemrose, William Hawkins, Christopher Wells and Helga Zimmerly for once again reading an early draft; and the Ontario Arts Council for providing funding during the research and writing.

My deepest thanks go to my first reader, Suzette DeLey MacSkimming, who gives me not only loving support and the inspiration of her creativity but intuition into the minds and hearts of my characters.